Praise for

Firedrake's Eye

"A talent for writing espionage makes her the le Carré of the sixteenth century.... Her work is as subtle, as complex, and as beautifully crafted as his—and she has a poet's enviable gift as well."

—Ruth Rendell, author of *The Bridesmaid*

"A rich and rewarding novel."

—*The Washington Post Book World*

"Historical fiction of a very high caliber. Patricia Finney creatively reimagines the past. She evokes the sights, sounds, and smells of Elizabethan England with remarkable fidelity."

—*Philadelphia Inquirer*

"Patricia Finney's political and religious thriller is an engaging and inventive as any modern spy novel."

—*San Francisco Examiner Chronicle*

"An intriguing puzzle of murder and high treason...historical fiction in the same league as Rose Tremain's *Restoration* and Umberto Eco's *The Name of the Rose*."

—*Cosmopolitan*

"Finney spins a magical and mysterious web...this is a wonderfully atmospheric rendering of an anarchist plot brimming over with vivid details of intrigue."

—*Booklist*

"Set in Elizabethan England, it sensuously reconstructs the era's vi·· ' pomp and splendor.... Historical and wholly invented figures mix ~   te to the author's careful research and panoramic vision."

; *Weekly*

Also by Patricia Finney

A Shadow of Gulls

The Crow Goddess

Firedrake's Eye

PATRICIA FINNEY

Unicorn's Blood

PICADOR USA
NEW YORK

Picador® is a U.S. registered trademark and is used by St. Martin's Press under license from Pan Books Limited.

For information on Picador USA Reading Group Guides, as well as ordering, please contact the Trade Marketing department at St. Martin's Press.
Phone: 1-800-221-7945 extension 488
Fax: 212-677-7456
E-mail: trademarketing@stmartins.com

Library of Congress Cataloging-in-Publication Data

Finney, Patricia.
    Unicorn's blood / by Patricia Finney.
        p. cm.
    ISBN 0-312-20039-0
    1. Great Britain—History—Elizabeth, 1558–1603—Fiction.
I. Title.
PR6056.I519U55   1998
823'.914—dc21   97-36063
                                                                          CIP

First Picador USA Paperback Edition: January 1999

10 9 8 7 6 5 4 3 2 1

To my darling Alexandra,
without whom this book might have
been finished a lot sooner—
but then it could not have contained Pentecost.

Foreword

A S I W R O T E A T the beginning of my first Elizabeth thriller, this is a novel, not a history book. I have used history as skeleton and scaffolding, but I have freely jumped off into fantasy whenever I felt like it, turned speculation into fact and rank conjecture into assumption—although I have tried to keep within the boundaries of what might just be possible, given the evidence. As I like to know when I finish reading a historical novel what was fact and what was fiction, I have included an extended historical note at the end. I have also supplied a glossary of obsolete words.

Again, I would like to dissociate myself from the opinions and prejudices of my characters, some of which I find obnoxious. But to attribute political correctness of any kind to the Elizabethans would be to commit the infuriating sin of psychological anachronism, something I have done my best to avoid. Their lives were far harder and more dangerous than ours—if simpler—and their attitudes to pain and death utterly different. And yet, underneath their fantastical costumes and strange notions, lay Shakespeare's familiar forked animal. If we look carefully and without prejudice, we are not so very different.

I have decided, that as I have received help from so many people over so many years, it would be politer not to thank any of them by name, in case I leave someone out. To all those who have patiently answered my occasionally mad-seeming questions or directed me to the right books, a hearty thank you. Even more gratitude is due to those who have read my book in manuscript and courageously suggested improvements (though I may not have thanked them at the time). All remaining stupidities, anachronisms, and mistakes are, of course, mine.

Unicorn's Blood

1

TO RISE FROM VIRGIN to Queen is one thing; to be cast down from Queen to Whore to Witch is quite another. Would you not kill to avoid such shame?

Once I was a Queen in England, and ruled on behalf of my Son, Jesus Christ. Ave Maria, *they praised me,* Salve Mater, *they sang to me.*

Now I am deposed, cast down from my throne in men's minds, a mere despised superstition. If I were mortal I would be a beggar on the road.

But I am not mortal. I am your Lady, always and forever, your true Queen of Heaven, the Blessed Virgin Mary.

I still spread my dark velvet cloak over all my children, apostates and faithful alike, protecting you from the cold blasts of your God's judgment.

For am I not the Star of the Sea, Tower of Ivory, Gate of Paradise, Refuge of Sinners, Comforter of the Afflicted, most Holy and Mystical Rose? I stand upon the serpent and the moon; I am clothed with the sun and about my head shines a diadem of twelve stars; I am Queen of the Angels, Queen of Virgins, Empress of Hell . . .

11

So WHERE SHALL WE begin, in this tale of unicorns and virgins? In the head of my usurper, the earthly Queen Elizabeth, I think. She lies peacefully in darkness on a clean linen pillow, the rose-water that took the red cinnabar and white-lead paint from her skin leaving ghosts of gardens about her cheeks. Her hair is cut short and no longer the fair burnished copper that men praised in her youth, but an ugly shade between grey and red, now hidden by an embroidered cap. Her alabaster skin is furrowed and freckled with the footprints of Time. But when she sleeps, the folds relax and the guile and statecraft melt away until it is as if a child peeks from behind a crumpled mask.

Just as earthly Queens must eat and purge themselves, so they also dream. In Elizabeth's dream she was in her Presence Chamber, as stiffly buttressed as a church in cloth-of-gold and black velvet. Above her was her Cloth of State, making an awning for her in the room, which was just as well, for the roof had disappeared and the rain fell clear from the heavy clouds above. And in her dreaming heart was a familiar dread which must be hidden behind the paint of her face and the riddles of her eyes.

They were bringing her a strange and magical gift. Sir Francis Drake had journeyed beyond the bounds of the world and returned, and in his holds he carried a beast that none in England had ever seen, a beast as mysterious as the striped horses of Africa or the giant deer of the Americas. The legend had travelled with great trouble and at hideous expense from Plymouth to London along roads lined with curious crowds to see the wonder. Now, in sign of his love and devotion to the Queen his Mistress, Sir Francis would present it to her as the perfect New Year's gift.

She had not been able to prevent it. How could she? Why should she fear a Unicorn, being a virgin? Indeed, the Virgin Queen. Therefore a unicorn must be a fitting present for her. For Pliny tells us that although the unicorn is full of rage and will stab lions through the heart with the horn on his head, still, if he be led to a virgin by strong men, he will lay his head upon her lap and be tamed.

And so, in the Queen's dream, strong men brought the unicorn into her Presence Chamber. It snorted and fought the ropes and swung its horn this way and that, its breath puffing with the heat of its rage. And all her people left her, being afraid of the beast until she stood alone, as she always must, under her canopy in the rain and waited for it. And the red silken ropes broke, and the unicorn stared narrow-eyed at her.

She could not speak. The unicorn tossed its head, trotted forwards with the raindrops splashing upon its gleaming white back, and its nostrils flared red as it snuffed her scent.

Its raging scream of hatred froze the rain to hail as it fell. It reared high and screamed again, set itself with its goat's tail lashing and charged at her, savage horn aimed squarely at her breast and the silver hooves breaking the rushes and the floor beneath it . . .

She shrieked in horror and humiliation and sat up, her arms flailing, feet kicking the covers off, screamed and screamed until the girl lying beside her sat up blinking and put her hand timidly on her Queen's shoulder.

"Your Majesty," she whispered. "Your Majesty?"

Tears flowed down the Queen's cheeks and she hunched over, clasping her bony knees, gasping and shuddering. Gently her bedfellow stroked her back and pressed her fingers into the stringy muscles of her shoulders and neck until the shuddering faded and the Queen could breathe again. At last the Queen turned her face to the girl and smiled a little.

"Was it the evil dream again, Your Majesty?"

The Queen nodded and shut her eyes, letting the girl's hands knead fear out of her back. Beyond the shut tapestry bedcurtains another of her women called out uncertainly, in a voice thick with sleep, "Are you well, Your Majesty? Are you in pain?"

"I am well enough," the Queen said, easing her shoulders. "Go fetch me some spiced wine."

There was a soft muttering beyond the heavy curtains and the sounds of covers being pushed back and a furred dressing gown wrapped around and feet finding their slippers in the rush-matting. The Queen ignored the muttering: if she was awake, why should anyone else sleep?

A door opened and shut, there were voices in the Privy Gallery, sleepy, aggrieved voices, and more argument.

Irritation burnt in the Queen's heart. Half-witted ninnyhammers, why did they never think to refill the pitcher by the fire? Why was there always the business of fetching and carrying? No matter what she wanted, it was never to hand.

At last the bedcurtain was pulled back a little and Blanche Parry's face appeared, underlit by a candle, creaking her joints down onto one knee and holding out a silver goblet covered with a white napkin.

"Hmf," sniffed the Queen, "about time. Bethany, you may stop that now."

She took the goblet and gave the napkin to Bethany Davison, who knelt there beside her in the tangle of blankets, exchanging glances with Parry that she thought her Queen could neither see nor interpret. The Queen drank to hide her irritation and the hot wine nipped her tongue. She blew on it and refrained from throwing the goblet at Blanche's head.

Blanche Parry's eyes were half-shutting blearily. She was still holding back the bed curtain, which let a sharp draught from somewhere pluck the Queen's flesh. The fire was banked and covered and the room cold.

"Oh, go to bed, for God's sake, Parry," growled the Queen. "I shall be well enough."

"Thank you, Your Majesty." She heaved herself off her knee and let the curtain fall back as the Queen sipped more cautiously at the wine: too much cinnamon, not enough ginger or nutmeg, she thought, but at least it is hot and sweet.

Bethany was shivering too. The Queen finished all but a couple of swallows and handed her the goblet.

"Finish it," she said, and the girl drank what was left and then delicately patted the napkin against the Queen's mouth and against hers. Well-trained, she wiped out the inside of the goblet and put it on the little shelf carved into the headboard, among the wooden grapes and vine-leaves and the wild gilded cherubs.

The Queen lay down again, the linen already glazed with cold, and Bethany drew up the sheet and rearranged the blankets and the fur-lined counterpane and at last lay down next to her, with her soft black hair escaping from its plait and spreading out behind her head like corporeal shadow.

In the dark you cannot see how beautiful she is, thought the Queen, how thick and sooty the lashes around her grey eyes, how pale and creamy her skin. It was Bethany's skin she had noticed when the girl was first presented for her inspection as a possible maid of honour: a miracle of clarity for a girl in her teens. Not a single pockmark or blackhead, smooth and soft and as lightly furred as a peach, and it was all the colour of clotted cream so that you half-expected her to smell of milk. She did not, though, she smelt of almonds and spice and the most expensive rose-water from Damascus. Someone had evidently warned her not to use musk, which the Queen abhorred, nor civet. She had been wearing a dark-crimson velvet gown then, the false-front of her petticoat of white satin embroidered with rainbows and butterflies. Her hair was loose and dressed with garnets that matched the jewels lying upon her breast, between those two soft hills that had sent many gentlemen of the Court gibbering into verse. This child's hair had the strange quality of being black, but not shining: it was too soft for that, it simply fell about her neck and down her back like still black smoke.

Her cousin, Mr Davison, who had brought her to Court, had known what he was about; while the Queen smiled and inspected his offering, she could feel the satisfaction in him at her liking. Just so, she remembered, had ambitious men brought pretty laughing creatures to Court for her father's inspection. To be sure, she was not Henry VIII. She did not want gigglers and made that well-known. And it was different for her; she prided herself on the fact that at her Court, the girl's maidenhood was safe.

Now with the curtains drawn tight and the air inside the bed's cave beginning to warm, Bethany Davison was turned to mystery again. All the Queen could know was the shape and smell of the girl. And that she was still shivering.

Why? Even the thin-skinned Queen was warming. Was she shivering with fear? This was no means to find Morpheus, and in any case the Queen had no wish to recall the fading rootlets of her dream, nor the heavy load of Christmas ceremonial awaiting her in the morning.

"Come, Bethany, my dear," murmured the Queen and gathered the dark head against her shoulder, wrapped her arms around and also her legs. "Don't be afraid. You are a good girl."

To the Queen of England, there was the same pleasure in stroking Bethany's cheek and shoulder as in running fingers across silk velvet. Her long, bony hand found its way to the square neck of the girl's smock, with its nubbling of black embroidery, and under it to the soft pointed cushion of flesh below. It quivered as she cupped it, warm in her palm.

Were mine once like that? the Queen wondered. Smaller, certainly, and more pointed, I think.

Bethany turned her face to the Queen and the Queen kissed her sooty black eyebrows and the straight nose—as cold as a dog's nose at the moment—and the warmer cheeks, and the soft defended rose of her mouth. The Queen's other hand moved down and down as they kissed, at length to find the outline of the girl's quim beneath her smock and rub there gently.

In a little while Bethany smiled and sighed.

111

ELSEWHERE, A MAN AWOKE in stinking darkness and knew that some terrible mystery had happened to his hands. Each of them was like a plate of meat, huge, amorphous, blazing in black flames that pounded from his fingers, bulged about his wrists, flowed down his arms and lanced upwards into his head. Aching cold struck into him from the stone under his flank and shoulder; every part of him was palsied with it, save his poor hands that lay somewhere in front of him.

He tried to sit up, find a tinder-box, discover what had befallen him, perhaps waken from his nightmare.

The black dream deepened. First, he cracked his sore head on a roof of stone only three feet above him. Then he stubbed his toes on a wall mere inches away, although he was lying curled over like a cat with his knees drawn up. There was a scraping clink of metal on metal, and he felt bruising, constricting weight on his ankles and his arms.

He blinked sightlessly, trying to understand. But understanding was a quicksand. Either he was dead and in an antechamber of Hell or he was a prisoner: so much was clear enough. But why? Who had chained him?

Breath sucked into his chest. He held it and let it out shakily.

Here was the man within, as it were an homunculus, setting out bravely to answer a mystery: why was its body cooped up in a stone cell with iron clasping him feet and arms?

No answer. The steady floor whisked from under his mental foot and so he stumbled to the next question.

Who could have done this? Again, no answer and the next step not where it should be.

And how and when had he come there? How had his wrists been so agonisingly wounded?

The homunculus within flailed, grasped out for a bannister and so found itself falling from a cliff edge and not merely a stair.

He had no idea who he was. He knew neither his name nor his condition, not his father's name nor his mother's face.

Within the dark sky of his skull was an echoing void, unstarred, unpeopled, barren. He had been robbed and stripped of all his mental furniture save this ugly present in which he lay trussed like a hog for the slaughter, stinking like a midden, and two great bladders of pain lying before him where his hands should have been.

He laid his head down again, gasping, his heart drumming, his ear crushed on the stone, his lips bruised and tasting of metal.

"Sweet Jesus," he whispered and found his throat raw also.

In the distance, loud and ugly, came an irregular distorted clanging.

I am dead and in Hell, he thought, appalled and strangely comforted because no further effort could be required of him. He was weary to the bone.

IV

THE ARISING OF AN earthly Queen from her bed is a matter of great moment. The fire must be made up and a brazier brought in to fight the frost flowers inside the windows. A dressing-gown must be fetched from the press and held up to the fire by one of the other maids of honour, who must herself be fully dressed and ready for anything. Maids of honour who singe the sable lining can expect to have their ears boxed for disrespect to His Majesty the Tzar of Muscovy who had sent the furs, so it is a job fraught with anxiety.

Blanche Parry and the other Gentlewomen of the Chamber who are on duty must bring Her Majesty's breakfast of bread and small beer and two red boxes of urgent papers. The Stool must also be ready, clean, empty and scented with lavender water. God forbid the Stool should smell, for Her Majesty has thrown it (full) at the head of the gentlewoman who was supposed to have seen it emptied.

Her Majesty Queen Elizabeth, the first of that name to rule in her own right, awakens officially at seven of the clock. Her women must be up by five and creeping about as they dress in the dark so as not to disturb her before the time comes for the bedcurtains to be drawn back.

The Queen is generally not in a good mood in the morning. On this particular morning she had woken at the first rustle and cautious creak of floorboards. Firelight and candle-light flickered between the curtains, reflecting and spangling on the cloth-of-silver tester making the roof of her elaborate den. Bethany Davison, her bedfellow, still snored beside her with the annoying ease of youth.

Somewhere in the cellars of the Queen's mind, the unicorn stamped and pawed the ground, but she had locked and barred the door and only kept the memory of terror and shame and the unicorn himself. She concluded that her melancholy dreaming was caused by that half-witted Royal whore, the Scottish Queen, whose badge is the Unicorn of Scotland, and she glowered. Every stealthy preparation and whisper beyond her bedcurtains fell crisp and clear to her ears, and she lay on her back and stared up at the gleaming tester and prayed for patience. Bethany sleeping beside her stirred and murmured something. It sounded as if it might have been a man's name, which it had better not be.

At last she could smell the new-baked manchet and the spiced warmth of the mulled ale.

Mary Ratcliffe and Blanche Parry, Mistress of the Maids, drew back the curtains while Katherine, Countess of Bedford, knelt by the bed with the dressing-gown.

"Good morning, Your Majesty. Merry Christmas," they chorused.

The Queen set her teeth and glared at them, sitting bolt upright and rubbing her arms.

"Did you sleep well, Your Majesty?" asked Mary Ratcliffe, who had the unfortunate gift of morning perkiness.

"No, I did not," the Queen growled. "And I am perishing with the cold."

All three exchanged glances. Lady Bedford rose to put the dressing-gown around the Queen's shoulders, while Ratcliffe knelt to put on her slippers, also lined with sable and embroidered with gold esses.

"Ratcliffe," said the Queen, "I have told you before: tawny does not become you."

Mary Ratcliffe tilted her head, not at all concerned by Her Majesty's normal ill-temper. She rose gracefully and offered the Queen her arm to rise from the bed. Behind the Queen, Bethany turned and muttered and let out a bulldog snore, at odds with her beauty.

"Christ's guts, Bethany," snarled the Queen, punching her shoulder, "enough of those foul noises. You kept me awake half the night with them."

Bethany sat up looking confused. "I am sorry, Your Majesty," she said.

"God save me from a bedmate that snores; I might as well have a husband," said the Queen as she ignored Mary Ratcliffe, jumped out of bed and went to warm her hands at the brazier. Behind her she could feel the glances weaving through the air, could predict how she had set in motion an army of warnings, rumours and assessments that would run through the Court and be in the wood-yard and the laundry before she had gone to chapel.

When she sat down in her carved chair, Parry knelt before her and asked how she would be pleased to dress this day. At the snap of her fingers, Ratcliffe produced the Wardrobe Book, which gave her a choice of five gowns, five kirtles and five bodices, newly brought up from the Great Wardrobe in Blackfriars, plus a vast variety of linen.

"Black," she decided, to match her mood, and the fashion for mourning which had swept the Court since the death of Sir Philip Sidney. "With silver and pearls—the French gown will do well enough, and the French wig to go with it."

This set in motion another hushed flurry as Parry called the orders to the chamberers waiting in the Lesser Withdrawing Room beyond the second bolted door.

Silently Lady Bedford brought up the red leather boxes to the side of her chair by the fire. The Queen opened their seals, took out sheaves of paper, warmed her hands and bit carefully into the white manchet bread with butter and cheese. The crust was too stiff, but at least it was still warm.

As she ate she read through the papers in the boxes, skimming through the Italic and Secretary hands and muttering to herself. She was currently caught in a vice of Mr Secretary Walsingham's making: he had begun its construction a year ago and she had found it out in the summer with the revelation of the Babington plot, in which Mary Queen of Scots was at last clearly implicated by her own letters in treasonable plotting against Queen Elizabeth.

In the autumn Elizabeth had made what she now knew to have been a deadly mistake. From sheer weariness and fright she had permitted her cousin Queen to be put on trial. The proceeding had filled Elizabeth with dread: put one regnant Queen on trial and God knew where it would end. Try one, you could try them all. But she had found it impossible to prevent; she had chosen men of ability and determination to surround her and in their loyalty to her and their bloody Pure Religion, they had nagged and reasoned and manoeuvred her into it.

Naturally the Queen of Scots had been found guilty. Naturally she had been condemned to die for treason against Elizabeth. Would that content them? It would not. God damn them all for half-wits, purblind fanatical . . .

The Queen put down the last paper and breathed deeply. She would not permit her anger to govern her. Anger came easily to her, as it had to her Royal father, but she had been forced to bridle it, to put harness on it and make it pull a kingdom.

The door to the Privy Gallery, guarded by two gentlemen who slept there at night fully-clad, was still bolted. Ratcliffe had unlocked and unbolted the second door to the Lesser Withdrawing Room where the wardrobe closets were. One of the maids of honour was pouring hot water into a bowl, and a second was standing by modestly holding a towel of Holland linen. Chamberers filed in carrying her clothes for the morning. The Queen rose, went behind the screen to the Stool. Parry was there waiting to lift the lid and hand her a book of Latin verse to entertain her. She withdrew tactfully.

If Elizabeth Tudor had been born a boy—apart from many other things being different, including perhaps the religion of her kingdom—she would have had a Groom of the Stool to attend her there. Sir Anthony Denny, who had been her father's Groom of the Stool, had directed much of the King's palace-building for the reason that His Majesty was pleased to overlook architects' plans while sitting. Elizabeth preferred poetry. Parry did the office of the Stool, as well as overseeing the Queen's robes, and drew income from half a dozen separate sources for a daily bulletin on the state of the Queen's bowels. It was a wry joke between them.

The Queen coughed and took the napkin handed to her. She stood and Parry came immediately to drop the lid and assess the results.

"You may tell them that I am utterly constipated," the Queen told her tartly.

"Again, Your Majesty?" Parry asked, amused.

"Ay, again. Tell them I am stopped up with bile and may well take purge."

Parry smiled and shook her head. "You are cruel, Madam."

"By God, if they will not heed me, let them fear me." The Queen's bowels were as healthy as ever, but only she, Parry and the chamberer who did the emptying knew that. Meanwhile Parry would pass the word of an unsuccessful Stool and the councillors would tremble, the Gentlemen of the Privy Chamber walk softly and the cooks in the Privy Kitchen prepare further messes of prunes and dried rubarb, which she would send back untouched. It cheered her to think of the ripples of consternation spreading from her humble (though velvet-covered) Stool throughout the Court and thence perhaps even into London.

She dropped her dressing-gown behind her for Bedford to catch, and washed her hands and face in the warm tincture of rose-water. Gingerly she rubbed her teeth with a salted paste of almonds and a cloth and winced when it hurt. Another tooth on the left side was twingeing her. Not badly yet, only when she ate comfits, but she had been down that road before and could see at the end of it, some time in the summer, the tooth-drawer waiting for her with his pliers and the sweat of fear on his face. She had threatened him with hanging every time he came in the past, but had paid him instead once the pain had died down.

They had a fresh smock ready for her as she dropped her soiled one at her feet and put up her arms and slid into its warmth. There was always the sense of falsity about warmed linen, whose heat dissipated so quickly, like the smiles of courtiers, she thought. The black damask stays with their fencing of whalebone went about her and she straightened her back and stood still while she thought of the letters she had read. Most were petitions that she sign the Queen of Scots' death warrant.

Ratcliffe had long slender fingers and a face that sat upon her neck like a lily on a stem. Deftly she wove the silk laces through the holes and pulled firmly to tighten the stays. Elizabeth squared her shoulders and settled herself into the reassuring women's armour, as she had nearly every morning of her life since she turned eight. In her youth she had had them cut narrow and pointed, and suffered for it. Sometimes after a long day's hunting she had found blood on the lining and her smock, but since she had put on weight after the Alençon courtship, she had been less insistent on fashionable shaping that made it hard to breathe. She would never be stout, but she no longer looked as if a man could pick her up and snap her in two, as the Earl of Leicester had said recently. She had laughed at him and punched his paunch and he had winced and bowed satisfactorily.

They brought a rose plush petticoat for warmth and fastened the straps over her shoulders so it would hang well. Ratcliffe knelt again as the Queen sat and slid her linen socks on over her feet, followed by her silk stockings, and gartered them.

"Which shoes will you have, Madam?" asked Ratcliffe.

Elizabeth pulled the dressing-gown round her shoulders again.

"What's the weather?"

"Cold, grey, perhaps the promise of snow?"

"Thames still frozen?"

"Yes, Madam."

"God damn it. Well, my fur-lined Spanish boots then. And they had better be clean."

They were, shining with wax. Parry wrapped a combing cloth about her shoulders and combed out her short hair. Then she brought up the trays of face-paint, broke and separated an egg neatly before dabbing her brush in egg white and then in the white lead.

Lady Bedford stood behind her while she held her face stiff to be coloured, and read her the list of likely petitioners to the especial Privy Council meeting at noon on the morrow, Saint Stephen's Day, and reminded her that she would be receiving the Treasurer of the Board of Greencloth after the Council Meeting.

"Christ's guts," hissed the Queen through stiff lips, while Parry dabbed red onto her cheeks. "Is the man mad? Cancel it and put it back to next week. If I see him after the Council, I shall likely skin him alive."

"Yes, Your Majesty," said Bedford, not smiling.

She sneezed as Parry set her maquillage with powder. The business of dressing went to its next stage: Bedford unpacked a fresh Flanders partlet of finely pleated and smocked linen, which she passed about Elizabeth's neck, buttoned at the back and tied under her arms. Ratcliffe was tying on a bum-roll and bringing her a farthingale, collapsed like a fan into a round wheel of linen. Over that went the second petticoat, with its red damask false-front, and finally the square-necked French gown of black Lucca velvet, laced bodice-wise all down the back, crossed with silver couching, spangles and pearls and garded with black satin embroidered in silver cobwebs. It took both Ratcliffe and Bedford to lift it so that she could dive in, arms first. Its weight settled about her shoulders like plate-armour as her women industriously laced and buttoned and hooked it on. As Ratcliffe set herself to pull out the little puffs of linen in the sleeves with a buttonhook, and Bedford stitched rapidly to settle the neckline properly, Elizabeth narrowed her eyes at the wire-stiffened rebato-veil they brought her.

"No," she said, not realising—because she did not remember—how her dream had dressed her in clothes like these, "I shall have a small ruff today."

They brought the ruff and tied it against the high lace-edged collar of the partlet and then at last Parry fitted the wig Ratcliffe brought, with its crowning freight of jewels and pearls already attached. It amused her now to think how she had endured anguish over her red hair all through her twenties and thirties— the washing, combing, setting with curl-papers and all the other tedious falderals. Finally one morning, tried beyond endurance, she had thrown an entire tray of pins, combs and unguents at Blanche Parry and ordered her to cut off the whole damned mop. It had been one of her best decisions: hairdressing now took place in one of the anterooms of the Privy Wardrobe and the result was brought to her and tied with tapes behind her head in a minute or two. Bedford was kneeling again to attach her gold belt with its hanging fan and case of scissors, needles, keys, penknife, bodkin and seal.

"God's death," she sniffed, "take the fan away; what do I want with a fan in this weather? Bring me a muff instead."

Eight rings slipped onto her fingers, alongside the Coronation Ring, which she wore as a wedding band on the third finger of her left hand. A jewel of a Phoenix was pinned by Ratcliffe on the breast of the velvet bodice, another hung from the rope of pearls and gold esses that Parry brought. Finally they held up a full-length mirror between them while Bethany arranged the train and Elizabeth frowned at herself.

"Hmf," she said, and her women visibly relaxed a little.

It was half past eight of the clock. Beyond the closed door of her Chamber lay the Privy Gallery where her gentlemen should be lined up by now, waiting to conduct her to chapel for the high ceremonies of Christmas Day.

She took another look in her mirror: the Queen was ready, although far, far beneath was still the young girl that all women carry locked within their maturity. That girl wanted to go back to bed, draw the curtains and hide from the world.

The Queen squared her shoulders, glanced at her women to be sure they looked as they should: why in Heaven's name did the fawn-coloured Ratcliffe, with her mouse hair and sallow skin, insist on black garded with tawny?—she looked liverish . . . And Bethany too was in black, which in all honesty did not become her either . . . This was a mourning Christmas, to be sure.

"Come," she said and swept to the door, which was being held open by one of her gentlemen—at least he was pleasing to look on, being one of her chestnut-headed Carey cousins, one of Lady Bedford's multitude of younger brothers, and immaculately turned out in forest-green velvet and black damask. She smiled at him as she went by, for the pleasure of seeing the broad shoulders bow to her, and passed on to the Privy Gallery where the rest of her gentlemen awaited. The brazen cries of trumpets echoed through the Gallery and beyond; deep voices rang forth in counterpoint to announce her:

"Make way for the Queen's Majesty."

"Make way for Her Majesty Queen Elizabeth."

"Make way."

"The Queen! The Queen!"

Damn it, she thought as she paced behind the red-velveted ranks and saw the double door to the Privy Chamber flung wide, the mob of petitioners and

Christmas gawkers waiting beyond. I am a prisoner of silks and trumpets; nothing I do is what I want and now those God-besotted fools of my Council will make me execute my cousin. Christ rot them all for cowards, why will not one of them do his duty and assassinate the Scotch bitch for me?

V

NOW I MYSELF HAVE awoken in fields and under haystacks on the way to Egypt, and also in a cold barn to the sound of angels singing and my Babe gurgling and laughing up at their brightness, which was outshone by His own shining.

And this other Mary, my poor daughter-in-law, once woke every morning in her stone cell to the sound of bell-ringing. More recently she has generally been under the table in boozing kens with a ragged skinny child curled against her body for warmth and the fumes of aqua vitae rocking their heads.

And latterly, of course, she has been prone to wakings in the watches of the night to attend some woman in labour, since she has been a midwife and a witch.

This is inevitable, oh you pure and scandalised gentleman: to be old, poor and not witless; and worse still, a woman in such adamant times, is ipso facto to be a witch.

MARY'S FACE TOO IS made gentle by sleep, for our souls do not age as our bodies do. But there the similarity to the Queen ends. The Queen's bed is curtained in tapestry, with a winter coverlet of sable fur. Mary's is a truckle-bed with a straw pallet and sheetless blankets and herds of lice and fleas. The Queen's breakfast is decorous compared with Mary's, which is aqua vitae, neat. The Queen's toilette is the final shining peak of a vast mountain of complicated effort. Mary's involves sitting up, scratching, pulling her part-laced stays shut and hooking her bodice across. She pauses to stroke her hands on the silk pile; even witches rejoice in blue velvet gowns. This one had been given to her long ago by a lover. Although it was not new when she got it, velvet is near as hard-wearing as canvas and she has it still, tattered at the hem and with new sleeves of brown homespun, darned, patched and darned again. It has become to her a second skin, since she never takes it off.

Ill-fitting shoes on feet innocent of stockings, a cap over her populated white hair, and a shawl over all, and there you have the completed picture of a witch. Change her round about by means of a miracle, give her the Queen's robes and the Queen hers . . . No doubt she could make shift to look Queenly and dignified.

She has no costly glass to admire herself in, only a rickety window backed with black night. Sinfully she rejoiced in mirrors when she first took her vows and desired to see her young face framed in white wimple and black veil. She used a window then too and did penance for it. She was a picture of piety once, it could make you weep.

Through the planks of the wall by her bed she can hear rhythmic thumping of some early-rising Court ram tupping one of the whores. At this time she is living in a little cubbyhole at the back of the Falcon bawdy-house, on sufferance. Very much on sufferance. They suffered from her and she is suffered on the unspoken condition that she should very soon suffer and die of something quick-acting. Julia, one of her granddaughters, is a junior-madam there, and excuses Mary when she drinks too much aqua vitae and swears at the customers and falls over in the common room and farts and so on. Sometimes she appeals to Mary to behave herself, but Mary remembers her as a snotty-faced five-year-old, running her poor mother ragged as they begged their way up and down the road to Plymouth, and tells her so.

Julia thinks she is well off at the Falcon and preens and prinks it the fine lady in velvet trimmings and cheap satins, and finds Mary an embarrassment, who saved her life when she took the plague at nine years old, by poulticing her buboes until they burst.

Julia prefers it if Mary does not remind her of these things. She prefers it if the witch does not speak to her. She prefers it, although she will not admit this, if she can pretend she does not know her own grandam: "Oh yes, the witch, to be sure, sir, we must have a witch for the girls . . . Yes, to attend them. Yes, to be sure, sir, would sir like another flagon of wine? And the blonde girl in red? Of course, sir, she costs fifteen shillings for the hour, or three pounds the night . . . Oh yes, sir, very clean, almost a virgin . . ."

Mary spits and snarls and then she remembers her duty, as she has every morning for three score years and more, no matter what the hangover. Creaking and groaning, she kneels in the musty straw and crosses herself, begins to make her morning devotions with words printed in her bones: *Ave Maria, gratia plena, Dominus tecum* . . .

Naturally I come to her and comfort my faithful liegewoman.

VI

To keep CHRISTMAS DAY at Court is the pinnacle of ambition for a place-seeker and has very little to do with the feast of Christ's birthday. Courtiers throng the palace of Westminster from before dawn and form long lines for admittance at the Court gate, snaking up and down between hurdles like the guts of a deer, to pack more precedence into a small space by a miracle of folding.

The day begins with the service of thanksgiving and Communion in the Chapel Royal, roundly sung (to the disapproval of Puritans), by the lily-white boys of the chapel. The courtiers of rank high enough to attend pay not the slightest attention to this, nor to the prayers, nor to the sermon that has taken many weeks of agonised preparation to pile up a confection of rhetoric until not even the preacher could say what it was about. The courtiers, having beggared themselves for new doublets of velvet and gowns of figured damask, and the dyers run clear through their stocks of black and indigo to feed the fashion, are a heaving tide of moving, preening and parading shadow, like cockroaches. They mutter softly to each other and bow and curtsey and ask after each other's tailor and bemoan the difficulty and expense of buying an heiress from the Court of Wards. Most of them are men, all of them desperate to catch the Queen's eye; to be tall enough and well-shouldered enough and polished enough to take her fancy, as the greatly hated Sir Walter Raleigh was and still is, damn him.

The Queen ignores all this desperate effort. Effort is not interesting to her, she sees too much of it. A kind of wild and witty nonchalance appeals to her, and for this reason she smiles and nods to Sir Walter, who bows lavishly back from his pew in the body of the chapel below her balcony. Raleigh is blazing in crimson satin and crimson velvet. There is his quality. If all the world is wearing black, in sheep-like homage to his own fashion, Raleigh must naturally wear shocking red and be like a drop of blood upon a field of pitch.

Impossible not to suspect he had planned it that way, which amuses her greatly.

Afterwards she walks like a secular goddess among the courtiers and receives their worship, accompanied by the strapping red-clad Gentlemen Pensioners of her Guard, and Raleigh, their Captain. Shadow-meadows of folk bend and sway before the wind of her sovereignty. She is gracious, chatting and laughing. She hears petitions, meets youngsters brought to see the wonder of Her Majesty, agrees affably to godmother at christenings, before she retires at last to her Withdrawing Room to catch her breath before the next round of pleasure. There, being what she is, she also attends to the papers that must still be signed in the great continual machine of her governance.

At Christmas, however, no one has had the courage to present a Warrant for Putting to the Question to her. About half of the interrogations of Papists carried out in her behalf by Sir Francis Walsingham and Mr Davison are thus legally signed and warranted, but her protectors have wide leeway and use it. She prefers not to know officially about the chamber of Little Ease in the Tower, lightless, airless, fireless and comfortless, being damp from the Thames and too small for a man to stand or lie in. When Little Ease has a new tenant, it is, in her opinion, no one's business save Mr Davison's and the Yeomen Warders.

VII

CAPTURED UPON THE FEAST of Saint Thomas the Apostle, first put to the question in a hurry the day after, to no one's satisfaction, the Queen's new guest in the Tower lay in a stupor of pain and exhaustion, waiting for the attentions of the Devil.

Not being theologically astute, it never occurred to him that he could hardly lament his sins if he could remember nothing at all. Hell would be better conducted than that.

No, what weakened his conviction that he was dead was the steady growth within him of the sordid fleshly necessity to piss.

Still, for a long while he lay there, shaking, sick and dizzy with fear and confusion, while his heart beat and his head pounded, and he could not get enough air. Because he was gasping for breath, he knew he could not be in Hell yet, for the dead do not need air. Therefore, alas, he must be alive.

So he set his chattering teeth against the dragging of the chains, bent his elbows and brought his hands close to his face, felt them gently with his lips. Their skin was taut and trailed prickles like fireflies from the roughness of his beard.

For all their hugeness in his mind's eye he felt they were only swollen, not crushed, not even bleeding. With great courage and some whimpering he could move them, flex the sausage-like fingers. But about his wrists were two pulsing swollen bracelets of flesh with a bruised and weeping furrow between. From these came most of his grief.

Whoever had chained his arms had found the wrists too swollen and had put the irons higher up, closer to his elbows. His chest ached already from the constriction to his shoulders.

Some men might have surrendered to terror at once, but he tried again to remember. He shivered and sweated with effort, wrestling mentally with the void, even as Jacob did with the Angel of the Lord.

Nothing. He knew nothing of himself. A man, to be sure, and not a maid, which was some relief to him. A man and not a beast; a child, rather, caught up in an aching body that seemed too large for it.

Perhaps he was indeed dreaming. But how could he be asleep? His hip and shoulder ached from the rough stone and also his head—particularly his head. The back was monstrously sore and griped him every time he lifted it. His hands—now he knew what shape they were in truth—had deflated from their extravagant size to become only sources of pain. He tried flexing his fingers and gasped as new rivers of fire woke in the muscles of his forearms and his wrists. He gritted his teeth and tried again, desperate to know more of the place he was in.

The void remained an ugly thing within him: the stump of an amputation, trees chopped down in an ancient wood, a lost tooth—like the familiar gap left by the loss of one of his dogteeth.

"I am . . . My name is . . ." he said to himself from time to time and then stopped. His throat was sore, his mouth dry and his stomach cramped, adding to the cacophony of pain that sickened him.

He flexed his fingers for a while, until they felt as if each were a separate swarming ants' nest. On reflection he thought perhaps he should be grateful to feel pain from them; it would be far worse for them to be completely numb and dead. How did he know that? He had no idea, except that he knew the smell of gangrene and feared it greatly.

At last his fingers seemed a little better. He moved them to his face, working to know himself.

His hair was short, curly, staring and wild with tangles and filth, and his scalp itched. There was a familiar crawling behind his ears, and he grimaced.

Around the trimmed margins of his beard was stubble, perhaps two or three days' growth. Below came some mystery again; he had no ruff but his shirt was linen and tolerably fine. He had on a doublet, velvet lined with taffeta, elaborately carved jewelled buttons and loops to fasten them. The sleeves had been slit to the elbows to allow his swollen wrists to pass the cuffs, his shirt-sleeves were untied.

One reason for his coldness occurred to him: his doublet hung open but he could not button it, his fingers were too clumsy. Nor was there a belt, something that surprised him not at all. They had taken his sword, of course.

The watcher within grasped the thought of a sword and brandished it.

"Of course I am a gentleman," he said. "What else would I be?"

With lice? said the homunculus mordantly and he answered himself, perhaps. Without a sword or with lice, why not? Then he stopped, because he did not know how he knew.

"Nevertheless," he muttered stubbornly and continued his awkward exploration, unbending his elbows. His hose were plain padded canions, also velvet, the points still mostly tied to his doublet points, and he still had his netherstocks but no boots.

Only one of his codpiece points was tied and that badly.

Cautiously he groped for a pot and found nothing save damp straw. Some of the stink is explained, said the homunculus smartly, although I cannot be the cause of all of it.

His sides ached, as if he had been carrying heavy weights, and his legs were cramping. There was no single part of him that had not some report of abuse to make, and he was so tired. Cramps knotted hotly in his bent calves. He wriggled until his back hit the wall and then sat up carefully as far as he could, hunched over under the pressing stone roof. At least that gave him just enough space to stretch out his legs, which was some relief.

This is not all of me, he told himself, nor is this all of the world. Men will come in time, if I wait, if I am patient, to . . . to . . .

It struck him like a fist in the mouth that such folk as could put a fellow-creature chained in such a hole would hardly be his friends. In fact, they were likely to be the men who had hurt his wrists.

Terror bolted from its lair in his heart and caught him by the throat, stopping breath and thought. He pressed his face against his useless hands and tried to stem shameful tears with his knuckles.

VIII

THERE IS ALWAYS MASQUING before Her Majesty on the afternoon of Christmas Day, supposedly a relaxation for her after the great feast for all the Queen's servants and attendants, packed like herrings in a barrel into the Westminster Hall. This year's masque was the fruit of many weeks' anxious rehearsal and dealt with a beehive wherein were two Kings, one rightful and one a usurper, and the whole very prettily danced and recited by the youngsters about the Queen, their mourning velvets lightened with tawny for the bees' coats, with wings of wired cobweb gauze, and the Queen of the Fairies coming in the nick of time to make peace.

"A pretty parable," the Queen said tartly as she clapped, "though I see no drones nor grubs among these bees."

Sir Walter smiled at her. "Perhaps they have removed to another hive, Your Majesty, where the honey is sweeter."

The Queen snorted. "Is there some parable to sermonise from this masque?" she asked, knowing perfectly well that there was, since the usurper King had ended miserably by execution and the true King had been crowned anew by Titania.

"I am afraid there is," said Raleigh, eyes dancing. "If Your Majesty is not yet sufficiently melancholic, I may parse its meaning for you, so well as I understand it myself."

The Queen groaned and then smiled and nodded graciously at Alicia, the nervous new maid of honour, whose wings were a little lopsided from a collision in the dance. The child curtseyed and shakily offered her a tray of honey-cakes. She took one, bit and winced. Smoothly, Sir Walter handed her a cup of wine to clean her mouth, disposed invisibly of the cake.

"Parse it pithily then, Walter," she snapped. "If you must."

"To be utterly brief, they desire that you should execute the Queen of Scots," he said, not bothering to keep his soft West Country voice low, "and I conclude that your subjects are as ignorant of beekeeping as they are of animal husbandry, sheep-keeping and tact."

"Hah!" said the Queen.

IX

Yes, I RECALL WHAT my faithful servant did upon Christmas Day 1586. Before dawn she was sitting by the fire in the Falcon's common room, sipping her breakfast and shivering while all the church bells clanged through the iron air of London. Over in the corner, ignoring the drunk huddled up by the wall, was sweet Pentecost, her great-granddaughter. Mary had forgot how old the child was, since she often blurred in Mary's mind into her mother and even her grandmother, but she was a fair little maid somewhere about six or seven, with brown hair and an oval face that tended to be solemn. No beauty yet, for which Mary gave thanks to me. Pentecost slept in her great-grandam's bed to keep her warm, but generally woke before her and went down to lay the fire and light it. We were careful that she should be useful, Mary and I, for Mary greatly feared that the little girl might catch some man's eye and be ruined as her dead grandmother Magdalen was, and as her own mother was, Magdalen's daughter, who died giving birth to her.

Her aunt the junior-madam, that Magdalen had named Julia, had already hinted to Mary that Pentecost could go to the Falcon's Chick, where the child-lovers seek out fresh meat. Julia herself was broken in at nine years of age by an upright man who was wapping Magdalen as well, so she saw nothing strange in it.

Mary had rather die than give her sweet little Pentecost to such men, ay, and kill her too. But Julia . . . The junior-madam was puzzled and offended when Mary slapped her face and screamed at her, and put it down to drink and senility. No doubt Julia's mind was as poxed as her cunny. Little Pentecost was the last of Mary's brood, and the last to be in her innocency and Mary was in fear and trembling for her great-granddaughter that she should be ruined by some drunk and go into the same trade as her mother, her aunt and her grandmother, and then die also of the pox or of childbed. If there had been convents in England still, Mary would have put her in one at once, to protect her from ravening men, but alas, the men had destroyed our refuges.

Well, sir, if you had seen men as I have seen them, as they come begging and confessing to me on their deathbeds, you would not be so affronted at what I say. Men revered the Virgin for they knew how much they need mercy, and they suspected that my Son, who was Himself a man, will have less truck with their excuses. To be sure, there are decent men who love women and consider them to be more than a warm moist place inconveniently supplied with legs to run away. Mary had never met one, however, and no reason why she should, since such a chimera would scarcely seek out the strumpets on the south bank of the Thames.

Now Pentecost was playing her usual game. From the long-ago wreck of her nunnery, Mary had taken away only her rosary beads and a precious image of myself. I was cunningly wrought about eight inches high in ivory, crowned with stars and standing on the moon, and if you were to open a little door in my belly, there was also the image of my Son, a carved ivory baby. The inner wall of His hiding place was painted delicately with the Cross of His Passion on Golgotha. There had been many such figures once, before the Reformers got to work at burning them, and this had been as old as the buildings of the nunnery itself, carved for the sick daughter of the man that endowed it and given to the chapel when the little girl died, two hundred years gone. Now the ivory was cracked and worn and yellow, although my face was as gentle and Queenly as ever. First Magdalen, the child of Mary's shame, had played with it; then the girls of Magdalen's brood, Martha and Julia, and at length it had come, through all vicissitudes of famine and wandering, to Pentecost.

First she set me upon a bench and came curtseying to me with a little horn-cup of wine, which she tipped carefully against my carved face, so as not to spill or mark, and then tossed down herself. Then she knelt as she had seen her great-grandam do, and she prayed as her great-grandam had taught her, gabbling a little: *Heavy Maria, grass a plenty, dominoes take 'em.* Then she caught me up and cuddled me, and opened my door and brought out the Babe to kiss, put Him very reverently away again and began to tell me her longings and delights, while I smiled back at her, my lips a little reddened with the wine. I am the Queen of Heaven and many times she had prayed that I would come to her as I did to her grandam and cover her with my mantle.

Her grandam never listened to what she said, but she was asking her invariable boon, which was to be summoned to meet me, the Queen of Heaven and to be my little girl, my foster child. It was her dream: she had seen the Queen

Elizabeth in the distance at the Accession Day tilts and, like many others she had become confused between that Queen and me. But her grandam never knew that then. Why should she pay attention to the notions of children?

Julia came hurrying in, making a great fuss with her new turquoise satin kirtle. She dared to frown impatiently when she saw how Mary wobbled on the stool by the fire. At her belt she had a bunch of keys, her badge of office, and very self-important it made her.

"Grandam," she said, with not even a curtsey, "what is this I hear about you speaking with Jesuits again?" Mary muttered and would not look at her. "Is it true?" she demanded.

Mary shrugged and gave no answer. Julia rustled over, pounced and snatched the bottle from her.

"Are you mad?" she hissed in her grandam's face, the impudent bitch. "I told you last summer what would come of this. You must not speak to these Papist priests, you must keep away from them."

Mary flinched. "I must make my confession," she mumbled. "I must shrive my sins before I die."

Julia spat like the urchin she once was.

"Oh, a fig for your confession, Grandam, it's too late for that. If the pursuivants get word of you speaking to a priest, they will arrest you for it and then where will we be?"

"You can find another witch," said Mary. "And I'll be dead. What joy, eh? No more drunken old grandam to sermonise, and you can send poor little Pentecost to the lecherous perverts at the Chick."

Pentecost looked up briefly at the mention of her name and then went back to her play, since she had heard both these arguments before.

Julia rolled her eyes and rattled the keys as was her habit.

"All you need to do is keep your mouth shut and away from Papist priests," she said, "Otherwise, out."

"You would put your own grandam on the street?"

"If necessary," she said, cold as the cobbles. "If I must do it to keep my place here, yes. Not Pentecost. But if you bring the City corporation down on our necks, out you go, Grandam, be sure of it."

Mary stood up and stretched her poor aching back which was barely soothed by the booze. She was in haste, for sunrise was only an hour away and she must go to her work and so must Pentecost.

Do you think work has surcease on Christmas Day? Think again.

"I'll never leave Pentecost where you could put your greedy claws on her," said Mary stoutly if indistinctly. "I know what you—"

"Never mind Pentecost," Julia interrupted, opening the door and going to fold back the red lattices. "Mind yourself, Grandam. That's my last warning."

One of the younger whores by the name of Kate was coming down the stairs in her stays and petticoat, scratching at the sore on her face, a filthy habit.

Ay, of course it is the pox.

"Kate," said Julia, very full of authority and key-rattling, "pick up that drunk and throw him out."

"He's not paid us yet."

"Well, take his purse first, then throw him out."

Julia was hurrying to open the other set of lattices. Kate bent to the man, found his purse under his crotch, then took him under the armpits and heaved him through the door into the street, where she left him in an icy puddle.

"Not gone yet, Grandam?" said Julia to Mary.

To be fair, it was she had found the place at Court in the summer, when Mary first thought to hide from pursuivants. Her Majesty's priest-finders only desired to know her business with a Jesuit who gave them the slip and later crossed the Channel in an almighty hurry, but Mary was not inclined to tell them and so required a bolt-hole. Julia's bolt-hole was an excellent one, working out of the Whitehall laundry, which is beyond the pursuivants' remit, being within the Virge of the Court and so subject only to the Lord Chamberlain and the Clerk of the Board of Greencloth. But God knows, that trade was hard on her poor bones, and her poor heart too, though perhaps better for her soul, being so humble.

She beckoned to Pentecost, thinking grimly of the evil times when the grandam must be meek to the grandchild. Her darling put her Madonna toy in the pocket of her petticoat and came trotting over, shivering a little in her thin old kirtle and wiping her breakfast off her face onto her apron.

She smiled at Mary and took her hand, plump living ivory in mouldy leather. "May we walk across the river again, Grandam?" she wanted to know and skipped and laughed when Mary said they could. To her it was a wonder to walk where the boats went, now the Thames was frozen. In general they had a longer walk to go round by London Bridge, to save the tuppence on the boat fare, through the City to Ludgate, down Fleet Street and the Strand and all the way round about the river to Whitehall, which was a walk of three miles and hard for Pentecost's short legs. Sometimes, when Mary was not too weary, she carried the child on her back, as once she had carried Magdalen. But with the ice that bit her old bones came the blessing that now they could walk dry-shod on the water like Christ and Saint Peter, and laugh at the boatmen too who were begging and starving in the frost, and serve the greedy bastards right.

X

PRIDE IS SUCH A strange thing, so lacking in logic. The man that lay crippled by torture in Little Ease set his teeth and endured unnecessary extra pain in his bladder, rather than wet like a child where he must lie. Although he knew he must have done it before while unconscious, now he was awake he could not bring himself to it. Water might come from his eyes, but not from his cock; thus he buttressed what little was left of himself.

Just as he thought despairingly that he must give way, there was a clatter of keys, rattling of bolts, and fiery daylight struck his face and blurred his eyes. An opening about a yard square had appeared.

A man in a morion helmet pushed in a tray bearing bread, meats, a leather jug and a mug.

"Sir," husked the prisoner, swallowing painfully against the flooding in his mouth, "Sir, please, a pot for my necessity . . ."

The man-at-arms turned his face as if to get permission from one in authority who stood out of sight. Then, blank-faced, he pushed in a small leather bucket.

The prisoner grabbed for it, dropped it, caught at it with both hands and fumbled to use it. While he turned aside, the door slammed back into place and was locked again, with only a Judas hole open to give light for his meal. None answered when he called.

Despite his hunger and thirst, he ate and drank as slowly as he could, made slower by his clumsy fingers. He was astonished at the quality of the food and wine. Why should they feed him such delicacies as white bread, only one day old, and roasted goose stuffed with chestnuts and apricots, ham basted with honey, cheese, and plum pudding with a hard sauce . . . ?

Suddenly it dawned on him what he was eating and what day it must be. Even inquisitors kept Christmas, it seemed, and he found himself sniggering. Such a cold nicety made him laugh until the stone echoed.

XI

Bⁱᴀᴄᴋ ᴠᴇʟᴠᴇᴛ ᴋɪʀᴛʟᴇ ꜱᴡɪɴɢɪɴɢ, Mistress Bethany was going at the half-trot down a narrow whitewashed corridor towards the Queen's chambers away from the tiny room she shared with two other maids of honour. She had told Blanche Parry she had left her needlework bag there, which she had, but not by accident.

A tall young man unfolded himself from a window-seat and fielded her neatly, with his arms around her waist to imprison her. Far from screaming and boxing his ears in defence of her honour, Mistress Bethany only giggled disgracefully and wished him Merry Christmas.

"At Christmas, the only roses to be seen are the ones blooming in your snowy cheeks," he whispered in her ear, a phrase he had carefully practised. Bethany's roses bloomed redder and she looked down at his hands.

"I have only a few minutes before I must be back," she hissed as he sat her beside him on the window-seat, checked to make sure that the winter Privy Garden outside the window was empty, and kissed her forehead. She shut her eyes as his kisses progressed over her eyelids, across her cheek, until they landed on her mouth where he kissed again, more dangerously. Her heart thundered beneath her stays until she was sure that the Queen ought to hear it. And then she rebelled against shamefastness. Why should she not enjoy his kisses, since she loved him? The needlework bag dropped to the floor.

"Have you written to your father?" she asked eventually, and did not allow herself to notice his infinitesimal check.

"Yes, but he has not written back," he said, "No doubt the rider was delayed with the snow."

"Do you think he will say yes?"

"I'm sure of it, sweeting, he's never denied me yet. Besides, we are already handfasted. What about your father?"

Bethany nodded, although she had not in fact written to him at all.

"He may take a while," she said, "but once we are married, he'll pay my dowry over in the end, rather than argue about it. He hates to see me unhappy."

"And so do I." There were more kisses and an expert exploration of the geography of Bethany's petticoats.

She stopped him at last, wriggling deliciously.

"I must go back or Parry will come searching for me," she said, jumping up ready to return.

"Let me give you your New Year's gift." He fished in a pocket in his sleeve and took out a little box wrapped in a scrap of cloth-of-gold. Bethany's eyes shone as she opened it, and she squealed over the little enamelled gold locket, delicately wound with dog roses of pink enamel on a midnight-blue background with sparks of diamond. But then she frowned to find there was no miniature within.

"I will have one painted when the Queen gives her permission. Until then it's too dangerous."

Bethany nodded, the frown almost gone. Then she grinned impishly, dived in amongst the tangle of her work-bag and produced her snips, caught a short lock of his hair and cut it off before he could protest.

"There," she said, as she put the golden strands carefully into the locket and shut it. "Now I have something for a token."

Her lover made shift to smile. "You need none of my hair to make your enchantments," he said. "Only your own beauty."

She laughed at him then, for being so solemn, kissed his cheek and trotted on down the corridor.

XII

I MADE YOU WHAT you are, the Queen thought as she stared at Lord Burghley during the Privy Council meeting the day after Christmas, on the Feast of Saint Stephen. I knew you when you were plain Sir William Cecil, and saw your quality. I made you Lord Burghley, I trusted you to make your fortune in such a way that it would not damage me. If Queens may have friends, then you are my friend. Why are you betraying me?

Burghley's pouched clever face showed no sign of any warlock's ability to read minds. His power came from the Queen and his value to her came from his unrivalled administrative intelligence. He sat on his padded stool at the long meeting table in the great Council Chamber and prosed on at length and in detail with his reasons for desiring the Queen of Scots' death. Opposite him sat Walsingham, occasionally his rival but on this occasion more in the way of his puppeteer. The whole damned garboil was Walsingham's, from start to finish. Walsingham's face was as different from Burghley's as a blade from a legal deed: a lean, dark face, black hair a little frosted with silver, eyes so dark a brown as to be black, skin sallow to the extent that she jokingly called him her Moor— especially when he had a jaundice as he had now. Walsingham's intelligence was more like her own, she thought, as he chimed in respectfully to support the Lord Treasurer Burghley. Now, *he* had powers of phantasy—politic rather than poetic. His mind was a sword, sharpened by the Bible and the classics and wielded ruthlessly. Unfortunately he also had a dangerous mental flaw, like too many others in these benighted times. One of its symptoms was in the dress: Walsingham wore black brocades and velvets, unrelieved by colour or jewels, and a snowy-white ruff. He was also in mourning for his son-in-law, for whom he truly grieved, as the black shadows under his eyes and the pallor of his skin attested. However, he always appeared in this stark cloth parable and the world through his eyes was much the same: all black and white, with no saving colours in it at all.

God rot you, thought Elizabeth as the Earl of Leicester chimed in, did you not know that the dyers and tailors have half a dozen names for white alone, as in burnt-lead white, and ivory white, and cream white, and alabaster white and marble white; each seems to be whiteness itself on its own but, placed one against the other, they are as different as men's faces. But then perhaps to Walsingham they would still all be white, until he saw a flaw or a spot in them, at which point they would no longer be regarded as white but relegated to the blackly damned nine-tenths of Creation. The thought brought fear with it. She was afraid of such a world. How many times had she hidden behind ambiguities much more subtle?

"Your Majesty?" said the Earl of Leicester delicately. "Are you offended with my plain-speaking?"

With a little effort Elizabeth reeled back the last few words of his speech in her mind and found a lot of charm, much flattery but hardly any plain-speaking. Leicester too was in mourning, and quite unlike his peacock self to be so sombrely clad in black velvet and brocade, even trimmed as his was with crimson: Sidney had been his nephew.

"In short, you desire that I should execute my cousin Queen," she said flatly. He bowed humbly from the waist.

"For your own protection, Your Majesty. Every single Papist plot has had as its end and object her usurpation of your throne—"

"Oh, give over your pleadings," she snapped. "God knows I have heard them all before, in multitudes and overplus. Has not a single one of you anything new to say?"

"Parliament, Your Majesty . . ." bleated Hatton, opposite Leicester.

Her headache worsened. "Parliament has been prorogued," she growled, "for meddling in matters it does not understand. Namely, these matters."

A decade or two ago that would have been the signal for some jewelled fool to pipe up the old tune: "If Your Majesty would but marry . . ." No longer. First they had learned to bridle their advice and then Time, her friend, had rendered the whole tedious subject irrelevant. And so they had pounced on a new obsession.

"The people, Your Majesty," put in a new voice.

My Court is ageing with me, she thought again, but here is a new face at least. She thought of him as a young man but he was in his thirties and had spent his whole adult life in her service. Unlike the others, he could barely remember a time when she had not been Queen.

"Yes, Mr Secretary Davison," she said, her voice deceptively mellifluous. "Teach me about my people."

Walsingham shifted surreptitiously on his stool and looked sideways in warning at his protégé, only admitted to the Privy Council the previous summer. William Davison had spent most of his career in the Netherlands and his dress betrayed how much the Calvinists had influenced him. Like Walsingham, he too wore black relieved only by the icy whiteness of his plain ruff and cuffs.

Davison bowed a little. "Your Majesty," he said, "I would not presume to teach you anything."

"Such as sucking eggs?" Her voice was tart. His face remained smooth and respectful and he answered without a pause. "That least of all. Only permit me to bring you facts."

"Well?"

"At the news that the Scottish Queen had been condemned, the people of London lit bonfires in the streets and let off fireworks."

"Firearms, too, so I heard," she said sardonically. "Were many wounded?"

"By the grace of God, not many," Davison answered, still straight-faced.

"Letters are brought daily to the Court from every county of the realm, beseeching Your Majesty to end the Scottish Queen's life. Ballads are written, Your Majesty, printed and sold in their thousands, that call curses down on the mermaid's head. A number of pamphlets have been written and likewise published that—"

"Oh." She shrugged. "So your paid scribblers and printing presses have not been idle."

He bowed slightly in acknowledgement, his flow of rhetoric momentarily dammed.

"And?" she snapped when he hesitated.

"And they commend your womanly mercy, your feminine unwillingness to shed blood—this is seemly, Your Majesty, and praiseworthy, but they fear that Your Majesty will pay for your gentleness and kindness with your life. And so do we."

It was almost funny how the other men at the table all winced in unison at Davison's patronising talk of her womanly mercy. The Queen looked in silence at him, considering. The others were bracing for a thunderbolt. She thought she would play with them a while.

"Do you know chess, Mr Davison?" she asked, still gently.

"No, Your Majesty. I abhor all games of chance as immoral."

She nodded gravely, wondering if he knew how often she liked to play primero. "But you know," she said, "if you do not throw dice when pieces of equal power meet, but hold that each skirmish is won by whichever is in place and may move, chess becomes a very different thing. It becomes a game no longer of chance but only of skill and logic, and in such a game you may learn many wonderful subtleties. For instance, a chessman rightly placed may hold in thrall a great attacking array."

His face was respectful and blank. "Indeed, Your Majesty. If you tell me so, I shall study the matter more closely."

"I advise it, Mr Davison," she said. "I advise it indeed."

"Your Majesty, in the matter of the Queen of Scots . . ." began the Earl of Leicester, presuming on their old friendship to nag her still further.

"In the matter of the Queen of Scots, the subject is closed."

"The death warrant?" said Walsingham, deliberately misunderstanding, "Shall we bring it to you, then?"

That impudence, finally, broke her patience.

Her fist hit the table and bounced. She stood up so fast, the two gentlemen behind her were not quick enough to move her heavy chair and she barked the backs of her calves on the carvings.

"*No,*" she roared, "you may *not* bring it! You may not speak of it. I will not sign it. Do I speak plain enough, my lords, gentlemen? The man that brings it to me will never serve me again."

Perhaps if loyalty would not keep them off her back, ambition might. They were standing politely as well, exchanging covert knowing looks. The Queen was often thought to use witchcraft to know the minds of men, but in fact she had no need of it for men are, beyond all things, transparent. They were weary and not at all put off, convinced that the poor frail woman must see their sense in the end. Damn them all for fools. She looked around for something to throw at Davison, and found nothing, not even a goblet.

"Now get out and leave me in peace!" she shrieked and they bowed, filed to the door, bowed again, backed from her presence.

She sat down and clicked her fingers for one of her gentlemen to bring her spiced wine. But he was there, kneeling at her elbow already, holding a tray with a steaming goblet on it. She took it, drank and smiled at her handsome young cousin, Robert Carey.

"What would you do, if you were Queen, Robin?" she asked him and he smiled back.

"Your Majesty," he said. "If I had been born to woman's estate, and further if I had been you, the Queen, I would have married twenty years ago."

Her smile stiffened and chilled. He was among the closest of her relatives, being not only her cousin through Mary Boleyn, his grandmother and her aunt, but also, unofficially, her nephew, since the man who had given him the name of Carey had not been the King who actually sired his father. However, this was perilously close to impudence as she defined such things.

"Oh?"

"Yes, Your Majesty." His hooded blue eyes crinkled at the corners and danced, perfectly aware of his gamble and enjoying it. "I should make a very poor monarch since I have so little virtue and far too much . . . er . . . sinfulness and so I would have married in order not to burn and the question would not have arisen."

"And it would furthermore have been your husband's decision."

"Precisely, Your Majesty. But then, if I were born a woman and a Queen, perhaps the Queen of Scots might have been born a man and a King, and so I could have married him and solved the problem entirely."

She had to laugh at the way he had given her perilous question the slip.

"It seems you are learning some Courtly talk at last, Robin. You used to be more plain-spoken," she said with a little edge, putting the goblet back on the silver tray.

"If Your Majesty desires me to speak plain, then I shall speak plain."

"Well, Robin?"

He frowned and looked directly up at her. "It seems to me kinder to execute the Queen of Scots than leave her cooped up and in doubt of her fate," he said, confirming her opinion that like his father, Lord Hunsdon, her Lord Chamberlain and unofficial half-brother, he did not really understand politics.

"Kinder?" she repeated wonderingly. Nobody else in the entire vexed saga of the Queen of Scots had ever mentioned kindness.

"Yes, Your Majesty. Are Queens to be exempt from kindness?"

"I had always believed so," she muttered.

Robin Carey shook his head, his face troubled. "But in this, as in anything else, I think Your Majesty should do what your conscience tells you is right."

"My conscience has more for which to answer to God than mine own soul. If I decide wrongly, I wreck the realm."

"Yes," he said simply. "That is why neither I nor anyone else can tell you what you should do. God will guide Your Majesty to do what is right."

If she had not been the Queen and he her nobly-born servant, she would have kissed him for his simplicity. Instead she sighed. "Give me your arm, Robin, and tell me where I can find your father, since it seems the household expenses are rising once more."

Deftly he passed the tray round the back of her chair to the other gentleman, held his green-velveted arm at an angle so she could rest her hand on it and came smoothly to his feet, supporting her as she rose. He towered over her and she had always liked well-made graceful young men, especially those who knew how to dress and how to charm. This one had a good voice as well, she recalled, suppressing the knowledge that she had been godmother at his christening, damn him.

"Come and sing to me," she said, enjoying the glower of envy he got from the other gentleman. "Soothe my ruffled heart."

He bowed and smiled.

"Your Majesty does me too much honour."

XIII

I T WAS SIX MONTHS before that black Christmas, in the summer of the Babington plot, the summer of 1586, when the Jesuits first got wind of the Book of the Unicorn. That morning all London crawled with Walsingham's pursuivants who broke into men's houses and hunted priests like the deer.

It was a rare morning of sobriety for Mary, since she had been attending a whore in the night to lighten her of her babe, a poor blue little thing that conveniently died without help. Tired and sad, at last the witch had broken her fast in a boozing ken east of London Bridge. As she started to drink away her fee she noticed a poorly dressed man at the next table. He had folded fine soft hands and was whispering Latin over his bread. At first all she thought was that he must be a careless and stupid priest, to be so public in his devotions.

Then, when she rose and hobbled to the door, she saw four men in the street, two on either side of it, armed with the clubs and coshes and warrants of pursuivants. For a moment she hesitated, afraid of Walsingham's men and also afraid of the priest. I stepped swiftly from my cloud into her heart and spoke to her, told her what to do. So she went back into the ken and sidled up to the priest.

By my small miracle she pulled together the rags of her Latin and told him in that tongue the pursuivants were waiting for him.

His square soldier's face was drawn and weary with long hunting, and he sagged like the fox that finds his last earth stopped up.

"Are they coming in?" he asked.

Mary shrugged. "How should I know," she said, still in Latin, "but the Blessed Virgin has ordered me to bring you away from here."

The priest looked cautiously at her, for it must be said that even the saintliest man will doubt a toothless old woman when she talks of visions. "Perhaps it's God's will I should be taken," he muttered, gulping the last of his beer.

Mary shook her head violently and pinched his shoulder. "If they take you, then to whom shall I make my confession?" she hissed. "What if I die unshriven and go to Hell? It will be your fault, Father."

He smiled briefly at that, reassured by her selfishness.

"The Blessed Virgin, eh?" he said. "What do you know about her, Mother?"

"More than you do," said Mary tartly. "And you should address me as Sister. Now come with me."

Blinking and calculating, the priest allowed her to take his hand, lead him softly past the bar while the tapster was busy with the farthest barrel, and through to the brewing sheds behind. They climbed over a wall, Mary grunting and struggling until the Jesuit, who was powerfully built, though not tall, boosted her up with no regard for her dignity. They crept through a yard filled with pigs, over another wall and into a tiny hidden passage between houses that wended down to the river. Just above the water-steps they tucked themselves into the lee of a garden wall that bordered the Thames.

"Sister?" asked the priest when he had caught his breath. "Were you a nun once?" His voice spoke volumes of how she was laid low and she winced at it.

"Sister Mary, Infirmerar and Mistress of Novices at the Convent of St Mary's, Clerkenwell," she said to him, bowing as she would have once to the nunnery's chaplain. And then the knowledge of all her sins caught round her throat like the devils of Hell and she blushed dark red with shame and looked away from him, down at the ground. "Once," she whispered. "Long ago."

The priest stared at her and shook his head. "I took you for a witch," he said simply. "I am sorry. You may know me as Father Tom Hart."

Mary's heart was too low and her hearing too bad for it, but the next moment he tilted his head. "Listen," he whispered.

It is hard to mistake when pursuivants enter a boozing ken to make an arrest, what with the bellowing of the Queen's name and the cudgelling of any that try to escape and the banging of doors and the breaking of windows.

"How did you know?" he asked.

"I saw them waiting for you and Our Lady told me what to do."

Father Hart crossed himself. "Praise be to her, merciful Queen," he said, and I smiled at him. "Now where do we go?"

Mary considered. "There will be pursuivants on the bridge and no doubt they know your appearance to stop you there." The priest nodded. "If we take a boat, the boatman will doubtless sell us to Walsingham as well. I think we should wait."

"Here?" he asked, for they were perched on a ledge above the foul stinking mud of the Thames and attacked by flies also.

"Why not? If it is not God's will that you die a martyr, then Our Lady will protect us, and if it is, you will be taken away."

Father Hart nodded at this good logic. "And you, Sister? You had better leave me so as not to be interrogated if . . ."

"Pooh," sniffed Mary, unwontedly brave, "what do I care for Walsingham and all his men. I'm too old to be frightened by a lot of pompous heretics. Besides, if I suffer a martyr's death, then it wipes out all my sins."

"Have you many sins to confess, Sister?"

Again the weight of them bowed her shoulders. "Too many," she husked. "Too many to tell."

Tom Hart's face softened. Within his breast I heard him give hearty thanks to my Son that he was made the means of helping her, old and ragged and stinking as she was. He put his hand on her shoulder right gently. "It seems we have time," he said. "If you want to wait with me, Sister, I can hear you now."

I smiled on both of them as my daughter-in-law crossed herself and composed her mind and began to whisper all the many evils she had done. Once the dam was breached, they poured out of her like a black waterfall, incontinent, uncounted. And the young man listened with his eyes closed to give her privacy, full reverently and gently.

She and the priest were not seen. Am I not the Star of the Sea, the Dew of the Ocean? Pursuivants searched the garden behind the wall that sheltered them and even checked the tiny path to the river, but my mantle was over them and a mist of insects came up and hid them. All the long afternoon while Mary unburdened herself, no once came near. By the time the river water lapped a couple of feet below them with the returning tide, Mary felt she had been cleansed to her soul.

The priest was all the wearier for what he had heard, but also exultant at having been given something he knew must be of vital importance to the cause of bringing England back to the Faith. Amongst the pelting rush of Mary's wickedness had nestled a story the more strange for being unremarked by her. An old, old story, many years forgotten.

Blessing her, he said the *Ego te absolvo* and she felt all the crusting of wickedness break from her soul and fall into the river. She did not like the penance he gave her, which was to avoid all booze but small beer in future. She would have found a pilgrimage to Jerusalem less difficult to contemplate. Never mind. She would think of it another time.

Then they said Vespers together and also the *Salve Regina*, which was Mary's favourite prayer and Mary wept at the beauty of the rosy sun on the water and the violet-petalled clouds in the sky while I smiled at her.

"Will you give me your Book of the Unicorn?" asked the priest carefully at last.

Mary shook her head. "I pawned it," she said. "And I have not the money to rescue it."

"Pawned it, where?"

For all her newly sinless state, she was canny enough to shrug. "I forget." Well, lying is only a venial sin.

The long summer evening was coming down and Tom Hart was full of joy. God would not have given him such a weapon for the True Faith if he was to be a martyr immediately and therefore he knew he would escape the pursuivants this time. He had already thought how he could do it.

"If I can find the money to redeem your book, will you give it to me?" he asked.

Mary nodded and began thinking hard, for his eagerness betrayed him. She was thinking about her great-granddaughter Pentecost, who was helping out at the Falcon, and what she was thinking was that if Pentecost could have a dowry, she need not be a whore.

"I don't know."

"Sister Mary," said Father Hart intently. "Do you know that God has His purpose in everything that befalls?"

She nodded, although she no longer believed it as she had once.

"Well, then, I see the means of a great good in all the sorrowful tale you have told me, a wonderful providence of God to rescue England from heresy."

He had caught her age-spotted hand, gazed into her red-rimmed eyes, full of ardour for his Faith, so she was almost afraid.

"This tale of yours, if it were generally known, it would destroy the Queen's power. It would break the false glamour of the spell she has woven over the people. Do you understand? Your tale could change the kingdom, if it were used right."

Mary did not answer, for she was all of a maze between hope restored and doubts. The priest paused, for what he was asking was no light thing.

"Everything you have told me is under the seal of the confessional," he said. "I will keep your secrets to death, if need be, with Christ's help. But if I have your leave, I will go to the Duke of Parma in the Netherlands and have the Queen's wickedness published abroad so all men may know what she truly is."

"And all men will know I am a witch," mumbled Mary.

"Your name I will never tell, but if I have your Book of the Unicorn, I can prove the truth of what you say. And besides, you are no longer a witch, for you have repudiated Satan once more and your repentance has saved you."

Mary nodded, for she felt it to be true.

"I'll get you the money for the pawnshop," said the priest, feeling sure he could persuade her. "Do I have your leave to repeat your story?"

For a moment she still hesitated, remembering. Father Hart recognised her scruples. "What do you owe Elizabeth the heretic? It was to clear her way to the throne that King Henry broke the nunneries."

Mary scowled. "You have my leave," she said. "Tell Parma what you like."

He kissed her hand as if she were the Queen herself. She smiled at him and then her face puckered with anxiety once more. "But how will you escape . . . ?"

He grinned at her like the daring knight he would have been, had my Son not called him to be His soldier.

"It's a warm day and will be a warm night, I think. I'll wait for the turn of the tide and then I'll let the river take me down to Tilbury."

"But the boatman . . ."

"Wherefore should I need a boat when I have my arms and legs still whole, thank God and thanks to you."

It took her a while to understand him and then she was horrified.

"Swimming?"

"Ay, of course."

"But your clothes . . . ?"

"Will be bundled up on my head. And the river will throw the dogs off the scent and much puzzle the pursuivants."

"You will catch your death, or the river water will poison you."

"Nonsense. Salmon swim in the Thames, why not I? Never fear, Sister, I feel sure this is God's will. With the tide to bear me, I'll have no trouble."

"What about the book?"

"How much to redeem it?"

"Five shillings."

Straight away he reached inside his shirt and brought out his purse, emptied it into her hand, to the amount of six shillings and eightpence. She blinked at such riches so casually dispensed and, newly shriven as she was, instantly fell into the sin of greed.

"Redeem it now and bring it to me here before the tide turns," he ordered, knowing her to be a nun and thinking that this meant she would be biddable and obedient.

Mary said nothing, only closed her fist on the money and sidled away. Tom Hart waited for her as long as he dared, but with the tide already running and

Walsingham's hounds, human and canine, still rousting out the City through the long soft evening, he dared not miss his chance. She had no faith that he could do what he said, but he did: clad only in his shirt for modesty's sake and with his homespun suit tied up and balanced on his head, he slid into the water and struck out under the stars for Tilbury.

XIV

AFTER THE PRIVY COUNCIL Meeting, the Queen suffered an afternoon glazed with tedium: there had been one meeting after another; the worst was an unpleasant cold encounter with Walsingham.

She had noticed with inward dismay that it was not only grief which was making his face so drawn and yellow. She recognised the way he would pause sometimes and grip hard on whatever he held, and from the sheen on him he was running a fever as well. When she accused him of hiding his sickness so he could harass her over the Queen of Scots, his lips had thinned to invisibility and he had not looked at her. She had ordered him to his bed and he had gone saying that he left the matter in Davison's capable hands.

Afterwards there had been another unsatisfactory passage of arms with the Scottish Embassy, sent to her Court by the Queen of Scots' undutiful son King James, the Sixth of that name, ostensibly to talk her out of executing the mother he had last seen when he was ten months old. They too wished her a Merry Christmastide.

She wanted the Scottish gentlemen—*gentlemen,* in God's name, not even nobles!—to say that King James would break their alliance and declare war if she executed his mother. That would give her the excuse she needed. Obstinately they refused to say it and took refuge in flattery of her mercy and enquiries after the subject of the play to be shown and whether the famous Fool, Richard Tarlton, would be in it. She dismissed the infamous fools and retreated to her Bedchamber to rest before the evening's festivities. Beyond many doors in the Presence Chamber they were laying the table with as much ceremonial as a Papist Mass for a meal she would eat in private. Great reverent mobs of petitioners were allowed to pay for the privilege of watching gentlemen serve an empty chair with delicate meats and complex sauces while the Queen munched winter herbs and farced goose and manchet and drank small beer at a table in her Bedchamber, and read more of the endless papers kept locked in her silver filigree cabinet. She was in desperate need of a good day's hunting to blow the megrims and cobwebs of deceit from her head, but with the weather so cold it was too dangerous to ride, even horses with studded shoes. The hunt planned for the Feast of Saint Stephen had been cancelled.

Still, she could dance. And the play in the Great Hall put her in an excellent humour, for all the heat from the candles and press of courtiers who roared delightedly as Tarlton poked his head from behind a tapestry and wriggled his eyebrows. When the mumming was done she gave Tarlton his bag of gold, and marked with a heavy heart the age-lines beneath his paint. At last she processed to her Privy Gallery and sat down on cushions with her women around her. There she talked to Lady Bedford about nothing whatever to do with the Queen of Scots while the musicians gathered in the far corner played quietly upon their lutes and viols.

Later the gentlemen rolled back the rush-matting and the musicians changed their instruments and began playing dances. The youngsters danced a volta, the men prancing like stags in rut, and, grasping the women by waist and stomacher, they threw them straight up and around so they came down in a flurry of petticoats with their feet placed so. The floor-boards resounded with it.

A couple of times the Queen rose and danced a more stately pavane, although she was still perfectly capable of a volta if she wished. Tonight she did not wish; with the passing of Tarlton's brief enchantment, she was in too dour a mood. Nor did the sight of the young people in the blaze of candles cheer her as they usually did, thanks to their dismal fashion of mourning for Sidney, which turned them all into an unkindness of ravens.

And then her women, who had been whispering among themselves, brought out their little plot to please her. They stood in a row and begged her in only slightly strained verse to guess which one of them was hiding a treasure. By the laws of the play she must find the truth by asking them questions and they could answer yea or nay but nothing else.

"Every one of the maidens is hiding a treasure under her skirts," said a gentleman gallantly from the press of them down by the doors to the Privy Chamber. Some of the girls blushed.

"I will not ask if Virginity is the treasure you hide, since 'yes' is the only answer any of you may give," said the Queen lightly.

The maids of honour looked at each other and tried not to giggle.

She established that it was not made of diamonds nor of silk and asked if it might be a book. They all shook their heads and looked at each other sidelong, while the gentlemen called out suggestions as ribald as they dared.

The only one none of them looked at was Bethany and the Queen began to smile. She passed up and down the line again, tapping her mouth with her fingers.

"Now it is not a man, I hope," she said.

More giggling, more sidelong looks. There was no mistake, they all avoided looking at Bethany. So she stood in front of the girl and smiled at her.

"Well, Bethany," she said. "And what have you got for me?"

The cream of the girl's skin coloured suddenly, like strawberry juice poured in a fool of sugared cream. The gentlemen cheered and prayed her to lift her skirts so they could see her treasure, which made Elizabeth turn and wag her finger at them. Felipe, one of her little dogs, took offence at the cheering and barked defiance, until a chamberer picked him up and held his nose.

The girls had devised a way to avoid embarrassment. They made a pretty dance of it and circled Bethany as if they were playing The Farmer Wants a Wife, so that, modestly screened by bouncing black kirtles, Bethany could lift her farthingale. Out rolled a tiny figure in gold and black, tumbling head over heels into the clear space.

In a high, piercing voice she sang a song of Arcadia while she danced and turned somersaults in the air until she sat down on her knees in front of the Queen, making herself tinier still and hailed the Queen as the greatest treasure of all.

The Queen swept her into her arms, kissed her face and settled her on her knee.

"Thomasina, sweeting, you must have been stifled under all of Bethany's petticoats." She laughed.

Thomasina put her wise little face on one side and nodded.

"It was very dark and what I could see was like a pavilion with rather plump tentpoles," she announced and the men laughed again while Bethany blushed. "Did my dance please Your Majesty?"

"Of course it did, my heart," cooed the Queen. "It was a wonderful dance. However do you turn yourself over in the air?"

Thomasina laced her fingers and looked up at the Queen. "You leap as high as a volta leap and then dive," she said, jumping from the Queen's knee. "Look, this is how."

She stood on her tiptoes, making herself a few inches more than a yard high, stretched up her arms, leaped, tucked and turned in the air, coming down on her feet with a flushed face and her miniature farthingale bouncing like a struck bell. "There," she said in triumph. "Now you try, Your Majesty," she added cheekily.

"But I am not a flea, Thomasina," laughed the Queen. "And not a frog neither."

"Well, nor am I. Will you dance with me instead? Please?"

With Thomasina the Queen danced a volta, leaping high and disposedly as she had twenty years before and occasionally usurping the man's part and hurling Thomasina up by her stays to watch her turn in the air. Sometimes she turned twice. Even the musicians smiled at the sight until the Queen threw herself back on her cushions and gasped with laughter. Thomasina turned triumphantly to the clapping courtiers, bowed to them and settled herself down at her Queen's feet like a kitten.

It would have been a perfect evening if that miserable bastard of a man, Davison, had not come in and stood quietly, waiting to be noticed at the back among the gentlemen, his melancholy suit blotting a whole candelabrum of lights behind him, a reproach to their elegant damasks and velvets. For a time, while three gentlemen lifted their voices in roundelays and Italian madrigals, the Queen tried to ignore him. Still he stood there, grating at her like a stone in her shoe. So she beckoned him over and he knelt beside her with his hat in his hands.

"Will you dance, Mr Secretary?" she asked.

"Alas, Your Majesty, I am too poor a dancer for your blessed eyes," he said.

"Then you should take instruction in the art."

"I have, Your Majesty, and my unfortunate teacher tells me that never has he met a more froward pupil."

"Hmf." She knew perfectly well he lied since he disapproved on principle of dancing, holding it like others of his doleful kind to be next door to dalliance and lewdness. Which, of course, was what made it fun. "They do say in Scotland: 'Never give a sword to a man who cannot dance.'"

"Do they?" prosed Davison, "Then how fortunate that although I am Scots by descent, I was born in England. We all have need of swords to protect Your Blessed Majesty."

How did he do it? the Queen wondered furiously, how could he take a perfectly proper and flattering thing to say and fill it up with untraceable menace?

"Well, what is it then, Mr Davison?" she said. "What urgent thing have you come to me about?"

"We have been searching for a woman," he murmured. "A witch who claims to be prophesying about you, Your Majesty."

What in hell had that to do with her?

"So?"

"She claims that Your Majesty will know no peace until you have found your Book of the Unicorn and destroyed it."

His face was as blank as ever. If ever he takes up primero he will make a dangerous opponent, she thought distantly. For a moment as she watched him, she felt that all her blood had turned to ice in her veins and stopped their flow like the Thames that winter. She could not speak.

"The Unicorn, of course," he went on, not seeming to notice her silence, "is the badge of Scotland."

She found her voice again. "It is also the name of a bawdy-house! Really, Mr Davison," she added in tones which had reduced other men to tears, "you bother me with this? Some old fool of a hag's presumptuous gabblings? I had thought better of you than that. Do you take notice of the sayings of an old witch?"

"We intend to arrest her, of course." If anything, his smugness had increased. Why? What had she let slip?

God damn it, she had said "old witch," she had told him she knew the woman was old, and therefore knew more about her than his information. Davison had carefully said only that she was a prophetess. A witch could be any age.

"Wherefore arrest her? To give her garbage the respectability of imprisonment? Has anyone published the prophecy?"

"No, Your Majesty."

"Well then, see to it that they do not," she told him, compressed malice in her voice. "Evidently you do not have enough work to do. I shall take steps to mend it."

At last he was silent, although his face gave no sign that he was abashed.

"Go on, get out of my sight," she shouted. "Get out, get *out!*"

He scrambled to his feet, backed between the silent gentlemen, bowed, backed again. She threw her muff at him and was pleased to see him trip on it as he went through the door.

All her courtiers looked at her, wondering what she would do next. She clicked her fingers at the musicians and nodded at the gentlemen.

"Come," she said in a false sprightly voice, "sing it again."

They did, but the evening was ruined.

XV

CLEARLY MARY WAS DAVISON'S old hag. If she had but known it, Julia had good cause to rate her grandam. Even little Pentecost had the sense to scold her for gabbing when once she had sobered up, but by then it was too late. Some maggot of a pursuivant had got wind of Mary's words and passed them on to Davison.

It must have been in the days before that evil Christmas that she spoke my prophecy and boasted her boast. On the day of Christ's Birth itself, when she had finished her rounds at Court, Mrs Ann Twiste, the Queen's Laundress, stopped her and gave her the Queen's bounty, which was two mutton and currant pies and some broken meats, a bottle of ale posset and a piece of the great plum pudding that was served in the Hall. Pentecost and her grandam drank all the posset to keep them warm on the ice and ate the pies as they slid giggling like girls over the Thames and made three attempts at the Paris Garden steps before they had the victory. And then they judged that Julia should suffer for her arrogance. They hid the meats and the cake under their skirts and swallowed their mirth as they crept in by the back door.

They went to bed in all their clothes because of the difficulty of taking them off, and the emptiness of the fireplace. Pentecost put her arms about Mary's neck and snuggled close and warm. She smiled ale into Mary's face and slurred that "To be sure, Grandam, you must not fear, the Queen will come one day, riding the clouds and wearing her crown of stars and give us all our desires." For Pentecost prayed daily to her that she would and now look how kindly she had given us a posset (hic) and the pudding for our breakfast . . . And so she fell headlong into sleep, while Mary slipped her bottle of aqua vitae from under the pillow and gave the ale some stronger help.

She told herself she needed it to sleep in the Falcon with Christmastide brawling above and around them. And there is this blessing to aqua vitae: it is, at first, a prime executioner of dreams.

XVI

YOUNG BETHANY HAD FALLEN asleep in the Queen's bony arms upon the night of the Feast of Saint Stephen. In her dreams she clutched the broad strong shoulders of a muskier lover than the Queen, revisiting the weight and warmth of her sin. In her dreams her passion rose until it compassed the world, and she was swooning and moaning with it when she was catapulted from her sleep by a horrible shrieking beside her.

The Queen was sitting up in the bed, both hands clutched to her belly, eyes staring, screaming like an Irish banshee.

Oh, living God, Bethany thought selfishly, she has been poisoned and I will be blamed. Stark terror froze her in place, her mind yammered at her to do something, help in some way, stop the terrible noise, but she could think of nothing to do while her mind was battered by the screams.

Footsteps beyond the curtains: Parry was up, the thunder of feet in the Privy Gallery, a man's voice shouting.

Icy air fell through the gap as Parry swept aside the curtains, took in the scene.

"Up," she snapped at Bethany. "Run, tell the gentleman to fetch the doctor."

"Y . . . yes, Mrs Parry," Bethany gasped, unfrozen by the order. She scrambled out of the bed and ran to the door to the Gallery, heard her own hysteria wobbling in her voice as she shouted the words, drowned by the banging of a male fist on the door.

"Nooo," skirled the Queen, eyes still staring like a madwoman's. "Do not let him in, Kat, never let him in."

Bethany fumbled at the bolts, got the door open a crack, found herself face to face with the handsome Robert Carey and gasped for breath.

"The . . . the Queen . . ." she whimpered.

A warm hand pressed on her own. "Mistress Bethany," he said, "is there an assassin?"

"N . . . no. Nobody but us."

"Is there blood, sweeting?"

He was calm and methodical and she was desperately grateful to him. She gulped down some more air.

"No. Her . . . her stomach hurts."

His lips thinned and the blue eyes narrowed. "Give her nothing to eat or drink that is in the room," he said. "I will run for the doctor."

The other gentleman on duty in the Privy Chamber was at his elbow, rubbing sleep from his eyes, sword in hand. Both had been sleeping in their clothes on truckle-beds by the door, as always ready for just such an emergency.

"Guard the door, Drury," Carey ordered him as he hopped about pulling on his shoes. "Wait for me."

Bethany saw him turn and run, shut the door and leaned her head against the wood.

The Queen's screaming had subsided to a short series of gasps. She was still not awake, but lost in the half-world between dreams.

"Kat, Kat," she moaned. "It hurts."

Parry had wrapped a dressing-gown around the Queen's shaking shoulders and was feeling Her Majesty's stomach gently.

"No, no!" cried the Queen, slapping her hand away. "It stabbed me, Kat, it stabbed me, the unicorn stabbed me . . ."

The two exchanged knowing looks.

"Well, do not stand there like a yokel, Bethany," ordered Blanche Parry. "Stoke up the fire."

She moved to obey, finding her knees gone soft as sugar-plate left in the sun.

"And fetch some wine."

"M . . . Mr Carey said we should not give her anything that is in the chamber," she said.

Blanche Parry frowned, then nodded. "Yes, he is right." She had her arm around the Queen, stroking her back as she shuddered.

"Shh, shh, Your Majesty," she said. "The doctor is coming."

Two more creaking breaths and then the Queen's eyes focussed suddenly on Parry.

"Blanche," she said.

"Thank God," said Parry. "Your Majesty, do you know me?"

"Of course I do. Ahh."

"Where is the pain, Your Majesty?"

"In my guts," said the Queen, rocking with it and biting her lip. "In my guts as usual."

"We have sent for the doctor, Madam."

"What for?"

"When Your Majesty screamed we were afraid you had taken poison," said Parry matter-of-factly.

"Screamed? When did I scream?"

"A few moments ago. We were . . . we were afraid."

The Queen squinted in the rising firelight at Bethany, who was trying to weep silently. Never in her life had she thought she would hear the Queen crying out like that, like a woman in labour.

"Well, do not sniffle, child," the Queen said gruffly to her. "I am sorry that I frightened you. It was no more than a nightmare and a bellyache."

Bethany came to the side of the bed and dropped to her knees, unable to stop the tears rolling down her cheeks, as if her eyes had turned to conduits. Absentmindedly the Queen patted her head as she winced and bent with another cramp.

"Put your gown on, Bethany," said Parry. "The doctor will be here soon."

Even as Bethany rose to obey, there was a knocking at the door. The Queen stiffened, wrapped the dressing-gown more tightly about her, tilted her chin. From an old woman in pain on her bed, she suddenly became the Queen again, as if her queenship were music that she could play or not play as she chose.

"Enter," she said.

Carey was at the door and opened it, his head politely averted. The doctor came in, portly in his dark-blue brocade gown and his round skullcap on his head.

Tensing against the cramps, the Queen held out her hand to the doctor as he came to her bedside and genuflected over it.

"Dr Nunez, how kind of you to come at this unseasonable hour," she said coquettishly. Dr Nunez watched her shrewdly as Carey drew the door shut after him and then rumbled something in Latin which made the Queen smile ruefully. "Off your poor knees, Doctor, and sit down."

Parry waved her fingers at Bethany, who realised what she wanted and brought a stool.

The doctor nodded at her, then stopped her with his hand on her sleeve. "Gather together all that the Queen has had to eat and drink which is in this room," he said, his voice flavoured with Portuguese. "Wash nothing that the Queen has used."

"Oh, stuff," said the Queen. "This is only my old trouble."

The doctor was holding her hand and wrist delicately, feeling the twelve pulses there.

"Breathe on me, Your Majesty," he said and she did, still talking.

"I tell you, this is nothing new. When I am harassed by loyal and stupid subjects, then all my evil humours fly to my belly and fight there."

"Mmm," said the doctor, "this may indeed be the case, but permit me, Madam . . ."

Gently and methodically he examined her, prodded her stomach, felt behind her ears.

At last he sat beside her and asked what her dream had been. She flushed. "Clear enough in all conscience," she said, "I dreamed that the Unicorn of Scotland charged at me and stabbed my belly with its horn. That is all."

Nunez had his fingers in his beard. "The warrant for the Queen of Scots' execution is still unsigned?"

"It is." The Queen's tone was frosty.

Nunez spread his large white hands. "I am your doctor, Majesty, not your councillor. I care nothing if it is signed or unsigned, only that such uncertainty may indeed cause the melancholy humours to fly to the gut. Also it may have an effect on the . . . ah, upon the women's parts."

"If you are about to tell me that my womb is wandering . . ."

"Never, Your Majesty; rarely have I found a more fixed and stable womb. We speak only of the humours which, being carried out of their proper places by uncertainty, may cause such symptoms as these. However, we must also exclude poison. Have you . . ." He raised his eyebrows delicately in the direction of the Stool.

"No."

"No vomitus, nor flux, unnatural voiding? Constipation?"

"No. None of these. Only cramping pains."

"Still?"

"They are fading as we speak."

"Hmm. I will prescribe for you a lenitive dose which will open your bowels."

"Oh God, must I purge?"

"A little, I fear, Majesty. And also a dose to help you sleep."

"Bah. You know how I hate to take physic."

"Yet I think we should not take such nightmares and cramps lightly."

"Very well. But I will not be bled; I have not the time for it."

"And of course it is not the season. But I see no signs that Your Majesty's sanguine humour is in any way unbalanced, only that perhaps the melancholy humour is in excess, for which I fear we must purge a little."

"God damn it."

"The Almighty (Blessed be He) is always Your Majesty's best physician."

XVII

DR NUNEZ HAD GONE, the Queen had reluctantly taken physic and half of the sleeping draught and lay on her side, her eyes staring ahead of her unblinkingly.

Parry had put the overwrought Bethany into her own truckle-bed to sleep and sat by the fire, stitching at a nightcap for the Queen. Occasionally the elaborate curling leaves and roses blurred together in her eyes and her hands would drop and her chin fall on her chest as she dozed.

She was up once to help the Queen to the Stool and give her watered wine brought in by a yawning chamberer. Then the Queen returned to her bed and curled like a cat under the covers, but ordered her to leave the curtains open a little so she could see the fire.

Bethany was already asleep and snoring again. Still the Queen lay staring at the fire, watching the outline of Parry against the glow, the fingers sometimes busy and sometimes slack.

At last the Queen's eyes drooped shut and her breathing deepened. But once again, there was my unicorn, forming himself of the firelight, pawing and prancing about the room, where strange lilies grew in a soil of manna, planted in pots of gold. In the far reaches of her mind, the Archangel Gabriel winded his horn and his hounds bayed for her blood, for the hounds are named Mercy, Truth, Justice and Peace. And here also was the rightful Queen of Heaven to ride upon the unicorn. I wore my raiment of blue and gold and my crown of stars; the serpent, my friend and victim, not crushed by my triumphant heel but wrapped about my arm, a living bracelet. Here is no meek and simple maiden of the Italian daubers; here am I, Holy Wisdom, terrible as the forest, mounted on moonlight, my hair flying black and wild behind me, laughing reproach at my mere mortal usurper.

Unicorns may mean more than Scotland. Tears began forcing themselves between Elizabeth's shut eyelids and dropping on the pillow until her cheek lay on dampness and she awoke, still weeping.

"Oh, Your Majesty," said a voice beside her. "Tell me what is wrong."

If only it were Kat Ashley's voice, the Queen thought greyly, she would know already. But Ashley is dead.

So she pushed Blanche Parry away, turned her back on the room and hid her face under the covers while her shoulders shook with sobbing.

It was impossible to stop. The sobs followed each other, one after the other, only pausing for breath, like carts on progress, and soon there was another damp patch on the sheets. Somebody gave her a clean handkerchief and she blew her nose, trying to regain her composure, but then the helpless misery rose up in her again and the sobbing started once more, endless, endless, rivers of tears dammed up for too long to stop now there was a breach in the dyke.

Behind her she could hear whispered consultations between her women as they arrived fully dressed, ready to begin the business of the morning once again. There was no end to it, no escape, only a long, slow leaking of water from her soul.

One of the maids of honour took a lute and began to play softly in the corner, she played well enough, she was a good musician, but the rippling notes only deepened the Queen's sadness and the tears flowed faster.

They tried to coax her to drink more tincture of laudanum, but her throat was stopped and her stomach cramped with sorrow. Another visit to the Stool and no wry jokes between herself and Parry, only more helpless sobbing and the shame of being seen by her women in such weakness.

Parry shut the lid and called for a chamberer to take the pot to Dr Nunez for his inspection.

For God's sake, Elizabeth berated herself, what is it, why am I weeping like this, what is it about? This is no new hurt, in Heaven's name. Parry and Bedford occasionally besought her to tell them, but she could not since she did not know herself. Or perhaps she did, but still could not tell them.

After half past seven had gone, Lady Bedford and Blanche Parry between them made the decision and passed the announcement to young Carey where he still stood guard at the door, hollow-eyed and worried.

By a quarter of eight on the Feast of Saint John the Apostle and Evangelist, the proclamation had been made in the Presence Chamber that the Queen, being sick with a distemper in her stomach, would keep to her chamber that day. All her meetings and consultations were hereby cancelled.

By nine of the clock the Queen was still weeping and had eaten no breakfast. Rumours were flying into the City that she had been poisoned and was lying near death. The traders at the Exchange instantly began buying gold and silver and there was a quiet rush to the armourers. Gunpowder tripled in price. Some of her councillors began wondering privily if it would be so impossible to contact the Queen of Scots at Fotheringhay and ingratiate themselves before the Protestant Queen died and the Catholic Queen succeeded. Others laid plans to carry out the terms of their Bond of Association, which promised death for anyone who profited by the Queen's killing. Ships bound for the Netherlands found a surprising number of gentlemanly enquirers after berths, particularly divines. And the special Scottish Embassy woke to discover themselves under a very polite house arrest. After frantic questioning of servants they began to wonder if they could find a man willing to ride for Scotland with the news if the Queen died, so that King James might invade and take the English throne from his Papist mother.

At eleven of the clock, Thomasina marched up to one of the gentlemen still on duty at the bedchamber door and tapped him peremptorily on the leg. As generally happened, he looked round, frowned and then down. He smiled a little on seeing her, as people did, finding her charming in her miniature velvet gown and seed-pearl necklace. She had a fashion doll clutched under her arm and a determined expression on her face.

"Mr Carey, let me in," she said in her high childlike voice.

"Have you been sent for, Mistress Thomasina?" he asked, politely squatting down to her so that their faces were on a level.

"Not exactly," she admitted. "But if the Queen is melancholic and sick, she had need of me. I am, after all," she added proudly, "the Queen's muliercula, the Queen's Fool."

His eyes became shrewd. "I have orders to admit nobody but her physician."

"Which surely applies only to full-sized bodies," Thomasina answered. "I am simply not included because my body is too small. Have the lap-dogs been let in?"

"Yes, Mrs Parry thought they might comfort her, but they have been sent out again because one of them ate a bowl of wet suckets and was sick on the mat."

"I have the same purpose as Her Majesty's lap-dogs," said Thomasina firmly, "so let me in."

He was looking worried and reluctant, full of responsibility and fear for his future, and, to be fair to him, concern for his aunt, whom he genuinely seemed to like.

"Come, Mr Carey," she said. "If the Queen had children, you would give them entry." His mouth had opened and he was staring at her in astonishment. "I am the nearest thing the Queen has to a daughter and I can help her."

"Well, I . . ."

"And further, if I am not wanted, I will be ejected just like the lap-dogs. So let me in, Mr Carey."

He stood up, swept her a bow, knocked and opened the door for her.

"Her Majesty's Fool," he announced as she marched past him, her head held high a little above the level of his knees, and shut the door behind her.

The women were whispering near the fire in the still-curtained and shuttered room. The sound of sobbing still came from the bed.

Thomasina clicked her tongue against her teeth. As usual, their habit of obedience to Her Majesty's hauteur left them utterly rudderless and silly if Her Majesty could no longer command. If I were you, Madam, she thought to herself, I would order them about less and expect more intelligence of them. It is a policy that works well with your councillors; why not try it with your women?

She dropped a curtsey to the couple of ladies who had noticed her entrance, trotted to the bed, took off her shoes and jumped up beside the Queen. Then she sat there, humming softly to herself and taking the clothes off her beautiful little fashion doll, waiting for the Queen to notice her.

XVIII

THE PURSUIVANTS HAD DINED well enough at the Old Swan beside London Bridge. James Ramme was careful to tuck a napkin under his chin; he thought himself very fine in a new black grosgrain suit slashed with tawny taffeta, his pointed black beard newly scented and curled by his barber in the fashion invented by Sir Walter Raleigh.

Elaborately neither he nor Anthony Munday mentioned their work of the day, but discussed the wicked ways of fighting cocks and the further scandalous vices of the bear-baiting men. Munday told ribald tales of the whores in Rome, of their striped petticoats and teetering high shoes. He had spent a year as a spy for Walsingham at the English Catholic Seminary there. Now he was claiming that the Pope made a personal inspection of the whores every week. Ramme laughed, willing to believe it, but wary of Munday's liking for improving a tale.

Munday ate and drank heartily, his appetite never affected by anything, so far as Ramme could tell. He was a short, round man, already greying, though he was about the same age as Ramme. He refused to wear silks and velvet, citing the sumptuary laws that everyone else in London ignored to the best of their ability, and went soberly in grey worsted and a plain white falling band. Ramme found this obscurely offensive.

"Why should I try to cut it the gentleman?" Munday demanded pugnaciously of Ramme, when Ramme spitefully recommended him his own tailor. "My father, may he rest in peace, was a draper, which is an honourable trade, and the most of his profit was made on fine silks and brocades, which I can assure you, Mr Ramme, are not worth a quarter of the money you fine courtiers pay for them. What did you pay for that?" He was offensive enough to grasp Ramme's sleeve and rub the cloth between thumb and forefinger.

"To be sure I cannot recall," said Ramme loftily, although the outrageous price was printed on his brain in letters of fire.

"Well, you should." Munday was impossible to snub, impossible to offend. "Where's the good of money if you throw it away to put duds on your back?"

"They show men what I am."

Munday laughed uncouthly and picked some shreds of boiled salt-beef out of his teeth with his fingernail.

"They do that. They shout 'gentleman's younger son that never did a stroke of honest work in his life and knows not the value of money, nor even the worth of his suit.' "

"Fifty pounds," growled Ramme, stung with irritation and cutting the amount by half.

"Lord, Lord, paid that, did you?" Munday clicked his tongue and shook his head in wonder.

"Of course"—Ramme was curling his moustache between finger and thumb—"I am not educated in the ways of cheapening at market."

Munday guffawed, reached for the wine flagon and emptied it out into his leather mug before draining it down.

"And so you must hunt Papists at Christmas for Davison to pay your tailoring debts."

"Why do you do it then?" Ramme demanded.

"To make my fortune," said Munday passionately. "To have the chance of taking possession of some traitor's estate. To collect a little acorn of money that I may then grow into a large shady tree and take my ease thereunder evermore."

"Very poetical," sneered Ramme as he put down the money for his half of the meal. Munday looked disappointed, but Ramme had learnt quickly that Munday never returned a reckoning.

Munday looked up at the sky and then at the Thames scarred with bonfires and the stalls of the Frost Fair.

"Will Mr Norton be at the Tower?" he asked.

"No."

"Why not?"

"How should I know?" said Ramme, although he did, it being a matter of some valuable Dutch tulips in Norton's garden needing protection from the frost. Munday liked to hear tales of the Court, which Ramme perversely preferred not to tell him. Suddenly beset with annoyance at his ill-bred colleague, Ramme came to his feet. Munday bounced to his and they put on their cloaks, went up the alley and around the bridge, down the steps at the other side to call for a boat.

On their way downriver Munday sat in the stern and dabbled his fingers in the dark-brown water, which was too salty and dirty to freeze, winced and withdrew them. The wind was still but the sky roofed with slate clouds and the promise of more snow.

"Mr Secretary Davison is coming to watch the interrogation this afternoon," said Ramme casually and Munday cocked an eyebrow at him.

"Is he now? I own I am surprised," he said. "I would not have said this one was a Jesuit. More of a soldier, if you ask me, from the way he was cursing."

Ramme looked away at the bridge and an expression of deep satisfaction crossed his face. "Whatever he was, he is clearly a traitor from the company he keeps."

"Of course, that could have been an accident," said Munday reasonably. "Could have been bad luck."

Ramme shrugged. "Mr Davison is particularly anxious to hear his tale."

"Jesuits hardly ever swear," Munday continued thoughtfully. "And they don't curse, neither, or at least not until they are further gone than he is. Speak the name of Jesus a lot, of course, but not cursing. Mind you, he was hardly in his right mind last time, even before we started. You hit him a mighty blow on the head, you know, Mr Ramme; it's a mercy he's still alive."

Ramme was still looking very pleased with himself. "It was he commanded the traitors' defence, what else could I do? He would never have let us take him alive else."

"Can't say I blame him, big heavy man like that."

Ramme shrugged and smiled.

Munday's eyes narrowed shrewdly. "Here," he said suddenly. "You don't know him, do you?"

Ramme looked away, shrugged again. "Certainly not," he said. "Why would I know a traitor?"

"We meet a few," Munday pointed out. "I'm always coming across fellows I met at the Roman Seminary, unluckily for them. You could have missed catching him some other time."

Ramme sniffed. "It is possible," he admitted, "but I really do not remember."

You lying slug, thought Munday to himself, delighted as always to find a new deceit; now what's going on here?

Aloud he said, "I wonder what he will tell us today?"

"Do you think he will?"

It was Munday's turn to shrug. "Of course."

XIX

THE QUEEN HAD FINALLY emptied her eyes of tears and lay exhausted from them, staring into space. At last she noticed Thomasina cross-legged beside her. She stared at her midget for a long time, as if considering her.

Now how shall I play this? Thomasina thought to herself. Shall I be her child again, or what? She had thought that would be the part she should play, which was why she had brought her doll, but now she hid the puppet behind her and stared steadily back at the Queen.

"Ah, Thomasina," sighed the Queen and turned her face to the pillow again. More tears were leaking from her reddened eyes. Thomasina leaned over and closed the tapestry bedcurtains against the prying frightened eyes in the room. Then she untied the strings of Her Majesty's nightcap, which was half over her ear, and began stroking the cropped greying red hair. A lump came in her own throat and she wondered what she would do if the Queen died. But then surely there would be war and soldiers trampling the land and she could always return to her first trade of tumbling if she must. You could get a living by making soldiers laugh, just as you could from Queens.

"What is the matter, Your Majesty?" she asked.

"The ladies think I must have taken poison." The Queen's voice was muffled and choked. "They have been feeding everything I ate yesterday to the pigs in Saint James's to see if they take sick."

"This is no bodily poison, I think," said Thomasina. "They say you have been dreaming of the Queen of Scots. Some say she has bewitched you and made a wax doll of you to stab with needles in the guts."

The Queen laughed through the drying tears on her cheeks. "She might as well, the grief she brings me," she said. "Though I am afraid the bitch is too religious a woman for it. I am surprised Walsingham and Davison between them have not come up with such a thing to accuse her of."

"Will you tell me the dream?"

"Why, Thomasina." The Queen rose on her elbow. "Are you a soothsayer as well as a tumbler?"

"Yes," said Thomasina. "You know I was first sold to the Egyptians who came by my father's house and they taught me to tumble and many other things as well. I can interpret dreams and tell the future from cards and bones, if I want."

"Is that not witchcraft?"

"No, Your Majesty." Thomasina smiled cynically. "Nor is it a science like astrology. It is a very profitable game. Say you were to come to me for a reading. I would look at you while I talked of spirits and hobgoblins and whatnot, and see the rings on your fingers and the quality of your clothes and the paleness of your skin, and I would say you were a great lady of much power, either now or to be—and you would think me very wise and if it were not true yet then you would still be flattered that I predicted it. And perhaps, by prognosticating your power, I may make you think differently and it might become true. Then you would think me wiser still."

"Hmm," said the Queen, looking at her differently. "How old are you, Thomasina?"

"Thirty-four or thirty-five, I think."

"Such wisdom in one so young."

"I have had good teachers. And I am not so young as I look."

"No indeed."

"Will you tell me of your dream, Majesty?"

"Well, it was the Unicorn of Scotland."

"How do you know? Did it bear a crown?"

"Now you ask, no. But the unicorn is Scotland's badge . . ."

"Your Majesty, any such beast may mean more than one thing: a lion can mean kingship, true, but it can also mean strength and, further, sweetness."

"Hm. Yes."

"What did the unicorn do, Your Majesty?"

"It stabbed me with its horn, in my belly, here." The Queen's hand moved to show her where.

"That was Mr Davison's message last night, was it not? That a woman was prophesying of a unicorn you must destroy."

Did the Queen pause fractionally there, taking a breath? "Bah," she snorted, "superstition and witchcraft. No doubt he made it up thinking thereby to persuade me to execute my cousin Queen."

"Yet it distressed you."

The Queen looked away and Thomasina wondered if she would be dismissed for impudence. No, for both she and the Queen knew the nature of her office: to say things to the Queen that others dared not and be held harmless for it.

"It reminded me . . ." The Queen looked away and her face was pinched. "It reminded me of something best forgotten."

Thomasina said nothing. The silence lay between them, like a thing of substance, not absence, until she would have sworn it dented the counterpane.

The Queen sighed heavily but there were no more tears. "Yes," she said very quietly, nodding to herself. "Yes."

Thomasina waited. At last the Queen spoke again.

"If I had one I could trust, one that did not serve Davison or Walsingham or even my lord Burghley . . ." The Queen's red-rimmed eyes held Thomasina's. "If I knew of such a one, who was loyal to me, not to the Queen nor to the throne, not to the realm nor yet to God, but only and solely to me, Elizabeth, I would ask a service of . . . her."

"I am only your Fool, Madam," said Thomasina. "I know nothing of thrones or realms." The Queen seemed not to hear. "I would ask her to find me a book I once made, when I was a foolish girl, of recommendations to the state of virginity, by Saint Paul and Saint Augustine and such like. It had a cover of blue velvet wrought with a white-and-silver unicorn in needlework and a ruby for its eye."

"A book, Your Majesty?"

"Yes, Thomasina. Only a book. Do you know of anyone that can find it? Quietly. Without telling my faithful councillors nor any other woman of my court."

"I am not a woman, Your Majesty, but a muliercula."

"It could be hard to find, for I lost it long ago, long, long ago, while my brother was King."

Why on earth did the Queen want her book now, after so long a time? wondered Thomasina but did not ask. Instead she sat up on her knees, took the Queen's hands and kissed them both.

"Would it ease your distemper if I found it for you?" she asked and the Queen laughed, a bitter laugh quite unlike her.

"Oh yes."

"Then I shall."

The Queen's smile was now sad and patronising.

"I think it may be too hard for you. Never fear if you cannot run it to earth."

A little puff of rage woke in Thomasina's breast although she understood why the Queen would underestimate her. It is hard to be taken seriously if you are both female and under four feet high.

"Your Majesty took me into your service when I was twenty-five," she said. "Since then you have given me whatever I pleased: food, lodging, servants, the most beautiful dresses and money for my old age. You have treated me only with kindness and gentleness and in return I have turned a few somersaults and sung a few songs."

It had not occurred to the Queen until then to wonder how Thomasina had lived before she came to the Court.

"Was it hard for you when you were young?" she asked.

"Yes, Your Majesty, very hard," said Thomasina, sitting up rigidly on her knees, her eyes turned to stony pebbles. "When once it was clear I would never be a woman, but always a child, men thought my understanding was only a child's. Worse, they thought of me as an animal rather than a child, a thing to be used for their pleasure and profit. They thought I would never remember what they did."

"Did they beat you?"

"Yes, but there are worse things than beatings."

The Queen frowned and Thomasina wondered how much of the world she knew, how much it was safe to tell her. Too late.

"Did they . . . ?"

"Yes," she said quickly, answering the Queen's gesture, not her words. "For there are men that fear women so greatly they lust after children instead."

The Queen's eyes narrowed with sympathy, her hands went out to hold Thomasina's arms. "Oh, my dear. But if you should get with child . . ."

"It would kill me, of course. But they never concerned themselves with that."

"Men seldom do."

Thomasina took a mighty breath to crush down the anger still living in her. "But at last I came to safe harbour and here I am now, Your Majesty's most faithful liegewoman, and all I desire is to serve you."

The words came tumbling out in a breathless rush. The Queen sat up and embraced her. "Thomasina, if only I had a Privy Council of mulierculae . . ."

"We would have to stand on the chairs to address you."

It was a very poor joke but it made the Queen laugh and that was good enough.

XX

THE CLATTER OF THE heavy door woke the prisoner from a doze. Some light filtered in, showing dried-up things among the sodden bits of straw that he had rather not think about.

"Out!" came the order from beyond.

Not knowing of anything he could do save obey, he eeled himself along a short narrow passage and almost pitched out of it onto his head. Someone caught him and set him on his feet.

"Thank you, sir," he muttered, too stiff to stand straight and swaying on feet too far away, his eyes blurring with tears at the brilliance of the daylight.

A tall thin gentleman and a short round commoner were watching him judiciously. Two other men in buff jerkins loomed behind them, holding lanterns.

He looked away from them and down at his hands, which was a mistake. The double braceleting of swollen flesh about his wrists was black, red, moist and ugly to see. But their combined gazes were worse: watchers in a bearpit had more sympathy with the bear.

"Well?" demanded the languid black-bearded one, who seemed to be laughing at him silently.

It was an English voice. So at least he was in England, a thought which surprised him by bringing him no comfort. There was another crumb to add to his store of knowledge of himself. Of course I am English, said his homunculus stoutly, what else would I be? Bloody Spanish? Dutch butter-eater?

They seemed to be waiting for him to say something. What colour is my hair? What colour are my eyes? he wondered distractedly. What should I say?

It came to him that generally, when in doubt, it was best to say nothing. Who had told him that? He could not remember.

The tall one rolled his eyes.

"Have you reconsidered, Ralph?"

The gentleman is addressing me, so that must be my name, he thought, wondering why there was no comfort in that either.

It would be offensive not to answer and he had no desire to offend.

"Reconsidered what, sir?"

"Your duty to the Queen."

"I cry you mercy, sir, but I know nothing of . . ."

The two looked at each other and he trailed off, his voice stopped with fear. Then the short round one came forward and touched his elbow confidingly, to turn him a little aside.

"Come, Ralph," said the man, "this is all foolishness. We want names, places, dates. We want your press and warehouses. And we want all you can tell us about the Book of the Unicorn."

He blinked down at the man, dizzy from hunger and thirst and the pain in his body. His hose felt loose on him, which was no surprise at all, though he still seemed to own a big enough belly.

"Are you a friend, sir?" he asked, still bewildered. "Will you tell me where I am?"

The short man laughed a little uncomfortably, shrugged his shoulders. His grey woollen suit was better cut than the other's silk.

"I'm the nearest to a friend that you have here in the Tower."

He blinked down at the man and then spoke out of his choking desperation. "If you are a friend, then I pray you will tell me your name."

The little man's square clean-shaven face darkened.

"You know me well enough."

He shook his head. "I know nothing, sir. Some dreadful accident has happened to my wits. I know nothing beyond waking up in this . . . this place. I remember nothing. I am"—he fought for control, found his poor swollen fingers trying to turn into fists—"I am like a babe newborn in a man's body."

The short one wrinkled up his face and laughed cynically. "By God, that's a new variation, Ralph."

"Shall we get on, Mr Munday," said the elegant one wearily.

"He says he remembers nothing before his last waking." Munday's voice had a mixture of spices in it: cynicism, amusement, a little grudging admiration.

He felt it was misplaced.

"We had best remind him then," said the elegant one.

"Come," said the short one, Munday. "This is amusing, but hardly to your help, Ralph."

"It is the truth. I was not even sure what country I was in until I heard you speak. I have forgotten my own name."

"Well, the name you've been using is Ralph Strangways, but I expect you have others."

They had at last said something which cut through the confusion; suddenly a skeleton in tawny velvet rags flashed past his mind's eye, jabbering nonsense. Then the moment was gone and he could recall nothing more. Munday had taken his elbow in a painful grip and was pushing him between the two men-at-arms.

He tried to take a step, was brought up short by the chain, his stockinged feet slipped on the stone and he nearly pitched on his nose. This time nobody helped him, though he kept his feet.

"Why would I lie to you, sirs? I am a loyal servant of the Queen."

Both of them smirked then.

"For the avoidance of pain," said the elegant one, "men will tell many strange lies."

At that deadly insult, despair boiled suddenly into rage and a knowledge from nowhere lifted him up. He lunged at an angle and drove his chained elbows into the elegant one's side, pinned him bodily against the wall, brought his knee up into the man's crotch and butted with his head at the aquiline nose.

Three others caught him, pulled him away because he was weak and hampered by chains and the two men-at-arms held him while Munday hit him in the stomach, a dispassionate wondering expression on his face.

The world was flickering around him. Gasping in a helpless bow in the grip of the two men-at-arms, he wondered in despair why he could not keep his temper. But fighting was a relief, something he understood. Oh God, for a sword and his hands free . . .

"You are something of a brawler for a priest." Munday's voice reached him from far away.

"A priest?" he croaked stupidly. "I'm not a priest."

"Then why will you not tell us what we want to know?"

The elegant one was less elegant now, he noticed as he began to be able to straighten up. Grosgrain silk had ripped across from a roughness on the irons, blood from the man's nose and mouth was decorating his ruff. He pushed himself away from the wall slowly, his teeth bared.

"Oh, now you have annoyed Mr Ramme," clucked Munday. "Steady, James, don't kill him, that's what he wants."

Ramme shook off Munday's hand and closed in on the man vengefully. Long, beringed fingers caught the open front of his doublet, straightened him, and the other hand cracked its rings across his face, once, twice . . . Munday was there again, hanging on Ramme's arm.

"Not his face, you fool," hissed Munday. "He has to look presentable for his execution."

Ramme blinked absently down at Munday, bunched a fist and let him see where he was going to punch before swinging up and into the prisoner's privates.

Moaning in a ball on the dirty stones, he heard Munday tutting again. They were dragging him, one of the Yeomen was cursing him for his weight. Their grip on his shoulders hurt, his toes scrabbled at earth and gravel, he could not see, he was too busy trying to breathe. There was a moment when his sight came back and he saw daylight and a square white tower. Then it was in at a door and down spiral stairs to a vaulted place half-piled with junk: cracked cannon, holed breastplates, strange bucket-shaped helmets of his grandfather's day. Under one of the arches was an ugly wooden frame and pulleys, covered with dust. Someone's brawny arm was holding his head in a lock while they released him from the irons, stripped off his clothes. But now somebody, Munday, told him to put his hands out. Terror filled him at the order. He would not, he resisted with all his strength, but they forced him, one to each arm. Then it was Ramme who crammed iron manacles, which had a bar between them instead of a chain, into the ulcered furrows on his wrists, locking them.

He whimpered, stumbled up steps as he was pushed, felt his arms lifted above his head by a man on a step-ladder and the bar was hooked onto a high bracket. The steps twitched from under his feet and he screamed as his wrists took his full weight, his bones cracking and creaking as he swung.

He thought the blood must be exploding from his fingers like fireworks. He scrabbled desperately at the void with his toes to find a relief for his wrists, and made the raging flames in his arms worse from the movement. At last he hung gasping, keening, wishing to scream again but without enough air to do it. Tears and sweat stung the graze on his face.

"There," said Ramme's voice, a little behind and below, rich with satisfaction. "We shall see if this reminds him."

"Names, dates, places, your warehouse, your press," droned Munday's voice. "And the meaning of the unicorn, this vaunted Book of the Unicorn. None of this is necessary, Ralph. We regret it, truthfully we do. If it were not God's work, neither of us would stoop to this."

Far away he heard his voice croak, "Romero . . . said that . . . too."

When? he wondered. Who was Romero? Why did I say that?

"Romero?" asked Munday sharply. "Who's that?"

"A Spaniard," smirked Ramme, "obviously. No doubt his master."

"Or another traitor."

"I am not . . . a traitor," he gasped. "I'm the Queen's loving subject."

Munday snickered. "Why do they always say that? Is your memory still defective, Ralph?"

Tears were running down his face from pain and despair.

"Yes," he whispered.

He was no longer in darkness. Light filtered down from high barred windows between the vaults and in the distance was a tinny clanging, but all he had to look at was the pillar he hung from.

There were footsteps, murmuring voices, the door slammed and locked. Christ have mercy, could they not even be bothered to watch him suffer? He wanted to shout and curse them but his ribs could not open enough, his breath wheezed through his teeth with each surge of blood in his hands.

The cold was dabbling experimentally in the sweat soaking his shirt. Oh Jesus, let me not shiver.

Anvils clanged like iron drums in the distance.

XXI

SINCE MR SECRETARY DAVISON would never waste in mere pleasure time that might be devoted to salvation, it was no accident that he met his cousin Bethany as she walked muffled in cloak and sealskin boots in the snow-covered Privy Garden with the Queen's three lap-dogs, to exercise them. They instantly set up an excited yapping when they saw Mr Davison coming towards them down the path by the knot-garden. The boldest of them started making little scurries and dashes to and fro from the safety of Bethany's skirts to growl at Davison's boots.

"Cousin," he said, lifting his hat and looking about to see that they were all alone in the garden. "How is the Queen?"

"She has a distemper in her stomach, has taken physic and the doctor will see her again this evening."

"So I had heard." Davison turned to accompany Bethany. The little dog kept making brave forays at his boots.

"Eric, stop that," said Bethany sharply. "Leave off, you bad dog."

Eric looked up at her and barked importantly, quivering with aggression. If we had eaten the magical salmon of the Irish which teaches men the speech of beasts, we could hear him telling her of Davison's hatefulness, and offering gallantly to rip his throat out. Or, at any rate, his calf-muscles. Eric's two friends, Francis and Felipe, backed him up, being his pack.

Bethany frowned and waggled her gloved finger. "Stop it, all of you," she scolded. "Go and . . . go and fetch." She found a stick broken off a yew tree by the wind and threw it for them. Immediately forgetting their enemy, the dogs yapped off to fetch it, bounding like deer through the snow and sneezing when it got up their noses. Bethany smiled wearily after them.

"I had hoped for more information from you," Davison said when his waiting silence had not done its work.

"Cousin, I do not want to be your informer against the Queen."

"Not against the Queen, Cousin Bethany, never *against* the Queen. I only desire more information than the Court is given, the better to serve her," Davison explained, believing it.

"Whatever it was you said to her upon Saint Stephen's Day, it upset her greatly."

"I know," said Davison, not seeming very worried. "I am forbidden her august presence."

"She woke in the night screaming with the pain in her stomach and then, after she had taken the sleeping draught, she woke again with some new dream that made her weep all morning."

"And what do you think is the cause of her distress?"

"The Queen of Scots. She is desperate not to sign the warrant."

"But she must. It is essential she stamp on the serpent she has nourished in her bosom for so long."

Bethany looked at him sidelong under her sooty lashes. He was so prosaic, it was always a surprise to hear him using the flowery phrases of the Court.

"Why is it so urgent?" Bethany demanded. "Why can it not wait? It has for twenty years."

"Twenty years too long. And it is urgent because I believe we have wind of a plot to release the Scottish Queen and no doubt to do away with our own Royal Mistress."

"Again?" said Bethany distantly. "Such a multitude of plots."

"Do you not believe in them?"

"The Queen does not, so why should I? She says they are all playhouse fantasies and theatrics cooked up by you and Sir Francis, and she has said that after the way you and he entrapped poor Babington she will never again believe either one of you."

After the Papist plotters had been safely executed, with such bloody adherence to the prescribed hanging, drawing and quartering for traitors that even the

London mob had been revolted, Walsingham had seen fit to explain to his mistress how they had been caught. Far from approving his cleverness, the Queen had flown into a rage.

"She said not one of the poor ninnies who were executed had the faintest notion of freeing the Queen of Scots or killing her until you and Mr Secretary Walsingham put the idea into their heads and that that was dirty dealing, to lead them on as weapons against an anointed Queen."

Davison was annoyed. "A Queen who was thrust from her kingdom by the outrage of Godly men at her behaviour, who is convict of adultery and petty treason and deserves to burn if only for those crimes, let alone what she has committed against Her Majesty."

He talks like a book, Bethany thought, every phrase and subphrase neatly rounded and stopped at the end. Also he has completely missed the point of why the Queen is angry.

"Well, she is determined on it," Bethany added. "She says she will not sign the warrant and that is the end of the matter."

Davison raised his eyes to Heaven, presently walled in by grey cloud. Where I sat watching at my ease upon their grey velvet cushions, he saw nothing at all.

"And the unicorn?"

Bethany's cheeks had been flushed with walking in the cold, but now she paled. "What do you know about the unicorn?" she asked.

It had been a guess, but a God-favoured one. Davison shrugged. At that time he still thought it might be a code-word for the Queen of Scots, although he was beginning to wonder about it. He smiled.

Bethany fell silent.

"Mistress Bethany, I require that you tell me what you know of this."

She pulled her cloak tight around her and looked at the ground. Francis came back importantly with the stick, followed by a circling of yaps from Felipe and Eric. Bethany took it and threw it again, and they were off once more, jumping and crashing through the short box-hedges of the knot-garden, running excited circles round the still fountain, and yelping continuously.

"Cousin," said Mr Davison, taking her arm. "Must I do my duty and tell the Queen of your dalliance with Mr Carey?"

Her mouth dropped open and the cream of her complexion turned to grey.

"Wh . . . what . . ."

"You heard me."

She swallowed stickily and shut her mouth. "I have had no dalliance with Mr Carey; what are you talking about?" There was an ugly pause, broken by the voices of the dogs arguing. "I have had no dalliance with anyone."

"Oh," said Davison. "Really?"

She looked at the ground and nodded, while the blood rushing back to her cheeks gave her the lie.

"At the Queen's Birthday in September you danced with Mr Carey and in the masque you were a nymph to his centaur. At the banquet you were with him and the other gentlemen once the Queen had withdrawn and whereas your tiring-woman believes you were the Queen's bedfellow that night, the Queen herself shared her bed with Susanna Broadbelt."

The dogs came back with the stick, Francis and Eric arguing over it and pulling it between them with many growls, whilst Felipe had uprooted a small rosebush and dragged it triumphantly in the rear.

Sworn as he was to God's service, tears had no power to move Mr Davison, which was a pity since Bethany's were likely to chap her skin in this wind. She had her hand clasped to her throat where some trinket hung under the embroidered Dutch linen. Grimly, he waited for her to bow to his will.

"If you must tell the Queen," Bethany said hopelessly at last, "could you not at least keep Robin Carey's name out of it? Please? He has done nothing wrong and you would destroy him and he has no money, no means of living beyond the Court."

"I think your father would not like him for a son-in-law, for all his high blood."

She shook her head. Her father had some respect for blood, but far more for land and money, neither of which Carey possessed.

"It is my duty to tell the Queen my suspicions," Davison told her. "Nothing less would be honourable."

The wind had got up and the three dogs were now standing in an outraged circle, yapping at her. Eric sniffed the air and then turned and nipped Davison's ankle through his boot. Davison kicked him and began to walk away down the path.

"No, Cousin. Mr Davison, stop!"

He turned courteously to her. Bethany breathed deep and coughed.

"She . . . she has been dreaming of the unicorn since December began, and every time it distresses her more. She dreamt that it stabbed her. That is all I know. I . . . share the Queen's bed, not her skull, Mr Davison, that truly is all I know." She clasped her hands together. "If I bring you news of the Queen, will you . . . will you not tell anyone your . . . your suspicions?"

Davison looked at her for a moment. "I shall consider it," he said, lifted his hat, and walked firmly away from her. The dogs yipped after him and returned happily to Bethany, convinced they had driven him off at last.

XXII

MR DAVISON TOOK HORSE in the Queen's mews opposite Charing Cross, having a universal warrant for them, and rode from there along the deep frozen ruts of the Strand past the great midden at the border between the cities of Westminster and London, where lay the half-buried skeleton of a dead dog, and on through Fleet Street, over Fleet Bridge and through London Wall at Ludgate. From there he turned down to the bridge to take a boat for the second half of his journey. He was alone, since Mr Rackmaster Norton had gone straight from his gardening to visit Walsingham's sick-bed at Seething Lane.

Parallel to his journey, the Frost Fair bellowed along the Thames, a second eddying river of people above the true one turned to metal. The booths set up on the ice by shopkeepers who had abandoned their shops were selling orangeadoes of Seville and sugar candy, metal pomander balls to hold hot coals as handwarmers, Dutch pattens with bone blades on them for sliding on the ice, and a vast variety of shoddy trinkets and ballads to mark the Frost Fair. A couple of bonfires were being piled on their old ashes on the ice ready for the night.

Mr Davison glanced at the wrapped and merry folk and looked away in contempt: God had turned the river to a paved road as a sign of His power, as a warning against sin, as a simile of the heart of London being like unto ice for sin and lechery, as was Babylon's. None of those who laughed and skidded and bought what they could not afford for the mere novelty of buying it a foot or two above the water, none of them could read what God's Finger had written thereon: "Repent or be damned to the frozen pit of Hell." Mr Davison could read it and he shivered at its clarity.

Downstream of the bridge, ice met oily water in a slow war, the ice fretted to petrified foam and razored icicles by the water, and the water made to porridge by the particles that broke off. There the once-proud boatmen scuffled over Davison's trade.

In the boat, as the oars sculled through the low stinking waters, Mr Davison prayed devoutly to his Lord God of Hosts: firstly that the Queen might be brought to execute the Queen of Scots; secondly that the Dutch might prevail over the Spanish Antichrist; thirdly that the evil Papist in the Tower might repent and disgorge the secrets he was hoarding. He had no prayers for Bethany his cousin, since she was damned and so they would be wasted.

At the Watergate of the Tower he paid off the hopefully servile water-man without a tip and climbed the slushy steps to meet Ramme and Munday at the top.

Both bowed, Munday twice.

"Well?"

"He has been up for much of the day," Ramme reported.

"Flogged?"

"Occasionally."

"Any change?" The humiliation of being beaten like a child or a peasant often broke a gentleman's pride better than the far worse pain of the manacles.

They shook their heads, hunching away from the bitter wind off the Thames.

Davison sighed and went ahead of them.

Under the White Tower the man hung limp.

"Wake him up," said Davison, taking a stool brought for him by Munday. Thames water crashed against the man's back, making him moan and shudder, dripped in rivulets of mud and blood from his limp feet.

"Come, Ralph," said Munday, looking up at him confidingly. "There is no need of this."

He was a big, broad, heavily built man, with shoulders like an ox and an ample gut on him, a little shrunken already. Black ringlets clung to his face from his sweat, and a beard that had been neatly trimmed now spread uncouthly across a square, ugly face. The river water made him smell no worse than he did already.

"Mr Davison is here," said Munday. "You should speak to him, he is the Queen's councillor, an important man. You should not keep him waiting, it is not polite."

"God rot Mr Davison," growled the man hoarsely. "God Almighty curse his Spanish bowels; Jesus Christ send he take a pox and leprosy, Spanish bas-tard . . ."

Davison frowned uneasily. "I am no Spaniard," he said.

"You lie in your teeth, you fucking Papist, servant of the Antichrist, bastard Spaniard-loving idol-kisser . . ."

Davison frowned more, an awful doubt beginning to gnaw at the roots of his perfection.

"How long has he been saying things like that?"

"Just now, sir," said Munday hurriedly, glaring at Ramme. "He was cursing us before, but not like that. Is he delirious?"

I hope so, thought Davison. "How was he captured, again?"

Ramme had a nervous look about his mouth as well. "When we broke in on the Mass, there were recusants there, worshipping at the altar of idolatry."

"This man, was he present?"

Ramme's finger began to twiddle nervously at his beard. "No, he was . . . er . . . he was in an anteroom, drinking."

"So he was not present at the Mass."

"No, sir."

"He was drinking while it went on?"

"Yes, sir."

"Go on."

"Well, as we broke in he came running out, shouting orders for his men to shut the inward doors, which they did while he delayed us, cursing and yelling to the priest to escape. In the mêlée, by God's help, I got behind him with my cudgel and brought him down."

"Clubbed him nicely on the back of the head a couple of times," Munday put in helpfully. "And down he went foaming at the mouth and twitching like a dog."

"The first time you interrogated him, what happened?"

The two looked uneasily at each other. "He . . . er . . . he seemed not to be in his right mind, sir," said Munday awkwardly. "He spouted a lot of babble about fire-drakes and some Book of the Unicorn before he fainted. So we took him down, sir, as per your orders, and put him in Little Ease over Christmas to think about it."

Davison nodded. "And then?"

Munday coughed. "Well, when we went to fetch him today, he seemed more sensible, you know sir, quite polite but . . . er . . . a mite confused. And then he told us this tale, sir, which I did not rightfully believe . . ."

"He's lying," said Ramme.

"Quiet, please, Mr Ramme," said Davison coldly, "Go on, Mr Munday."

Munday put his hands behind his back and stood with his toes pointed outwards, like a grammar-school boy saying a lesson.

"He told us he had no memory. He said he had forgotten everything before he woke in Little Ease and did not even know my name."

Davison sucked air through his teeth.

"Said he did not even know his *own* name, and wanted me to tell it to him."

"But you did not believe him."

"Of course not, sir, why would I? It was a new story, but there again, why not say that if you were desperate, sir . . ."

The man was gasping and wailing now, had run out of strength to curse.

Davison went to the pillar, stood beside it with his head flung back to look at the man, whose eyes were shut.

"Quiet," he rapped out. "Stop that noise."

The man took a shallow breath and held it, turned his face to squint down at Davison. His eyes were grey and bloodshot, rimmed with startlingly long lashes, like a woman's. Blood had oozed down his arms into his shirt, joining that which soaked the upper part of it, and his lips were bleeding where he had chewed on them earlier.

"What religion are you?" Davison demanded.

"I am an English Protestant, you Spanish catamite, you bastard—"

"Do you swear it by the living God and your hope of salvation?"

"Jesus Christ, yes, I do . . ." His voice was whittled down to a breathless croak. "And you can . . . shove your Pope and . . . and your fucking crucifix up your arse with your candles, you . . ."

"Enough," snapped Davison, full of horror. "Will you swear it on the Bible?"

"Ay, and spit on your cocksucking . . . idols too, you boy-loving . . ."

"Get him down from there." Davison turned his back and paced to the end of the basement. He contemplated a pile of shields, the bright paint on them faded and flaked, and tried to ignore the cries as they put the steps under the man's feet, unhitched his arms and supported him down. As if he heard them for the first time in his life, he winced at the sounds of pain. They laid the man on his side in the sawdust sprinkled on the cobbles to soak up ordure. He screamed and writhed as they forced his arms down slowly from where they had been frozen in place by his weight. Then he wept like a child as they took off the manacles and some blood began returning to his hands.

Davison had paced back by then and stood looking at the wreckage on the floor with his fingers clasped tight over his mouth. After the sobbing had died a little, he fumbled in his penner and brought out a little fat book, bound in black leather and tooled with gold. He went down on one knee.

"This is the Word of God, the Gospels, Acts, Epistles and Psalms in English," he said to the man when he thought he could understand. "In English, not Latin; do you hear me?"

Now the man nodded once, his eyes half-shut.

"The Word of God, in English. Do you swear on this that you abjure the Pope of Rome and all his unclean works and hold to the True and Pure Religion?"

The man could not move his arms, so delicately, distastefully, Davison lifted one of the swollen purpling hands and slipped his book under it.

"I swear," croaked the man.

"Do you accept the Queen as the rightful and only Governor of the Church of England and as your lawful Sovereign?"

"Christ, yes, always . . . have. I think," said the man, panting a little.

Davison took his book of Scriptures back, finding one edge soaked with blood and wiping at it abstractedly with his hankerchief. He looked bleakly at Munday. "No Papist would endanger his soul like that," he said. "This man must be one of ours."

"Never," hissed the man, "never one of yours, you . . . Spanish bum-licker, cocksucker . . ."

His eyes were rolling and although Davison said urgently that he was English too, it seemed the prisoner could no longer hear.

Davison stood straight with one hand on his sword and the other on his hip, looking down, while Munday dry-washed his hands nervously.

"It seems he was telling the truth that his memory is lost," Davison said. "Evidently he was a pursuivant himself, and would have reported to us immediately save for the accident to his wits. It is . . . he has been . . . This is a terrible mistake. A terrible mistake."

"What shall we do with him, sir?" asked Munday. "Release him?" Munday was too tactful to make the suggestion at the forefront of his mind, which was to slit the man's throat and slip him in the Thames before Burghley or Leicester found out what they had done to his agent.

"No. Not like that. Put him in a clean comfortable room, in a bed. Change his shirt. Keep him locked up lest he wander, but not chained. I shall send a physician to him."

"Might need a bone-setter," said Munday. "One of his arms looks to be out at the shoulder."

"The physician may judge of it."

"Yes, sir."

"Has he said anything of his mission that might make sense?"

"Well, no, sir, we never thought he could be . . . what he seemingly is, sir. Except early on, about the Book of the Unicorn that could break the Queen. But that was babbling, sir."

"Quite so," said Davison, "babbling. Any names?"

"Only one, but it made no sense, for the man is dead."

"What was the name?"

"Simon Ames, sir. Ramme said he was a Jew in Mr Secretary Walsingham's service about four years ago, sir, but it meant nothing, since he died in '83."

Davison's eyes narrowed. "A Jew? Hmm."

The man was too big and heavy to be dragged now they had some concern for his health, and so they put him face-down on a litter and carried him to the Lanthorne Tower, to one of the round rooms. Davison saw him into his bed and the fire lit, but he was still unconscious, though he woke enough to swallow the tincture of laudanum they forced into his mouth. Then, still frowning deeply, Davison left the Tower by the Lion Gate and walked to Old Jewry in the City.

XXIII

FINDING THAT DR NUNEZ was not at home, Davison immediately returned to Court. There he waited in the Presence Chamber until Dr Nunez came out after his evening consultation with the Queen, and approached him.

Dr Nunez was courteous and willing to have a private interview with Sir Francis Walsingham's deputy. They went into the Guard Chamber and stood in the corner, away from the gentlemen who sat playing cards while they waited to be summoned to assist the Queen.

Dr Nunez listened courteously, his hand on his beard and his chin on his ruff. When Davison had finished his peremptory request that Nunez come with him instantly to the Tower and treat a prisoner they had been interrogating, his dark eyes flashed with anger.

"Absolutely not!" he snapped.

Davison was nonplussed. "I beg your pardon, Doctor?"

"So you should, sir. What you ask is an insult."

Davison frowned with puzzlement. "I had no intention of—"

"Which is, furthermore, a worse insult in itself."

"But—"

"You ask *me*, a doctor, a physician, one who has sworn oath to the Almighty (Blessed be He) that wherever I go, I do no harm, I hurt no one save to cure them, you ask *me* to go and treat some poor creature in your dungeons that you may better torment him next time? No, no, no, I will not do it. How dare you, sir? How dare you!"

"How if I tell Sir Francis you would not help?" hissed Davison.

Nunez's eyes narrowed and he muttered something ugly in Portuguese as he drew himself up.

"Certainly," he said. "Let us go and speak with him at once. I have never done this, no, and I never shall. Sir Francis is an honourable man and he is well aware I am a physician."

Cynically Davison thought the Jew's anger overdone. Nunez was known to dabble in intelligence. On the other hand, he was also known to be well-thought-of by Walsingham. He and his people were under the protection of the Queen on that account, if no other.

"Sir, Doctor," said Davison more temperately, "wait. This prisoner is not . . . he is not a Papist, he may be something else. We may have mistaken him for something he is not."

Nunez looked amused. "What, he is a pursuivant, a creature put among the Catholics to tempt them to rebellion, the better to accuse them and arrest them and steal their lands?" Davison nodded. "And you tortured him by mistake?"

Davison nodded again, annoyed. Nunez's big laugh boomed out through the Guard Chamber, until the card-players looked up wondering what the joke was.

"Serve him right," said Nunez. "It is a dirty business. Why should I help?"

"Because he let slip the name of a Jew," said Davison coldly. "And since you are the chief of the Jews in London, I thought you might know the man himself."

Now Nunez's black eyebrows had come down over his nose. "Hmm," he said. "What was the name he gave you?"

"Ames, Simon Ames, although he died four years gone."

The broad-ringed hand went up to stroke Nunez's beard again.

"What is this man called?"

"We know him as Ralph Strangways." Davison saw Nunez's face become intent. "But that is never his real name, be sure of it."

"And what is? No doubt on the rack he told you it."

"We do not use the rack now," said Davison disdainfully. "It bursts the joints and makes the traitor unable to stand for his hanging. Which gives the crowd mistaken cause to pity him."

"Mistaken, eh? His name, Mr Davison?"

"We do not know. He has not given it. He says he has lost his memory. I desire a physician to examine him and treat him and bring his memory back. Which is why I have come to you."

The doctor was nodding slowly. "Very well," he said. "I shall send for my surgeon colleague, and on this one occasion, I shall come and treat your victim."

XXIV

FROM MY THRONE IN the clouds, I may see all the busy scurrying of God's creatures, and angels bring petitions to me, prayers and beseeching and flowers of gratitude. I am the merciful, the benevolent Queen, and no matter what the sinner, those who come to me are never wholly unsatisfied.

And so that night in another part of the Tower a man knelt in prayer and promised me the most extravagant presents if I would see to it that he was not tortured. He feared it extremely, for he is honourable and brave but did not believe he could remain true if tested. Slyly Munday had allowed him a view of his friend in the manacles—to edify him, as Munday said. Although Munday never told him so, he believes that is how he was betrayed and arrested. In fact, Munday happened to see and recognise him by the most ordinary bad luck while he was waiting in a queue at a pie-shop.

While he prays, an idea of Machiavellian cunning occurs to him, as it were, a gift from me. If he can but coney-catch Her Majesty's pursuivants, perhaps he could rescue all of them, and their enterprise as well. The hope of it tickles his arrogance and offers him a relatively honourable way out.

Accordingly, when Munday comes for the preliminary interrogation, he finds to his astonishment that his Jesuit prize is quite co-operative.

XXV

UPON THE FEAST OF the Circumcision of Our Lord, the first of January, many months of anxiety for the courtiers and servants of the Queen come to their consummation. In the September previous had begun whisperings and worryings—what gift to give Her Majesty, of how much worth, of what kind, and with what allegorical and symbolical meaning.

By November the better goldsmiths had ceased taking orders and those maids of honour who had begun in time were beginning to look smug. Others dashed about asking what was the fashion and what had Her Majesty disliked last year. By December the goldsmiths and broiderers that had been fully booked before were taking rush-commissions for triple the usual price and desperate men were visiting the money-lenders and pawnbrokers in the City.

The Queen likes to receive presents. They should be elegant, expensive and appropriate to the giver's station and calling, and if they make her laugh, so much the better.

James Ramme had spent more than he could afford on a jewelled stomacher. Last year Munday had used his father's old contacts to present Her Majesty with a sixteen-yard dress-length of strangely painted silk, blue and white with delicate interlacing cranes that he was told had come from the mythical island of Cipangu. It had disappeared into her Great Wardrobe, never to be seen again.

This year he had written and caused to be printed a book of sonnets praising Her Majesty's glory and beauty of which he was quite modestly proud, and had it specially bound in red and green velvet with gold tooling, and had hand-written in his best script a dedication in the front.

By eight of the clock on the first of January he was standing in line waiting to pass into the Presence Chamber, where the Queen's Lord Chamberlain, Henry Carey Baron Hunsdon, stood massively in black Lucca velvet and gold before the blazing allegories of the Queen's best tapestries. Gentlemen shuttled to and fro from the chests lined up in rows on the left, carrying a magpie's festival of painfully considered and worked gifts, and clerks wrote lists and issued tickets at folding tables behind him.

Not all the largesse went into the chests. Some, like the Clerk of the Pastry's elaborate palace of a raised pie, filled with sparrows and figs, must be carried to a sideboard for tasting and later unheeding consumption at a banquet.

Two hours later, Munday reached the head of the line and bent the knee to Lord Hunsdon, whose eyes were glazed with tedium.

"Mr Anthony Munday," Munday dictated to the plump clerk. "A book of his own devising, by name *A Pithy Basket of Verses to the Praise of England's Eliza* and richly bound in red and green velvet with gold."

". . . green velvet with gold," muttered the clerk.

Munday genuflected again and held out the book in its wrapping of silk. Hunsdon nodded wearily.

"Her Majesty thanks Mr Munday right heartily for his generous gift," he rumbled, "and wishes him, with God's grace, all honour and prosperity in the New Year."

The Gentleman of the Presence Chamber hurried up to take the package and Munday drew him aside slightly.

"An extra small present for yourself here," said Munday quietly, and the gentleman nodded without showing notable gratitude, since courtiers commonly bribed them to draw the Queen's attention to their gifts. "No, do not trouble the Queen, I have no doubt the merits of my poor verse will be sufficient. Only I would be grateful if you could hand the letter beneath it to my lord Burghley."

Nicely shaped eyebrows rose, and the starched ruff creaked as the gentleman tilted his head.

"It concerns Her Majesty's safety and is information my lord Treasurer will wish to have," Munday hissed urgently. "I shall pay the same again to you if I receive any reply from his lordship."

Quite a friendly smile broke out on the gentleman's face and he nodded gravely, took the package, and they flourished bows at each other.

"Your ticket, sir," snapped the plump clerk as Munday made to pass by the table. "Do not forget your ticket."

Munday had been so concentrated upon the necessity of getting his ciphered letter into Burghley's hands without using any usual channels which might be known to Mr Davison, he had quite forgot that the Queen always gave a present in return.

"Oh. Ah. Yes. Thank you," he stuttered, feeling hot and foolish while the elegant creature behind him in the line smiled patronisingly at him for a country bumpkin.

Ticket clutched in his hand, he followed the steady stream of people to the Jewel House to pick up his carefully weighed-out twenty-ounce piece of silver plate.

XXVI

A WEEK LATER A small man rode into London late in the afternoon, accompanied by a consignment of cloth from Bristol and guarded by six outriders. They knew him as Mr Simon Anriques, which had only been his name for the past four years. Before that, while he served Sir Francis Walsingham, he had been called Simon Ames.

He had made a good journey from Bristol, if you did not count two falls from his horse and an attack of the flux, from which he still suffered. His wife, ominously pregnant with their third child, had wept on his neck when he left and given him a package of pasties she had made with her own hands. They were excellent pasties, of lamb mixed with currants and spiced with ginger and cinnamon, but unfortunately he had forgotten all about them after the first day and they had gone mouldy.

His small cavalcade joined the stream of folk passing down Fleet Street to Ludgate. Ames had his cloak round his ears and his new black beaver hat pulled down nearly to his nose. There was no sign of anyone he knew well, although Eliza Fumey's linen-shop was still there and doing a brisk trade, if its new shutters and awnings were any guide. The name over the top had changed but he was too short-sighted to read it without his spectacles.

Ames sent one of the men ahead through the crowds to warn his uncle of his arrival, and jostled his way through the City throngs while the Bristol men with him gawked happily at the displays of the Cheapside goldsmiths.

"Remember," he said to them, "London has more coney-catchers, footpads and thieves than any place else in the world."

"Yes, sir," they said to him, their ears stoppered by greed.

Ames sighed and eased forward in the saddle. Only a little farther to go, thank the Almighty (Blessed be He); he was sure the journey had given him piles. No doubt his uncle would recommend some awful medicine for them as well.

Hector Nunez and his wife, Ames's Aunt Leonora, were waiting at the gate of their house in Poor Jewry, the five servants of the house in attendance behind them. Hector came over with a cry of welcome in Portuguese to embrace his nephew as he dismounted slowly and painfully from his horse and hobbled over. Leonora embraced him as well, weeping over the long time since she had seen him, insisting that marriage agreed with him and furthermore that he was looking very tired; did his wife feed him well enough? And furthermore he had put on weight; how did she do with the babe? Did he not think it was too soon after the last one? And furthermore, blessed be the Almighty to have given him two strong children so quickly, when she had quite despaired of it, and perhaps this one would be a son like the first one, and furthermore . . .

"Leonora," said Nunez gently in Portuguese, "shall we let him into our house?"

They dined on partridges, salt-beef, mutton in mustard, fried cakes of salt-cod and a spit-roasted chicken. Over the pippin fool and saffron bisket-bread Leonora cross-examined her nephew about his children, how they had fared with the dangerous business of teething, and picked over every detail Ames could remember of Rebecca's symptoms, appearance, appetite and sleeping habits, until two hot spots burnt in his cheeks. At last Leonora withdrew so the men could drink tobacco smoke.

Nunez surveyed his nephew critically, with a physician's eye. He seemed to have put on some weight at last and his cheeks had filled out. There was even a small encouraging potbelly under his belt, although his hose wrinkled around his calves as before. He now dyed black what was left of his hair, whose natural shade was straw, and he also dyed the beard he sported, which did nothing for his looks, since it grew in an awkward frill around his mouth and on the margins of his chin. Rebecca had evidently taken control of his wardrobe, since he was very well dressed in a sober dark-red brocade suit and the long black velvet gown appropriate to a married man of substance, topped with a small white ruff.

"Marriage agrees with you, Shimon," Nunez commented genially in Portuguese. "How is Rebecca?"

"As well as any woman in her sixth month." Ames was wary after Leonora's questions and Nunez smiled.

"Is she a good wife?"

"The Almighty (Blessed be He) has truly blessed me with a wife more valuable than pearls," said Ames, and then tempered the formality of his praise with a shy smile. "She is . . . she is a very comfortable woman. I had not realised . . ." His voice trailed away with embarrassment.

Nunez leaned over and patted his hand. "How have you been occupying yourself in Bristol, Shimon? Do you not find yourself dull after your work here in London?"

"My father-in-law is kind to me and asks of me only that I cast up his accounts for him at the end of the month, and encipher his sensitive business correspondence," Ames explained. "I keep track of his money in the Exchange in London and at Amsterdam."

"No more intelligence work at all?"

"Well, I have been building a network of correspondents to warn me of happenings at Court and in Holland."

"Do you pass on this information to Walsingham?"

"I would like to, but have no safe way to do it."

"Why not through me? You may rely on my discretion."

"Perhaps. If we could devise a safe enough cipher and find trustworthy messengers to carry the letters."

Nunez sucked on his pipe.

"And what else?"

Ames's face took on the strained modesty of someone who is actually proud of what he does, but will not admit it.

"I am studying Cabbala a little, in my own fashion. Joshua Anriques has a Rabbi who visits from Amsterdam sometimes. He has been instructing me."

Nunez raised his eyebrows. "Are you not a little young for such studies?"

Ames flushed with irritation. "I am above the age of thirty and married. I think there is no danger. Besides, my study is different from most."

"How?"

Ames squirmed in his seat and picked up a piece of bisket-bread, began breaking it apart, mathematically, into halves, quarters, eights, sixteenths.

"Only it seems to me that as the Almighty created the world (Blessed be He), so the world must reflect His thought."

"Of course. Though not all of it."

"Naturally not. But some of it. Now I know you have heard of Thomas Digges and the calculations of Copernicus that he describes, for I have expounded them to you . . ."

"Many times," rumbled Nunez, a little sadly, tamping his pipe.

". . . and I am attempting to reconcile the Cabbala with those thoughts."
Nunez blinked. "Why?"

Having failed to produce exactly equal thirty-seconds of bisket-bread, Ames now absently drew concentric circles in some slopped wine with his finger.

"There are so many riddles to be answered," he said. "Firstly, the problem of Holy Scripture."

"What problem?"

"Either Copernicus speaks the truth or the Bible does."

"Why cannot they both be true?"

"Unlikely. Genesis describes Creation beginning with the earth and continuing with the sun and moon as lights in the sky. Which is as it should be if the sun and moon alike circle the earth, as Aristotle has it."

"Yes," Nunez admitted cautiously.

"However, if Copernicus be true, then Genesis cannot be. The sun must have been God's first Creation, as the centre, then Mercury, then Venus; then, and only then, the earth and moon."

"Oh. Why must it be so?"

"It would seem logical."

"Surely the Infinite is not bound by logic?"

Ames sighed. "Of course not. I have had this argument many times with the Rabbi and I am still confused. But you see, Copernicus's calculations are beautiful. They so clearly account for all the observed strange behaviour of the planets—the checks and retrograde movements and occlusions which anyone with patience and good eyesight can observe and Ptolemy cannot explain. Unless you begin multiplying cycles and epicycles and end up with an ugly unbalanced thing that makes no sense."

"No human sense."

"No mathematical sense either, which is what offends me. Besides being beautiful mathematically, Copernicus's world has a fitness about it."

For perhaps the hundredth time at that table, the candlestick became a miniature sun and round about it went further pieces of bisket-bread.

"You see: here we have the sun at the centre, a fitting figure for the Almighty, and then around it the planets on their spheres, with the earth at the midpoint of the planets. It is . . . it is beautiful."

"I find it hard to imagine."

"One of the beauties of it is that we can know for certain: if, as saith Aristotle, all beyond the sphere of the moon is perfect, then the slightest imperfection will show that not to be true."

Nunez nodded.

"Therefore if one of the planets were found to have moons or perhaps even creatures upon it . . ."

Nunez laughed. "This is fantasy."

Ames smiled nervously. "True, it is speculation, perhaps worthless at that. But my query is simpler, more founded on logic. I wish to know what the spheres are made of."

"The spheres?"

"The crystal spheres whereon the earth and other planets must travel. Copernicus's theory does nothing to these, only creates a new one, perforce that the earth hangs on and so is carried around the sun."

Nunez's mouth fell open. It had never occurred to him to wonder about such a thing.

"So the sphere must be crystalline or we would see it as the earth rotates."

"Do we not see dawn and dusk?"

"Yes, that may be a solution, that the sphere is made of light; but then, think of the sun as it pours out light. Merely the shadowing of the earth by itself could explain dawn and dusk. And the sphere must surely be transparent or we could not see the outer planets through it, nor the stars. And it must be strong to carry the weight of the earth. But why then . . . Why then does it not shatter when the moon passes through?"

Nunez nodded slowly. "Why indeed?"

"I was greatly perplexed by this and then it came to me. The spheres themselves must be patterned in some way after the Almighty who made it. Therefore to understand the world we must seek the mind of the Almighty Himself. And vice versa."

Nunez nodded again. "Indeed a holy quest."

"But how may I make the enquiry if our chiefest teacher, Scripture, proves mistaken upon the very construction of the world?"

"Aha."

"Precisely. I have considered the Hermetic knowledge, but am not satisfied. And so I return to the Cabbala, a very ancient knowledge, partly mathematical, partly verbal. Perhaps it gives a clue to the nature of the spheres."

"Are you sure they are spheres and not some other shape?"

"Of course they are spheres. The sphere is the perfect shape. What other geometry could they be?"

Nunez lifted his shoulders. "If we must use the world as if it were Holy Scripture, the Word of God, should we not observe it more? We know little enough about it."

"True. But I cannot help wondering. It is a question which hammers in my brain. If there were no moon, the question would not arise: each planet must be borne upon a sphere of crystal—simple. But with the moon—here is a riddle, a mystery made for us by the Almighty, as a good schoolmaster will give a conundrum to his children, that we might learn more about Him by the world He made."

"Amen," said Nunez. "I wish you well of your study, Shimon. It seems you are happy in it."

Ames turned his face to Nunez. "Considering I am supposed to be dead these four years gone, I am extraordinarily happy," he said seriously. "What more could I ask for?"

"Hmm," said Nunez, very unhappily.

"Why did you want me here?"

"If I had known the importance of your studies I might not have . . ."

"You used our emergency code word, Uncle," Ames said quietly. "And further that you dared not write of what had happened. May I ask what—"

"I have found David Becket."

Ames sucked carefully on his clay pipe and waited.

"The last I heard of him myself," Nunez went on, "was that he was in the Netherlands, as Sir Philip Sydney's sword-master. After Sir Philip died last autumn, he disappeared. I had been making enquiries about him, quietly, in case he had chosen to drop from sight. It seems he did so choose and that he was engaged in some matter of intelligence."

"So where is he?"

"At the moment he is in the Tower."

Ames blinked a little. "And?"

Nunez told him the full tale. ". . . Snr Eraso and I have been attending him every day since then," he finished. "Snr Eraso has successfully resolved a dislocated shoulder and has made some progress with the damage to his arms and hands. I have been treating a fever he had taken. He has had two episodes of the falling sickness, which I believe to be the result of the injury to the back of his head sustained when he was captured. The injury to his mind, however, is much worse."

"He genuinely has no memory?"

"He recognised neither me nor Snr Eraso, as I expected him to. Occasionally, in delirium, he makes references to the past, but he then denies that he understands them himself."

"He gave my name."

"In extremis, the first time he was tortured. Perhaps at that time his memory was still intact, I do not know. These are matters of mystery to any physician. I have known a similar case where a blow on the head rendered the patient like a baby, with no speech and no understanding even of dressing himself. This is the first time I have known a case where a man remained palpably sane and yet remembers nothing beyond a couple of weeks past. He does remember his tormentors and is afraid of them. He now knows me and Snr Eraso and has asked me if I will appeal to the Queen on his behalf."

"He knows his religion."

"Yes, though again that seems to have burst from him unknowing while he was in agony. He tells me now that until he began cursing Davison as a Spaniard and a Papist, he was not aware of it."

"Who were his inquisitors?"

"A Mr Anthony Munday and a Mr James Ramme."

Ames nearly dropped his pipe and swore in Portuguese.

"Mr Ramme at least should have known him," he said angrily. "The last time he and Becket met, Becket knocked him down and ruined his clothes and further broke his new rapier. He complained to me of it."

"Perhaps Mr Ramme did know him."

They exchanged glances. Ames's jaw set. "And what does Mr Davison say? How was he captured? How was the mistake made?"

"Mr Davison refuses to tell me. No doubt he feels I am not to be trusted, seeing I am a foreigner."

"Walsingham?"

"Sir Francis is unwell again. Partly it is grief for the death of his son-in-law but I very much fear he has another attack of the stone on the way as well. Whatever the matter was, he has left it in Davison's hands and will not overrule his deputy."

"Surely Becket will be released?"

Nunez sighed and helped himself to more tobacco from the little box on the table. He puffed for a few moments. "Myself, I very much doubt it. I think that Davison believes Becket knows something of vital importance and he will not let his man go until he has it from him. Becket of course denies any such thing, but admits that he might not know it if he did. It seems that the first time he was tortured, he babbled matters such as the fire-drake and also of something else, whereof I have not officially been told. However, Becket himself remembers them discussing it while he was 'up,' as he puts it. He says it was something about a Book of the Unicorn which he does not rightly remember now, except that it fills him with fear."

"What papers were captured with him?"

"None. I understand, by implication, of course, that the arrest went wrong."

"Hah," said Ames. "With Ramme running it, of course it did."

"Do you know Mr Munday also?"

"I have never met him, but we had one A. Munday in place in the English Seminary at Rome, which I assume is that same man."

"No doubt."

Simon sat in silent thought for a while. "I am in a very awkward position, Uncle," he said at last. "By my pretence at being dead, Sir Francis has been planting some wonderfully wrong information with the Spaniards through the Reverend Hunnicutt in his dispatch office. Hunnicutt still believes he is undiscovered. As with all Sir Francis's operations, it is being run with artistry. Not even Davison is aware of the deception. And yet, if I am to use my influence to save Becket, I must come back, as it were, from the grave."

Unconsciously, Nunez made an avert gesture with his hand.

"Have you spoken to the Queen about him?"

"No, Shimon, I wanted to consult with you first. I know there are a number of delicate considerations in this business."

Ames took his pipe from his mouth and tapped out the dottle into the bowl for the purpose. The tapestry-lined room was graceful with candles, and the blue smoke hung in the air; with approval Nunez noted that he handled his pipe as if he had become accustomed to tobacco, which was certainly doing him good for he had not coughed or blown his nose once since he arrived.

"Further, my influence may not be what it once was. I have been away from intelligence matters for four years. Moreover, I do not know Davison personally, but I have decoded letters from him while he was in the Netherlands, and he strikes me as being a clever, subtle man, utterly loyal to their Protestant religion. I have no knowledge at all of his operations against the Catholics and I dare not endanger them. Davison has been appointed to the Privy Council. Walsingham is ill; if he were to die, then Davison . . ."

Nunez nodded. He did not need to finish the sentence. There was silence for a while and then Simon's fist came down on the table, causing Nunez to start.

"We cannot leave Becket in the Tower. I owe him my life several times over; no matter what he has been up to, we must help him."

"Of course," murmured Nunez. "I had no doubt of that, Shimon. My doubts are simply over how we are to proceed."

"Davison will not release him and Walsingham will not interfere?"

Nunez nodded once. Simon smiled at him, his rather cold pale-brown eyes glittering in the candle-light.

"Then we go above both their heads. We talk to the Queen."

XXVII

MARY NEVER CHOSE TO be a witch, nor made a pact with the Devil. In a way, the witchery chose her.

Consider the sorrows of a land without the Queen of Heaven. When King Henry's clerks and pursuivants destroyed the monasteries fifty years ago, all they did was cast into the world a number of men who knew no trade but writing and reading and singing. To be sure, they gave them pensions and then some became schoolmasters and some married and they all did well enough save the inevitable few who turned to drink and vice.

But when they destroyed the nunneries—ah, then they did a far different thing, for then they stole from women our very last redoubt from men. If a woman cannot be sanctified by Christ as a nun and if she further cannot marry or is not married—until she is too old, she is every man's prey, and when she has at last become old she is likewise prey. Then they call her a witch, the better to justify their cruelty.

When the men came to break up the convent and take their lands, Mary was thirty-five, an Infirmerar and Mistress of Novices. Hers was a good nunnery, a quiet place with blossoming cloisters and lay-sisters who took good care of the vowed Religious. They treated the sick of Clerkenwell and their granaries were

opened when the harvest failed. Their Mother Superior was not like those tra-
duced in Cromwell's reports; she managed the convent as she would have run
her husband's estate, well and firmly, if a little unimaginatively. They say the
nunneries were rife with vice and with nuns giving birth to bastard babes. Perhaps
there were some like that and there certainly were many that were badly managed,
but riotous vice was not their sin. Mary and her sisters in Christ carried on the
old comfortable sins of carping and sarcasm, gossip and sulking; of over-nicety
and fussiness; of unspoken hurt and the little prickles that women make for each
other. No man came to riot with them, because they did not want him. This
was a matter of great disappointment to some of the inspectors sent out by the
King, who had convinced themselves that houses full of manless women would
be desperate for the starved red meat that flourished between the honourable
inspectors' thighs.

In their chapel they sang right beautifully to me, their Gracious Lady, and
Mary sings it still. Listen: *"Salve regina, mater misericordia, vita dulcedo et spes
nostra salve . . ."*

"Help us, Queen, mother of Mercy, our sweetness of life and our hope, save
us . . ." *"Ad te clamamus, exules filii Hevae, ad te suspiramus, gementes et flentes,
in hac lacrimarum valle . . ."* "To you we cry, exiled children of Eve, to you we
sigh, groaning and weeping, in this valley of tears . . ."

Well, it was gracious singing but they knew nothing of which they sang,
God knows. Beyond a romantical wistfulness, Mary had no notion of exile, nor
of weeping then. The greatest threat to her soul came from complacency.

It was no liberation for Mary, to be told at the age of thirty-five by a greedy-
eyed clerk to make her own way in the world. She was given a small pension
barely enough to live on that in any case was not paid. How could she marry?
She had no dowry, she was old as men reckon their bedmates, and if she married
or fell with child, they said, the pension would be withdrawn (if it had ever been
paid, which it was not). So she must be chaste but could no longer be a nun;
must have no man, but could find no women either. This they called liberation.
Mary called it robbery.

What could she do? Dame Mary Dormer, Infirmerar, Mistress of Novices—
no one had need of her. By spinning she could only starve more slowly, by
needlework the same. Some nuns became nurses and cared for the children of
others; some went home to their families to be resented and pitied as a thing
out of place, out of time, useless, tolerated. She was too proud for that.

Why should I wonder at her rage? Think on it. She had known one Bridegroom that never took her maidenhead, that had promised her pure eternal love and protection from the world. And then, to her mind, He cast her out, spurned her. Even her prayers to me boiled with her corrosive anger at my Son. "Speak not to me of the love of Christ," she would hiss, "what love did He show me?" Ay, poor lady, give her a hammer and nails and she would crucify Him again for what He did to her. Bang! you gave me no children and the name you gave me, you took away again. Bang! you put me on the road and gave me no means to help myself. Bang! bang! (for the feet) you made me a laughing-stock and you made me a whore.

XXVIII

THOMASINA BEGAN HER QUEST for the Book of the Unicorn by realising that although she had spent ten years in the Queen's service, she knew almost nothing about the Queen's past. After some thought she went to Blanche Parry and asked her about the Book of the Unicorn.

"I have never seen such a thing," said Mrs Parry, very positively.

"She lost it during her brother's reign, she says."

Parry's plucked eyebrows went up nearly to her hair-line.

"But she was only a girl, only the Princess Elizabeth. Mrs Kat Ashley was her chief gentlewoman then."

"She does not expect me to find it, Mrs Parry, but I thought I would try."

"Hmm." Parry thought hard. "You could look at Mr Parry's account books—they are in the Library here, along with some other record books."

Thomasina thanked her and went to the Library at the end of the Privy Gallery nearest the Holbein Gate. She had been in there sometimes to find a book, but had never had the run of the place. She found it wonderful to think of all the books and papers stored there, although it was hard to find anything if you did not already know where it was. And so she began methodically looking at the books on the bottom shelves, and then the second shelves and there she was lucky, for she found a whole group of leather-bound volumes that had never before been taken out, from the dust on them.

Coughing and struggling with the weight of the ledgers, she drew them out and found her way back to Edward VI's reign. Strange to think that the Queen had once been a fourteen-year-old girl, with a penchant for rose-coloured damask and cloth of gold, badly served by Thomas Parry, a cofferer who could not, it seemed, add up. There, amongst the other entries, was one for the spring of 1548, an order for blue velvet, another for white silk and silver threads, and a pattern-drawer's fee for the outline of the work. Then, nothing.

Carefully Thomasina checked through the rest of the ledgers, until the light coming through the windows from the Privy Garden began to change and she realised it was past noon. She put them back and hurried off to attend Her Majesty at her dinner.

As she arrived she found the Queen closeted with Mary Ratcliffe, who was carrying the Wardrobe books. When they had finished, the Queen turned to her and smiled.

"My dear," she said. "Will you run me an errand?"

Thomasina curtsied and smiled. "Whatever Your Majesty desires."

Thomasina was to go down to the laundry, the long building facing the Thames in the woodyard, and speak to Mrs Ann Twiste, the Queen's laundress, taking with her a small blue seal ring of Her Majesty's and a purse of money. She would have one of the chamberers to go with her, carrying the laundry bags.

Thomasina hardly ever went outside the central part of the Court where the Queen lived, nor usually desired to. She had seen enough of the world. But she put on pattens and a cloak to preserve her from the ugly wind and the snow and went meekly with the chamberer.

The chamberer delivered the bags of linen to a harassed red-faced woman standing at a desk by the door to the place. She noted down the bag in her ledger and took the laundry list, checked it through and separated out the sheets and Holland towels from the underlinen, and the partlets and ruffs from the smocks.

They passed through the passage and Thomasina found it strange to find so many women bustling about, most of them in their bodice and petticoats, with their smock sleeves rolled up and cloths around their heads. At Court almost all of the servants of the *domus providenciae* were young men, except for tiring-women and maids for the Queen's gentlewomen. Wherever you went in the whitewashed corridors and passages behind the outward show of magnificence, there were men of all sizes, ages and conditions milling here and there, a shocking contrast to the cloistered femininity of the Queen's Privy Chambers. At the laundry the case was opposite. Small girls also ran about in their petticoats, carrying bags of grated soap or scrubbing brushes. There were many rooms in the long building: one, labelled the Ewery, dealt with table-linen for the Court; the largest was for the household linen, where two vast coppers boiled clouds of steam into the air; the next for the smocks; and the smallest room—though still large and airy—for the partlets and ruff-starching. The Queen's silk-woman was in charge there and personally washed the Queen's linen, although there was never-ending demand for her services from the rest of the Court.

The heat and noise of boiling, scrubbing, flapping and wringing was outrageous, but it was almost drowned out by the continuous babble of talk. In the ruff-laundry, the women standing by the fire dipping the ruffs in the warm starch suddenly broke into shrieks of laughter.

The chamberer was still talking to the woman at the desk. Thomasina reached up to twitch her sleeve.

"Where is Mrs Twiste?" she asked.

"At the end of the passage, dear," said the woman clerk kindly. "Why do you want her?"

"I have a message for her," Thomasina said, flushing slightly. It always annoyed her to be taken for a child, unless the Queen did it, when it was a game between them. Many people looked no farther than her size and the roundness of her face.

"Well, do not forget to knock."

Pulling her cloak about her, Thomasina picked her way along the tiled corridor, carefully avoiding the puddles. Before she came to Mrs Twiste's office, she found the passage opened out into a room full of cloaks and pattens and kirtles hung on hooks, where a small gang of tired little girls were sitting on benches eating bread and cheese.

"Excuse me," she said politely to them. "Is this where I can find Mrs Twiste?"

A couple of them nodded while the others stared at her curiously.

She reached up to knock. A voice said, "Enter," and she went in to find a small room lined with shelves for ledgers and laundry-books, with rush-matting on the floor and a high desk where a woman sat frowning as she wrote.

"Mrs Twiste?" Thomasina said.

"Yes?"

She went round the side of the desk so that Mrs Twiste could see her. But again, what Mrs Twiste saw was a little girl. For a moment Thomasina was annoyed: I am the Queen's Fool, you fat old cow, she thought, damn you, get up and curtsey to me. And then she started to smile inwardly and decided to have some fun with Mrs Twiste. She curtseyed and came forward shyly, holding out the ring and the purse of money.

"Please, ma'am, the Queen sent you these."

Ann Twiste's eyes swept over her a little curiously, then saw the ring and nodded. She took the purse of money, put it in a small heavy chest under the desk, and began drawing sheets of paper from another locked drawer.

"Now," she said briskly, "what is your name?"

"Thomasina, ma'am."

"Well, Thomasina, the Queen has trusted you with an important office."

"Yes, ma'am. The Queen is very kind, ma'am," Thomasina added artlessly.

Mrs Twiste smiled indulgently. "Of course she is, providing you are a good girl and do as you are told."

And that is the truth, Thomasina thought, hiding her urge to snigger with a curtsey and a modest lowering of her eyes.

The papers were being sorted, tapped into neat bundles and tied with tape before Mrs Twiste put them in a small canvas bag. She looked about her and frowned.

"Run and fetch me a light for the sealing-wax, there's a good girl," she said.

Thomasina dropped another curtsey and went through the door. She hesitated when she saw the group of girls and then went over to them.

"Mrs Twiste wants a light," she said. "Where should I go?"

One of the little girls, wrapped in bossy consciousness of being the oldest, pointed to the smallest, an oval-faced sensible creature with pink-and-white skin and dark-brown hair hanging out from her cap.

"You show her," she said as peremptory as the Queen.

The child jumped to her feet.

"This way," she said, took Thomasina's hand and pulled her down the passage again. They got a candle from the woman by the door and then went into the big main room full of steam and water where women pummelled huge white table-cloths and bunches of napkins in vats of cold water. The copper in the fireplace was being stoked to a boil, as two broad women piled soaked and scrubbed napery into the water and another stirred with a long stick.

"I am called Pentecost," said the little girl. "What's your name?"

"Thomasina."

"Are you at Court, Thomasina?"

She nodded, play-acting shyness successfully because she did in fact feel shy.

"Mistress," yelled Pentecost at one of the red-faced women, "may I take a light?"

"Oh ay," said the woman irritably, slung another armful of linen at the copper. She turned her head and gave tongue like the captain of a ship, "Mary!"

Pentecost frowned unhappily. What had appeared to Thomasina as a pile of velvet rags, dangerously dropped by the fire, moved and became an old woman, her face weather-bitten and crumbled, her bloodshot eyes ringed with white in the iris. She muttered and heaved herself to her feet, came shambling over to the woman and stood there swaying.

"Fetch me a taper, then give Pentecost a light," ordered the woman, still briskly throwing table-cloths into the copper.

The hag focussed uncertainly on Pentecost and smiled, showing a couple of insecure brown teeth.

"Now, sweeting," she said, and her voice was surprising. Old to be sure, but not harsh. "How are you, poppet?"

"I am well, Grandam," said Pentecost gravely, and dropped a curtsey. "Are you better now, Grandam?"

The old woman shook her head. "Not well, sweet, not well. It's desperate dry work here."

"Hah," said the other woman, who had stopped throwing table-linen and was now stirring the copper with a long wooden stick. "Fetch some wood as well, Mary, and I'll give you a nip."

There was a momentary flash of anger across the ugly face, and then Mary shrugged and struggled to the wood-box by the door. High above it was another box. Pentecost trotted after her, helped her fetch out sticks.

"The taper, Grandam," she whispered and Mary grunted, reached up and fetched down a good taper from the box on the wall, gave it to Pentecost, who picked up the logs that Mary had dropped all over the floor and carried most of them in her skirt to the woman by the copper. Mary followed, holding a log in each hand and one under her arm. As she passed by Thomasina, a many-layered wave of stenches went with her; the smell of feet and old teeth and bad bowels, overlaid with a powerful stink of piss, and on top of that bad aqua vitae. The woman with the copper had opened the fire-door underneath and was piling the logs in from Pentecost's apron, flapping her own apron at the fire to get it to catch, opening a lower door to let air in. Gravely Pentecost lit her taper from the flames and gave it to Thomasina, who used it to light the candle which she held like an acolyte in the Queen's chapel.

"Pump the bellows, Mary," said the woman.

"How can I do that, when I'm dry as your cunny," demanded Mary rudely.

The woman sighed, fetched a bottle out of the ample front of her bodice, gave it to Mary and watched hawk-eyed while she drank, sighed and wiped her mouth. The woman snatched back the bottle and sullenly the old woman set herself to pump the bellows by the lower door. Her bony hands were chapped, age-spattered and red with work, but fine-boned.

The candle successfully lit, they went back down the passage, carefully cupping it with their hands.

"Why does she smell so bad?" Thomasina asked, taking advantage of the nosy freedom of all small children.

Pentecost frowned. "She does not," she said, not asking whom Thomasina was talking about.

"She does," said Thomasina.

"Well, she is the night-soil woman for the Court," said Pentecost. "How can she help it if she splashes herself sometimes?"

Thomasina nodded and kept to herself her thought that the old woman might splash less and smell better if she drank less. On the other hand, what other help did she have? It was a frightening picture, to be old and poor and despised by the young; why should she not drink? Thomasina shuddered a little and comforted herself with thoughts of the gold and silver plate she had at the goldsmith's, the houses she had bought in London for their rentals, the small estate she had managed to pick up from one of the Babington plotters.

"Are you a princess?" Pentecost wanted to know.

Thomasina shook her head.

"Why do you have such beautiful clothes if you are not a princess?"

"The Queen gave them to me. I . . . I am her tumbler; I turn somersaults and dance for her."

"Ohh." Pentecost's eyes were round. "The Queen. You dance for the Queen? What does she wear? Does she like it? Is she tall? What do you do when you dance? Show me."

For a moment Thomasina wanted to temporise, but then she found herself slipping her feet out of her pattens, pulling her cloak around her as she found a dry piece of floor, and bounced a couple of times on her toes before springing up and turning a somersault in the air. Pentecost stood sheltering the candle with her mouth open and lights in her eyes.

Thomasina put her pattens back on. "Mrs Twiste will be waiting," she said a little breathlessly, pushing her cap straight again.

"Ohh," Pentecost said, a flush in her cheeks, "that was wonderful. How do you do it? Is it hard? Could you show me? Would the Queen like another little girl to dance for her?"

"It is very hard to learn," Thomasina said gravely, "but it is easy when you know."

Pentecost nodded. "No wonder the Queen gives you such beautiful clothes," she said as they came to Mrs Twiste's office again. "Do you have a dowry as well?"

The question was so unexpected it twisted Thomasina's heart in her ribs. "I . . . no," she said at last "No."

Kindly Pentecost patted her back. "Never mind, Thomasina," she said, "I expect the Queen will give you one when you grow up and need it. My grandam says she is the kindly one."

Pentecost slipped back among the other little girls and was clearly telling them all about her. Thomasina took a moment to recover her composure before she knocked and went in with the candle.

Mrs Twiste made an elaborate business of sealing the bag with the Queen's blue signet ring, and another one she wore on her forefinger. Then she gave the bag to Thomasina and told her to tie it safely under her petticoat.

"Now there is one piece of news I have not had time to write down," she said. "Are you listening carefully, Thomasina? I want you to remember this."

"Yes, ma'am."

"A guest arrived at Dr Nunez's house today. He was short, slender, well-dressed, his hair was dyed black. He had a strong look of the Ames family and Dr Nunez called him Simon and embraced him like a relative. He brought with him six attendants, a manservant and four pack-ponies bearing bolts of cloth with a Bristol merchant's mark on them. Did you hear all of that?"

Thomasina nodded.

"Repeat it for me."

She did, getting it right after only one repetition.

"Off you go then, Thomasina," said Mrs Twiste kindly. "Oh, attend one minute, child."

Thomasina turned at the door. Mrs Twiste had risen and taken something from a jar on her desk. She handed it to her. "This is for you." It was a ribbon of sugar-plate, twisted and patterned with red sanders and yellow primrose juice. Thomasina smiled and curtsied.

"Thank you, ma'am."

Once outside the door, she sighed and felt suddenly old. Once upon a time she had loved sugar-plate and gorged herself with it at every banquet. Now she had two teeth missing and could no longer crunch sugar with abandon.

"Pentecost," she said to the small flock of loudly arguing children in the corner, and Pentecost came over, followed by all the other little girls.

"Is it true you can jump in the air and spin?" they all wanted to know.

The tall imperious girl at the back said contemptuously, "I bet she can't. Pentecost is telling stories about Queens again."

Why did she care what the little girls thought? But she did and also cared that Pentecost was looking flushed and unhappy. Once there had been children who were vicious to her as only small girls can be, asking her pointedly when would she start to grow, when would she have breasts, when would she have babies? Their brothers had thrown stones which hurt less.

"Here," Thomasina said roughly and gave Pentecost her bag of dispatches and the sugar-ribbon to hold. "You," she said to the girl who had sneered, "clear a space for me." Her voice had suddenly taken the tinge of London to it which she had lost at Court.

Cloaks and pattens were shoved back, leaving a clear stone-flagged space with gutters for water. Thomasina slipped her feet out of her pattens again, dropped her cloak behind her, causing a satisfactory gasp as the girls saw her damask kirtle and farthingale sleeves. Then she took a short run, stretched her arms and did a cartwheel, a flip-flop and a jump, tuck and double-twist, landing on her feet, facing them with her arms out. They squealed with amazement and some of them clapped. With dignity, Thomasina put on her cloak and pattens again, took back the bag and nodded to Pentecost who was still holding the comfit, her eyes shining.

"You have that, Pentecost," she said a little breathlessly. "Share it, if you so wish."

And then she walked out, leaving them open-mouthed behind her.

XXIX

NUNEZ EXPECTED TO SPEND several days in the delicate pursuit of an audience with the Queen. Now she was recovered of her stomach cramps he had no reason to consult with her, and in any case he would not have confused the therapeutic relationship by using such a time to ask something of her. Besides, she would have regarded it as impudence.

However, the following morning a summons to Court came to his house, carried by a young Gentleman of the Privy Chamber named Gage who looked harassed and in need of bleeding. The summons itself was in Secretary hand and peremptory in tone.

Wondering uneasily how he could have offended her, Dr Nunez combed his beard, changed his shirt and put on his gravest and soberest brocade suit and velvet gown. Ames insisted that all he was to do was ask the favour of an audience for Ames himself.

After being kept waiting for three quarters of an hour while the Queen walked in the garden, Dr Nunez at last knelt before her as she sat under her Cloth of State in the Presence Chamber. She was fully dressed and not in bed, so this was not a professional consultation. However, it was private: she ordered all her gentlewomen and gentlemen out, leaving only her muliercula reading quietly on a cushion in the corner, looking something like a large stiff puppet in her pale blue damask garded with cloth-of-gold.

"Doctor, how is that nephew of yours?" the Queen demanded after she had stared down at him for fully five minutes.

Nunez blinked stupidly for a moment. How had she known? How did she . . . Who was the spy in his household? For a heartbeat he felt angry that she should have information on him and flaunt it and then he thought more carefully. Naturally she would have a spy upon him, given his activities. It was by way of a compliment that she was letting him know it.

In case it should actually be a matter to do with one of his many other young nephews, Nunez asked hesitantly, "Your Majesty? William? Francis?"

She waved a long white hand. "No, no, Doctor," she sniffed, "I can hear about either of them from Walsingham. I mean the runt of the Ames litter, the valiant little scrawny one with the running nose. The one that protected me from the Papist assassin, four years ago."

"Er . . ." said Nunez unhappily, wondering which tale Walsingham had told her: the one for general consumption which said that Simon had died of lung-fever four years ago, or the secret. Surely he had not kept her in the dark. Or had he? Walsingham was extremely close-mouthed about his counter-intelligence operations.

Nunez lifted his head and looked at the Queen. Considered dispassionately, she was an extraordinary sight: quite a small red-haired woman, as it were, almost eaten alive by the extravagant heraldic beast of her kirtle and gown, and her face rayed like a saint in an old picture with the delicate cambric lawn of her veil. It was an elaborate confection, a carapace like a hermit crab's and designed deliberately to hide the fact that beneath it all was only the soft flesh of a woman; a compound of four humours, wetted with some divinity and a great deal of unwomanly intellect. And yet the time he had attended her for her stomach cramps she had still been very much the Queen, despite being in bed and in pain. Turn her from her realm in her petticoat, as she had boasted once, and she would still be a most formidable lady.

Hoping it was not true—as he had heard—that she could read minds, Nunez cleared his throat again. She was waiting patiently for his answer. Whether Walsingham had told her the truth or not, it was not his business to lie to her.

"He is well, Your Majesty. He has married . . ." The high arched eyebrows came together. The Queen was extremely averse to any of her servants' marrying.

". . . as we are enjoined very strictly by our religion," Nunez added, and wondered at the stickiness of his mouth and the heat generated by the furnace of his heart, which made him sweat. "He has . . . ah . . . moved to Bristol and changed his name, the better that the Spaniard should believe him dead."

She laughed. She kept a wardrobe of laughter as well as of gowns and kirtles; she could tinkle merrily like bells when flirting with an ambassador, but this was a deep and humourless sound.

"Walsingham is fixed in his belief that truth will grow from a sowing of lies," she said. "In this case, it seems he was right."

Nunez coughed delicately. "The ploy has been successful."

"Then why is Ames endangering it by coming back to London?"

"Your Majesty, I would have sought audience with you anyway," Nunez said hurriedly. "I was intending to ask you the favour of audience for him, as he has a matter of extreme urgency to discuss with you."

"And what is that?"

"He has asked me most particularly that I not broach the subject without him."

"Hmm," she said consideringly. Her eyes held his for a while and then suddenly the weather of her face changed for the better. She smiled and beckoned him.

"Come, Doctor, off your knees. Come and take my pulses."

Nunez creaked to his feet and waited for a minute to let the blood go back down his legs. It was a hard thing for a man as well-stomached as he was to kneel for a long time, and growing harder. Soon he would have to bring a cushion, like Burghley.

He approached her throne smoothly, putting on a grave professional face. Her Majesty held out her slim jewelled hand again and he took it, spreading his blunt fingers to sense the little pulses that whispered of the balance of her humours. There was silence for a while, he standing with his eyes half-shut, concentrating, she watching him, head on one side, her perennial restlessness briefly stilled.

"I have rarely met a woman in such an excellent humourous balance as Your Majesty," Nunez intoned.

She smiled and wagged her finger at him coquettishly.

"What, no physic, no bleedings, no emetics? You shall be drummed from the Physicians' College."

Nunez bowed.

"I would like to have a sight and taste of Your Majesty's water," he said, "but with that proviso I had best pray that none of my other patients should fall so healthy."

"Save my lord of Leicester, of course."

Nunex bowed again and decided against flattery and euphemism.

"Your Majesty knows he is not in good health."

She nodded. "Ay, he eats and drinks too much, shouts too much and is of choleric complection."

"If the disposition is too heated, the heart may be brought to spasm."

"And what makes the heart overheat the body?"

Nunez shook his head. "All we can say is that an oversupply of blood and also of bile will greatly tire the heart's furnace. I beg Your Majesty will urge him to be leeched more often, as I advised last month. His pulses are very fast. Perhaps he will obey his sovereign, if not his physician."

"He has not been my obedient servant recently," said the Queen wither-ingly, "and the Netherlands did him no good at all, neither body nor soul. He was greatly distressed when that silly poet nephew of his died. Is your own nephew's business to do with that business of Sidney's?"

"Your Majesty," Nunez began uncertainly, "I am only a physician . . ." What was she talking about, "business of Sidney's"? Sir Philip had never been involved in espionage. ". . . with a few commercial interests and—"

"A network of spies throughout Europe and Turkey that Walsingham would covet if you did not put them at his disposal."

"Your Majesty is too kind. They are but friends and family who—"

"Put their lives at risk to send me information. Come, Doctor, must we play veney sticks with words? What made your most wise and circumspect nephew desert my service? I would have rewarded him well for his actions in my defence. I was even considering a place on the Privy Council."

"His health was bad—"

"Bah. I do not turn off the least of my door-keepers for ill-health. What was the reason?"

Nunez took a deep breath, wishing wistfully that she were not so sharp. "He has said to me, very vehemently, that he will not return to his old work of inquisitor."

The Queen sniffed. "I shall see him. Bring him to me at this time tomor-row." She held out one hand for him to kiss while she rang her bell. The ladies- and maids-in-waiting, who had been banished to the Waiting Chamber, came filing in with their work, books, parrots and lap-dogs. One of the small fat furry creatures leapt down from a pair of green velvet sleeves and galloped across the rush-matting, yapping excitedly. The Queen laughed and plucked it up, caressing it and feeding it little pieces of chicken from a silver dish brought by a dark-haired girl with extremely pale skin. The dog lapped deliriously at the Queen's face, got a tongueful of white lead, and shook itself. The Queen patted it, coddled it with more chicken and then plumped it into Dr Nunez's arms while she flicked her fingers at one of the younger girls standing about.

"Fetch the velvet purse."

Whilst he waited, Nunez felt the little dog in his arms heave convulsively. He put it down on the floor and moved the edge of his robe so the dog could be sick out of sight of his mistress.

Gimlet-eyed, the Queen saw.

"Now what ails Eric, Doctor?" she asked.

Nunez looked down gravely. "It has eaten something that disagreed with it," he diagnosed.

"But what?" demanded the Queen sharply, looking sideways at the plate of meat.

Nunez was in a quandary. Clearly it was the face-paint the horrible little creature had slurped off his mistress's face, but on the other hand it was never wise to mention the fact that the Queen painted her face, since this detracted from the notion of the Queen as a great and immortal beauty.

He gave himself time to think by picking the dog Eric up and opening its jaw. It snapped at him irritably. Inspiration came.

"A hairball, no doubt, Your Majesty. Any creature with fur that licks himself will suffer from them, and they are only upset until they have vomited it out."

"What of his humours?"

Did dogs have humours? If dogs, why not horses or cattle? But surely mere dumb animals could not be complected as men were—though, on the other hand, presumably they were complected somehow, and in which case, of what? There was no question that animals had blood, the sanguine humour. It was a fascinating question, and Nunez had never considered it before.

"Good, for a dog," he said gravely, not for the first time making it up as he went along. Eric snapped again and nipped his wrist. "Perhaps a little choleric."

The girl sent for the purse puffed towards the Queen with it, who handed it to him magnanimously. Nunez took it, found his arms too full of dog to look inside, but gathered that it contained his fee. Lackadaisical about paying her courtiers, the Queen was punctilious about paying her servants. Paying him personally meant she was very pleased with his service to her when she was ill. Nunez suppressed a shudder. The Almighty forfend that she take it into her head to appoint him her Chief Physician; the last thing he wanted was a dangerous office like that.

Having repented of nipping him, the dog licked his face, blasting him with its breath. The Queen stood up impatiently, causing a tumble and creaking among the older ladies who had sat down on stools and cushions, as they got hastily to their own feet.

"You have our leave to depart, Doctor" was thrown over an imperious shoulder as the Queen walked briskly to the door, trailing two more little dogs who had apparently been taking refuge amongst her petticoats. Eric left a pattern of nail scratches as he jumped down from Nunez's arms and yelped after his mistress.

XXX

LORD BURGHLEY STOOD SHIFTING from foot to foot uneasily while he waited for his mistress to admit him to her presence. Generally speaking, she had mercy on his gouty knees and saw him at once, but now she was furious with him for siding with Walsingham, Hatton and the Earl of Leicester on the question of the Queen of Scots. Behind him his son carried a cushion and a large sheaf of papers. He was a skinny hunchbacked youth with a dark, unhappy face livened by intelligence and a surprising wit.

At last a gentleman opened the door and they went into the Council Chamber where the Queen already sat at the head of the long table under her Cloth of State.

Burghley shuffled forwards, wincing at the pain in his big toe and ankle, and slowly folded himself down on the cushion Robert placed in front of Her Majesty. Unusually she left him there for a while, hammering the point home that she was the Queen whilst he, however rich, however powerful, was the servant.

"How are you today, my lord?" she asked kindly enough after a while. "How is your gout?"

"The cold weather does not agree with it, Your Majesty," said Burghley. "I am taking a new physic which I hope will be more efficacious."

"Pray God that it is," said the Queen distantly. There was a pause, a distinct gap in the conversation into which her command to him to rise would usually have fitted. The absence was marked. So that is the way of it, Burghley thought wearily and decided to get the unpleasantness over with. If she threw her ink-pot at him and told him to get out of her sight, at least he would be off his knees. But no, he had to sort out the business of the prisoner first.

"Your Majesty, we have a number of matters to deal with," he said. "First is a petition from a Mr Coulson to have the Clerkship of the Ewery revert to his son when he dies."

"Granted," said the Queen, who preferred continuity even though Mr Coulson was hardly ever seen near the laundry-house.

"Second is a matter of a man that was taken in a raid on a house in London two weeks ago."

"A Papist?"

"A complex matter, Your Majesty. I would have consulted Sir Francis if he had been well-enough, since it concerns his deputy."

"Mr Davison." The Queen's lip curled in distaste. "What has he done now?"

"Has there been a warrant granted for putting to the question?"

"No." The Queen signed dozens of documents a day, and somehow seemed to read every one. "No such thing."

"I have here a letter from one of Mr Davison's pursuivants, a Mr Munday, who questioned the man in the Tower. He is concerned because they have discovered this man was a Protestant and not a Papist. They had not realised it before because he has somehow lost his memory. Mr Munday thought perhaps he might have been working for me and so wrote to me secretly."

"Wise of him."

"Yes," said Burghley, "very wise. I do not in general employ pursuivants against the Catholics, leaving that to my learned colleague Sir Francis. I fear I do not know this man, but it occurred to me that perhaps Your Majesty . . ."

She leaned forwards and twitched the paper out of his hand. He shifted his weight to his less painful knee and wondered how long he could last. Lord, she was in a temper with him.

Her eyes scanned the writing describing Munday's prisoner—very clear and well-formed, Burghley had thought—and the decipherment of the code-words. Her eyes narrowed. "Hm," she said, took breath to speak and then stopped. "Hm," she said again and looked at him. "And what is this operation of Davison's?"

"Extremely secret," Burghley said. "I have not yet been fully apprised. I am told by Sir Francis that the matter is of such delicacy—"

"Like that damnable and wicked charade, the Babington plot?"

Burghley, who had not been involved in it, coughed modestly and looked down. He shifted to his other knee.

"As far as I know," he hazarded cautiously, "it does not directly concern the Queen of Scots."

"What then?"

Burghley made a small moue of embarrassment. "I take very little part in such things now, I prefer to—"

"Oh, God's bowels, Cecil," shouted the Queen. "Will you cease from fencing with me and tell me what you know?"

Burghley bowed. "The rumour is that it has to do with a wicked libel against Your Majesty, known as the Book of the Unicorn. That is all, I fear."

"A libel. Worse than before?"

"I have no idea."

"And Davison is investigating?"

"So I understand."

"And why have I received no report on the operation's progress?"

"Your Majesty, I can only answer that I have received no report either. Perhaps we had best ask Mr Davison."

"And have the long-nosed po-faced Calvinist read me another impertinent lecture upon the necessity for executing the Queen of Scots? I think not, my lord."

"It *is* necessary, Your Majesty—"

Thank God, she threw a slipper, not an ink-pot. Burghley ducked just in time, but it hit his son, who squeaked inelegantly.

"Necessary, by Christ? Necessary? Execute an anointed Queen—*necessary*? God-cursed tomfoolery and half-wittery, that's what it is, Cecil, and I will have no more speech of her before me . . . Get out, get out!"

With his son's inadequate arm to help, Burghley got to his feet just in time and bowed with as much dignity as he could muster while another slipper, a muff and a book whizzed by his ears. Fortunately, rage made the Queen's aim bad. They bowed again at the door, and slid past as the gentleman opened it.

She still looked magnificent in a temper, Burghley thought fondly, and her roar had exactly the timbre of her father's, only two octaves up. He bent and rubbed his knees, wincing at the shooting pains lancing up to his hip. They had left the cushion behind in their hurry.

"Go back for the cushion, Robert," he said to his son. "And leave the papers on the table."

"Ah . . ." Robert looked nervously in the direction of the closed door and the sound of swearing seeping through it.

"The more often you bow, the less likely it is she will hit you. Off you go."

Looking like a man on the way to the scaffold, Robert scurried over the floor and slid round the door. Moments later he scrambled back, looking frightened and upset.

"She said she will have me in the Tower by morning and treat my hunchback with stretching," Robert said.

Burghley nodded. "She has threatened me with the same many hundreds of times; it is to her like a hobgoblin to frighten children. I have yet to see the inside of the place unwillingly."

"But she has committed others . . ."

Burghley put his hand on his son's arm. "Robert," he said, "get no maids of honour with child and serve her faithfully and honestly and she will never desert you."

XXXI

THE FOLLOWING MORNING SIMON Ames knelt before the Queen in the Privy Chamber and quailed inwardly at her wrath. He had begun badly by telling her the news of his wife and then made his position worse by informing her without prompting that he could no longer act as her inquisitor. Nunez knelt behind him and winced.

"How dare you!" roared the Queen in peroration. "Viper, son of Belial, damned puling little clerk, how dare you tell me what you will or will not do?"

"Your Majesty, if I may have leave to speak my mind—"

"Leave, by God? When did I ever give you leave to snivel that you have not the stomach to find out traitors to the State, and me, damn you, when I am surrounded by fools and pompous Puritans that think themselves full of God-given wisdom when all they are fat with is bile, choler, arrogance and ignorance!"

"Nonetheless, Your Majesty, it is true," said Ames when the tirade had slackened. "I have neither the stomach for it, nor the body."

"Walsingham is tortured by the stone and he serves me."

"I would not compare myself to His Honour."

"Yet your father finds he can act as my Comptroller for Groceries without any of this lily-livered niceness."

"I believe the offices are not comparable, Your Majesty. And alas, I am a very ill son to him."

"My favour is not imperishable."

"Your Majesty is a most just, patient and gracious Prince, the Nation's jewel and our only Shield from Spain," said Ames steadily, while Nunez wished to put his head in his hands and moan. He shut his eyes.

"Are you bargaining with me, Ames?" The voice was a dangerous hiss. "Are you jewing with me for a price?"

Nunez's eyes snapped open at the insult. To his astonishment, Ames said nothing, kneeling before the Queen and watching her steadily. Only the flush climbing up the back of his neck told of his anger. He continued to say nothing and it was the Queen who spoke first.

"Well?"

"Your most gracious Majesty is aware of my religion," Ames said, with an unsuspected flintiness. "It is for us a sin to persecute for religion's sake."

Oh my God, thought Nunez and began to wonder if there was any way he could get a message to Leonora to dig up the gold and get herself and the Ames children out of the country. Their family had bought land in Constantinople, just in case.

Ames seemed not to be aware that he was dancing on the lip of a volcano.

"Are you daring to insinuate that *I* persecute for religion's sake?" The hissing was softer and more frightening now.

"I would not dare to presume upon Your Majesty's sacred mind, nor is it a subject's place to guess at what may lie therein," said Ames, still steadily. "It is further a tenet of our religion that we must serve faithfully the land wherein we dwell. I am Your Majesty's liegeman and whatever you order me to do I will do, save that I may not imperil my immortal soul."

Expecting a further roar of fury, Nunez was even more alarmed when it failed to erupt. The air crackled with the Queen's dangerous silence.

After a decent pause, Ames continued firmly.

"Your Majesty is well aware that there is no prohibition in Christianity against persecution; indeed, there are many injunctions to extirpate heretics and unbelievers wheresoever they may be found. What a Christian may do with a clear conscience, I may not."

More silence. Nunez risked a glance under his eyelashes at the Queen, who was studying Ames carefully.

"What of reasons of State?" she enquired with curiosity, as if they were carrying on a philosophical conversation.

Ames gestured apologetically. "I had thought . . . I had excused my former work with that reason, but I fear that, thanks mainly to the Pope's Bull of

Excommunication against Your Majesty, I find the politics impossible to distinguish from religion. It is a nice distinction and I ask your forgiveness if I have distinguished wrongly, but in all conscience—"

"Yes, yes," said the Queen, flapping an ostrich-feather fan hanging from her belt, "I understand your discourse. Though I had thought we worshipped the same God."

"So had I, Your Majesty."

Shimon, Shimon, you have ruined us, thought Nunez.

There was a further desert of silence. Nunez's knees were paining him but Simon now seemed relaxed, the hat he held under his arm not even slightly crushed.

The Queen rose from her seat under her Cloth of State and rustled towards them. Nunez looked warily for dogs but they must have been banished with the Queen's women.

She stood before Ames, who seemed to be examining a magnificent jewel hanging from her golden belt, of an ermine made in white enamel with rubies for eyes. Rebecca has certainly steadied him, Nunez thought, a pity she will be a widow.

The Queen was extending her hand to Ames. He blinked at it, confused for a moment, and then took it and kissed it.

"Up, Mr Ames," she said quite calmly. "I desire you to attend me in my Withdrawing Room, where I will expound to you the difference between religious persecution and reasons of State."

Ames got to his feet ungracefully and the Queen took his ungallant arm, nearly knocking him over with her farthingale.

"Come," she said sweetly and smiled. For all the brownness of her teeth, it was a smile of extraordinary magic, one of her prime weapons.

Ames went with her meekly, leaving Nunez to stand stiffly after his nephew had opened the door for the Queen. He was alone again, apart from the muliercula sitting in the corner, this time in pale-pink tissue shot with gold and edged with black velvet. She looked up and smiled at him wisely. Nunez smiled back, wondering how much she understood, if anything, and longing to ask her a number of personal questions about her women's courses and her bodily functions. He restrained himself.

A little later the music of virginals floated through the shut double doors. Nunez sighed, took his own pulse and thought that if he was not in the Tower that night, he would have Snr Eraso bleed him to ease the strain on his heart.

A full hour passed and Ames bowed himself out alone, looking pale and his thin lips almost disappeared with compression.

"Well, Shimon?" Nunez whispered in Portuguese. "Are we under arrest?"

Ames blinked at him. "No," he said abstractedly.

"She is not going to fine you or rescind Dunstan's patent for the Groceries?"

"She may do those things and worse whenever she pleases," said Ames, "but not immediately, I think."

"Well then? Will you return to her service?"

"Not directly. She has convinced me, but I have also convinced her and we are to proceed by my advice."

"To do what?"

"To rescue Becket."

"But Davison . . ."

"I have a warrant for him."

"But?" asked Nunez warily, recognising his expression.

"I must find out his secret first."

He was hurrying to the door, putting on his hat and lapping his cloak around him. Nunez followed.

They took horse at the Court gate, Ames wincing as he sat down in the saddle.

"The Almighty send the thaw comes soon," Nunez said sympathetically.

"Hm?" Ames said vaguely. "Ah yes. The Thames." He smiled. "I wonder if I would have the courage to take a boat under the bridge again?"

They walked the horses, since the ground was frozen and slippery. As they passed Charing Cross, Nunez asked in Portuguese, "How will you proceed, Shimon?"

Ames sighed and bit some chapping off his lips. "I am not at all sure, to tell you the truth, Uncle," he said. "First we must break Becket out of the Tower."

"Break him out?" asked Nunez in horror. "But it is impossible."

"I mean, we must talk to Walsingham, which will be difficult if he is ill. But I cannot possibly attend him in the Tower: there are too many people who know me, not to mention James Ramme himself. He must be moved somewhere else."

"If he could be released to my care . . ."

"I tried that. It is the obvious answer. Unfortunately the Queen will not countenance it. She says he must be kept imprisoned until she knows what he has forgotten." Ames sighed again. "It seems I am fated always to be an inquisitor."

"His loss of memory is genuine," Nunez said. "I will swear to it. Nothing can be got from him by further torture."

"Of course not. Even the Queen understands it. I hope that once we have transferred him to a different place, if I can come to him, he will remember me and that will open the floodgates. Then it depends on whether he is willing to trust me with his secret or not."

"He did not remember me."

Ames shrugged. "If that fails, then we must try something else."

XXXII

WHILE MARY SERVED THE Queen as night-soil woman, she knew the Court as a wood-louse sees a garden. The Court by itself feeds and clothes and houses much of Westminster City, for it is like a great beast curled by the river that takes in beer in rivers and beef in mountains and pays out streams of silver, gold, embezzled poultry and kitchen scraps, misappropriated linen, paper and ink, dishonestly gotten candle-ends, firewood and stolen soap and a vast variety of different forms of political interest.

The Queen never lives at Whitehall for longer than a couple of months together, after which the whole swarm of them, courtiers and servants alike, set off up the road to Nonsuch or Greenwich like ants on the march. Then a new swarm descends to sweep out rushes and burn mats (or resell them at a premium to strivers in the City of London) and scrub floors and stairwells with lye and whitewash the walls again.

Now one of the chiefest problems for my lord Hunsdon, the Lord Chamberlain, is always the matter of lodging—less serious at Whitehall than elsewhere for the size of it since, after all, it is the largest palace in Christendom, and the fact that the greater courtiers like Leicester, Hatton or Burghley, and now Raleigh, also, live in their palaces on the Strand with their mobs of servingmen and not at Court. However, in order to attend upon the Queen and perhaps snap up a parcel of lands or an office going begging, it is needful for the lesser fry to live as close to the palace as possible.

Therefore, south of the Whitehall orchard and the tennis courts is a scurry of ancient and mainly damp buildings, let at exorbitant rents to the hordes of young men who attend upon the Queen. Living exempt from direct female interference, the young gentlemen of Queen Elizabeth's affinity put their nether-stocks to dry on strings over their fires, cook collops of mutton on skillets, in summer hang their crocks of butter on long strings through their windows directly into the Thames, and would on occasion rent out window-space for fishing. The stairwells and alleys stink of piss because young men who average a gallon of beer apiece per day and spend long periods standing about in ante-chambers can see no point in dirtying a pot.

These young men, as young men do, spend much of their time in idolatrous worship of their own pillicocks and a good segment of that in the plotting of lies regarding women—lying *to* them first, and *with* them in due course if it could possibly be achieved, and certainly lying *about* them afterwards if not before. The Queen was a wise woman indeed. She absolutely forbade, on pain of instant dismissal from Court in disgrace, any of her maids of honour to venture anywhere south of the orchard into the forbidden dens of young men.

But chastity is such a hard thing for a girl-child who knows she has five years at most to snare her a husband, for there is no honourable life open to her save that. And her veins throb with the sap of youth and her mind is all afire with flowery platitudes and punning sonnets and the young men parade past her, tall and broad and arrogant and set her heart to trembling most deliciously. Nor do they pray to me for strength in temptation, for they have not been taught about the Queen of Heaven at all.

XXXIII

MR ROBERT CAREY, GENTLEMAN of the Privy Chamber, came bounding up the stairs to the room he was currently sharing with his friend John Gage, tossing up his racquet and catching it and whistling because he had just won five much-needed pounds off Drury at the tennis-play. He stopped as he ducked through the door. He was not as pleased as he might have been to find a woman sitting on the other bed and his manservant Michael nowhere to be seen. On the other hand, it was not the first time.

She was tightly wrapped in the striped cloak of a strumpet, with a hood and a velvet mask that hid her face. He thought he recognised the cloak.

"Now then, Kate," he said to her kindly. "Gage will be along soon, he was losing last I saw. Will you have some wine?"

He turned his back on her, slung his racquet under his bed where it could fend for itself amid a turmoil of shoes, boots, weapons, balls, books, packs of cards, an untuned lute and some empty plates. He took off his doublet, stripped his shirt off over his head and began to dry himself with it in a way that would have greatly grieved his mother who sewed it for him.

"If you look in the pitcher by the fire, there should be something left and if there is not—"

"Robin," said the woman and he spun round, looking comically frightened.

"Christ, have mercy," he gasped. "What the hell are you doing here, Bethany?"

She was crying silently into the hood of her whore's cloak. He gaped at her for a moment, made to offer her the shirt to dry her eyes with, thought better of it, realised he was half-naked alone with one of the Queen's ferociously protected maids of honour—worse still, one of the Queen's own bedfellows—and began delving desperately in the chest standing next to him.

"Bethany, you . . . what is it? I can't . . . I . . ." He finally found a clean shirt, hauled it over his head, fumbled his doublet back on.

She had taken off the dampened mask and groped for her handkerchief. She blew her nose noisily on it while he managed to stop gabbling and found half a cup of wine left in the pitcher. It went into a nearly clean goblet and he gave it to her, mainly to have something to do. Then he sat down on the narrow bed opposite and stared.

When the tears stopped he gathered his wits and said, "In God's name, what's amiss, sweeting? Where did you get Kate's cloak?"

Bethany hiccuped. "I borrowed it from her for a crown."

"How did you . . ."

"I waited for her at the stairs when I saw her walking over the ice and talked to her and she gave it me."

"But . . . but why?"

Bethany swallowed hard and looked up at him. "Mr Davison thinks I am your mistress."

Carey put his hand over his eyes and leaned his elbow on the chest. "But . . . but it's not true," he croaked desperately.

"He did not believe me."

"Has he told the Queen yet?"

She sniffed again. "He says he will not if I will be his informer about the Queen."

Carey's face reappeared from behind his hand, dawning with hope. "Well then, do it. For God's sake, Bethany, tell him whatever he wants to hear. As long as you can be useful to him, he'll be silent to keep you at Court and then you can marry the next man that offers for you. Why did you have to come here to tell me that? You could have—"

"Robin, I must see John Gage."

"Why?"

"I am . . ." She choked on it. "I am . . ."

Carey was suddenly looking ten years older. "Oh, Bethany, you are not with child? Are you?"

She nodded.

Carey stared for a moment, took breath to speak, thought better of it, stood up, sat down again. Then he stood up decisively and began sorting through a box of ruffs. He reached up to unhook a cramoisie velvet suit from a nail in the wall, changed his mind and took a black velvet doublet and trunk-hose slashed with red taffeta. He laid them on the bed.

"Whose is it?" he asked. She made no answer. "Gage's?"

"I th . . . think so."

"You *think* so?" For the first time his voice was tinged with disgust.

"I . . . I never intended . . . I do not know . . . Do you remember the masquing at the Queen's Birthday in September?"

Carey did not answer that as he had played the part of a Venturesome Knight, wearing borrowed armour, and had done quite well in that the Queen had applauded his dance and laughed at his speech, he did indeed remember it. Gage had been a centaur.

"Do you remember the banquet after?"

"Er . . . yes." September had been mild and golden and they had taken the risk of using the Whitehall canvas banqueting hall, tricked out with tinsel streamers and icicles of cast sugar. There had been a particularly ferocious flower-water for the ladies, and his own lady-love had been well-seasoned by it, he remembered fondly. But she was married. He was extremely careful to deal only with married women at Court because he was not a romantical madman like Gage, and intended to make sure he married a wealthy widow who could please herself. In any case, the rage of horned husbands was a minor risk compared to the deadliness of the Queen's jealousy.

"That was when I . . . I drank too much," Bethany explained dolefully.

Carey nodded, hoping she would not go on. "But you were with Gage, were you not?" he asked.

"I do not rightly remember," she said in mourning for her lost memory. "I think so."

"Well then, it's simple. Marry Gage at once."

"The Queen will be angry."

"Not a quarter so angry as she will be when you come to bed of a babe with no father."

For a moment she thought about it and then looked up at him tremulously. "Do you think he will?"

"He must," said Carey positively. "Is that why you came here?"

She nodded.

"Does Mr Davison know of your . . . er . . . condition?"

She shook her head.

"Come then, it's mendable." Carey heaved a private and very selfish sigh of relief. "Marry at once and the thing is solved."

There was the sound of someone climbing the stairs below. "I'll warn him you are here." Glad of the excuse, Carey grabbed his change of clothes and scurried out the door.

Bethany sat, looking at the counterpane and plucking at the worn crewel embroidery on it, wondering how it was possible to have such a yawning space within the narrow compass of her bodice, and far away, at the end of it, a drum. She heard the sound of their voices, the hurrying of John Gage's feet up the stairs.

Carey was due to go and wait upon the Queen but now could not change in his own bedchamber. Muttering to himself about maids who had no sense and men who had less, he began the complicated process on the landing, cursing furthermore that his manservant was nowhere about to help with the fiddly business of tying the doublet points to the back of his paned hose. And he had brought his shoes but left his pattens behind in his chamber.

The door slammed and Gage reappeared, his blond hair standing on end where he had run his fingers through it.

"What the devil did you let her in there for, Carey?" he demanded.

"She was there when I arrived," Carey answered evenly. "Should I congratulate you on your—"

"To hell with your congratulations, I can't marry her."

Gage tried to shoulder past him, but Carey somehow got in his way.

"Why not?"

"Because I am betrothed. My father wrote to me at Christmas; he has bought the wardship of Annabel Prockter, paid a fortune for it. She is fifteen, guaranteed a virgin, got a thousand pounds in land, shares in four ships and five hundred in jointure, the Queen has given her consent and I'm going home at Easter to marry her. It is all arranged."

"But Bethany is—"

"So the little bitch is with child? So? How do I know whose it is?"

"Yours."

"Mine, yours . . ."

"Not mine."

"Cumberland's, who knows? I'll not have her; she would horn me before the year was out."

Carey stared at Gage disbelievingly. Gage refused to look at him.

"Silly cow should have kept her legs closed," he muttered and moved to shove Carey out of his way. "You have her. Your family is used to bastards."

Carey instantly punched him in the face. Gage fell back against the wall, grabbing at his cheek; Carey punched him again and this time hurt his hand on Gage's teeth. Gage made to draw his sword but was hampered by the narrow landing; Carey grappled to stop him, they lurched about grunting for a few seconds, evenly matched, equally fit, until Gage missed his footing at the head of the stairs and they both slithered and crashed painfully down to the next landing.

Footsteps from above stopped them. Bethany was standing there, still wrapped in her striped cloak, her face white and frozen and now tearless, looking down at the undignified muddle of men below her.

They looked up at her and found neither could think of anything to say. Silently Bethany walked down the stairs, stepped over them and continued down the next flight to the alley running into King Street.

Carey jumped to his feet and followed her. Gage picked himself up, holding his bleeding mouth and shouted at him, "Carey!"

Carey paused at the next landing. "What?"

"I want satisfaction from you, you bastard's get."

For a moment Carey's hand tightened on his sword-hilt and he looked ready to lunge back up the stairs, but then he stopped himself.

"Better a bastard than a maker of them," he said coldly. "Whenever you want, Gage, I am at your disposal."

He turned and ran after Bethany.

XXXIV

SHE HAD REACHED THE street door, but instead of turning left to King Street, she turned right, heading for the water-stairs.

Carey caught up with her and touched her arm.

"I hope you were not fighting about me," she said tonelessly. "I'm not worth it."

Half a dozen things to say battled in Carey's throat, so all he answered lamely was, "Not really. It is . . . well, he has the right, I did hit him."

"A duel?"

Carey shrugged and sucked his knuckles. "Probably. Unless he calms down."

"Will you apologise?"

"Certainly not."

Bethany shook her head wearily. She seemed to be shutting herself away from him.

"Listen, Bethany, I never knew he was betrothed."

"Nor did I."

"Well, betrothals can be broken . . ."

"Why should he? She has money, youth and her virginity. Why would he want me? I would not, if I were a man."

"Perhaps somebody else . . . ?"

"Marriage negotiations take months. I have a few weeks before I must buy longer laces and the Queen casts me out." She shook her head, put her fingers up against her brow-ridges to stop the tears again.

Impulsively Carey caught her arm and swung her to face him.

"Bethany," he said softly, smiling at her. "Marry me."

She laughed a little. "You are not in love with me."

"What has love to do with it? Besides, you're so very beautiful, I could come to love you. And as Gage so kindly pointed out before I hit him, my family has some experience with bastards."

"Everyone will think it's yours."

Carey shrugged. "They do already, it seems."

"The Queen would be . . ."

He waved a long hand dismissively. "Ah, the Queen is always enraged when one of her bedfellows marries. Envy that they have a man in their bed and she has not, no doubt, poor lady." Bethany smiled inexplicably at that. "I expect she'll banish us from Court for a while, but after that she'll surely . . ."

"She will call it treason and put us in the Tower, Robin," Bethany said, "You're too closely related to her to marry without permission. She would never receive you at Court again. How will we live?"

Carey waved his arms. "The Lord will provide. *Behold the lilies of the fields, they toil not, neither do they spin . . .*"

Her face twisted as though she was still laughing at him.

"This is impossible, Robin. If either of us had any money or any land or even if you were a lawyer or a physician, but . . . but . . ."

"Then I'll go and fight in the Netherlands, sack a city or two and come back rich as Croesus."

She watched him from a mountainous distance as he tried to convince her of his excellence as a match. From the dark-red curls on his head, the hooded blue eyes and the arrogant Tudor nose, past the broad shoulders, narrow waist and long legs, he was the very picture of a romantic suitor, and one day he would make a woman very happy.

He was now burbling about shepherds and shepherdesses being happy in Arcadia. She thought of breaking the news to him that neither of them lived in Arcadia and that the shepherds she knew at home were taciturn, weary men who stank of sheep and dogs and went out in February snowstorms to help their ewes to lamb.

He does not understand and he cannot be serious about it, Bethany thought. He thinks this is a game, something to gamble over. Suddenly she felt very much older than him, although he was her senior by seven years. And tempting though she found him, she could not bring herself to let him ruin his life out of kindness.

She turned away from him and walked on to the water-steps where Kate was waiting for her, she hoped.

He followed her, talking about the Queen's liking for him and how he could always talk to his father, who would understand. Hiding a shudder, Bethany stopped him.

"Tell no one," she said, fumbling with her mask to put it on again. "Keep your mouth shut, Robin, please."

"Of course, sweetheart," he said, patting her shoulder familiarly. "I am not a fool."

Kate was still there, leaning against the wall by the stairs, her hands stroking the velvet and silk of Bethany's cloak. She straightened and smiled when she saw who was with her.

"Now then, Mr Carey. What's your desire today? Is it you or Mr Gage Michael brought me for?"

Carey kissed her on the mouth in greeting. "I have no time, sweeting," he said. "I'm late for the Queen already."

He kissed Bethany as well, on the cheek while she stood like Lot's wife, and then hurried away. Kate stared at Bethany insolently.

Not knowing anything she could say, Bethany pulled off the striped cloak and gave it back to Kate, who parted with the velvet very reluctantly.

I can ask her, thought Bethany, she knows. "What do you do when you fall with child?" she asked in a rush, feeling her face heat up under the black velvet. Kate's expression became even more knowing and more insolent. She tutted.

"Been careless, have we, dear?"

I am standing here talking to a whore who patronises me because there is no one else, Bethany thought. She thinks I am a fool too, look at her. She was too desperate for hauteur and nodded.

Kate shrugged. "Get rid of it, what else?"

"How?"

"It depends," said Kate hintingly and waited.

Bethany understood and fumbled in her purse, pulled out another crown and gave it to Kate.

"How long is it?" Kate asked with an attempt at delicacy.

"Since I . . . ?"

"No, dear. Since your last woman's trouble."

Trouble, thought Bethany, so distant from herself that phrases she had heard all her life became suddenly alien. For all the mess and inconvenience and the little bags of rags that had to be washed, it was much less a curse than a blessing, more of an old friend who had suddenly gone missing.

"I . . . Before the Queen's Birthday."

Kate tutted again. "Always the same," she said. "Well, it's too late for the easy way."

"What is that?"

"Our witch says there's two kinds. Either you're with child of a frog or a babe. When you miss the first time, then you drink a tea of tansy and pennyroyal mint to bring on your courses and keep drinking it every day until the frog comes out. If it doesn't, what's in your belly is a babe. So then you go back to the witch and she does it for you."

"Does what?"

"Kills the babe inside. With a knitting needle."

Bethany felt sick and swallowed hard. "Does it . . . does it hurt?"

The contempt in Kate's stare hurt her. "Of course it does," she said. "Sometimes you die, just like in childbed. But if you live and the babe comes out dead, then you can lace your stays tight again and nobody the wiser."

"Do you . . . can you . . . ?"

Kate rolled her eyes. "There's a price."

"How much?"

"Ten pounds," she said, obviously naming the largest sum she dared. Bethany simply nodded.

"Can you ask your witch for me?"

Kate sucked her teeth. "I'm not sure. I mean, it is a crime, it's dangerous for her too. If anyone finds her out, she burns for it. And you hang."

Bethany could not move her feet, she felt she was in a nightmare and her feet had frozen to the ground.

"Will Mr Carey not marry you then?" Kate asked solicitously. "I would have thought better of him . . ."

"No, it's not his," Bethany said sharply. "And if you must know, he offered and I refused him. He has no money."

"Can't see why you did that." Kate grinned knowingly. "I'd have him in his shirt, or nothing at all. Nothing at all for preference," she added and elbowed Bethany in the ribs.

"It is impossible," she said distantly. "Will you ask your witch for me?"

Kate laughed. "Not the first time she'll have helped a maid of honour," she said. "All the same, you courtiers are all the same. You always think you're the first to love a man and the first ever to lie with him unwed and then you think you're the first and only maid that fell with child."

She climbed down the water-steps and set off across the dirty ice, slipping and sliding occasionally on her worn pattens and laughing.

Bethany pulled her own cloak tight around her and ran to the worn place in the orchard wall where she had climbed over. It was hard, but she had found a fruit-picking ladder to help her, and if she was very very careful and gathered up her skirts and farthingale and tied them in place with a hair ribbon, she could manage it with streaks of earth on her under-petticoat and shift that only she and her tiring-woman would know about.

At last she dropped down, to be greeted by the little dogs she was supposed to exercise, who bounced throttling themselves on the ends of their leads tied to an apple-tree root. She put away her mask in the pocket of her petticoat, then untied them and threw sticks for them on the way back.

XXXV

THE MAN WHO THOUGHT his name might be Ralph Strangways lay in his bed in the Tower and looked up at the sharp sunlight cutting between the bars on his high window. The floor was warmly covered with straw, he had three covers to his bed, though no sheets, and they had given him a new shirt to replace the foul one. He was wearing all his clothes because the room was bitter cold; the man who had been asigned to tend him was filching his firewood and the fires he made rarely lasted until dusk. At least someone had mended the sleeves to his doublet so they no longer hung down like clothes in an ancient arras.

I am . . . he thought wearily. My name is . . .

It did no good, had never done any good. The first time the Jewish physician and his surgeon had come, he had been raving with pain and fever and in terror and rage lest they hurt him again. The physician had told him that his name was Dr Hector Nunez and said it with a kind of significance as if he thought perhaps he would recognise it. He did not, though something in the way the doctor pulled at his beard was familiar. The doctor had reassured him that they had come to help, had reassured him many times that he would not be put to the question again, but that it was necessary to hurt him to make him better.

The pain Snr Eraso then caused in his shoulder to put it back almost made him pass out, but afterwards it did feel better so he was more inclined to trust them with his arms and hands. His back and legs they left alone, since they were healing well.

Occasionally he could stand away from himself and know that once he had not been so fearful. He could look at his hands and know that once they had been pale and strong, not helpless moles' paws of raw meat. Nunez and Eraso had put leeches to the two swollen rings about each wrist to bleed the bruises of bad blood. They had put maggots on the places where iron and weakness had made ulcers in the swelling. Nunez then poulticed and bandaged his wrists with care and spoke to him at length of the sanguine humour; how flesh that was without it died and became blackened with gangrene and so must be cut off. If he would keep his hands, he was told, he must move them continually and suffer them to be rubbed and massaged by Snr Eraso.

And so they came every day and forced him to work his hands and made him drink draughts so foul that very often he puked them straight up again, which seemed to worry them not at all, for then they made him drink more. For a long time he had no appetite to his meat, and they tutted over the way he lost weight. It had been days before he could pick up anything with his hands at all, but must be tended to and fed by an old man with foul breath and a wall-eye, who rammed the spoon into his mouth carelessly, almost knocking out his teeth. God save him, he was afraid of the old man too and asked him with pathetic politeness not to spoon so fast, to be rewarded with a loud "Eh? Can't hear ye," and another spoonful of pap.

He was slow to recover, for loneliness wore him down like a whetstone. He would sit for hours staring at the sunlight or the dull greyness at the window, listening to the clanging from the mint and the sounds from the Queen's beasts down by the Lion Gate. He was afraid to be alone because without other men to watch and talk to, he felt like a wisp of thought that might blow away in the wind. Once perhaps he might have thought of his past and remembered the good times therein to cheer himself, but that was forbidden him too. As in Little Ease, a black mood came often upon him, latching down the dark lid of his mind and whispering that he deserved to be in Hell for his many forgotten crimes. In truth, he would rather have been a slave in the French galleys, heaving an oar to the crack of a lash than idle, fed and rested as he was in the glacial isolation of the Tower.

Sometimes as he lay and watched the barred sky darken from pewter through iron to lead, a kind of horror would whelp itself from his fear and expand like smoke to fill the whole room with its bulk, squeezing him tighter against the stones, as if he were being invisibly pressed to death. Death seemed his only friend then; he would wonder for hours together how much it would hurt to take a run at the wall and ram his head on it, but was always too paralysed by self-hatred to do it. If there had been hemlock in his cell then, he would have drunk it gladly.

Worst of all was the way he could not stop himself from searching endlessly in his mind for some traces of what he was. He begged for something to read to help pass the hours, but it seemed the request must pass up through layers of command and back down again. Nothing happened and he watched himself whirling down and round in the evil whirlpool of his mind until he was so drowned in it he could not even weep. There was no bottom to it, no end. He was nothing, hanging by his fingertips over an abyss of black nothingness. He cursed God for his abandonment, but if my Son heard, He gave no sign, for to the man it seemed He had taken on the form of Davison. That made him angry, and anger brought him to such a pitch that in his dreams he faced God and rated Him for His wickedness and demanded to know where was this Grace they heard so much about in church. Perhaps God in His ambiguity took that as a prayer. Certainly, the next day, the old man brought him a Bible and a book of sermons.

Sullenly rebelling against the triteness of it, he would not look at it for a while. When he did, it was only to confirm his opinion that God was nothing but a foul inquisitor with a whip for his wit. But when he opened the Bible, it was as if for the first time. He thought vaguely that if he had read it before, it had not been with any great attention, and if he had heard the stories he had not been listening. Only the shorter tales of Jonah and the Whale and Tobit and Daniel in the Lion's Den were familiar to him. It struck him how strange it was to read of the Lord God of Israel and come to Him afresh. Considered dispassionately, as a general, even as a man, the Lord God of Israel had many serious faults. The Book of Job brought him no comfort at all.

But the tales of David fascinated him. Here was a soldier, someone he could understand, perhaps even like: from his fight against Goliath to the battles against Absalom, David was a man of his own mettle. Half-shamefacedly, for fear of being mad, half-pleasurably in his desperate need, he made of King David a friend to talk to, and sympathised with him over his woman troubles—and even cracked a joke or two that he personally would delight in such troubles, having forgotten completely the last time he lay with a woman.

Perhaps that is as I was, he thought, smiling as he reread the story of David coming on Saul while he slept and disdaining to kill him, and then thinking with shame of his shrinking from the old man with his spoon.

Still, as he felt better and it was less painful for him to move about, he grew tired of reading. By that time he had come to the end of God's Word in any case, since he passed quickly over the accounts of the Passion because he could not bear to read them and found the Apocalypse as incomprehensible as a fever dream. Angry restlessness burnt in his bones, until he must rise and pace about the little room in his nether-stocks, since they had not seen fit to give him his boots. He would pick up bits of wood and juggle with them and drop them because he was so clumsy. By careful stretching and bending he could unkink the stiffness in his much-scarred back, but his damaged shoulder ached when it rained and quivered with weakness when he tried to lever himself up by it. To be so weak frightened and enraged him; he sought heavy things to lift and push until the sweat came.

Once he thought he remembered something about fighting: he took a position that seemed familiar and tried sword-passes with his spoon and dropped it because he had no strength in his hands. The deaf old man no longer came to feed him, since he could do it himself and they were giving him proper food now, meat and bread and cheese, which he could chew. Gradually his appetite came back.

And then a thing happened that frightened him greatly. He had been pacing and straining to remember his true name, not the one Munday had given him. He was determined on it, for his name had become a kind of Grail to him. But none of the names he tried seemed right and nothing came up from his drowned memory and he filled up with frustrated rage until he cursed and kicked the bed and hurt his toes.

Then he saw that the room had filled with haloes and rainbows, as if the sunlight from the window were passing through a great many crystals and he smelt roses, as if a garden were growing invisibly from the flagstones of his cell. He saw me standing under the window, with the roses growing about my gown and my hands full of the serpent Wisdom, but knew me not and was afraid. I smiled at him kindly, but then all his world went black and he fell to the straw. By the time he woke, the sunlight was gone and so were the rainbows, he could see me no more. He was bewildered like a child and so exhausted he wondered if he had been in a ghostly battle.

In the Bible he read accounts that sounded like what had happened; he wondered briefly if he was becoming a prophet and then found himself laughing bitterly, because there was no mention of a prophet who could not remember his own name. Only old Saul, who went on all fours and ate grass. At least he still had the power of speech and walking and knew the difference between grass and food. Yet it seemed to him, what with his childish friendship with the long-dead King David and now this, that he was becoming mad and he wondered if he would end with a begging bowl by Temple Gate, like Tom O'Bedlam.

Now there was someone . . . He tried to seize the thought as it went by, tried so hard he unknowingly reached out with his hands, but the memory slipped away from him again. By the time the Jewish doctor and surgeon came in the afternoon, he was too low for speech. He held out his hands meekly like a boy and waited for them to do what they did.

Snr Eraso the surgeon unwrapped the bandages and turned his arms this way and that. The swellings were much reduced and had stopped sloughing black skin. The sores were scabbed over while his hands were almost their normal size, though still weak and poor to grip. Eraso told him to make a fist and to point and he managed these things. Then the surgeon knocked for the Yeoman to let him out and Doctor Nunez sat beside him on the bed.

"How is it with you?" the doctor asked.

He shook his head and shrugged. "If you mean my memory, I can tell you nothing."

"No. I meant, generally. You seem melancholy again."

"I think I have reason."

"No question but that you do. Has something else occurred?"

He was too ashamed to admit that he had fallen down and dirtied himself like a baby, but he had none of the reserves that might have let him brazen it out.

"I . . . I was wondering how a man might know he was mad? If he was becoming mad? Would he know it?"

Nunez stroked his beard. "Hm. Why do you think you are becoming mad?"

He shrugged again, unwilling to reveal himself. But then his loneliness and the doctor's kindness conspired to unlock the gates of his shame and the words tumbled out. "I do not know my own name, I . . . I am afraid of . . . everything, of shadows. My heart pounds when I hear the Yeoman's keys in the locks, even though I know that he is bringing my food. I was afraid of the old man that was set to feed me. I'm afraid of nothing and everything; sometimes I'm afraid that I will drown in fear."

"To be afraid in your situation is not madness, but sanity," said the doctor judiciously. "Have you seen any strange things, things that should not be there?"

Bitterly ashamed, he hung his head and nodded. "Will you tell me of them?"

"I . . . I saw rainbows in the room, and smelt roses. And a woman was standing there, by the wall, smiling at me."

"What did she look like?"

"Fair and bright like a window in a church. She smiled and I fell down in blackness, in a kind of faint, and I woke again much later and she was gone."

The doctor sighed. "I am sorry to hear it."

Fear wrenched his heart again. He could hardly talk through the dryness of his mouth. "Then I am turning into a madman?"

"No, I think not. I believe that you have contracted the falling sickness."

"What? That makes men foam at the mouth and kick and scream and they know nothing of it?"

"Yes. It is not madness and I do not believe that it is possession by devils either, though some do. I have seen this before, often after one has been struck hard on the head. Is the back of your head still sore?"

His hand came up to rub the place, which was ridged and tender. "Sometimes. But surely to fall down and know not what you do is madness?"

"No. I would go so far as to say that if you are able to wonder whether you are mad, then your sanity is not in doubt. True madness seems to me to reside in being unable to know the difference between what is real and what is in your mind. I have known one madman well enough to talk to him and this is what struck me about him: he spoke of devils and angels as his friends and looked at me pityingly when I said I could not see them."

"Ay, poor Tom," he said absently. "One minute playing chess and the next minute doing desperate battle with devils of green and purple climbing into the cooking pot."

It was only the way the doctor looked at him so carefully that let him realise what he had said.

"Do you remember him?"

For a moment he thought he did, and then the memory fled once more. "No, no, it's gone again." He thumped his fist on his forehead and fought not to weep. "God damn it."

"Listen to me," said the doctor. "Unlike the falling sickness, I am not experienced in this thing which has happened to your memory. You are the first I have seen. I have been consulting my books and they are as ignorant as I, and so I think we must devise our own answers. I believe that your brain has been hurt by the blows Mr Ramme gave you on the back of your head. I suspect that your phlegmatic humor which feeds your brain has been disarranged and no doubt unbalanced. And this is having its effect on your thinking, so much is plain. The falling sickness is one side of it. The other is your loss of memory, but I do not believe that your memory is truly destroyed, so much as lost, hidden away behind walls in your mind. If we could but break those walls, then I think your memory will return. Perhaps not all of it, but enough."

"If we both knew this madman, Doctor, then you know my true name."

"Are you sure it is not Ralph Strangways?" asked the doctor.

"No, I am not sure, but Ralph does not feel . . . right."

"Excellent. I am more than ever sure that there is hope."

"My name, Doctor. Please, I beg of you, give me my name."

"You have no need to beg me, sir, I am not your tormentor. Your name is David Becket."

It was like putting on a breastplate that had been made for him by a good armourer.

"Yes," he said after a moment. "Yes, it is. I am David Becket."

The doctor smiled and patted his shoulder. "I must go now . . ."

"Wait." He caught at the doctor with one hand and winced at the dull pain. "You know my name, we both knew the madman. Are you a friend?"

The doctor hesitated. At last he said, "Yes, I am."

"Will you speak to the Queen for me?"

"I already have, Mr Becket, but there is more than your fate involved here. We are working in your behalf. Alas, I can tell you no more."

"Can you tell me who was Ralph Strangways?"

"Yes, that I can. He was a madman that called himself Tom; it was his real name."

"Ohh. Now why did I use it? Did he not need it?"

"I fear not. He is dead."

"Yes. Yes, he is. I saw him die . . ." Becket gripped his face again as the memory hid itself once more.

Nunez waited a little and then spoke softly.

"There is a great power in names, Mr Becket. In names, according to Hermes Trismegistus, lies also the power of control. Rightly name a thing, and you have, as it were, put a bridle on it."

"And yet . . . I fear I am not the same man that David Becket was."

"How could you be? Heraclitus made it clear that we are none of us the same as we were even last week. Who can step twice into precisely the same river?"

"No, but I think David Becket was not so . . . so afraid."

"Perhaps he had less to fear. And he was yourself, only an earlier, less-abused self. Do not be afraid to use the name David Becket. Only I would advise against giving Munday or Ramme, or indeed Mr Secretary Davison, any hint that I have told you it. They know you as Ralph Strangways."

Becket smiled humourlessly. "The only thing I will give any one of them willingly is six feet of land and a box to house them."

"Well said, sir."

The doctor rose in his customary rustle of brocade and the faint scents of blood and tobacco. That reminded Becket of something that might mend his mood.

"God, what I would give for a pipe," he said wistfully.

Nunez nodded gravely. "Rightly is it said that the patient often knows his own physic. I could not have prescribed better myself. It is a drug sovereign for the rebalancing of phlegm. I shall at once ask that tobacco be brought you. Good day, Mr Becket."

XXXVI

SO FAR THEY DID not suspect her; thank God, Bethany had not been troubled with morning sickness, although she sometimes felt ill in the evenings, and still her woman's trouble had not come back. She had gone out in her velvet mask and a borrowed gown and cloak once to an apothecary's shop by Charing Cross to buy dried tansy and pennyroyal mint. Nothing came of the tisane she made with them, neither frog nor babe, although she had stomach cramps and diarrhoea for a day that kept her away from the Queen's bed. She was relieved at that: the Queen was in a bad mood much of the time and often paced half the night in some strange anxiety. No matter what Bethany did, no matter how she stroked and massaged and caressed, the Queen would not be mollified and took out her temper on whoever happened to be near.

She was worst of all after Privy Council meetings, when they could often hear her shouting that she would not be badgered about the Queen of Scots and she would have every man jack of them in the Tower if she heard another word on the subject.

So Bethany made the most of her illness and kept to her bed for another day before she decided she could bear the tension no more. But how could she talk to Kate? She did not know her surname, far less where she lived. She certainly could not send her tiring-woman for her, nor could she ask Alicia Broadbelt or Jane Drury, her room-mates, for any one of them would tattle of her and word would inevitably reach the Queen, wasting all her care. She had been very careful. She had even pricked her thumb with a needle at the times when her courses should have come and smeared blood on her smocks, to fool the laundresses.

And *still* her courses refused to come and every day her stays were more of a struggle to lace. When she pressed herself between her hip-bones she found a small hard ball there, like a canker, instead of softness.

She dreamt she staggered into the Queen's Privy Chamber with her belly swollen out before her and gave birth in front of the Queen and all her Privy Council. She dreamt it several times, each time waking in the Queen's cloth-of-silver bed, crying with remorse and humiliation, until the Queen lost patience with her and took another bedfellow. Her room-mates sympathised with her delightedly, but she was relieved. She missed the Queen's caresses and those she gave the Queen, but she was in terror lest she talk of her trouble in her sleep and the Queen dismissed her from Court.

Being so favoured of the Queen, being her nightly bedfellow with the opportunities that offered of bribery and influence, had made her no friends at Court. The other maids of honour were the more jealous because they could not tattle to the Queen of her accepting over-extravagant gifts from office-seekers in exchange for a kind word behind the bedcurtains. All she had accepted were small precautionary presents to keep her sweet, which the Queen cynically winked at as being unpreventable. She was not outgoing in any case, one of the things that had first endeared her to the Queen. She had always preferred to watch than speak. Before her catastrophe it had not mattered to her that she had no confidante.

But now there was no one to turn to, no one to ask. Once she took out her steel knitting needle and went into a closet with it, but it hurt to poke herself and she had no idea what to do, and so she stopped. She rated herself for cowardice. Once as she stood in the chapel on a Sunday she wondered if anyone could help her there, but one glance at the round pale faces of the Clerks of the Choir, satisfied and pleased with themselves and their God, working their mouths above their white surplices, told her she was a fool to think it. Certainly she could not pray to God, who would be as angry as her father and the Queen at her unchastity—worse, since her father would only beat her, whereas God would send her to Hell.

Once girls in her predicament might have prayed to me for help, might have gone and hidden away in a nunnery until the babe was born—no easy thing, with the nuns tutting over her and dropping catty hints while she wore haircloth and scrubbed floors in penance, but less wounding than to be so alone, so utterly condemned, so escapeless.

At last she could bear it no longer, and on the Sunday she decided to lie in wait for Robin Carey and ask him where she could find Kate. She caught him on his way to play primero with the Queen, dashing and fine in black velvet and crimson taffety, polished from head to toe.

He bowed to her lavishly while her curtsey was a mere automatic dip.

"They say that if we could hear the speech of the swans on the Thames and understand what they were saying," Carey told her, "it would all be a discourse of how they could outrival the whiteness of Mistress Bethany's skin with their feathers." She struggled to smile and match his flourish, not wanting to annoy him when she needed him. Pleased with himself, he paid out more elaboration. "And the crows are likewise jealous of you, for they would delight in it could their plumage be as black as your hair. And the—"

"You should try that compliment on the Queen," she interrupted him, "but you will need to find another bird than crows for her hair."

"It is good," he said, smiling complacently. "I got it from a horse-holder at the Curtain Theatre. But it needs polishing before I can put it to its true use; what kind of bird would be the colour of the Queen's hair?"

It was a ridiculous thing to be thinking of. More and more Bethany felt as if she had been turned into twins; one behaved as it should at Court and even managed to return elaborate Court courtesy; the other, hiding behind its sister, tore its figurative hair and wrung its invisible hands and wept tears that scalded down the inside of her face.

"I cannot think of one bright enough," she said after a moment. "Could you not say sunbeams?"

"Well, but the Queen is tired of being compared to sunbeams; I heard her snip at Drury for tediously comparing her yet again to the damned sun that none of us have seen in days. And besides, it is yellow and she is red and she hopes he is not so ill-mannered as to compare her with the setting sun, and so now what will Drury say?"

Carey had a gift for mimicry and could almost bring a ghost of the Queen into the passageway with them. Despite herself, Bethany laughed.

"You had better never let her hear you doing that. She would put you in the Tower."

"Too late, Mistress Bethany. Last week she caught me imitating my father and my lord Burghley arguing over the costs of the Court and said afterwards that if ever I needed a trade, I should straightaway go to Burbage at the Theatre and be a player."

"How rude of her. You are no mountebank."

Carey shrugged his beautifully tailored shoulders. "They would never have me, in any case, and my father would . . . Lord knows what my father would do, once he had finished beating my brains out, though he likes players well enough. Otherwise I would go today to find honest work—well, nearly honest work—and then marry you."

She managed to keep her countenance. "I shall await my father's pleasure," she said, even achieving demureness.

He smiled. "Are you better of your . . . your sickness, then, sweeting?"

The lie was so longed-for, it almost seemed true. "Oh yes," she said, "I can take my time over marrying now."

"Thank God," said Carey, very heartfelt, and kissed her cheek. "What was it you wanted? I dare not keep the Queen waiting."

"Only . . . only the place where Kate lives."

"Why would you want to know that?"

"She . . . I know she is a whore, but she was . . . she was kind to me when I was distressed and I wanted to send her a gift. That was all."

He smiled again approvingly. "She works out of the Falcon Inn, by Paris Garden Stairs. I have no idea where she lives. She would like any one of your old kirtles, and the red-and-white velvet would suit her extremely."

"Thank you, Robin," said Bethany, her heart pounding with triumph. "Good luck in your game."

He bowed to her again and walked away whistling like a bird. Which he is, she thought, a very long-legged bird with about as many worries: seeing he was wearing cramoisie hose, a red-shank, perhaps, which thought made her giggle a little hysterically as she hurried away.

While he waited to be admitted to the Queen's presence for the game, Carey thought vaguely that Bethany was a kind girl to think of giving a gift to a whore. He was glad she had not asked about the duel he had pending with Gage, which was looking more and more likely to happen. He didn't want to worry her. Of course, he was not afraid; well, no more than was right and proper, but he could see no good come of it. If he won and wounded Gage, he would be in deep trouble with the Queen, who abhorred duelling. If he won and killed his man, he might have to flee the country or face a charge of murder. If he lost he might be wounded, and certainly in trouble again. Or alternatively, and worst of all, if he lost badly enough, he might be dead.

Morbidly, he had been thinking that perhaps the best solution for the pair of them would have been if he married Bethany and then got himself killed on Gage's sword: then she would be a widow, her child would have a name and she could remarry someone better. But he only thought that late at night while he was wondering whether he should choose guns or swords and whom he should pick for his seconds. He had heard that his friend George Clifford, Earl of Cumberland, had opened a book on it and that he was not getting good odds at all.

Still, there was no help for it. He had to fight Gage or be laughed out of Court.

At least he had his little room to himself now, since his father rented it for him, although he needed to find another room-mate soon because he always needed money. He neither knew nor cared where Gage had moved to, although rumour said he was spending two hours a day learning sword-play from Rocco Bonetti at his sword-school in Blackfriars. Carey had enquired after Sir Philip Sidney's sword-master Mr Becket, who was reckoned the better man and had tutored him before. He had been very fashionable a year or two before, but now he had disappeared.

The door was opened for him by a maid of honour. He walked forward, carefully avoiding one of the Queen's small dogs asleep on the rush-matting. As he swept his best bow, he took in Her Majesty and the Earl of Leicester, already at the card-table. Then his heart sank, because there, magnificent in pearl-grey damask and diamonds, his black beard and moustache curled and scented, stood Sir Walter Raleigh.

Carey knew the man and had no illusions about his ability to shine in such company. It was the pity of the world that the Queen was so much older than Raleigh, for it was he, not the pompous and conscientiously arrogant Leicester, who could have been a proper match for her.

Carey knelt reverently to the Queen and mentally said goodbye to the fat purse he had brought with him.

XXXVII

THE DAY AFTER HE had spoken to the doctor, they brought Becket a pipe and tobacco and he found that his fingers were clumsy about filling the bowl and lighting it, but that nonetheless they knew what to do. As the smoke bit its way down his throat, he coughed and then sighed, feeling a little of his fear depart. Only a little, perhaps a pebble off the back of a black mountain.

But two nights later the nightmare became real again. They woke him as they entered his cell, carrying lanterns and wearing cloaks. Becket started up in bed, wildly staring and plucking for something that was not under his pillow.

There was Ramme, there was Munday, and behind them were three large Yeomen of the guard with the dogged disgruntled expressions of men who see no earthly point in rising so long before sun-up but must bear the whims of their betters.

"Dress yourself and gather your belongings," ordered Ramme and stood with his arms folded whilst Becket struggled with the points of his hose and doublet. It took him an hour to dress himself in the morning, like a great lady, which was another reason besides the cold for sleeping in his clothes, although it had done the wrecked velvet suit no good at all. Watching them out of the corners of his eyes, Becket gathered up his pipe and tobacco pouch and the Bible, leaving the Book of Sermons because they had miraculously combined the incomprehensible with the stupidly banal. One of the yeomen handed him a lumpy package tied in a cloth. He wrapped it and his few belongings with a cheap falling band in the other shirt they had given him.

Another Yeoman came forward with a pair of shoes and helped him put them on, then gave him a cloak and hat.

"Where are we going?" he asked Munday, who shook his head.

"Put your hands out."

Becket's heart almost stopped with fear and misery. The third Yeoman was carrying chains, manacles. For a moment he was unable to move at all.

"If . . . if I am to be executed, may I have a l . . . little time to prepare myself?" he heard himself whisper.

Munday stared at him coolly for a moment.

"We would give you such time, Ralph," he said. "Do as we ask."

He delayed, crossing his arms and hiding his hands under his armpits, hoping they could not see him shaking. Drops of sweat tickled his nose. He had backed from them as far as he could, his calves pressed against his bed-frame.

Ramme made a short noise of impatience and contempt, and that pricked Becket where he was rawest. Anger steadied him. With enormous effort, he put out his hands as directed and managed to watch impassively as the yeoman locked the manacles in place. His wrists were still bandaged, so the iron did not chafe but it felt bruisingly heavy. His hands began to tingle and burn again.

All five men surrounded him as they passed through the door, Ramme on his right gripping his arm. He saw the spiral stairs for the first time and found they had been worn by feet, so he missed his footing several times and must be supported by Ramme. The nails on their boots clattered like an army.

Out the door and into the dusk before dawn, with a further two men waiting for them, carrying lanterns that made the soft rain into clouds of golden stars. Becket looked about at the looming towers and crowded buildings, sniffed the smell of wood-smoke from chimneys, lifted his face to see the dim clouds and feel the wetness of the icy rain. It delighted him. As suddenly as he had been terrified by the order to put out his hands, he was lifted by being out of doors at last.

They matched paces as men do when walking close-packed together and tramped across the cobbles, frightening a broad black shape from their way, which flapped and cawed. A gust of wind brought the smell of carrion from somewhere eastwards.

Down through a gate and past the stench of animals in cages—men or lesser beasts, it was impossible to say, until something large made a coughing roar as they passed which no human could have made. Their boots boomed on the boat-landing.

A wherry was waiting, with two rowers staring into space, boatmen's cloaks over the Queen's livery of scarlet. Ramme jumped in lightly and Munday nodded that Becket should follow him.

For a second he was undecided, thinking perhaps to jump into the murky sewer of a river and take his chances with the current, but the manacles promised only death for such boldness, and besides, where would he go after, and in what state?

Munday understood his hesitation and his eyes narrowed but at the same time Becket decided against jumping and stepped across into the boat, sat down hastily before he fell. Munday sat beside him and put his dagger point against Becket's side.

"If you wish a clean, quick death," he said quietly as the guards clambered in and the lantern in the prow was lit, "you have only to call out or make any sudden move."

"May I speak?"

"No."

One of the yeomen was busy with yet more chains.

"Put your foot out, Ralph," said Munday.

"Is this necessary . . ." he began and felt the sharp prick of the poignard against his skin. Ramme leaned over, took a handful of his doublet-front and pulled him nose to nose.

"We'll not warn you again, scum," he hissed. "Put your foot out."

Becket licked his lips in fear as he saw the man's anger and did as he was told. They chained his ankle to a ring-bolt in the bottom of the boat where a little water washed and glittered in the lantern-light. Ramme let go slowly but his eyes never left Becket's face. Becket wanted to look away, found pressure in the stare and fury again within himself at his womanish cravenness. Why are they angry? he wondered like a child about his parents. Then it came to him, as if someone had spoken in his ear, that perhaps they were angry because of something entirely unconnected with him. He already knew there was no point in trying to placate them. If they wanted to hurt him again, then they could and they would, no matter what he did. So he could at least try and act as if he were a man and not the empty broken thing he knew he was. He crushed the urge to swallow, managed to stare back levelly at Ramme. To his satisfaction, at last Ramme looked away, and he had to hide a small victorious smile.

Feeling better, he held his bundle tight and rested his hands in his lap to take the weight of the metal. Then he looked about, screwing up his eyes against the needles of rain.

Somewhere inside him, a door opened and some knowledge trickled out. They were rowing on the Thames, upstream but with the tide—perhaps to see the Queen in her palace at Whitehall. He was afraid of that idea, very much afraid of seeing the Queen, whom it seemed he had offended grievously, although he had no idea how. They would pass . . . Images of familiar buildings passed processed before his mind's eye: Baynard's Castle, the Temple, the palaces on the Strand . . . And the door shut once more.

Becket looked again at Munday, who was also watching him intently. His poignard was gripped in his hand and the blade still pricked Becket between two of his ribs. He drew back from it a little and the blade followed the same couple of inches. Munday did not seem a wantonly cruel man as Mr Ramme was, but he was determined and looked like one who could kill when he said he would, and for no further reason. His expression seemed more interested than angry. Becket tried smiling at him to show he knew his mind, but it manifested as more of a death's-head grin and revealed his fear.

It came to him again then that to be afraid all the time was a new thing for him. Once he had felt other emotions and fear had come and gone as the world suggested. Now it was riding permanently on his back, sucking at his strength. He sighed. Even if all his memories should fly back to their old roosting places, surely he could never again be the man pictured therein.

The thought dismayed him and he gulped hard, focussed for distraction on the careful rowing of the boatmen as they bent their backs into the oars. The wind caught at his hat and, without thinking, he tried to put one hand up to catch it, jerking his wrists cruelly. He could not keep from gasping but the poignard forbore to stab him. The guard in front of him caught his hat and gave it to him, and Becket nodded his thanks and sat holding it as well as he could. What if the boat sank? Was drowning a better death than execution for treason?

Ugly butcher's images rose out of the black waters of his mind and this time he shrank from them too, inwardly, staying still and silent as Munday had ordered. It all depends, he thought, it all depends on whether the executioner had been ordered to cut me down alive or dead.

He wished, longed to ask them what the executioner had been told, but could not because his throat was too swollen with fright. He could not even swallow now. The black mountain of terror inside him seemed to swell and grow and tremble like Mount Etna, until he was astonished that the pursuivants could not see it and ashamed that it made him shake.

They are taking me to Tyburn, to Tyburn, where Campion died, he thought, and the ghostly smell of blood filled his nostrils until he thought he would puke.

And then something broke or changed inside him, as if the pregnant volcano had at last given birth to fire. It seemed to him that dying was no bad thing if it meant release from such fear, even a traitor's death was better than his loneliness and emptiness and the branded-in memory of hanging from the pillar in the White Tower.

It occurred to him that he might well end in Hell for the sinfulness of his life, but then he thought that as he could remember nothing of it he had nothing to repent and surely God would grant him special circumstances? From his reading of the Bible he felt sure that Jesus Christ was a more merciful man than Davison, and might well be persuadable and would at least give him a fair hearing, which was all he asked.

Upon which thought his trembling faded a little. To occupy his mind with more than future pain, he looked about him at the night, at the blurred earthly stars of occasional lanterns marking water-stairs on the Thames banks, at the rhythmic shadows of the boatmen and the creak of oars and the scrape and gutter of icy water under the boat's keel. In honesty it was a filthy night, but still better than his dry empty cell, and he smiled up at it.

The cheap black felt of the hat they had given him was dewed with water, there was wind and sleet in his hair. He liked it. If he was going to his death . . . well, at least he could bid farewell to the sky and the river.

XXXVIII

THE QUEEN'S SECRETARY SITS at his desk and takes a pen, examines it, takes his penknife and trims a tiny sliver from the nib. Before him his desk is neat as a chessboard, with piles of paper squared off and held down with books, his sander placed just so by his ink-pot and not a single splatter of ink to mar the smooth polished wood.

He has a triple candle-stick to give him light, with wax candles bought thriftily by his wife from clerks at Court with rights to old candle-ends, and remelted in her own moulds. Every book on the shelf is straight, the floor swept as clean and clear as a Dutchman's with a fire of Newcastle coals burning soberly in the grate.

To Mr Davison a pile of papers slightly off true gives pain. A speck of dust on the floor shouts at him like the voice of doom. When one of his sons commits the blasphemy of leaving a toy horse on wheels out in the middle of the floor, Mr Davison does not lose his temper and shout and bang about as some might: his face tightens and tightens and the child is summoned from bed and made to put the abandoned horse, personally, on the fire and watch it burn.

His children also are very neat.

The pen perfected to his satisfaction, he dips and begins to write, slowly and hesitantly, unused to the exercise he now imposes on himself.

Sunday 22nd January 1587

I, William Davison, in the 36th year of my life, have resolved to keep a daily record of the progress of my soul to salvation, hoping that Almighty G-D shall vouchsafe to me the power to write only His Truth in these pages, and so make better known to me wherein I have sinned and wherein I have pleased Him. It shall be like a mirror for me, a matter between myself and G-D.

All that I do is in the service of G-D and all that I do has prospered thanks to His merciful aid, until now. To reprise the matter which seems so far beyond belief, two days before Christmas my men broke in upon a nest of Papists while they were at their blasphemous mumming of Christ's sacrifice. It seems the raid had been ill-prepared and the hall was well-defended against them so that they captured only women and servants and one gentleman that had been commanding the defence which gave the Jesuit traitor and the others time to escape.

It being for the safety and quietness of the Commonwealth and further likely to benefit his soul, in that a foretaste of Hell may often prompt a man to repent him of his sins before he suffer the true Eternal Fire, this man was put to the question, to wit, the manacles, our usual engine of instruction, in the Tower of London.

Being as we thought obdurate in his sin and treason, he was questioned thus twice. At last, in extremity, we found that he thought us to be Spaniards, Papists, which tormented him to abjure the true Protestant religion and that he had in very truth lost his memory as he claimed (and as we had not believed).

In error, he cursed me for a Papist and an idolator with such defiance and courage as makes me proud to be of one religion with him. The man that we had thought was only a blasphemer of Christ, a worshipper at the altar of the Beast of Rome, was rather, in a strange manner, a noble Protestant martyr.

Being himself upon a mission of intelligence against the Papists, the blow Mr

Ramme gave him on his head to pacify him had driven out his memory but not his wits nor his manly bravery. Unable to tell us, who were rightfully his friends, what service he was about for the True Religion, knowing not where he was nor why he was in the manacles, he had taken us for priests of the Inquisition and cursed us.

Never before has such a miserable chance happened. Never before has a foul and loathsome devil of Popery turned so strangely and sadly to a fair angel of the True Religion.

Mr Davison pauses, dips his pen, pauses and dips again.

I have sworn that I shall write truly as I feel, that this record may be a true mirror.

I own I am at a stand. If I were a heathen philosopher I might take this for a cruel jest of the gods, a demonstration of their power and the power of Fate.

Being rather, as I thought, a partaker in salvation, a Christian man of the ancient and Pure Religion, then there is a question I cannot keep myself from asking, blasphemous though it be.

Wherefore did G-D permit such a thing? And wherefore was I, who am his stoutest and staunchest servant, used in so black a twist? G-D may indeed permit his creatures to be tried unto their uttermost, that they gain Heaven thereafter, as we have seen with poor sailors taken by the Inquisition in Spain that witnessed so stoutly to the truth before their burning.

But I am concerned with cleansing the realm of Papist wickedness, and protecting the Queen from the evil machinations of her enemies. Wherefore should I have been used as G-D's tool herein? Surely it was a sin to torment a man witnessing to the True Religion? Wherefore then should I have been cozened into such a sin?

Again he pauses, for his last question shakes him.

If I were less certain of my soul's salvation through G-D's Grace, I would wonder . . .

Very unusually, Davison's pen catches on a fibre in the paper and spatters a few drops of ink. He stops, looks down at it, sands it and blows off the sand, then sets the paper aside. Deliberately he blinks, takes a new sheet.

This evening I went to visit my master, Sir Francis Walsingham. He is sick again of the stone, very grievously, and has given into my hands all the business of defending the realm from the Jesuits. Which I pray G-D to give me the strength and wisdom to do as it should be done. I brought him papers and warrants to sign and had meant to apprise him of the moves against us by others of the Queen's Councillors. However, when I saw how diminished he was by pain and how discoloured his skin, I felt it better not to trouble him therewith and only brought the papers.

Our business being finished, I asked him of the documents that I had marked to be missing, judging from the sequencing of code-numbers, and relating especially to Sir Philip Sidney while he was in the Netherlands and also to the Jesuit that had given us the slip in summer while we were busy about the Babington plot.

He must needs consider for a while but then he gave me the key to his privy office in Seething Lane where he lay, being too sick to remove to Barn Elms, and also the cipher sheets.

After I had taken my leave of him, I went forthwith to his privy office and there, in the space of a few hours, had the full correspondence with Sidney that gave something of our noble Protestant's mission.

To be brief, an informer at the Rheims Seminary (or nest of devilish vipers) had sent us some strange information. In the summer of 1586, Father Thomas Hart SJ had taken the confession of a witch in London. He had given us the slip but as soon as he reported to his master, the Duke of Parma, every Spanish or Papist agent in London was ordered to search the secondhand book- sellers and pawnbrokers for a thing they termed the Book of the Unicorn— presumably some libel against the Queen. We did not know what it might be, though we knew it could be to no good purpose and therefore attempted to find it ourselves. Alas, after much effort, both we and the Papists drew a blank.

After that, long silence upon the subject of the Book of the Unicorn until we thought it had been merely a chimera to distract us. At last a letter came in cipher from Sir Philip Sidney at Arnhem, praying Sir Francis to protect Sir Philip's faithful servant, Mr David Becket, that was now working as an informer among the Papists if he should ever chance to be arrested and promising further information upon the matter of the Book of the Unicorn by a later letter.

This Becket, it seems sure, is our poor prisoner who gabbled of the same book while under pains.

Alas, now I cannot ask him of his service to Sir Philip. For there are enemies of True Religion at Court, that connive with the poor feeble womanly cowardice of the Queen who will not stamp out the enemies of G-D.

Once more the ink sprays on the paper, once more Mr Davison pauses and put it aside, then stops again, takes both sheets and locked them in a secret drawer of his desk. He kneels in prayer, stiff and straight as if at audience with the Queen, struggling to turn his mind from the angry memory of his last meeting with Lord Burghley.

XXXIX

BURGHLEY HAD BEEN AT his most infuriatingly bland.

"The Fleet is not safe enough for the keeping of a traitor," Davison had protested angrily. "The place is crawling with recusants and debtors . . ."

"But Mr Davison," Burghley had answered mildly, "this prisoner of yours is plainly not a traitor since he has professed himself of the True Religion. Do you tell me now that you were mistaken, that he lied on oath and that he is in fact a Catholic?"

"No, but he is hiding a secret of great importance."

"And what is this secret?"

That Davison had not been able to answer. "If I knew that, I would not need to keep hold of him," he said through his teeth. "I do not know his secret, only of its existence."

"Are you saying that he has not in fact lost his memory?"

"I do not deny that."

"Then presumably he no longer has this secret, whatever it may have been."

"He might remember."

"Then, as he is no traitor, he will no doubt tell it to the proper authorities."

"If we set him at liberty . . ."

"Mr Davison, we are not setting him at liberty. We are putting him in the Fleet. He will not be in the Knights' Commons, in any case, but in Eightpenny Ward, from which no one has escaped yet."

"No one has escaped from the Tower."

"Of course not."

"Then why—"

"This is a fruitless discussion," said Burghley. "He is going to the Fleet, and there is the end on it."

"You need a warrant to move him."

"I have a warrant," said Burghley, and showed him the paper, signed by the Queen, that took the prisoner out of Davison's power and into his own. "The Queen said she will execute no more fools and cat's-paws like Babington. She said, and I quote, that she does not trust you. She is afraid that you will invent some startling treason for the poor man, torture him into signing the confession and execute him, and that God will require it of her when she dies."

"The Queen said that?"

"I am afraid she did. She was most vehement about it."

"Thus she requites faithful service."

"Faithful service she requites very well, as I have good cause to know," said Burghley with the smugness of a cat. "To other manner of service, perhaps she is less kind."

"Are you insinuating, my lord, that I am not her faithful servant?"

"Not at all." Burghley was picking up his papers, shuffling them, tapping them straight and handing them to his silent and attentive son. "I am sure you believe that you are. And I am sure that the Queen believes you are not. At the moment. And I am also sure, Mr Davison, that the Queen is our Sovereign and you are not."

Too furious to say any more, Davison had left him there. It was madness to put the prisoner in the Fleet, a sink of corruption and uncleanliness, where no one could know whom he would meet or what he would say.

Kneeling still in prayer in his house, truly believing that he directed his thoughts only to God, Davison turned devices of power in his mind. He needed a weapon as the shadowy play and counter-play of the Court tightened around him, all of it seemingly plotting to save the wicked Queen of Scots. Walsingham himself had taught him that the best weapon was knowledge, and so he had gone seeking it at the fountain, and found it.

Who would have thought that the poet Sidney could have been so circumspect, he thought. At last he knew the prisoner's true name, now it was too late to do anything about it. And there was the mention of the libel, the book against the Queen. Sidney called it that: a Book of the Unicorn, he said, and the repetition almost made Davison snuff the air like a dog following a hart. There was something, clearly something. Perhaps it was a code-book, perhaps a plan for the invasion of England; perhaps it gave information on the Queen of Scots' affinity in England.

It came to him as he knelt that he was wanting in faith. There could be no chance in the accident that had happened to Sidney's agent. It was all in God's plan, as all must be, in God's service there could be no sin, nor was there blame to Davison, who was only a sincere seeker after truth. In some way the Book of the Unicorn would give him what God desired: the death of the Queen of Scots.

Unheeding how far his mind had strayed as he knelt before the idol in his mind, Davison said, "Amen," and rose to his feet again, his face a little less tight on its bones. He could see clear at last. God had put Davison on his path so that he should be able to serve the cause of the True Religion by bringing the Queen of Scots to the block at last. The Book of the Unicorn was also a weapon to that end. It was the only possibility: Becket was part of God's plan to snuff out the viper of Scotland.

Davison too was part of God's plan and it was his task to circumvent Burghley.

A moment's thought brought a thin smile to his face. Burghley did not know all that took place; not even Walsingham knew of the other arrest Davison's men had made a few days after Christmas, nor its result. There had been no need of the manacles that time.

Snuffing out the candles with infinite care not to spill wax, Mr Davison locked and left his office.

XL

ON HER WAY BACK from chapel, the Queen received four petitions that she execute the wicked Queen of Scots. By the time she reached her Withdrawing Room her gracious smile was wearing very thin and her long hands had begun removing and replacing her rings. Bethany discovered that the spiced wine she had brought the Queen was too hot and too gingery and furthermore stale, and that she herself was a white-faced little fool who knew nothing of anything and snored like a sow in farrow. She was sent scurrying to fetch better. The Countess of Bedford found her in the Lesser Withdrawing Room, weeping helplessly. Lady Bedford, who had served the Queen for longer than Bethany had been alive, impatiently tipped the offending wine from one goblet into another, added a spoonful of powdered sugar-loaf. Then she sent Bethany to fetch the Queen's Fool while she herself took the miraculously transformed wine back to the Queen.

This the Queen pronounced bad but adequate and drank it, wincing as the sugary heat touched her teeth.

By the time Thomasina arrived, Her Majesty had calmed herself by sarcastically shredding another maid of honour's taste in clothes and ordering a third to quit her sight until she could wipe that miserable scowl off her face and furthermore do something about the pimple on her nose.

Thomasina came with her fashion doll, prepared to prattle, but found that the Queen wanted to take her on her lap and pet her instead.

She played a pretty game with one of the canaries in its cage, singing to it a song that teetered on the edge of the obscene about birds in bushes and shepherds finding satisfaction therein until at last the Queen laughed and the miasma of anxiety began to dissipate from the Withdrawing Room.

As the maids of honour settled sighing to their embroidery, the Queen bore Thomasina off to a pile of cushions in the corner of the room to admire a book, gaudy in red and green velvet, which had been presented to her by a poet. They both laughed over the miserable straining of the man to get his rhymes properly in line and the Queen kindly corrected his grammar for him.

"Thomasina," she said quietly at last, "I have golden opinions of you from Mrs Twiste."

"She is very kind," said Thomasina with mischief in her eyes.

"She compliments me on your good manners and obedience, which she finds wonderful in one so young."

Thomasina tilted her head graciously. "Mrs Twiste tends to see only what she looks at."

"And so you have been playing a game with her."

"Yes, Your Majesty. Only a little game. I will tell her the truth if you want me to, next time I go."

"No need for that. She says you have been entertaining her little girls with your tumbling and asks if you would like a gift."

"Your Majesty's kindness is payment enough."

"Hmm."

"What is it, Your Majesty? Have I offended you?"

"No. I am thinking."

Thomasina had learnt the gift of repose when the gypsies had shown her in a cage to the peasants as A True Pygmy Queen of the Amazon, painted with walnut juice, tattooed with woad, decorated with beads and dyed chicken feathers. Now beautiful and clean in Lucca velvet and gold tissue, she sat neatly on her cushion with her hands folded and waited for the Queen to finish thinking. At last the Queen began to speak slowly. "I am in a quandary which I think you might solve for me, if you will. Only I fear to lose you."

"Lose me?"

"Let me tell you a tale."

There followed a very strange account of a man who had been taken by Mr Davison in mistake for someone else. His memory was somehow gone, yet he held a secret, vital to the Queen and the welfare of the kingdom. The Queen was in perplexity how to get it from him, but he had been moved to the Fleet prison to take him away from Davison and his men, and the Queen required to put someone to watch him whom neither he nor anyone else would suspect.

At last light began to dawn. "Certainly there are children in the Fleet," Thomasina said, casting her mind back to the days before she had been the Queen's Fool. "Do you wish me to pass as one of them?"

"I believe they carry messages in and out for those who have not been granted liberty. Could you do that?"

Thomasina thought for a moment and then nodded. "Only . . ." she said hesitantly. "Only . . ."

"What?"

"I am . . . very small, and not powerful or strong. It is an ugly place, the Fleet, and I am afraid I might fail. Is there nobody better Your Majesty could ask?"

A line appeared between the Queen's plucked eyebrows. "If there were, be sure I would not trouble you, my dear," she said sadly. "I am Queen of a great realm and yet I have trouble finding those I can trust in this matter."

"What matter?"

"I want you to take particular note of anything this man says regarding the Book of the Unicorn. If he has it, steal it from him as soon as you can and bring it straight to me."

"Oh? Do you think he took the book you lost?"

"No. But I greatly fear he knows the person who did. In particular, if you see him speaking to any old women, tell me at once. I shall arrange for you to pass messages through the Earl of Leicester's household, in their linen."

Thomasina knelt and quietly straightened her doll's petticoat.

"Will you do it?" the Queen asked anxiously.

"I still have my old clothes," Thomasina said distantly. "I take them out sometimes to remind myself how blessed I am." She smiled up at the Queen radiantly. "But this is only play-acting. Is it not, Your Majesty?"

"Thomasina," the Queen answered very seriously, "I do not require this of you, nor do I order it. It is too dangerous. If you refuse, you will still be my Fool and I will love you none the less."

Thomasina paused, wondering if she dared ask. Yes, she must. "Please, Your Majesty, has this anything to do with the Queen of Scots?"

She waited for the storm to break, but it did not come. "Only I do not want to end like Babington, nor yet be mistaken for a traitor like your poor prisoner," she added.

"I do not know. Perhaps. Perhaps not."

"Why will you not sign her death warrant, Your Majesty?"

"These are matters of state, Thomasina, and I do not permit any one of my women to dabble in such matters. It is not fitting."

"Your Majesty, I am too small to be one of your women."

"How much less fitting for you, then."

"And yet I am large enough in your esteem for you to ask me to spy for you, like a man."

"It has nothing to do with this."

"But it might."

"Has someone put you up to this?"

"No, Your Majesty. I am only a Fool who is curious."

There was a long ugly pause while Thomasina wondered if she had forfeited the Queen's love so simply and so easily.

At last the Queen spoke slowly and softly as if to herself.

"Walsingham, Burghley, Davison, they all want me to execute an anointed Queen, as if she were no more than any other woman."

"But she encompassed your death?"

"Of course she did. What else could she do? It was her duty. I have held her here for twenty years, since she threw herself so stupidly on my mercy. I have been deaf to her pleas that I release her even to go to retirement in France. I have helped her rebels and made alliance with her most unfilial son, James. I have shown myself her enemy again and again. If she wishes to return to her kingdom—as she should because God gave it to her—then she must escape from me, and since I hold the key so tight, then in all duty she should try to kill her gaoler. She has been a great deal more restrained in her plotting than I would have been in a like position. Though, perhaps," she said, with a small snort of conceit, "I would have fared better at it."

"But is her plotting not treason?"

"How could it be? This is what Walsingham and his cohorts will not see. The Queen of Scots cannot commit treason against me because she is a sovereign Queen, chosen and anointed of God. This is not her realm, she is not my subject, she owes me no duty of loyalty—therefore she cannot commit treason. All she is doing, all she has ever done is try to win back her throne."

"Does she not desire yours as well?"

"In vengeance for her imprisonment, in zeal for her religion, yes. And she is in fact my successor; she must be, her blood dictates it. And you see, here is another reason why she must not be executed and should not be killed. She inherits the throne of England before Philip of Spain. Why would he wish to bring Parma across from Flanders and send his ships up through the Bay of Biscay in order to bring a Guise Queen to the throne? The Hapsburgs hate the Guises, and always have. No, he never would."

"But they are both Catholics."

"Philip is Hapsburg first, Catholic second. So you see, *imprimis* the Queen of Scots cannot commit treason against me because she is not my subject; *secundus*, she is placed squarely in the path of an invasion from Spain."

"You sound as if you are sorry for her."

"I was sorry for her; she was a fool and still is, she has less political sense than a flea. She had everything and she threw it away; she could not even assassinate her husband sensibly. The stupidity of it! Blowing him up with gunpowder."

"What should she have done?"

"Get him blind drunk and put a pillow over his face. And then scream."

Thomasina hid a smile. She did not ask if the Queen could have done it if necessary.

"If you are sorry for her, why have you kept her prisoner so long?" she asked instead.

"Well," said the Queen with a slow smile, "firstly, for policy. Wherever she went as a Queen, there was uproar. She could not govern Scotland, she could not even govern herself. I cannot have such madness on my northern border, it would canker half the kingdom and leave an open door to France. Furthermore, while she is here as my captive I have a leash to use on the Scots and on King James. And secondly, also for policy. There she sits, the sad romantical Queen, and every Catholic hothead in the country thinks of her first in his plotting. Watching her, I can watch all of them at the same time."

"So she is in the nature of bait."

"Lord, Thomasina, I wish you were a man so I could appoint you Privy Councillor. You are the first to have seen that. She is bait, she is a sword to hold over the Scots, and she shields us from Spain, all in the one royal person. Wherefore in God's name should I execute so useful a creature?"

"Does Davison not understand this?"

"God alone knows what Davison understands. He is a man besotted by the Apocalypse; he believes Armageddon is near. He is convinced that the Queen of Scots' death will bring closer the day he hotly desires, when the Antichrist of Spain and God's English soldiers face each other across, no doubt, a wasted blasted land such as they enjoy in the Netherlands. He expects the English to win."

"Would they not?"

The Queen laughed. "No one who has read the accounts of our doings in the Netherlands could believe that. We have neither the money, the men nor the experience to do it."

"But with God's help . . ."

"God's help comes to the better soldiers, depend upon it, Thomasina. I, who have never been near a battlefield, know that. However, Davison . . . Davison believes in the Lord God of Hosts."

"So you will never sign the death warrant?"

"Most problems solve themselves if only you can content yourself in patience and wait. No, I will never sign the death warrant. Not willingly. Not in my right mind. Not unforced. In the last resort, I may yet manage to have her assassinated."

"But how is that better?"

"It is unofficial. It is doubtful. She dies of a sickness. A tragic loss, a sad story. She is unwell already. Men will mutter all over Europe that I poisoned her, but I shall go into mourning and lament her with great lamentations and keep them all in doubt a little longer."

"But is not an assassination immoral?"

The Queen shrugged. "The Queen of Scots fears it, I know. God send that the fear of it is enough to kill her, though unfortunately she seems as tough as

I am. If she must die for policy's sake, then let it be quietly, let there be no song and dance, no martyr's scene. Lord, how she would love to be a martyr and wipe out all her sins, the silly incontinent bitch."

"But, Davison . . ."

"Davison is made blind and deaf by his religion. I, the Protestant champion, must not stoop to poison. All must be open and above-board and beyond doubt. But if I were to sign the death warrant, then all that men will remember of me beyond doubt is that I killed a sister Queen."

The Queen sighed heavily. "He has been pressing me hard and he has convinced most of my councillors to back him, so I cannot simply dismiss him and make an end of his idiocy. It may be . . . if he lays hands on the Book of the Unicorn that he could force me to it, and worse besides. I believe he is searching for it as we speak. So yes, Thomasina, in a way, your quest has to do with the Queen of Scots."

"What is in the book?"

The silence this time was too strained to pass unnoticed by the other ladies. They were casting anxious glances across at the Queen and her muliercula.

"No doubt you will read it if you find it," said the Queen bleakly. "And then you will know. If you will do this thing I ask of you."

Thomasina stood and kissed the Queen on her stiffly plated pink-and white cheek.

"Of course I will do it, Your Majesty," she said.

XLI

THEY HAD LEFT THEIR boat at the bridge and marched strangely on the ice, past the night-time remains of the winter fair—empty booths and piles of offal and market rubbish that no one could be bothered to move because once the thaw came they would be carried out by the tide. Behind them the Queen's boatmen returned to the Tower, unable to pass the bridge where the great frothing curlicues, pillars and daggers of ice marked how the frost had come down like a thunderclap at slack water, to dam the river and make of it a playground.

As soon as his legs were freed and he was out of the boat, Becket had straightened his back and looked around, putting his hat on his head with care.

The sleet had stopped as the world chilled. Early-morning darkness shrouded and silenced all the mass of humanity living in the city; it seemed as if he and his guards were the only men awake. Their breath puffed into the stiff air as if they were chimneys and frost prickled at Becket's cheeks. The river ice had been roughened by thousands of boots and some skates since it formed, though Becket was uncertain enough of his feet to slip occasionally. Their steps scraped and creaked on it and occasionally startled a skinny rat away from the rubbish heaps.

At last they had passed the closed and shuttered City and climbed the steps of the boat-landing by the derelict palace of Bridewell. Becket was getting breathless from weakness and lack of exercise but they took no notice and marched him briskly up the path that ran beside the Fleet River. He knew the path, knew the river. He knew that generally it stank like the open sewer it was, but now it was frozen and all mortality with it, so that the turds and bones that had been in it when the frost came before Christmas were still there, miraculously preserved in rough dirty glass. At one place, close against the stone, he glimpsed the waxy remains of a whore's deadly sin, one small fist in its mouth and its eyes closed tight.

He looked away from it quickly, blinking up at the teetering four-storey-high buildings on their left. He knew them. He nodded as they passed Bridewell Bridge and nodded again as they turned left up Bride's Lane past the little old church.

"If I did not know better, I might think you were taking me home," he said facetiously to Munday, who had put his poignard away again.

"Be quiet."

"This is all familiar to me, sir. Are you not pleased?"

"No. Quiet."

"There is a boozing ken up that way. I forget its name," Becket went on, seized with an urge to tease his tormentors. "Will you take a quart of beer with me, for sentiment's sake?"

"I'll not tell you again," interrupted Ramme. "Silence."

Becket tutted, full of ridiculous pleasure to be seeing something other than stone walls. His mind was fizzing with images. Yes, he knew this part of London. It was as familiar to him as . . . well, the back of his hand has become strange to him, considering its colour and shape. And here was Fleet Street, and that way was Temple Bar and that way was Ludgate and that way . . .

"Ah," he said, "the Fleet Prison. I see."

Ramme growled, turned suddenly and hit Becket in the belly. Now they had to pause while he doubled over and must lean against a wall until he got his breath back. So unprovoked and casual a blow alchemised Becket's black fear in a heartbeat to black rage. For seconds together he shook with the red blind urge to kill. When he could breathe again, Becket said softly, "Pray they hang me, Mr Ramme. I have a great deal of satisfaction to take from you."

"He did warn you," Munday pointed out self-righteously.

"A famous deed, to strike a gentleman in chains," Becket pointed out, still sustained by his anger at being treated like a slave. He was also emboldened by the familiarity of the buildings, as if he were backed by friends who would fight for him. "And all because Mr Ramme's writ does not run in the Fleet."

Neither of them answered, nor did they look at each other. Becket showed his teeth as he rubbed the bruise in the pit of his stomach and jangled the links. Something had happened, high up amongst the courtiers around the Queen. He knew perfectly well that he was a pawn, but now he also knew that he had just been captured and transferred to someone else's power. He had no idea whose, only the fact that it could not be Davison's made him feel as if he were really being freed, rather than simply transferred from one prison to another. In the Fleet he might meet someone he knew, might find someone who would answer the questions marching round his head as pointlessly as Dutch soldiers doing drill. And if he was out of the Tower, perhaps there would be no treason trial, no hanging, drawing and quartering at Tyburn after all. Doubtless they would hang him in any case, to be on the safe side, but at least he would be whole on the Day of Judgement and able then to hunt down Ramme and Munday, if not before.

They moved him on while he was still coughing, over Fleet Bridge, up Fleet Lane and into the gatehouse of the prison.

He was bidden to stand and wait respectfully with his hat in his hand while they called for the Deputy Gaoler. Joachim Newton came lurching out of his private lodgings, still pulling on his jerkin, growling and grumbling. Soft words passed between them, Munday produced a paper which provoked Newton to take his hat off, put it back on and address a great many sirs and your honours to both of them.

A Privy Council warrant, Becket thought to himself.

The next thing that happened was another long wait. At last Newton returned with a fistful of leg-irons and a mallet. Becket sat on the end of the bench and looked knowingly at him. They were not irons that could be unlocked: rather, once on, they must be removed by a blacksmith. He yawned ostentatiously and put out his left foot. It was the Deputy Gaoler himself who did the honours with the rings and bolts and the mallet.

"Christ," he said conversationally, when the hammering was over, "what is it about me that frightens you so?"

Ramme boxed his ears as if he was a servant to silence him. Becket made no protest, but sat and stared at Ramme. The mountain of fury inside him warmed him like a baker's oven, all the more for its being unexpressed. His soul basked in its unaccustomed glow. Then there was business with keys and a lantern, and money must be paid before they could pass through the great double gates. One locked behind him before the second was unlocked, and then they were in the courtyard, empty except for the stocks, pillory and whipping post in one corner.

Another iron-bound door, more rattling of keys in Newton's clanking bunch of at least twenty. Up the stairs, through another locked door and into a dark vaulted chamber that stank muskily of men. Becket picked his way carefully between the tight-packed beds, freighted with dreaming souls huddled up in their blankets, mostly two to a bed. Newton's candle-lantern swung and caught shoulders and noses and made unreliable encroachments on the kingdom of shadows. Some of the men were waking up and their eyes glinted as they watched what happened. One man, made hideous by an old sword-slash down his face that had taken out one of his eyes, sat up and scowled at them.

"What do you want, Newton?"

Newton instantly lifted his cudgel and took a few threatening steps towards the man, who sneered at him.

"No business of yours, Cyclops," snapped Newton and Cyclops snorted and leaned back with his hands behind his head. Nobody else dared to say anything. Most pretended to be sleeping. They tramped to the end farthest from the door, where an old fireplace showed no sign of a fire despite the bitterness of the night, unless one could be made with old turds. They stopped in the corner beside a bed with only one man in it, Becket scraping and jingling as he went.

Whoever had tenure of the bed was one of those pretending to sleep, huddled up with his cloak over his head.

"Sit," snapped Ramme, as if to a dog.

They were being watched covertly by most of the men in the room now.

"You might as well put me in Bolton's Ward straight away, Mr Newton," said Becket, insolently ignoring Ramme and Munday. "I have not a single penny to give you as garnish."

"Fourpence a bed per night if you share," put in Cyclops helpfully.

Newton growled at both of them. "Your friends are paying," he said to Becket and Becket smiled sweetly as he sat on the edge of the sagging straw mattress.

"What friends are those?" he asked. "I was not aware I had any in the world."

"Shut your mouth," snapped Ramme.

"Lord, what have I done to deserve such kindness," said Becket rhetorically as he took off his new shoes and decided against removing his nether-stocks, since they gave some protection to his ankles against the rough leg-rings.

Ramme leaned down to him and growled, "Tell us, and all this will be done away with."

The relief to his soul that he was out of the Tower, his warming spine of anger and their ridiculous precautions against someone who could still barely hold a sword turned strangely to laughter. Becket thought it might be the first time he had laughed properly since he came to empty wakefulness in Little Ease. Perhaps he made a point of it. Ramme's lips tightened and almost disappeared.

"Give me back my cloak," he demanded meanly.

Becket grinned at him, laid himself clinking down beside the other man and pulled the cloak tightly over him.

"My need is greater than yours," he said insolently.

Ramme started forward to take it from him by force, but Munday held his arm and whispered at him. He stopped.

"You had best learn some manners," Ramme hissed.

"Go and find someone else to bully, you pox-brained Court catamite," Becket said, putting his head on his bundle and his hat over his face. He ignored the passing punch in his ribs that his insult earned him. It was worth it.

XLII

TO ACCOUNT FOR HER absence from Court, it was given out that Thomasina must visit her mother, who was on her deathbed. The story made Thomasina wonder wistfully if the woman was in truth still alive; she had not seen her since her father pocketed the silver he got for his daughter and the gypsies tied a rope around her neck and led her away.

Thomasina left the Court before dawn in one of the Queen's own carriages and rattled and rumbled her way past Charing Cross and up the filthy, slush-ridden, frozen-rutted disgrace of the Strand to the Earl of Leicester's London palace, which gave onto the river. There, in the spicery, she changed quickly to the patched velvet rags that still carried the smell of incense and horses and brought back to her memory things she had fought to forget. In that guise, the Earl introduced her to Mr. Benson, his major-domo.

"You are to admit this child at any time she wishes," he ordered and the major-domo's face remained bland and obedient while his intelligent eyes took in her size and shape and the cleanliness of her hands and considered it all.

She used walnut juice to stain herself a little and then sat and dabbled in the ashes of one of the fireplaces. She had lost the habit of dirtiness at the Queen's Court. While she was not so fanatical about stenches as the Queen, the mere ability to shift her smock every other day kept her clean and fresh as a lily in comparison to what she had been.

She had her knife hidden up one sleeve, strapped against her forearm, but she knew better than to think it would be any protection. The money she had brought she rolled in a cloth round her waist.

And then she took a deep breath, passed through the kitchen to filch some bread and a small pie for practice, and slipped out the back door that gave onto Leicester's magnificent stables.

Here she sat on the neatly raked manure heap for a while to warm herself and look about. For ten years she had hardly ever left the Court, except on Progress, when she travelled in a carriage or a litter or sometimes on a little fat white pony. The Queen's favor and her bright velvet and silken embroidered clothes marked her apart from others even more than her size, as if she herself were an ornate jewel worn on the Queen's breast. She had had no longing for freedom, had not felt herself to be a prisoner at all. True, she was numbered among the Queen's pets at first, before the Queen learnt to know her better. So? Would the Queen's lap-dogs prefer a life on the streets to the chicken and pheasant they ate every day? Of course not. Even brute beasts had more sense, although she recalled that one of the courtiers had taken the trouble to ask her once if she minded. She had laughed at him, but made allowances later when she found that he was Sir Philip Sidney and also a poet.

And here she was, stripped almost naked in comparison to what she normally wore, shivering as the cold gathered itself around her and found the spaces between her rags, willingly venturing beyond her safe haven on an ill-defined quest for a mysterious book. Without any doubt, she was mad.

She ate the pie and hid the bread in the pocket under her skirts and jumped down from the dung-heap to wander out into the noisy street.

She passed the length of Fleet Street from Temple Bar to Ludgate and back, getting her bearings. As always before, the world was full of broad gowns that jostled her and gentlemen's swords that poked at her, baskets that swiped at her head, horses whose hooves threatened her skull. She saw some children playing by the huge midden on the border between Westminster and the City and they stopped their game to stare curiously at her. She stared back as insolently. Otherwise the street was full of giants who saw only a beggarmaid. She did not beg, though, since she no longer knew where the regular pitches were and who had tenure of them and had no desire to offend anyone.

For a while she stood and listened to a ballad-seller's singing of his latest broadsheet, and resisted the impulse to cut any purses for she knew she was out of practice and rusty at it. Once she had been an upright man's valuable property: by day she had filched for him and by night she had climbed amongst the roofs of London and crept into the citizens' bedrooms to steal their jewels and gold. As the man boasted before he pawned her to Paris Garden, she was better than a child because while she was as nimble, she was stronger and more sensible. At the time she had been proud of her skills.

Back on Fleet Bridge she jumped to peek over the parapet and wonder at the strangeness of a still river, turned to stone like its banks, and then she ran to Fleet Lane to take a look at the prison.

The gate was being opened for those who had given bond for their good behaviour and were allowed to go out into the City during the day. Many of the men worked, trying to pay off their debts, while others simply dug themselves in deeper by boozing all day in taverns. Some of the women wore masks and striped cloaks to ply the only truly profitable trade a woman could learn.

She took a chance and slipped in amongst the skirts and then dived through the gap behind a woman who had come out to kiss her husband goodbye. While she waited between the gates for the second to be opened, she stayed as still and quiet as she could.

There was nerve-racking byplay between the woman and one of the turn-keys, who wanted a kiss as his garnish for letting her back in, and in the end the woman yielded to him.

And then the gate opened and she could slip into the wide courtyard and join one of the gangs of children playing amongst the rags and scraps of the ruff-making circle. She took out her knuckle-bones from a purse and began throwing the ball and gathering up as practice and nobody took any notice of her at all, since she was small.

XLIII

MORNING IN THE EIGHTPENNY Ward was marked by some dim light coming through the high barred windows along one side, the sound of one of the turnkeys opening the door and a chorus of groans and farts. As the queue formed to use the malodorous jakes just outside the door, Becket opened his eyes and looked up into the face of his bedfellow.

For a few seconds his world lurched and heaved in confusion and horror: he should not be seeing that face, it was impossible. Why? he wondered muzzily, and the memory skittered away again like a rat.

"Good morning, sir," said the other man softly.

Becket sat up on his elbow and blinked. "Good morning," he said automatically. "Er . . . do I know you, sir?"

The other was a balding little clerk with a worn woollen doublet and a nervous expression. "Perhaps you do," he said quietly. "Can you recall me?"

For a moment the name was on the tip of Becket's tongue, but refused to come. Growling with frustration, he shook his head.

"Does the name Simon mean anything to you?" asked the clerk.

It did, there was no question but that it did and he had forgotten why.

"I ask your pardon, sir," Becket said sadly. "An accident has happened to me and . . ."

"I know," said the clerk, Simon, very softly. "Your name is David Becket."

Becket smiled at him and at the repetition of the talisman of his name. "Oh, so Doctor Nunez has—"

"Shh," said Simon, with his finger on his lip, "no names, please, Mr Becket. Yes, the doctor has asked me to help you."

Greatly cheered, Becket moved to sit up properly and whined as he jerked the manacles on his bandaged wrists. He swore and rubbed his buzzing hands until the pain went away while Simon the clerk watched sympathetically.

"Do you know why they have loaded me with irons?" Becket asked. "If you know of the accident to my memory, perhaps you know that."

"I know they fear you, Mr Becket, so much is plain. But perhaps we can have those taken off."

"How?"

"It is remarkable what money will do, here as everywhere else. Have you anything to sell?"

Suddenly frightened that he had been robbed, Becket reached for his bundle and found it where it had been. He opened it, discovered his pipe and tobacco and the Bible, then the package the Yeoman had given him. He opened that too, and found two flat pewter bottles, a loaf of bread, a lump of cheese and a sausage, and a small knife in a leather sheath.

The knife pleased him most of all. Somebody had paid for it in gold and influence. He felt more and more like a proper man again, to own a blade once more. He took it out, careful at the clumsiness and heaviness of his hands, tested the edge, felt the weight, checked the balance. It was an old friend, he knew its worn hilt and where he usually wore it, but the chains stopped him when he tried to fasten the strap at his neck.

"Here are riches indeed," said Simon, staring at the bread.

"Well, sir, help me put on my knife and I will be glad to share my breakfast with you."

The clerk had an unusually sweet and knowing smile. "Done, Mr Becket."

While the clerk's thin fingers busied themselves with the strap about his neck, Becket wondered at their immediate intimacy, that he felt no qualms at allowing the stranger to do it.

"If I put the buckle where it was before, it will be too loose," Simon said after a moment. "How is it if I take it in a notch?"

"Excellent," Becket said. He had the feeling that he was properly dressed at last, now he could feel the cold knob of metal against the back of his neck and the sheath in the valley between his shoulder muscles. What was left of them. Evidently he had been a better-built man before he got into Davison's clutches . . .

The sudden piercing memory of Davison looking down on him while he wept like a baby with pain completely destroyed his happiness. He ducked his head to hide his expression from the clerk and tried to break the loaf in half. This time the clerk did not offer to help and it took several moments of struggle before he managed it.

"You must excuse me, sir," he said, ashamed at his weakness. "My hands still do not obey me properly, though they are a great deal better than they were."

"Indeed," said the clerk politely, took the bread eagerly and chewed and swallowed.

They shared half of what was in the bottle that contained beer quite companionably. The other had been filled with rough aqua vitae, which was a blessed thing to find. Becket cautiously put that one inside his shirt for emergencies. The clerk accepted half the cheese but regretfully refused the smoked sausage.

"I have a delicate stomach, sir," he said. "Not all meats agree with it."

"Oh," Becket said with his mouth full. "I knew a man like that once, almost sickened on a plain dish of bacon and peas."

The clerk nodded attentively. "Who was he?"

"Why, he was the little inquisitor . . . the . . ." Becket stopped chewing and grunted with the effort of trying to remember. His hands fisted and ground into each other but mere effort would not bring it back. "God damn it."

"Please, sir, do not distress yourself. Eat."

Thinking ahead, Becket kept half of his share of the food back, though he was still hungry. "What is the food like here, sir?" he asked.

"I have tasted better," admitted the clerk. "And much of it disagrees with me."

"What are you in for, sir?"

Simon shrugged, a gesture subtly foreign that seemed to come naturally to him. "Debt," he said. "I owe five thousand pounds and my creditors caught me at last."

"Bad luck. Why did you not try hiding in the Liberties of Whitefriars?"

"I did, only they lured me out of it. And you, sir? Do you know why you are here?"

"Perhaps for treason," Becket said casually, watching under his lashes to see how the clerk took it. "Only, thanks to the Devil taking my memory, I am not sure myself."

"Then why are you not in the Tower?"

"Why indeed? Do you know, Simon?"

The clerk looked away and patted the sorry fringing of beard around his mouth delicately with his fingers.

"I think you do," Becket said. "Are you a friend of mine?"

Simon nodded. "I believe so."

"Then tell me what I have done to offend the Queen."

Simon shook his head and sighed. "That nobody knows but yourself, Mr Becket, alas. I may be your friend, but I do not know everything."

"Then tell me what you do know. Tell me about myself."

"I dare not . . ."

Frustration peaked the mountain of rage inside him. Becket growled like a dog, reached out double-handed and caught the front of the clerk's doublet, pulled him close.

"I may be chained," he snarled, "but chains make good weapons, used right. Tell me."

With humiliating ease the clerk freed himself and moved away a little, swinging his legs to the floor.

"Mr Becket, please," he said. "Calm yourself."

Becket lunged for him in fury, was jerked short by the chains attached to his legs catching on the end of the bed and squashed what was left of the loaf as he came down hard on an elbow.

"God damn you to Hell!"

Something was wrong with Becket's eyes. All about the clerk's head were rainbows and dancing lights while the sombre tapestry of stenches about them melted suddenly into a sharp perfume of roses. Among them he saw me standing, smiling, crowned with stars and shaking my head. I would have spoken with him, comforted him and helped him, but the disorder of his brain that let him see me at all suddenly crested and broke. The rainbows engulfed all the room and blackness hammered through his mind.

He woke exhausted and sore with a strange taste about all his thoughts and saw again the face of the clerk and believed it to be a ghost. He could have wept. Once more his heart was clenched inside a great fist of fear, retransformed from more comfortable rage.

"For God's sake, Simon," he whispered. "Get me out of this."

The clerk put a bottle against his lips and he drank a little of the aqua vitae mixed with bad-tasting water. Simon's face was drawn with distress.

"David, David," he said softly. "What have they done to you?" There was more, but Becket could not understand it since it was in a foreign language. The words sounded gentle enough.

He knew he had to wait patiently for the world to return to its right moorings. Patience came hard to him, but every time he lifted his head he was not entirely sure where it was. The light was stronger and the ward was now empty of all but one man, who lay tossing in some fever by the door. Eventually the strangeness faded like the tide.

It took great effort, but he dug coherence out of the depths. "I am not mad," he told the clerk anxiously. "Do not believe that I am mad, for all I look it. The . . . the doctor said I have taken the falling sickness from being hit on the head."

Simon nodded. "So he told me, but I had not realised how gravely. Do you know me now?"

I am too tired for this, Becket thought as he shook his head; too tired, too afraid. It was misery to look inside his heart and find there such weakness that it took much of his strength to hold his voice steady. He preferred the times when he was full of black murderous fury; it felt cleaner, more like himself. His hands were prickling and burning and his wrists throbbed; he must have jerked them about while he was . . . wherever he went when he fell down.

"I know you as Simon because you told me," he said, his voice stopped down to a mutter because his Adam's apple ached. "For a moment I thought you were a ghost, but I see now you are solid. That's all I know. I wish you would tell me of myself so I am not empty."

"Well, when the doctor spoke with me we talked of this at length. He is against any of your old friends' telling you what you should remember. Rather he feels it would be better for your reason that you remember by yourself, for he is convinced that your memory has not flown away but only hides chained in some . . . some dungeon of your mind. If I tell you, then you might never be sure what you remember and what you have only been told."

It was cruel to hear that there would be no easy refilling of his empty chambers. Even so he could see the sense in what the doctor said. He sat up with difficulty, jerking his wrists again and bit his lip to stop the cry. Simon was kneeling on the bed beside him, took his hands and turned them over, examining them as Nunez had.

"It is imperative we have you out of these chains, Mr Becket. I am afraid of the damage they are doing to you."

Becket tried to smile. "They'll never free me until they know what I have forgotten, and once they know that, then I expect they will hang me."

"Your legs, I fear, must remain in irons, as you say," Simon answered. "But I see no reason why your manacles should not come off if we can find the money to do it. Come, sir, what will you sell of your possessions?"

He spread out what there was on the mattress. Becket was touched to see he had gathered up all that remained of the food, every crumb, and put it back in its cloth. There were the shirt, the falling band, the pipe and a small pouch of tobacco and the Bible. Neither mentioned the bottle of aqua vitae, which Simon had put back inside Becket's shirt-front once he had taken a little to cleanse the river water he brought.

"Can we sell the Bible?" Becket asked, extremely unwilling to part with his tobacco, though he suspected it might gain a better price.

"We can but try. Are you able to walk?"

With effort he could sit up, put on his shoes and swing his legs to the floor. He jingled down the narrow passageway between the beds. The clerk had taken it upon himself to carry the bundle.

Only for a second, Becket hesitated, wondering if he could trust the clerk. And then he shrugged mentally. To be sure, if Simon planned to rob him there was nothing he could presently do about it. After they had each used the jakes they went down the narrow stairs and out into the courtyard.

It buzzed and writhed like a hive, was as full of activity as Gresham's more famous Exchange in the City. There were craftsmen working wherever the light was good and a sewing circle of women sat under one of the awnings, feverishly making new ruffs.

Simon hurried over to one of the trestle-tables set up by the prison gate, covered with books, cards, bales of dice, candles, meat pies, shoes, leather laces, leather scraps, a purse, sewing gear, articles of clothing, a chafing dish and a lump of iron pyrites labelled as gold ore from the New World which could be bought for a trifling sum by anyone interested in financing an expedition to find the rest.

After a moment's thought, Becket jangled his way over to stand behind Simon, who was looking frustrated.

"How you can suggest a mere one shilling for a brand-new—"

" 'Tain't new, neither, Mr. Anriques; look, it has plain marks of reading on it and a gravy stain at Genesis Chapter One, what's more."

"How can we put mere money to the value of the Almighty's Word, Mr Arpent?" demanded Simon rhetorically. The plump man shrugged.

"Well, Mr Anriques, it's in the matter of what the market will bear, not the value, as you might say. And the price of that Bible, which I will venture to say I doubt I can sell inside a week, is a shilling, take it or leave it. Though if the gentleman was thinking of selling his buttons to gain garnish for striking off of his irons . . ."

Mr Arpent left the suggestion dangling. Becket looked down at the numerous buttons decorating his velvet doublet and noticed that they had purple and red gems set into the jet they were carved from and were in fact very fine indeed.

"Ah," he said. Simon looked at them closely and let out a soft whistle of admiration. "I must have been living high on the hog when I got these," said Becket self-deprecatingly. There were twenty-four of them, alternating garnet and amethyst, all down his peascod-bellied doublet. No doubt about it, that had been a fine and fashionable suit before Ramme and Munday got to work on him.

"What will he close his doublet with, if he sell them to you?"

Arpent squinted up his eyes. "Well, I'll only take six of the garnet ones, see, because I happen to know a tailor that is looking for work like that, and I'll pay . . . ah . . . fifteen shillings for them, seeing as it's to free the poor gentleman from the manacles."

"Forty shillings," said Simon instantly. "See how finely they are carved, and how deep-red are the garnets."

"How do you know they are only garnets?" put in Becket. "They might be rubies."

"Or they might be glass," said Arpent. "I am taking a risk as it is; my friend might have found what he seeks elsewhere. Twenty shillings and it's my last word, sirs."

"Twenty-five and you shall have them," said Simon.

"Wait a bit," said Becket, driven by a half-understood instinct, "I might find someone else to buy them off me. And I want some trade as well."

Arpent rolled his eyes. "Do you think I am in the Fleet for my health, sir? I have need of money too . . ."

"I only want some of those leather laces, Mr Arpent, and I also want you to tell Mr Gaoler Newton that you gave fifteen shillings for the buttons."

Arpent lifted his chin and looked sideways at Becket. "Why would I do that?"

Becket kept his smile stuck to his face, although his heart had gone cold and weary. "If he should ask you, sir, only if he should ask you."

There was a strained pause. "I pay my protection," said Arpent. "I don't want no trouble."

Becket leaned over, making the most of his small advantage. "No trouble, Mr Arpent," he said softly. "But do you think I got these buttons and my velvet doublet for the beauty of my face?"

Arpent made no answer and Simon wondered how it was that Becket managed to convey menace simply by the way he stood. Nobody had ever feared Simon because he leaned over them.

"Done at twenty shillings," said Arpent after a moment.

"Twenty-five," Becket reminded him, still gently. "I shall remember you kindly, Mr Arpent; indeed I shall."

Arpent looked as if he might cry. "Twenty-five then," he said sadly, "and the laces."

"Splendid, Mr Arpent. I shall remember you in my prayers. May I borrow your snips?"

They accomplished the trade simply, leaving Arpent with the six buttons which he tied up in a scrap of leather, and while Simon took ostentatious delivery of fifteen shillings, Becket received an extra ten by sleight of hand. They tipped their hats to Arpent and moved away to stand in the cold sunlight.

"Now we had better hope that Mr Newton comes soon to rob the charity box," said Simon Anriques.

Becket leaned against the wall and scratched his head.

"He takes the lot, does he?" Becket asked. "Where there is money there will be robbery, so they say."

"Precisely," said the clerk, looking nervously around. It occurred to Becket that they were being beadily watched by a number of skinny ragged men who were not hobbled as he was. "It all depends how soon he comes."

He came soon, perhaps to take a look at his important prisoner, for he did not go directly to the box bolted to the wall where charitable passers-by in Fleet Lane might put money or food through a small hole in the bricks. Instead, he came over to them as they sat on a stone step that led up to the Eightpenny Ward.

"I hear you have a garnish for me, Anriques," he said without preamble to the clerk. "Where is it?"

"It is a garnish to strike off these irons," said Simon, pointing at Becket.

Newton bent down to him and leered, and Becket enviously caught the smell of old aqua vitae on his breath.

"What makes you think I won't take the garnish and leave the irons?"

"I know you have the power to do that, Mr Newton," said Simon Anriques humbly. "But I hope that consideration for your future will prevent you."

"Consideration for my future, eh? Why?"

"This man is here on a Privy Council warrant. It is not unknown for such a man to be released and even to return to favour at Court." Simon was steepling his fingers and examining the shape, while the sunlight fell on the tuft of hair in the middle of his head, moated by baldness. Becket let him get on with it, since he felt he was not good enough at play-acting to treat Newton with the respect he wanted, and menace would hardly help him with the gaoler, who never went anywhere without his cudgel and three bully boys at his back. "Once the Queen held him high in her esteem. Now he is fallen to the depths. But he may rise again. Others have."

Newton breathed hard and stared at Becket, who stared back as blankly as he could, heart beating fast, fear again unmanning him.

"He may not."

"Then you will have lost nothing."

"Doesn't look like a courtier."

"Looks may be deceptive, Mr Newton. Though it is true he is less of a courtier than a soldier."

"Better keep him chained then."

"Better to have him remember you with kindness, Mr Newton, as I will."

Newton laughed. "Give me the fifteen shillings before I beat it out of you and put you in irons too."

"Think on what I have said, Mr Newton."

"Give."

Simon handed over the money and Newton slid it into his purse and laughed at both of them, spat close to Becket's boot and marched over to the charity box, fastened to the wall with a marvellous number of iron bars and padlocks. He unlocked it, took it down, gathered up the pennies and shillings in it and threw the stale loaves and legs of chicken at random at some of the prisoners who had gathered like ravens at an execution. Then he put it back while a couple of fights broke out over the food.

"I am sorry," said Simon to Becket. "I mishandled that as well. I am not used to being so utterly without power."

For a moment Becket was puzzled to know what Simon was apologising for, since he had been more steadfast than Becket.

"Newton only wants us to understand we are at his whim," he said wisely after a moment. "If he were too easily bought, he would lose much of his terror."

The bell rang at noon for dinner and caused a rush to the greasy-walled refectory and a struggle amongst the benches to be nearest the serving hatch where Newton's servants stood with platters. Simon had disappeared on some errand of his own and Becket as a newcomer found himself in an end-mess. The platters slammed down in front of them, meagrely piled with meat in a universal anonymous brown sauce, followed by grubby baskets of coarse bread cut into thick trenchers with the cinders still on. Becket found as mess-junior that he was supposed to divide the dishes, but when he held up his hands to show the manacles, another man took the office.

The chicken was stringy in its brown sauce, the beef salted, imperfectly soaked and boiled just enough to make it solid, there was a pease pudding of wonderful vintage and a hunk of bacon, also anointed with brown. Simon arrived in a hurry just as one of Newton's deputies said grace, with a look of tight-mouthed satisfaction on his face. He stepped over the bench and sat down, then looked at the bread trencher in front of him and shook his head in wonderment. Becket was already stoically doing his best, chewing patiently through the gristle. Out of kindness he swapped some of his chicken and beef for Simon's bacon and pease pottage, washed it down with as much of the thin ale as he could decently lay hands on, and finished the meal with his belly full enough. Simon found the going much harder and only ate half of his portion.

The noise of talk, chewing, spitting and complaining was enough to deafen the dead, and yet Becket did not regret his cell in the Tower where, he had to admit, the food had been far better. Here at least there were other men to look on and things to watch. Absurdly, he began to feel happy. At the other table where they were serving the Knights' Commons, he saw the women sitting and discoursing and spent a pleasant few minutes speculating about uses that pretty buttons could be put to in a prison.

Please, Lord, please, he prayed silently while one of Newton's servants gabbled out another grace, and he laughed when Simon followed his gaze and flushed.

In the afternoon he spent an hour constructing a web of laces to hold his leg-chains off the ground and stop them from tripping him up and then shuffled over to the other end of the courtyard to find out what was causing the circle of cheering men. It turned out to be a rat fight, with two brutes the size of cats hissing and squeaking at each other in a ring made of the masonry blocks by which some of the men were hobbled. Becket watched for a while and put sixpence on the smaller of the two, on the grounds he had more to fight for and nimbler paws and gave better odds. He lost, which depressed Becket greatly as he struggled back to the step where he had left Simon.

The clerk had taken chalk and cleared straw from a space on the cobbles. He was busily chalking marks and shapes on it.

"What's this?" Becket asked curiously. "Witchcraft?"

Simon sighed. "No," he said. "Only the Cabbala."

Becket grunted and squatted to look closer. "What is the design?"

"The Tree of Life."

"What does it prophesy?"

"It prophesies nothing. I am not trying to prognosticate the future."

"What then?"

Simon sighed again. "It will no doubt seem a strange thing to do, but I am trying to understand the world."

"With chalkmarks?"

"I wonder if you recall the sayings of Copernicus about the movement of the earth about the sun?"

"Not that old song again, Simon. How can such a thing be? What would hold up the earth? Depend upon it, the sun and moon are lights in the sky, as they always have been." Becket was vehement because the whole idea always made him feel queasy.

"Perhaps the earth is carried on a crystal sphere like the other planets."

"Pooh. What would the sphere be made of? And why would we not hear of it from travellers? Surely someone would have bumped into it by now. Think what a tale it would make. 'As I journeyed in foreign lands I fetched up of a sudden against an endless wall of crystal . . .'"

"Perhaps it is in the sea, dividing one from the other."

"'. . . and our ship rammed against a solid but invisible thing.' Someone would have found it. For God's sake, Drake would have found it while he was sailing around the earth and burning Spaniards in their beds."

"Your objection is a good one. I had asked the same question a little differently: if the earth is held on a sphere, then how come the moon can go round without breaking it?"

"Well, there you are. Clearly the thing is nonsense and Copernicus was a little distempered by drink when he published the thing."

"And yet mathematically it is beautiful. Mathematically it—"

"Mathematics this, mathematics that . . . You talk as if numbers were Holy Writ."

"Perhaps they are." Becket saw that Simon was flushed with anger, as if his woman had been insulted. "See here," he rapped out. "I draw a right-angled triangle, and upon this and this side a square, divided in four, and if I add the two together, then they will give me the size of the third square, which will always, always, no matter where I draw it or what condition of man I am, it will *always* thereby give me the length of this side of the triangle. Always. It is true and it is provable; what more could you ask of Holy Writ?"

"Pff. That is only an old soldier's trick for finding out the right length to make a siege-ladder. What makes that Holy Writ?"

"Its simplicity, its universality."

"And what has it to do with crystal spheres?"

"Everything," murmured Simon, gazing down at his diagram in frustration. "If only I could understand it."

"What does it matter? Who cares if the earth goes about the sun or the sun about the earth?"

"Matter? Tell me, Becket, who made the world?"

"God made the world, everyone knows that; it is in the catechism."

"Agreed. In which case the world must in some way reflect the mind of the Almighty. Yes?"

"Why? If a courtier poet writes of living as a shepherd in Arcadia or some like tedious foolishness, does that mean he has been a shepherd?"

"No, but—"

"A Popish painter draws Heaven upon a church wall: has he been to Heaven? Is Heaven in his mind? By looking at his limning, shall we learn what manner of man he is?"

"No, admittedly, but . . ."

Becket jangled aggressively as he wagged his finger at Simon. "This is the arrogance of the clever man," he said. "Here is logic, true, but you have forgot that to make something new which was not made before has more than logic in it. It has a touch of divinity."

"You are reading me a lesson I already know," Simon said hotly. "I would never claim to confine the Almighty by logic—"

"But you just have. The world was made by God. Therefore, to know God's mind, study the world. Yes? A syllogism, though I forget which kind."

"Where would you have me study the mind of the Almighty then, eh, Becket? In the Bible?"

"Why not? Better men than I am have done so."

"The Bible says nothing of the earth going round the sun."

Becket leaned forwards with his face reddening. "Because it is not true," he bellowed. "The sun goes round the earth, always has, always will. Look up there and you can see it in its course."

"Bah," snorted Simon. "What about the cycles and epicycles upon Aristotle's explanation? How can the Almighty have made a thing so ugly and unbalanced when He also made this"—he gestured fiercely at his Pythagoras theorem—"and this." With his chalk he drew a circle and wrote letters within. "Maimonides saith, 'To know the size of ground within the circle, take the radius, square it and multiply it by seven twenty-thirds, a number which is as infinitely changeable as the mind of the Almighty itself . . .' "

"Why would I want to do that? Will that get me out of here? No. Then what good is it?"

Simon threw down the chalk and glared at Becket, who glared back.

"All this with circles and triangles," he growled. "If I knew no better, I would think you a pagan Greek, not a Jew."

Simon turned his head sharply. "How did you know I am a Jew? I never told you."

Becket screwed up his face and then shook his head. "The Cabbala?"

"Dr Dee is a famous Cabbalist and a Christian. How did you know?"

"I . . . I don't know."

They stared at each other. Becket's belly gave a great triumphant rumble which broke their irritation with one another and he grinned ruefully at the commentary.

"Do we get supper?"

"Sometimes," said Simon. "If you like stockfish that last saw the ocean in Queen Mary's reign."

Becket shuddered. "Good God, not stockfish; I cannot abide the stuff. So shall we finish our good manchet loaf or keep it till tomorrow and risk being robbed of it, Mr Anriques?" he asked more peaceably.

"Eat it," said Simon at once.

They had finished the last of it and Simon had gone to refill the bottle at the water-seller's barrel. Becket was trying to devise a way to scratch the small of his back where a flea had bitten him. It maddened him because the chain between his wrists was just too short to let him reach. Finally he scraped his back against a doorpost like a bear. While he was immersed in that simple pleasure a shadow fell over him and he looked up at Joachim Newton.

"Mr Strangways," said the gaoler. Becket looked blank for a moment.

"That is . . . er . . . yes."

Newton was waiting for something, so he stood up and made a moderately respectful bow.

"Put your hands out."

Suppressing his instant instinctive swoop of terror at the order, Becket did so. The keys rattled, the manacles unlocked and at last he could stretch his arms and rub some more feeling into his hands.

"Ahh," he said, "I shall remember your kindness, Mr Newton."

Newton made a fist and held it under Becket's nose while his three henchmen surrounded Becket and looked as ugly as they could.

"You get no ideas from this, Strangways," he snarled. "These irons still have your name on them and I'll keep them safe for you, never fear. Just because you have a friend in here that pays garnish for you and has some pull at Court don't mean I favour you."

"No, sir," said Becket quietly, addressing the fist. "I shall do my best not to offend." Newton took back his fist and put it on his sword-hilt. "My legs . . ."

"Your legs stay as they are. Not all the garnish in the world will take them cramp-rings off. They're on your warrant, and if I loose you from them I must answer for it to my lord Burghley."

While they were talking, Simon Anriques had come back unnoticed and was standing where he could hear, listening intently.

"So," said Newton triumphantly, "we understand each other."

"Perfectly, sir," said Becket, still quietly.

Newton stumped off, spinning the cuffs on their chains suggestively, and kicking a child in colourful rags playing knuckle-bones by the gate as he went. Fortunately he was too full of importance to notice the copious spittle from Becket that followed him. The keys rattled and the gate crashed behind him.

Becket gave Simon a tense smile. "Jesus, that's better," he said and stretched his arms voluptuously as far to the sides as they would go. "Ahhh." He flexed his fingers, rubbed them together, circled his arms, linked his hands behind his head and stretched his shoulder muscles until they creaked. "I would put even the taking off of a breastplate second behind the taking off of manacles, eh, Simon?"

Simon was muttering to himself, a peculiar expression on his face as he sat down on the step in the setting sun's long shadow and twiddled his thumbs.

"I am indebted to you; was that what you were about when . . ." Becket said and paused. He would have gone on, but cunning stopped him. Why blabber out what he had just understood with Newton's help? So it was a strangely convenient thing that he should be put in the Fleet and wind up sharing a bed with a friend? He knew that all about him strange puissant shadows moved and countermoved against each other, and as a pawn there was no reason in the world why anyone should tell him what they were doing. But if this Simon Anriques was some species of informer set to question him under the guise of friendship, then why let the man know he had been spotted? And if he was not, but a genuine friend indeed, why insult him and perhaps offend him mortally?

He laughed and clapped Simon on the back, not quite accidentally nearly knocking him over, and offered him a sip from the aqua vitae bottle to celebrate.

XLIV

SO OFTEN A SIN is expedient; the blacker it is, the more expedient it seems. Poor child. If there had been any Bethany could have spoken to, or anywhere she could have taken refuge or anything she could do at all, save what she did . . .

Mary also believed she could do nothing else. Should she let the girl be attended by Julia or Kate, who knew so little? Bethany had threatened to kill herself, to cut her wrists and kill the babe and herself both. She offered good money, which Mary had need of suddenly.

But this was one sin Mary had not committed since she shrived herself to Father Hart, and it took her most of the bottle of aqua vitae she carried to bring herself to agree to do it.

Bethany crept over the palace orchard wall in the middle of the night, her heart banging in a sick whirling terror, so that she was afraid it might echo through the empty passage ways. She was dressed in her tiring-woman's kirtle and she had dosed the woman herself and both of the other girls in her room with laudanum. She carried gold under her cloak and counted it a great mercy that the Thames was still frozen, so she needed no boat.

I rested on a cloud and wept crystal tears for her, so that she was speckled with white and shivering when she came into the back room of the Falcon, and this was the bravest thing she had done in all her short life. In the smoky light of tapers she looked away from Mary, who swayed muttering on her stool, and when Julia told her to, she put the money on the table, took all her clothes off and her shift as well, so it would not be marked. Then, with her teeth clattering, she climbed on the straw-covered bed and opened her legs. Kate and Julia held her down, as Mary ordered them, for the pain was very bad.

At last it was done. When she could walk reasonably straight, and was clothed again, Kate led her out and helped her back all the long way to Whitehall, a long icy road through the centre of the sleeping City, and the tears freezing on her face. For all her hardness, Kate had pity for her and let her rest as much as she desired, being also careful to see that there was no blood in their tracks that might give them away. There were a few spots she missed, but they were thankfully licked up by starving rats well before the dawn.

Bethany went to her bed as quietly as she could, huddled up under all her blankets in the soft gown-filled darkness, while the others snored their way through golden vivid dreams. She shook and wept silently at the pain in her groin and the pain and emptiness in her belly. At last the mantle of my mercy went over her and she dozed a little before dawn came at last, and all four of them overslept.

XLV

BECKET TOO WAS PLAGUED by dreams. He had caught it, though it snarled at him and swung its horn and had schooled it on a lunging rein in a churchyard, in the midst of a wide flat land scarred with burnt houses and ruined fields. The unicorn leapt nimbly over the gravestones, and when he looked up again, the world was blotted out by fog. Then he had brought a golden saddle for it and the unicorn had suffered him to put it on its back, and with a strange high certainty he had swung himself up and found the stirrups just as the unicorn screamed in rage and began to buck. He rode it, whooping, hand tight on the pommel while the sky darkened and the circle of soldiers watching him cheered him on. Sir Philip Sidney smiled at his prowess and led the Queen into the ring. There she stood, blazing with jewels and smiling strangely at him. Father Hart stepped out too, and made the sign of the cross, blessing him and smiling. His dreaming self knew the man and wished to smile back, to make up for the fact that his waking self was still mired in ignorance. But such smiles enraged the unicorn further, and while Becket fought desperately with the suddenly tangled reins, the unicorn lowered its horn and charged squarely at the Queen in all her velvet magnificence, stabbing her deep in the breast, breaking her in pieces with his tossing and riding over her. Becket found one of her broken hands caught in his own and woke sweating out of his dream.

He still had hold of a bony hand, though this one was still attached to its owner, whose breath stank in his face. Someone was trying to steal his little bundle of possessions.

He reacted without thought, flung his arm around the man's neck, rolled off the bed on top of him and headbutted viciously. There was a bubbling animal-like cry, he kneed upwards as hard as he could and was rewarded by a whoof of charnel breath. Whoever it was went limp.

"What was that?" asked Simon's voice beside him, sharp with fright.

Becket was panting for breath and greatly pleased with himself as he got up off the floor.

"Some God-damned thief," he growled.

Simon was fumbling with his tinder-box, striking flint on steel and managing to light a stub of wax candle. In the flame they saw other eyes watching and Becket could look at the human skeleton he had just bested. That diminished his victory, because from the look of him the man should barely have been able to walk. He was writhing silently, bleeding from the nose.

"Stupid bastard," Becket said in disgust and then looked round at the watchers. "Anyone else want to try it?" he demanded aggressively. One pair of eyes after another looked away. "Which one of you put him up to it, eh?"

Everyone was lying down again, busily asleep. Simon was still holding up his stub of candle. Becket was revolted at the sores visible through the rents in the man's ragged shirt and hose, the pressure of the man's bones against his blue skin.

"Christ have mercy," he said to himself and then to Simon: "Blow it out, damn you; when will you get another candle?"

Simon blew quickly and stopped the glowing end with a licked finger. "It is the man with the fever," he said. "I heard he is being moved to the beggar's ward tomorrow, since he has no money left."

The man was now sobbing and coughing cavernously. His hot, bony hands were plucking at Becket again. Becket pushed him away.

"God damn you, what do you want?"

He was whispering something. Unwillingly, Becket bent as close as he could bear the stink to hear him. "Cold," the man was saying, "cold." Shivering rattled what was left of his teeth.

"No doubt he wanted your shirt to cover him," Simon said impersonally out of the darkness beside him, lying down once more. "After all, you have two."

"Christ's guts," muttered Becket. He stayed sitting on the side of the bed for minutes together, listening to the man's sobbing, staring at the freezing darkness. At last, after looking around furtively to be sure no one was watching, he unwrapped his other shirt from his pipe, tobacco pouch and bottle, and put it in the sick man's hands. As an afterthought he fished a shilling out of the roll round his middle and handed that over as well. "Go away, for God's sake," he whispered.

"Th . . . thank you, sir," came the answer, the voice shockingly educated. "God bless you."

There was painful shuffling, a few more muttered curses as the man tripped on the corners of beds, and he had gone.

Becket lay down and turned himself over, hating the sour jingle from round his feet, pulled his cloak around him again. Then he found that Simon was still awake and, from the gleam of teeth and eyes, was smiling at him. He scowled.

"Anything to get that stench away from here," he hissed defensively and shut his eyes.

XLVI

HE WOKE AGAIN IN the grey foredawn with a cramp in his belly. He remembered his stupid impulse of the night-time and cursed himself because, after all, he could have worn two shirts and been a little warmer. On the other hand, until he ran out of buttons, he was rich as things were reckoned in the Fleet. Simon was still asleep, curled neatly under his worn cloak, one of the few silent sleepers in that whole ward—a welcome attribute in a bedmate. Becket thought sadly of breakfasts he had eaten a couple of months before in the Low Countries: one in particular when the perennial Dutch fogs had whited out all the land around. They had crossed the river in front of Zutphen before dawn and found Sir John Norris where Becket had expected him to be, entrenched in Warnsfeld Churchyard. There they waited for the fog to clear so they could ambush Parma's relief force to Zutphen. Swaddled in the mist, the camp had been full of the smell of breakfast. The best smell in the world, he thought it— collops of looted bacon frying, and autumn field mushrooms and sausage, and big hunks of bread fried in the same fat. Dyer and Fulke Greville had been there, laughing at him as he shook the skillet over the camp-fire between two grave- stones and swore when the fat spat on him. He was doing the cooking because he had bet them all that he could, each of them five shillings or a Spanish ear, whichever they could come by first. Greville's servant had brought out silver plates looted from somewhere and served up the feast, and Sir Philip had come out of the vestry where he had set up his command post and joined them. Being Sidney, he could not simply enjoy the breakfast, but he had to reduce them all to fits of laughter by making ridiculous poetical discourse ad-lib on the glories of fried bacon and . . .

A firework of excitement made his heart thunder inside him. At last he had remembered something! Indeed the memory shone and echoed in the empty cavern of his skull, so strong the smells were making his mouth water. There was more: afterwards, since the fog had still not lifted and nobody could see more than a couple of yards in front of his face, Sidney had wanted another lesson in sword-play, to make him ready for the battle. Becket had taken one of the blunt swords and gone through a veney with him; as it were, almost a dance. Every move was there, bright and clear against the dreaming fog, as if it had happened moments ago instead of last autumn, before . . . before . . .

Whatever door had opened to let out the happy memory suddenly swung shut again. Still, it was something. It was true. It was real and his breath came short with excitement. He shook Simon's shoulder until the clerk came frowstily awake, muttering and scratching at flea-bites.

"I remember," he said, eyes blazing with it. "I remember being in the Neth- erlands last autumn."

That got Simon's attention. He sat up, yawned and smacked his lips. "Tell me," he said.

Becket told him, far too happy to recall his caution over his convenient friend, and Simon nodded and asked pertinent questions.

"So you know you were Sir Philip Sidney's sword-master," he said. "And he took you with him to the Netherlands. Was that all you did there? Were you helping him in his soldiering?"

Becket shrugged. "I must have been, though I do not remember it at all."

"Were you with him when he was wounded?"

Becket shrugged again and spread his hands. "I told you all that came to me. It has neither a beginning nor an end to the tale. I know not even why I am not still Sidney's sword-master—it was a pleasant office, though I think he had not paid my fees."

"That I can tell you, since anyone else will. Sidney died at Zutphen."

Becket's face darkened and he put his hand to his eyes. "I told him," he muttered. "It was nothing to do with his not wearing his cuisses—damn it, I had none either, there's no armour made will stop an arquebus ball, and it is better to be nimble. No, it was that they did not cut his leg off."

"You were there, at Zutphen?"

"Oh ay, somewhere about. In fact, now I think of it, I was riding one of his horses. Once the fog lifted so we could see, there we were—about five hundred of us; and there they were—the Spaniards had four and a half thousand, well dug in, horse arrayed, arquebuses poking over every bank of turf. God's blood, I nearly voided my guts."

"Why did you not know they were there?" This question was harshly put from another bed by the strongly built man who had lost an eye, Cyclops.

Becket laughed. "Well, sir, there are generals who are curious to hear what is coming towards them and send scouts to find out. And then there are generals who think scouts are a waste of good cash because they *know* what Parma would send with a convoy, and that could be hardly more than a couple of hundred men, what? And they know it by God's gift and because they are the Queen's favourite."

"It was my lord of Leicester's fault then?"

"Who else? Oh ay, he was on the other side of the river, dug in with the rest of the army and safe enough. We came across the river to Sir John with the noblemen and their horses, all afire to fight the Spaniard and win honour for the Queen."

There was a certain amount of muttering. Becket showed his teeth again.

"But Leicester has not the wits of a . . . of a spring lamb. Of course it was his damned fault we were caught napping because we had no scouts. And most of the English knights there egging each other on and in terror of being discovered to fear. I am no knight, thank Christ, I told them to withdraw. But it was not so simple as that, for we had the river at our back, between us and the rest of the army, and the Spaniards knew it." He fell silent for a moment and then continued, a far-away sound in his voice.

"We saw them. I said, 'In God's name, withdraw; they are entrenched, we can ford the river now.' But Sidney said, 'The Spanish horse will surely charge us while we are going down to the water and then they will bring their arquebusiers out of the trenches to the bank and shoot us at their leisure. Those on horses will no doubt mostly live, but all the commoners will be trampled and drowned and shot to pieces.'

"To be sure he had the right of it, he was a good pupil. He decided that honour dictated the English knights must keep the Spaniards busy to give the footmen a chance to cross. He ordered the foot to begin crossing over as soon as the cavalry fighting started. So we mounted and lined up and we charged them."

"What was it like?" asked another voice. "What happened in the battle?"

Becket was in the full flood of reminiscence, too enraptured at his new-found memories to improve on them or notice he had acquired an audience. "It was a better battle than most, for at least I was not in the front line of a pike square, where I usually end up."

"Ay," pointed out the man with one eye, "but if you had been a pikeman you would have crossed before the cavalry."

"Well, Sidney gave me one of his horses; how could I refuse?"

"He knew Sir Philip Sidney?" someone asked reverently from behind Simon. Simon was afraid of breaking the spell and only tilted his head a little.

"He was Sir Philip's sword-master," he whispered. "Quiet."

"Still, it was a damned luxury, riding a horse, not hefting a pike and only a little toothpick of a lance to carry."

There were whispers travelling like waves of the sea, far back to the other end of the ward, and movement, as many of the men came closer to listen.

"There we were, charging together, and the Spaniards so surprised we would attack them when we were so outnumbered, they were not ready for us. We punched straight through them, scattered them."

There was a muted cheer. "Did the Spaniards run?" asked someone eagerly.

Becket spat and grinned. "Jesus, no, they gave us better sport than that. Wherefore should they run when they outnumbered us and had us in a crossfire? We charged them and pushed them back, but then we had to pull back again ourselves, because they were shooting us down. Second time we charged them, Sidney's horse went down, so I gave him mine."

"Why?" asked the eager man who was now sitting on the next bed with his head thrust forward, listening intently. "Was it the love you bore him?" Cyclops snorted.

"What?" asked Becket. "No, he was our captain and he had to be seen, and it was his horse anyway. Besides, it was safer from the musketry on foot, I thought, and I saw some good pickings from a few of the dead Spaniards."

There was a ripple of laughter.

"What happened then?" Simon prompted, praying hard.

"Well, I saw him coming back, at the head of the retreat, and I saw he could not control the horse, which always was a headstrong nag, so I caught its bridle."

"Why could he not—"

"His thigh-bone was shot to pieces," Becket said. "I told you it was. But he wanted to be sure we crossed the river orderly while the Spaniards were disarrayed and their cavalry were having trouble with their horses bolting, so he told me not to lead him and he took the lot of us across the river after the third charge went in, as if nothing had happened."

"And so he got his death."

Becket made a sour face. "No, he got his wound from an arquebus ball, which could happen to any man that ventures on a battlefield. Not his death."

"What was it killed him then?" Simon asked.

Becket shrugged. "Vanity. He would not let the surgeons cut his leg off."

"Would that not kill him by itself?"

"It might," Becket agreed. "About half the time it does, but to try and have the surgeons search and set a broken thigh . . . He could not bear the thought of coming before the Queen with a wooden leg. She cannot abide ugliness, he said so often."

"Did you see him giving his water to the common soldier that needed it?" asked the eager man. "There was a ballad that told of it."

Becket seemed to see his audience for the first time, and as Simon had feared it would, it broke the spell and his eyes lost their far-away look. In fact, he looked like a man awakening from a fever dream.

"Er . . . no," he said, confused. "But he might have done it, that sounds like him."

"What I want to know," asked a ragged bearded man with bloodshot eyes, "is what brought a soldier who was at Zutphen so low as the Fleet Prison so quickly?"

Becket's face stiffened to a mask. Simon was anxious that the sudden excess of phlegmatic humour that had brought back a part of his memory might give him another attack of the falling sickness.

"He has suffered terrible misfortunes," Simon put in quickly. "Among which is a strange loss of his memory."

"Seems to remember Zutphen well enough."

"For the first time," said Becket, thoughtful and pleased. "For the first time in . . . in weeks."

"You could have made it up?" sneered Bloodshot-Eyes.

Becket's eyes narrowed and his fists clenched. "Do you give me the lie, sir?"

"No. It's the truth," said Cyclops authoritatively. "I have fought with Drake and in France, and his tale is the first I heard that made sense of it. All the ballads talk of heroic chivalry and a desperate battle, but not one of them said it was a fighting retreat."

Becket nodded at him. Cyclops was sitting up on his bed with his legs crossed, tailor-fashion. "Moreover, a man inventing himself into a battle will generally come out of it sounding more heroical."

Becket misunderstood, being sensitive on the subject, and his face darkened again.

"Are you saying I am a coward, sir?" he demanded.

"Not at all." Cyclops put his hand up placatingly. "Never at all, sir. But I have heard many soldiers reminisce and being one myself, it is wonderful how invariably we have been in the forefront of every charge, and struck the enemy captain's head off our very selves. Is it not?"

Becket made a grunt of agreement and continued looking at Cyclops. The turnkey opened the ward door and many of the audience scrambled to get to the jakes, but Becket and Cyclops ignored the rush. It came to Simon then that they were assessing each other, and if they had been dogs they would have been walking around each other, sniffing arses and wagging tails high and slowly.

"It is," said Becket. "But I would not claim so much."

"Why not? At the moment, you could turn that story into beer and beef in any boozing ken you chose to enter."

"Alas," said Becket wryly, "I see no beer." He began constructing his suspenders of laces to hold up his ankle chains.

"What brings you here on a Privy Council warrant?" Cyclops asked directly.

Becket did not answer for a while, concentrating on tying knots with his disobedient fingers.

"How did you know . . . ?" Simon asked.

Cyclops turned his attention and looked Simon over, dismissing him, as many fighting men did. "I know most things about this ward, Mr Anriques," he said. "I was awake when they brought him in and I saw the two that brought him, that had 'Walsingham's pursuivant' written all over them. And yesterday I heard Gaoler Newton talking to him and I was curious to learn that his hobbling is in the warrant itself, for generally speaking, Newton is only too pleased to strike off any irons at all for the right money." Cyclops paused and smiled sourly. "Of course, he puts them back on a week later, the better to milk you, so you should be warned. But that was a curious thing in itself, and stranger still to find that Mr Strangways was at Zutphen also. Generally, we do not find heroes in the Fleet. Nor yet traitors."

The words were ugly and hung in the air between them. Ah, thought Simon to himself, his thinking a little dishevelled by lack of decent food, the older dog has just lifted his leg.

Becket's fists were clenched again, but then he looked at them and made them open, sighed quietly.

"Sir," he said, "I will be straight with you. I have taken the falling sickness from a wound to my head, and as my friend here has said, I have somehow mislaid my memory. I have been as strange to myself as you are to me now. This is the first time I have remembered so much, but this much I know. I am no traitor, nor yet no Papist."

"A Privy Council warrant is generally for treason."

"No, sir," contradicted Becket levelly, "it is generally for those that the Privy Council believes to be traitors."

"Are they not traitors then?"

"In the end I expect they confess treason," said Becket bleakly, "whether they are traitors or not."

Cyclops grunted and held out his hand to Becket. "My name is Simpson," he said, "but most men here call me Cyclops."

Becket shook hands and found that he could not match Cyclops's grip. He smiled to hide the pain. "And you are the King of the Eightpenny Ward?"

Cyclops smiled back shrewdly. "Mr Deputy Gaoler Newton might dispute the title."

"I think none other does," said Becket. "Do they?"

"Not twice," agreed Cyclops.

There was a little space in the talk, as something hung in the air unsaid between them. Simon was watching, fascinated. "Shall we come to business?" Becket said quietly. "How much for your protection, Mr Cyclops?"

Cyclops paused. "I generally charge sixpence garnish a week, but I am happy to remit half of this week's contribution in return for your tale."

Becket nodded. "Will you include my friend here?"

"Hm," said Cyclops. "Are you so sure of him?"

Had they forgotten Simon was there? No; they thought so little of him, they did not care. He suppressed the urge to argue and waited to see what Becket would say.

Becket was thinking. "Being the way I am," he answered at last, "I am not sure of anything. But I would like him to have your protection too, in any case."

"Done," said Cyclops. Becket fished money out of his shirt and philosophically handed over the ninepence.

Becket looked consideringly at Simon after Cyclops had gone. "Are you offended at my doubt?" he asked.

Yes, thought Simon, although I know there is no reason why you should trust me so easily if you do not remember me. Perhaps even if you do. But Becket could not hear his thoughts and so he dissembled and shook his head. After all, Becket had paid his protection.

Be not so high-stomached, a cynical commentary inside him said. You have always needed the help of those stronger and better-visioned than yourself; how was it different at school when your elder brothers thrashed anyone who laid a finger on you?

I never much liked it even then, Simon answered himself, feeling suddenly dispirited.

"What made you remember?" he asked Becket as he waited by the door.

"Easy to tell. I was wishing for breakfast and remembered how we fried bread in camp."

Simon swallowed and smiled a little painfully. "That explains it."

"How can I make it happen again?"

"You have not remembered everything?"

"No. Only that island of Zutphen. That I was a sword-master seems right to me. It was a trade I loved."

"You may ply it again when your hands are well."

Becket emerged, smiled sadly, and flexed his hands as Simon went past him.

"What is the final border of your memory?"

"I think . . ." He had wrinkled up his eyes again as if it hurt him to think at all. "I think, when we crossed the river . . . One of the others, Dyer, perhaps, let me hold his stirrup to help me through the water, seeing I had no horse. We got on the bank under cover of the arquebusiers, who had crossed first, and Greville and Norris were helping Sidney down from his horse onto a litter. I went with him."

"Why? Did he ask for you?"

"No . . . I . . . There was blood. Yes. I was bleeding."

"You were wounded?"

"Nothing bad. A sword-cut to the shoulder, I think. One of the surgeons sewed me up when we got to Arnhem."

"You were with Sidney afterwards?"

Becket stopped on the stairs, shut his eyes for a moment, wrestling inwardly until the sweat shone on his face. Simon reached over anxiously and touched his arm.

"Please. Do not over-try yourself. If some came back, then surely the rest will. It is only a matter of patience."

"Mr Anriques, if you only knew how sick I am of patience," said Becket sadly, staring at his feet as he jingled his way down to the courtyard.

XLVII

ETHANY SHOULD HAVE STAYED in bed for at least the next day, only the Queen summoned her and in terror of having a doctor sent to her sick-bed she dared not excuse herself. She put red cinnabar on her cheeks, plugged herself with rags and went to serve her mistress.

All day she stood and sat and fetched and carried and held up her hands so

Lady Bedford could wind wool. When they cleared the floor for dancing, she asked to be excused on account of a megrim and went early to her bed.

But it was not her head that hurt.

Mary saw her there still the next day when she went in to empty the chamber-pots. Did you think chamber-pots and stools empty themselves by magic? Even at Court, where the office of Third Clerk to the Poultry is highly sought after because of the money to be made in it, even there no one becomes a night-soil woman willingly. But Mary had been in fear of arrest.

Young Julia had found her the place at Court through Dame Twiste and through my help. Ann Twiste gave young Pentecost a place in her laundry, and to Mary she gave the work of carrying covered buckets round the back corridors of the Court to collect up the effluvium of the great. It was hard on Mary's old back and bony collar-bones to carry a yoke, but there again, she had no choice. All of the Court within the Virge was out of any pursuivant's jurisdiction. Pliny, or some such learned man, hath said that there are birds that make their dwelling even in the mouth of the crocodile and their nest in his teeth, to clean them, and are safe.

Yes, there is a great house of easement at Court, near the woodyard, that drains into the Thames and plays no small part in colouring that river brown. But it is for the hordes of young men at Court. A woman would be shamefast to walk into such a place and lift her skirts to sit over a hole in a bench surrounded by untrussed men, all talking and smoking tobacco and telling each other evil and lying tales of women. And a Queen's lady must void herself no less than a man, whereof her chamber-pot must in due course be emptied by some such as Mary.

Wherefore should anyone bother to collect and keep night-soil? Well, sir (and I take pleasure in telling you this, which was known also in my day, in Palestine, but, as now, only to women), the finest whitener and cleanser of linen is to scrub it in ten-day-old piss, and accordingly there are barrels in the basement of the laundry, down by the water. So it be well-rinsed, it does not stain yellow but rather takes out stains.

Therefore every two hours or so, in trudges Mary and tips her buckets into the cloth sieves and after much straining and sieving it passes into a barrel to mature. The rest goes down a chute into other large barrels in the foulest cellar in Christendom, by reason of the Queen's niceness with regard to smells. The dung from the cart-horses that haul supplies in by the Court gate and through the woodyard likewise ends there, for the Queen will have no midden in her sight.

Every week the barrels are taken downriver by boat to Essex, where the ordnance men pile it up in great heaps and after several years come and dig it over to find the white saltpetre below. There are other ways of making saltpetre, and none of them can make enough, for there is an endless crying need of it, whether for curing bacon or fixing dyes or making gunpowder. You find this distresses you? I cry you mercy for your delicate stomach. Perhaps you had best run and find yourself some pretty book of sonnets or some great lolloping description of an Arcadia where men have their pillicocks sewn up tight and their arses also and women likewise, and all is as delicate as can be.

So it was that Sister Mary came in upon Mistress Bethany, not knowing her, nor who she was at the time, save that she was a maid of honour and in her truckle-bed at an unseasonable hour. She was curled up there with the great curtains of her kirtles hanging up on either side, her face flushed and her forehead dry as a bone.

Mary was not so drunk as usual. She saw the child and recognised her at last and something from forty years before rose up inside her. Mary went to her, hearing her moan, and touched her to find her burning. Bethany woke then but was disordered by the heat, and pulled away. Or perhaps she found Mary as frightening and foul as a witch in a fairy-tale. Or perhaps she knew her as the witch that attended her.

"No," she said, and muttered.

"Shall I fetch your tiring-woman?" Mary asked her.

"No," Bethany said, forcing her eyes to focus. "Thank you, I need nothing."

Mary liked her for a polite child that did not tell her to begone with her stinking buckets. She found her pot and saw what was in it, which could not be put with the rest, but must be tipped quietly onto the fire instead. And whose fault was it she was in such a state? Mary knew she had been drunk the night before last, sin piled on sin, and a beautiful girl that might have been her own granddaughter destroyed by it.

"My dear," Mary said, pity and shame blocking her throat, "young mistress," she added lest she offend, "you must see a doctor. I fear you are distempered with fever."

Bethany shrugged and tossed herself over.

"Please leave me alone; I shall be well enough."

Mary brought her a cup of wine from the flagon by the fire. She drank, being made thirsty by fever, and then huddled the blankets up over her shoulders. So Mary put a cloak across the bed to keep her warm, made up the fire. Then she hesitated before she took her buckets on the yoke across her shoulders again. It was only a kindly thought, but she must still have had her thinking disordered with booze or she would never have been so foolish. Certainly it was no command of mine.

All she did to bring her doom was to write a note for Bethany's tiring-woman, that the girl needed a doctor and quickly and must be tended and not left alone in a poky airless little back room of the palace. There were pens and paper on a table, scented for sending to lovers and rejecting sonnets therefrom, all part of that ardent complex lying foolery they call Courtly Love. It pleased Sister Mary's vanity to be able to write as fair a hand as she wished still, for all the arthritis knotting her joints and the long time since she last had anything to turn into writing. She thought to herself that if only she had been a man, she could have been a good screever, better than some of the old monks that did such work. So it was self-indulgence. But what could she do, guilty as she was? Either she left ill enough alone, or she tried to help the poor maid what way she could, and that was all she could do. She had no gardens to pluck feverfew, no willow-bark nor garlic to give. Certainly she could not wait there for someone to come since she was late on her round as it was, and had to make a journey to the wheelbarrow with full buckets to replace them with empty ones before she could continue. Still, she should have known better. What did it matter to Mary if the silly bitch died?

The children of Eve help each other to ease their own hearts, I think. That night Mary sat in a boozing ken by Charing Cross, refusing to look at me or speak to me, smoking her pipe and drinking the world to softness, bright lights and a whirlpool of blessed forgetfulness.

XLVIII

THERE ARE SHOPS AND stalls in London where you may buy ruffs to wear at Court; some starched with blue or yellow starch, some plain white. Those who wear them or admire them never know how painful thing it is to make a ruff: yard upon yard of white Holland linen drawn up and stitched to the compass of a neckband. What you have then is a flabby thing, not the glory of fashion that it will become. After making, it must be dipped in starch and part-dried carefully upon a line. Tubes of metal must be put in each fold to tease it out evenly with the help of a metal rod hot from the fire. And at last comes wax to seal the open ends, alternately, to make a multiplicity of figures of eight. And then it can be worn at most for a few days or a week, if you are not serving the Queen herself, and then it must be washed and starched and ironed and sealed with wax again. In every single ruff around every single courtly neck is a week's work for a woman.

The recusant Catholic gentlewomen in the Fleet had never needed to win a living before, but the expenses of the prison and recusancy fines are such that they would soon be destitute if they did nothing. All the skills they had, apart from the efficient running of large manors and many servants, were their needles, and perhaps the making of banqueting stuff, for which there is scarcely any need in the Fleet. And so they sat in a circle, every day including Sundays, and stitched frantically at one part or another of the ruffs. Those they finished were sent in their flabby state to a nearby starching-house to be finished off and then sold throughout London. Each woman was paid a penny for each ruff finished in a day, and so, by working all the hours of daylight, they could just keep pace with the costs of shared beds and bad food without resorting to the other profession of womankind. It is a poor trade and an invitation to immorality for any girl who thinks herself too fair to stitch linen until her eyes squint.

The gentlewomen making their ruffs were sitting where they could watch the great inner gate of the Fleet Prison yard. At ten of the clock, it opened to admit friends and relatives of the prisoners who could pay Newton the right garnish. Their eyes silently sorted among the new faces and at last there was a rustle and shift among them, for some of them saw the man they awaited.

He was not tall, though he was strongly built and walked with a swordsman's swagger. His hair was black and his square face had a sharp canny look. This time he was not wearing homespun, but a good gentleman's suit of berry-brown wool. He strolled as if he were not on the list of every pursuivant in London, to be captured dead or alive, and tipped his hat coolly to Newton. Then he began by examining the trestle-tables and bought several of the things thereon, before sauntering over to speak to the one of the ruff-making ladies as she unpicked the stitches that had mysteriously gone crooked. Intent on them, he had not noticed who else was in the busy yard, over by the steps up to the Eightpenny Ward.

That was the moment when Simon, who had been artistically forging the signature on a counterfeit Bedlam begging licence, looked up and saw Becket staring at a visitor talking to the gentlewoman making ruffs like a rabbit at a stoat.

He came to his feet, almost upsetting his ink-bottle, and took the shillings from the beggar without even noticing the man had underpaid him. Becket had gone the colour of old putty and was shaking.

"What is it?" Simon asked, taking his elbow. "What has happened?"

Becket's mouth opened, worked; no sound came out. He looked at Simon and swayed.

"Come," said Simon briskly. "Let us fetch you upstairs now and lay you down."

Becket was resistless and his cumbered feet stumbled on the worn steps. Clucking him along like a child, Simon got him into the Eightpenny Ward and all the way to the end, where he sat down on the side of the bed and put his head in his hands.

"Lie down now, sir; perhaps we may avoid another fit if you rest."

Obediently Becket hefted his feet up and lay straight, looking at the stained ceiling where some flakes of paint still clung. The man with fever was still in his bed by the door, but seemed to be sleeping. Simon sat down next to Becket.

"Go and . . . go and stop anyone from coming," said Becket slowly, "especially the . . . the man that was talking to the . . . the ladies. Keep him away from me. Please."

"Are you sure?"

Becket looked at him for the first time. His eyes were terrible.

"For Christ's sake, go."

Worried and puzzled, Simon got up and went to the end of the ward. He paused by the bed of the man with fever, concerned at his ominous stillness, then shrugged and carried on.

The Eightpenny Ward was silent and dim, smelling of unwashed men and worse linen, mouldy straw and damp plaster, of rats and fish and the foul jakes.

Becket turned on his stomach and pressed his fists into his eyes. After all his agonising and straining, the thing when it happened had been simple enough. He had looked at a man across the courtyard and known him as Father Hart. He had known . . . Somehow a petard had been laid against the gates of his locked memory and blasted them open and knowledge was boiling round his mind like a battle.

All the weight of what he had been doing since Zutphen had come slamming down around him and it terrified him no less than ever. No wonder his memory had gone a-wandering; a man might well run witless at the thought. If the Queen knew what he knew, she would . . . Well, to be sure she would hang, draw and quarter him, but she would also cut his tongue out and probably his eyes to make certain he could not pass it on. And to be fair to her, he would have done the same if he had been in a like position, for reasons of state.

I am a dead man, he thought. Oh, Christ.

Other lumps of knowledge came swirling to him in the mêlée. He knew now that Simon Anriques was in fact Simon Ames and he had thought the man dead four years gone.

"The bastard," he muttered, writhing with rage. "That bastard bloody Jew, I wept for him."

Simon had been an inquisitor for Walsingham. Once an inquisitor, always an inquisitor, and there could be no coincidence in his being in the Fleet, none at all. Kin as rich as the Ames and Nunez families would have bailed him out and paid his mere five thousand pounds of debt before Newton so much as clapped eyes on him. And Nunez had treated Becket in the Tower when he was helpless as a child . . . God damn them for their cunning kindness, God damn them all. They were working for the Queen, they were trying to find out how much he knew . . .

He was panting now with fear. If they knew his memory had come back, they would . . . The least of it would be a return to the Tower. Little Ease, no doubt, and then into the basement of King William's Tower and hanging by his arms again, now they were better. God knew what else they would do if they thought it worthwhile, or rather he did know, too well, and had no false expectations that he would now be able to keep his mouth shut if they did them.

What could he do? How could he save himself? Part of it was obvious enough: he must give no sign to anyone that he had remembered. On the other hand, Father Hart would want to talk to him, to make contact and perhaps even tell what he had found. Presumably he had not caught up with the witch or the Book of the Unicorn because he was still in England and not on a boat to France.

Becket could admit to a partial remembrance and perhaps learn how much Father Hart had discovered. Father Hart believed Becket to be a repenting Catholic called Ralph Strangways who was helping Father Hart to find out the holder of the Queen's deadly secret so it could be used against her by Parma. Only Becket had known what he planned to do if they found the Book of the Unicorn, if it contained what it was said to contain. Which he must not admit to knowing.

"If I stay in the Fleet, I'll let it slip somehow," he said to himself. "I must get out."

And then where?

"The Netherlands, of course," he muttered. "Not even Davison could find me there."

Davison's name alone had the power to cause his throat to stop with fright. If Davison ever laid hands on him again . . .

"No," he said to himself with finality, "not alive. Never again."

But he could not go back to the Netherlands immediately. He had given his word to a dying man that he would find the Queen's Book of the Unicorn.

12

IN THE TWO WEEKS after the battle of Zutphen Sir Philip Sidney went from being a lanky, elegant man with a face a little like a sheep to a skeleton with great bruised eyes. Becket had pitied him, for Sidney had never been wounded before, was inexperienced in pain, and his leg was about as bad as it could be and still be attached to his body. By one of the strange miracles of musketry, the ball which shattered his thigh-bone had not touched the great leg artery and so he had not bled to death, although he had bled a great deal. Sidney would not be separated from Becket, refusing to let him be treated in the main camp by the trenches of Zutphen, clinging to him surprisingly. Becket could not remember much about their journey by barge to the house of Mlle Grui-thuissen, since he too had lost blood copiously from his shoulder slash and the surgeon had bled both of them a further four ounces on the way, to guard against infection.

Becket did remember trying to talk some sense into Sidney, who turned out to have a surprising degree of obstinacy in him, despite his loss of sanguine humour.

"Have them take your leg off," he remembered saying gruffly, while they lay side by side on their pallets and the barge wallowed its painful way behind the plodding horse on the tow-path, through the rocking and scraping of innumerable locks, to the little town of Arnhem. "Have them cut at the mid-thigh where the bone is sound, and good riddance."

"No," Sidney had said through his clamped teeth. "I will not be a cripple."

"Christ's guts, man," Becket had said brutally. "You *are* crippled. No more tournaments for you, no more battles. The only choice is to be a dead cripple or a live one."

"No."

Becket was the stronger, had not in fact wanted to go to Arnhem at all, only Sidney had insisted on it. He was weak with blood-loss and his shoulder burned monstrously, but it had only been a long sword-cut from above, easily washed with aqua vitae and sewn up. There had been no need for boiling oil in the wound to sear out the poison of gunpowder, no need for the surgeon's fingers, nails in mourning with old blood, to go probing about in it looking for a ball and wad. To be sure he was weak, but beef and beer three times a day and a week's rest, and he knew from experience he would be well enough, providing the wound did not go sick.

At the moment, though, he was no more able to move than Sidney, since his head reeled and pounded and his breath came short if he so much as sat up.

"Listen," he snarled sideways at Sidney, who was looking mulish. "The bone is shattered above the knee, it was poking through like kindling wood, I saw it. How can you ever get it straight?"

"I have heard it could be done."

"Where? When? Who by? And I want to meet the man it was done to as well, I want him to walk in here and show me his two straight legs. I am no surgeon, but I know this much: if broken ends of the bone have gone through the skin, that's it, that is the end, for bad airs get into the flesh and it sickens and blackens and if it be not cut off at once, you die screaming. Do not argue with me, sir, I have seen it, I have seen it too bloody often. Call the surgeons and have them cut."

Sidney was clamping his mouth again, the boat's rocking was moving him against the splints on his leg. He shook his head.

"Are you afraid of the pain?" Becket demanded rudely. "There's no blame to you if you are, only have courage. If the surgeon is good enough, it takes but thirty seconds . . ."

"I am not afraid of the pain."

"Why then? Why do you want to die stinking?"

"I . . . I must be able to serve the Queen. I must not be . . . hideous to her. She will have no man about her at Court if he is not whole and good to look on and she likes me little enough as it is."

"For God's sake . . ."

"I owe at least thirty thousand pounds, some of it to the Queen. I must try and recoup it, and where else can I do it but at Court? Would you have me search for Raleigh's El Dorado with my wooden leg, eh, Becket? Now be silent."

"No, you can order me no more, sir; I am no longer your sword-master since you have no further need of one. If you want, I'll sit by you and hold your hand, but I say to you again: have the surgeons cut it off. At once. Before it goes black . . ."

"No."

Sidney shut his eyes and pretended to sleep, which Becket knew was a lie, since his hands were clamped to the side of his litter until his knuckles shone like dice.

For days Becket stormed and begged as far as his lack of blood would allow him and Sidney remained obdurate. A French surgeon was found for him by the Earl of Leicester, chewing his moustache and red with worry and misery. Apparently it was the very man who claimed to have searched and set just such a wound before, successfully. True to his promise Becket let his hand be crushed while Sidney lay strapped to a table and the surgeon did his work. After an hour of probing, cutting and moving bits of bone around, the surgeon shook his head and said in broken English that it was beyond his power to know where the ball had gone, but at least he had found the wad. Instead of boiling oil, he advised a mixture of honey and rose-water to be poured in the wound to counteract the gunpowder poisoning, and said it was possible the wound might heal even with the ball still lodged.

Becket felt sorry he had accused Sidney of being afraid of the pain of amputation; he doubted it could have been much worse than such a long hour of searching and Sidney had said nothing throughout.

In the days following, to Becket's astonishment, Sidney seemed to be getting better. Every day, morning and evening, he sniffed suspiciously at the bandages for the deadly smell of gangrene, and did not find it. To be sure, Sidney lost flesh like a wax puppet left by the fire and after a week had sores on his back from lying so long, but considering he should have been dead by then, was remarkably well.

By that time Becket was up and moving about, a little doddery, but gaining strength every day. The surgeon returned to take out his stitches and considered that if he moved his arm enough to keep the wound soft, he would find no harm come to him from the slash.

Sidney's leg was dressed and it seemed to be well enough; it was wasted and pale below the crater left by the bullet but had not gone blue or black and he had feeling in his toes and could move them. It was only the way he would keep flaring up into fevers and then fall into heavy sleep that concerned the surgeon, who believed that the bullet was releasing its gunpowder poisons within.

Becket, being the man he was and in the rare condition for him of having some money, soon found the boozing kens of Arnhem and a couple of pretty punks. With them as an incentive his Dutch returned to him, which gave him great satisfaction, quite apart from the buttery charms of the girls themselves. Whenever Dyer or Fulke Greville or the Earl of Leicester was there to keep Sidney company, Becket would quietly slope off to drink geneva and aqua vitae with his girls.

Late one afternoon—Becket had just done telling them for the fifth time the sad story of how a woman he loved in London had fallen with child by him and then refused to marry him, but instead married some bastard burgher with a fatter purse—he noticed that there was another man in the taproom who kept looking at him, as bony-faced as a horse, wearing the buff coat of a soldier and a nervous expression. Becket toasted him in Dutch and invited him over.

The man wanted a private talk, so Becket regretfully left his girls and went out into the street with the man.

"Is it true you are Sir Philip Sidney's sword-master?" the man wanted to know. Becket agreed that he was, and being a little drunk, added some stirring stuff about how he had saved Sir Philip's life at Zutphen.

"Sir, I will be straight with you," said the man in English. "I am a Catholic Englishman in the service of Parma."

Becket's hand instantly went to his sword-hilt.

"Please sir, I have . . . important information concerning the Queen. Please."

"Why would you care about her, being a traitor?" Becket demanded, thrusting his face close to the man's.

"To be a Catholic is not necessarily to be a traitor," said the man steadily, "although those around the Queen would make it so. If the Queen would allow it, I would far rather fight for her, but she will not and I must live, knowing no other trade."

"Hmf," said Becket, moving back but still keeping his hand near his sword.

The man smiled a little. "Besides," he said, "it may well be the Providence of God that sent me to fight for Parma. Otherwise I would never have heard of this matter."

Becket and the man had reached the canal-side, and they sat themselves down at one of the sentry-places.

"Well?" Becket wanted to know.

"Parma has got wind of a deadly libel against the Queen, something that would turn most of her subjects against her."

"This is nothing new," sniffed Becket, thinking sadly about his two blonde pigeons who had no doubt found other company. "The Papists are always publishing some such filth about her. What is it this time? That she has borne three children by the Earl of Leicester and Raleigh is her new paramour?"

The man grinned. "No. This is a different thing altogether. I want to show it to your master, Sir Philip Sidney."

"Why not me?"

"With respect, sir, you are not Sir Francis Walsingham's son-in-law."

"Why not tell it to Sir Francis himself?"

"Because, sir, Walsingham is in England and I am in the Netherlands and I have no wish to risk the rack. I want to pass the knowledge I have to someone who can see it investigated and then my conscience will be clear."

Becket nodded. "Well, what kind of proof do you have that this libel is not some chimera you have dreamt up for gold?"

"A letter from Parma to the King of Spain concerning it."

Becket raised his eyebrows. "How did you get it?"

"Among other things, I am the courier."

Becket laughed and shrugged. "Very well, I'll get you in to meet Sidney."

The meeting happened that night, while Sidney was working on a song to be called "La Cuisse Rompue," upon what he called the sad and hilarious matter of his wounding. He was in good spirits and had eaten well, showing no signs of fever.

Sidney had never had much to do with Walsingham's intelligence gathering, but he knew enough to be able to open the courier's bag secretly by taking a plaster-of-Paris impression of the seals.

Within was a number of letters, some militarily quite useful, but only one double-sealed in oiled silk. With great care, they unpicked the stitching. Parma had used a simple numerical cypher combined with code-names in clear: some were easy to understand, such as "Jezebel" for the Queen, and some more difficult, such as the Book of the Unicorn.

Sidney called one of his secretaries to make copies of all the letters, while he talked affably with the courier who insisted that his name was Smith.

When the copying was done, they resealed the silk and the bag itself and gave Smith gold for his service and safe conduct out of Arnhem—although, as Becket said, it was equally likely he had been sent to show them a wild goose to chase, to distract them from something else.

Becket knew Spanish and Sidney had been learning it. They spent much of the night on cracking the cypher, over a jug of wine and some sausage. After a few hours' sleep they went back to it, Sidney quite merry to have something to keep his mind off his various pains and his boredom. Becket told him of the little Jew, Simon Ames, who could undoubtedly have cracked the cypher in an hour, but unfortunately was dead and Sidney agreed. He had known the man, who had in fact recommended Becket as his sword-master, but this way was more amusing.

At last they had prized open the oyster, to find within a very black pearl, as Sidney said, if it was a true one.

A Jesuit had come to Parma straight from England, saying that he had met an old woman, once a nun. The old nun claimed to have come by a manuscript book of the Queen's, embroidered with a unicorn, which contained her last will and testament, written when she was fourteen, that named the Queen of Scots as her heir. It also contained a confession as to how she had come so close to death, and that was the gunpowder in the bomb.

There was no amusement in it at all when the cypher finally yielded. Sidney had gone white when they realised what was emerging from their work. Becket, who was far less of an idealist, had begun wondering uncomfortably how far he could get from England and still live somewhere reasonably civilized. Constantinople, perhaps. He had heard that Turks could keep six wives if they wanted.

Sidney's bony hands were shaking as they held the scrawled paper.

"If Parma's 'Jezebel' is the Queen . . ." he whispered.

"She must be; who else commands the Earl of Leicester?"

"Then . . . then she is no virgin, nor never has been since she was fourteen."

Becket nodded glumly. "If it be true. It could be a ruse."

Sidney rallied a little at the suggestion. "Of course it could be a black Papist

lie to dissever us from her allegiance," he said. "But . . . but see here, it seems
Parma believes it. This is addressed to Father Parsons in Rheims, asking him to
send another priest to track down the old nun and buy her book from her."

"That might be a lie also. For our benefit."

"It seems genuine."

"Well, it would, if it were a lie. Why did the Jesuit not buy the book at
once, when he heard about it last year?"

"See here, it says he was hunted and could not stay to search for her again."

Sidney was silent, staring out of Mlle Gruithuissen's long glazed window,
watching the people in the street distort and ripple as they passed by the glass.

"If it is a lie, it is a black and wicked one which must be stopped," he said
at length, "If it is the truth . . ."

"Depend upon it, they lie."

"But if it is the truth . . . then the Queen is no better than a whore." Sidney's
voice shook.

"Well, Sir Philip," Becket said uncomfortably, "the Papists have always said
she has the Earl of Leicester in her bed and Sir Christopher Hatton in her bed
and now Sir Walter Raleigh; God knows they have given her the entire Court
as her lovers before now. Why are you so distressed?"

Sidney's wraithlike fist came down on the table next to his bed with a
surprising crack. "Because no one could live five minutes at Court and think it
true," he shouted. "No one could know my father-in-law or my uncle and believe
a word of it. Jesus Christ, Becket, if Walsingham thought for a second she was
not chaste, he would never serve her, never in a thousand years. Knowing the
man, if he thought her a woman of such immorality, he might well work against
her. At least he would remove to the Netherlands. He would have nothing to
do with her. And my uncle of Leicester also. I have heard him talk about her,
how in their youth she would dance with him and ride with him, and tap his
cheek or lean on his shoulder and it would drive him wild because he desired
her and she would never yield."

"Surely it is a lie, Sir Philip . . ."

"But it is a plausible lie," shouted Sidney, his hollow cheeks flushing un-
healthily. "It's the most plausible lie they have ever told. Not Leicester, not
Hatton, not now when her every move is surrounded by eyes, but long long ago,
in her brother's reign, when she was a chit of a girl. And there was scandal then
about her, I know, my uncle told me of it. There were rumours that she was
with child of Thomas Seymour, the Admiral of England."

"Who?" Becket asked, puzzling at the new name. Sidney huffed with impatience.

"The Lord Protector's brother, who married King Henry's last Queen. They say he tried to oust his brother from the Protectorship by kidnapping the boy-King Edward one night; only one of the Court lap-dogs raised the alarm and King Edward's guards were roused when he shot it. He died on the block for treason and nearly dragged the Princess Elizabeth down with him."

"He was her paramour? When she was a girl?"

"She was his ward, she lived in his household after he married Catherine Parr. There were evil rumours, it was said that Catherine Parr found her in Seymour's arms. Certainly she was sent from the household. When Seymour was arrested, they arrested her servants as well and the Council had her interrogated for a week on suspicion she was part of Seymour's plot. She stayed away from Court for nine months or more. And then she returned. My uncle said he himself believed ill of her, as the whispers passed around, but then when he saw her, so slender and pale and always thereafter until she came to the throne, always dressed in grey or white, as almost a nun . . ."

Sidney buried his face in his hands and struggled for breath.

"Sir, sir," said Becket, "be calm, please. This is only a Papist lie."

"You know it could be true," Sidney whispered.

"I know simply talking of it as we are doing is certainly treason," said Becket grimly. "I say we burn the papers, forget the whole thing . . ."

"We cannot. The original letter is on its way to Rheims."

"Intercept the man, kill him; burn those letters also."

"To put such a thing in train, I must tell my uncle," Sidney answered quietly. "Do you think I should do that?"

Becket took a breath to answer, then thought a little further. "Perhaps not," he allowed.

"Do you think I should tell my father-in-law?"

Becket winced. "No."

"If the Queen is not our Belphoebe, if she is not our Astraea, if she is no more a virgin than a strumpet at the Falcon, then she is nothing. She has founded her Court on a lie, a most corrupt and abject and wicked lie."

Becket shrugged. "So? Why are you so distressed?"

"Do you not care? Why does it not distress you, Becket?"

"I have known many whores. They seemed no worse than other women, and some of them better because more willing to please." He tried to make a joke of it, to lighten the atmosphere, but it fell flat. It came to him then that one of the things that made Sidney what he was lay in a kind of willed innocence. The ethereal ladies of his phantasy were one thing; real women were too practical and earthy for him. As far as Becket knew, he had had no carnal dealings with women at all until he was handfasted to Frances Walsingham.

For the first time Becket wondered if Sidney was a boy-lover, like the Earls of Oxford and Southampton, but no, that was too simple an answer. As the Greeks said, the only real friendship was between men: how could a man be friends with creatures as unpredictable and passionate as women? True, the Queen had a mind like a man's, but was herself alone, the only Phoenix of her age. The Virgin Queen. And if she was no virgin . . . The people of Scotland had risen against their Queen and thrown her out when she had proved to be ruled by her quim; the same might yet happen to the Queen of England. Certainly none of the Puritans would ever again hail her as God's Protestant Champion.

Sidney was shaking his head violently. Becket knew that Sidney too was something of a Puritan: one who thought that the pristine purity of the reformed religion was the only thing that mattered. By extension, one who valued purity above all. "We must find out the truth of it," Sidney was saying. "We must. God who brought Smith to us, God requires it of us."

"Surely it can wait until you are well," Becket said, not liking the brightness of Sidney's eyes nor the flush in his cheeks.

"It will have to," Sidney agreed, "although you could make enquiries for me, could you not?"

Becket sighed. He had thought that was coming. Sidney believed his soldiering and skill with a sword meant more than it did, and had refashioned Becket in his poet's mind as a chivalric knight of the Queen, such as Sidney wished to be.

"Well, I am no intelligencer, nor yet a pursuivant," he said unhappily.

"But you are the only man who can do it," Sidney blazed at him. "We can tell no one else; this is too grave a matter."

"Not even Walsingham?"

"Certainly not Walsingham. For the sake of his health, if no other reason. If he learnt of this, he might sicken again."

"And so might you, Sir Philip; this is overmuch excitement for you."

"Then find out the truth of it, Becket. Go to Rheims and seek out the priest

Father Parsons sends and learn whatever he knows. Will you do that for me? Will you learn the truth of this?"

Becket groaned inwardly.

"Well, I . . ."

"Come," coaxed Sidney, with the smile that had charmed so many Princes, "you found out the Queen's assassin, you saved her life, and saved mine and my father-in-law's credit also."

"Most of that was done by Simon Ames."

"But without your courage it could not have been done at all. She would have been dead and we would all be prisoners of Spain by now."

"But I . . ."

"I can do nothing." Sidney said. "You are healed of your wound. You can act for me in this. Say that you will?"

"But how can I discover this priest?"

"Go to the English Seminary at Rheims."

"They will not trust me."

"See here." Sidney was pawing amongst the bits and pieces on the table by his bed. "Take the seal-moulds and the cypher. We will make you a letter of recommendation from Parma, that you are to help whoever Father Parsons sends in his search, that you are a Catholic Englishman working for Parma against the Queen."

"Christ Almighty," said Becket, appalled at the thought. "If I am caught in England, they will hang, draw and quarter me. At least."

"Never fear, Becket." said Sidney. "I will write a letter to my father-in-law explaining what you are doing. There will be no danger to you there."

"Hmm." Becket was very unhappy. "I want a letter from you in your own cypher to carry with me, in case of accidents."

"Very well. What name will you use? Ralph Strangways might be good— an old Catholic family and they will not know what became of him. We could draft the letter now."

"I have not said I would do it."

"But you will." This was Sidney at his most dangerous, his most charming. "This is a noble adventure, David; no other man could hope to do it."

"Never pour out your Court-honey for me, Sir Philip; it is wasted," Becket growled.

Sidney paused, as if recoiling after a cavalry charge and considering how he would change his attack to get through.

"Then I put it to you like this. Think of the Book of the Unicorn as it were a long-buried siege weapon, a store of gunpowder, a petard directly under the Queen's throne. Or no, rather the rumour of one. We do not know if it be there or not, only we have heard that it might be. If such a thing were so, would you not bend every effort to find it out?"

"Ay, but a man may be blown up by his own petard, let alone someone else's."

"Would that stop you in the face of real gunpowder? I think not. Come, let us be done with arguing, let us draft the letter and encypher it and I will make an attempt at Parma's signature and use the seal-moulds. It will be a work of art."

Becket sighed. "Oh, very well," he said grudgingly. "On condition that then you will put all this aside and calm yourself."

Sidney immediately put down the papers and settled himself on his pillows. "There," he said, "I am calm. I will put it from my mind on the instant the letter is sealed. Now give me your word you will hunt down the truth of this matter?"

Unwillingly, grimly certain it would lead to his death, Becket gave his word.

L

THE SURGEONS BLAMED IT on the musket-ball still lodged somewhere in Sidney's thigh muscles, but Becket blamed it on the weight to Sir Philip's mind of suspecting the Queen's chastity, the destruction of his belief in England as a blessed land next door to Heaven, ruled by an earthly Virgin Queen. If there had been proof come to the Vatican that I, the Blessed Virgin Mary, was no such thing, but a well-known legionary's drab, there might have been a similar upset among the faithful. Although no doubt most would have refused to believe it and the Inquisition would have dealt with those who found and published such blasphemy. Behold the weakness of heretics: they set such store by truth and so little by faith. For truth is a hard and cruel thing, and faith, not always opposed to it, beautiful and comfortable for those who can keep hold of it. For what am I but a thing built of faith, many centuries of devotion, founded on a far more ancient love? Do you think that a peasant girl from Nazareth is all that I am? I too sit upon an usurped throne.

But none of this could the misfortunate poor young man consider, being entranced by that chimera truth. Not even in delirium could he take comfort from my mantle, believing me either a she-Devil or a dream of his old idol, the Queen of England. Nor could he any longer take refuge in the Arcadian garden of his mind, since that, too, he believed, was founded on a lie.

Sidney's wife, Frances Walsingham, arrived from England and took over the care of him from Mlle Gruithuissen's servants, although she was pregnant again. She served her lord as a good wife should, well-trained by her mother, gentle and quiet and dosing him with feverfew and comfrey and willow-bark for the headaches and sweats and fevers that were plaguing him, against the advice of the surgeons and physicians. She even shame-facedly brought out a supposed saint's knuckle in a silver-chased bottle, which her old wet-nurse had recommended as a sure bone-knitter, but Sidney refused to have it near him since it was superstitious papistical trash and probably a pig's knuckle anyway. Though it would have helped him could he have had faith in it.

Becket fed the copies of Parma's letter and their translations of it into the fire, although he kept their forged letter of recommendation from Parma, and made enquiries about the man who had named himself Smith, but could not find him. With Lady Sidney now attending Sir Philip, he was free to practise sword-play again with some of the other convalescing soldiers, and drink with them in the boozing kens. He did not feel more than a couple of twinges of guilt for abandoning Sidney, since Fulke Greville and his other noble friends were now with him most of the time and half their talk was in Latin and the other half in what sounded like English but was too abstruse and allusive for Becket to understand. And yet he could not leave for France without knowing how Sir Philip was faring.

And so it was several days after the incident of the letter before he called on Sidney's sick-room again, to find it full of the scent of incense and herbs and Sidney more cadaverous than ever.

"Oh, Christ," he said, snuffing at the stink of mouse under the sandalwood and frankincense. He came and sat by the bed, and found that Sidney seemed to be sleeping, though shaking with chill under a mound of coverlets. His colour had looked better from a distance, but that was an ugly rash boiling up from under his shirt. Close to him the smell was unmistakable.

Dumb with regret, Becket sat down by Sidney's bed and touched his hand.

"I wish you had had the damned thing off, like I told you," he muttered eventually. "Stupid bloody vanity."

"*Vanitas vanitatem, omnes vanitatem est*," whispered Sidney and heaved his eyes open. "*In principio erat mortem et in saecula saeculorum . . .*"

"Leave off your schoolmastering, Sir Philip," Becket said. "Daily beatings in my youth never got any Latin into my skull, and where they failed you will certainly not succeed."

Sidney focussed his eyes on Becket and smiled vaguely.

"Then the fault lies with your teacher, not you," he said. "Latin is by far an easier language than Dutch, and you needed no beating to acquire that."

Becket grinned. "Alas for it, but there are precious few whores that speak Latin, unless there be a few in the Vatican City."

A faint frown wrinkled Sidney's forehead. "I was garbling my Latin in any case," he said. "Half dreaming. Have you made any progress in . . . in the Queen's Great Matter?"

He had very much hoped that Sidney would have forgotten the whole thing, but was not surprised to find he was wrong.

"No sign of Smith. As you said, I will have to travel to Rheims to discover anything about him," he said unwillingly. "Never fear, it is all in hand, you must bend your mind to getting well."

Sidney shook his head infinitesimally. "Everyone must die, Becket."

Becket shut his eyes, although he had expected nothing else, given the smell. "You were mending last I saw."

"The surgeons say the poisons from the bullet . . . They say, given a strong body I might have fought them off, but . . . not strong enough. Too weak."

Becket patted his hand, which was bluish and cold. "Never blame yourself."

"And . . . and I have not put you in my will. How could I forget . . ."

"For God's sake, Sir Philip, I expected nothing."

"At least your fees . . ."

"To hell with my fees. I saw the way you were spending on the troops; I never expected them."

Sidney reached for the little silver bell on the table and could not manage it.

"Ring for Frances," he said, and Becket did.

She came, soft-footed, and stood respectfully with her hands clasped. She had the ivory skin and black hair of a Spanish lady and rings under her eyes.

"Frances, will you fetch my black Court doublet from the chest, the second-best, and cut off all the buttons, give them to Mr Becket," Sidney ordered.

"You cannot give me your—" Becket protested.

"I am reliably informed I will not need buttons in the grave," said Sidney.

"Well, but to be buried in . . ."

"That's why I told her to fetch my second-best suit," said Sidney with a ghostly smile, and Becket had to smile in return.

Frances Sidney had gone and Becket sat next to the dying man and wished Sidney were more like the Earl of Leicester or even the cold and correct Greville, so his heart would feel less squeezed by his loss. But Sidney could no more help making friends of the men he met than he could stop breathing, and Becket had been chastely seduced with the rest.

"Are you afraid of death, David?" Sidney asked.

Becket had to struggle to answer evenly. "Yes," he said, which he would have admitted to no man else. "Of course."

"You give no sign of it."

Becket shrugged. "I suppose, like most, I am more afraid of being known for a coward."

"We play-act courage," said Sidney.

"Nothing wrong with that," Becket told him. "Besides, I have seen cowards die as ugly deaths as heroes." Sidney had shut his eyes.

"It is judgement that . . . terrifies me," he muttered. "Justice."

Becket coughed awkwardly. There was nothing he could say for comfort, being afraid of judgement himself. At last Sidney's mind wandered back to the thing that fretted him worst.

"I have been . . . thinking about the Queen."

Becket sighed. "Damn the whole business. You were mending until we read Parma's letter."

Sidney seemed not to hear him. "When you find . . . the book . . . burn it. No matter what is in it."

"Had I not better give it to Walsingham or Leicester?"

"No. Nor to the Queen, for she will put you in the Tower for expediency. Burn it, say nothing."

"If you say so. But I thought you wanted the truth?"

"Whatever it is, I will know it sooner than you," said Sidney. "And other than that . . . Think on it. If such a Book . . . of the Unicorn fell into Spanish hands, or even . . . Walsingham's hands . . . Think what a curb-bit that would be in the Queen's mouth, how she could be . . . controlled by it?"

Convinced he would never find the book, Becket shrugged. "If you say so."

Sidney was breathing short and fast and seemed very tired and anxious. His fever was rising again, and he moved uneasily against the pillows. "You will do it, David?"

"I gave you my word. Consider it burnt already. Now lie still and rest."

"I cannot." For the first time misery crept into Sidney's whisper. "I itch. I stink. I burn. How can I rest?"

"Is there laudanum? Can I give you some?"

"In the bottle, there."

Clumsily Becket did his best with the bottle and spoon and Sidney calmed a little. "It gives me dreams. I hate to dream," he whispered. "I dream all the time of unicorns and she-Devils."

"God damn it."

Frances Sidney was standing there again, arrived like a fleshly ghost, holding a small heavy leather bag.

"Here are the buttons, sir," she said. "The smaller ones are gold and the larger ones jet with amethysts and rubies set in them."

"It is too much," Becket protested.

"You will need funds," Sidney said. "Take them."

Becket took the lumpy bag and put it inside his shirt.

"He needs to sleep," said Lady Sidney. "Have you finished your business with him, sir?"

The laudanum had pulled Sidney back into its velvet pit, he was only half-awake. Becket bent down and kissed his forehead, which burned his lips. He was ashamed to weep in front of a lady and unable to talk without uncorking his throat, and so he only patted Sidney's hand again and left the place.

That night he got roaring drunk so he could cry on the comfortable breasts of his Dutch girls. The following morning, his head beating like a gong, he headed south for Rheims and the English Seminary there.

⌊|

THOMASINA CLIMBED THE WORN stairs to the Eightpenny Ward clutching a horn-cup full of aqua vitae. After spending days wondering how she was going to talk to the man the Queen thought might have the Book of the Unicorn, she had been running past when the Queen's little Jew who called himself Simon Anriques had stopped her and sent her upstairs with a drink for Becket/Strangways and instructions to find out what he was doing.

She peered cautiously between the beds. Mr Anriques had warned her that if he was rolling around or foaming at the mouth, she was to come straight down and tell him, which had quite frightened her. She had known a counterfeit crank once who used to pretend he had the falling sickness and she was supposed to be his daughter, but she had never seen the real thing. At least he was not doing any of that. He was lying on his back with his head resting on his folded arms, legs crossed at the ankles, staring at the ceiling as if he were reading from it.

"Sir?" she said.

"Hm?" He looked all round for her and then spotted that she was short and came to the usual conclusion. Lord above, did no one ever actually use their eyes?

"Yes, sweeting, what is it?" His voice had the special timbre of patronage that grown men often use to children.

"Mr Anriques sent me with some booze, sir."

A shadow crossed his face but he sat up and swung his legs to the floor.

"That was kind of him."

She brought it to him and stood looking at him. Now what do I do? she wondered. Do I tell him the Queen sent me and has he got the book? Not hardly, I don't think. So she smiled and sat on the bed opposite, swinging her legs. He drank and watched her with the caution of the childless. She had spent enough time as a counterfeit child to stare back at him with all the guilelessness of a girl of six. He was the first to look away.

"Mr Anriques said if you was in a fit to tell him," she said artlessly. "Are you?"

He darkened. "No," he said shortly. An adult would have known he was not inclined to talk and would either have gone away or waited in silence. But children are less subtle and are permitted to make social gaffes.

"Is it true you have no memory, sir?"

"Who told you that?"

"All the gaol knows it, sir."

Becket nodded. "It's true."

"What happened? Did a Devil fly away with it?"

Becket's mouth curved sourly. "In a manner of speaking."

"What was the Devil?"

"It was in human form, by the name of Davison."

And there's the truth, thought Thomasina, who was grateful she had had no dealings with him. "How did he do it?"

"He hit me on the head."

"Did it hurt?"

"Yes."

This was going nowhere. "Can I do you any service, sir?" she asked. "Only, I can run messages if you want, or get you things."

His eyes narrowed. "What kind of things?"

Thomasina was pleased with herself. She shrugged and twiddled a bit of velvet that had come adrift from her bedraggled kirtle.

"Booze, tobacco." She smiled slyly. "Girls."

Becket snorted. "What do you charge?"

"Only a penny for a message."

"Can you get me paper and pens without letting Mr Anriques know?"

"Oh yes, sir. When do you want them?"

"Now. As soon as you can."

She nodded, picked up the empty cup. "What shall I tell Mr Anriques?"

"That I am asleep."

An adult would be advised by his tone of voice not to ask any more. A child, however . . .

"He says he's your friend. Is he?"

Becket was staring up at the ceiling again. "I doubt it," he said, bleak as a winter gibbet.

Hmm, she thought, he has not lost cunning. She trotted downstairs, told Anriques that Mr Strangways was asleep, and whisked into the crowd. It was the work of a minute to collect a scrap of paper thrown away by one of the screevers working in the courtyard, and a little more complex to acquire a penner from a trestle-table by the gate. With both things hidden inside her bodice, she waited her moment to go up to the Eightpenny Ward.

At last Anriques obeyed the bell for dinner. She hid behind a rain-butt and then made a dash up the stairs.

She found Becket/Strangways still staring at the ceiling the way she had left him. He sat up when she came, took the writing tools and gave her two pennies. She sat on one of the other beds, swinging her legs again. Becket wrote for a while, with difficulty, as if his hands still had not their proper feeling. Every so often he chewed the end of the pen and then had to spit bits of unstripped feather onto the floor.

At last he finished, folded the paper and looked at her under his heavy black eyebrows. He has lovely eyes, she thought, but they are tired and sad.

"Can you read?"

"Oh yes, sir," she said stoutly, making it sound like a lie. "I can do my alpha beta and my name."

"Will you take a message?"

"Yes, sir."

"Do you know the man that came in by the gate this morning and talked to the ladies making ruffs?"

"Yes, sir. The Lady Dowager called him Father Hart, and he said he was to be Mister Hart. He asked about you, sir."

Becket nodded. "Take the message to him and no one else. Do not let Mr Anriques see you do it."

She almost said she would, she was so anxious to lay hands on the letter, but no, that would be too easy.

"Then it's two more pennies, sir."

"You said a penny . . ."

"That is for an ordinary message, sir. This is a secret."

He smiled cynically at her. "How old are you?"

She shrugged. "I don't know, sir." Which was true.

"And your name?"

"I am called Thomasina. Shall I come back?"

"Only if there is an answer."

She curtseyed to him, took the letter and the money, put it inside her bodice and skipped down the stairs. She opened the letter quickly, just within the door, and read what he had written. He only wanted an immediate secret meeting with Hart, that was all. But he had drawn a little stick figure instead of signing it, a stick figure of a horse with a horn on its head.

LII

WHEN SIMON AMES CAME from the dining-hall after dinner, faithfully carrying half a loaf of bread, some cheese and salt-beef, he found Becket sitting cross-legged on the bed in the Eightpenny Ward, whistling through his teeth.

"How are you?" he asked.

Becket did not look at him at first. "Well enough."

"Was it the falling sickness?"

"In a way. I saw the rainbows and smelt the roses, but after I lay down they went away and I felt better."

Simon smiled with relief. "The doctor said it was possible if you were careful that the falling sickness would go away again. Here, I have brought you some vittles."

"What makes it happen?" Becket asked with his mouth full. Simon shrugged.

"Some excess of phlegmatic humour, no doubt."

"He prescribed tobacco for it."

"Then let us smoke a pipe," said Simon, feeling he could do with one.

"Dr Nunez is very hot for tobacco," said Becket. "Why?"

"He imports it from New Spain . . ." said Simon, ". . . I believe."

"If he is so rich, why does he not bail you out of here?"

Simon paused. "Perhaps he will when he thinks I have learnt my lesson."

Becket had taken out his pipe and was filling the bowl. Now he looked at it before lighting it.

"What a pity to smoke something that puts money in the pockets of bastard Spaniards."

"Perhaps we should grow our own."

"Ay." At last Becket lit his pipe, sucked gratefully at it and passed it to

Simon, who did the same. Becket smiled. "At least the doctor's medicine agrees with you better now," he said casually.

Simon's eyes narrowed. "You have remembered some more?"

Becket wanted to kick himself. Simon Ames had always been too sharp to fool for long.

"Well, it comes back to me," he said. "Above all when I am not trying to remember."

"Excellent. Surely soon it will all come back."

Becket nodded, took back the pipe. "If only I could free my legs," he said, "then I think I would be quite happy."

"Are the irons so very irksome?"

Becket sighed. "Not as bad as if it were still my hands as well, but . . . Yes. Now I am recovered I want to run, not shuffle. I want to try some sword-practice." He rubbed at the bruises the rings made on his ankles when he forgot and tried to take a longer stride, and was irritated to find a hole worn there in one of his nether-stocks.

Simon was blinking down at the chains thoughtfully. "We could try filing one of the links," he said, doubt in his voice.

"Too slow. And depend upon it, there will not be any such thing as a file here."

"Perhaps aqua fortis, a very strong solution of aqua fortis might weaken the iron enough to snap it."

"What is aqua fortis?"

"A kind of liquid fire, an alchemical paradox. The elements of fire and water are opposed, as you know, but if the right counter-elements of air and earth be combined, then a water may be made which is in appearance like water but in quality like fire, since it chars anything it touches."

"How could I make it?" Becket wanted to know.

"To be sure, you could not, but an alchemist or a goldsmith might have some."

"Hm. Aqua fortis, you say."

"Very strong aqua fortis. But there is the other problem that if Newton finds out he will beat you and put you in the stocks."

Becket shrugged. "So? By my reckoning he might do that anyway."

"His rule, though tyrannical, is not irrational. His main concern is to prevent escapes and rioting, since he is fined for them."

"Ah."

"Now, will you come out of the ward, sir? There are many down in the courtyard who want to hear your tale of Zutphen and anything you can recall of Sir Philip Sidney."

"Lord, why is everyone so hot about a skirmish over a fort?"

Simon shook his head. "Sidney has become a hero for the way he died."

"There was nothing heroical about it. If he died like everyone else I have seen who took sick from a wound, then he was raving or unconscious."

"For the Almighty's sake, sir, keep that to yourself. Besides, it was the way he commanded in the skirmish before Zutphen that was heroical. It is not so often that the flower of the Court's chivalry spend their lives to let common soldiers escape. More often they ride the commoners down in their haste to get away. All the people know it was Sidney's doing that they dealt so honourably and only lost thirteen men."

"Well, that is true, at least. I was astonished myself."

"Zutphen has become a watchword. The ballad-sellers have printed a dozen tales of him, and the stories have gone round of how he gave the water to the poor soldier. He has become a Protestant martyr, a pattern of chivalry."

"Hmf," said Becket cynically. "No doubt it suits the Earl of Leicester to have everyone praising Sidney for his heroism and nobody asking how it was we had no scouts."

"No doubt. Will you come and tell the tale, sir?"

"Oh, very well." Becket was ungracious. "Tell them they will have to wet my whistle first."

In fact, as Simon had suspected he would, Becket told the tale very well, once someone had passed him a cup of aqua vitae. He stood by the ruff-makers so they could hear while they sewed and Cyclops sat nearby as his bear-leader. Afterwards they passed a hat round and gave him three cheers. When Cyclops had had his cut, Becket poured quite a respectable number of pennies and groats into his purse and said he would have been less willing to sell his buttons if he had known the value of mere hot air. One of the ruff-makers smiled up at him.

"To be sure, sir, have you never seen a lawyer posing it in marten and brocade, which is very fine-looking stuff but mortally expensive?"

Becket grinned and bowed at her. "I had forgotten," he said. "Along with much else, ma'am. Had you heard the accident that happened to my wits?"

"Then it is true you lost your memory?" said the recusant lady, trimming a vast long strip of linen with needle-lace that she was working at an extraordinary rate.

"Yes, ma'am. After Zutphen, all is fog."

"What a terrible thing," mused the lady. "I had wondered why . . . er . . . why a hero of Zutphen was in the Fleet."

"It is not so bad as the Tower, ma'am," Becket said meaningfully.

"Indeed not. Lord above, I would not wish my worst enemy in the Tower; there are so many ill tales of the place, especially of poor Catholic priests that have suffered there, like Father Campion."

Simon, who was one of the inquisitors who had interrogated Father Campion, looked at the ground and found himself glad that Becket had forgotten so much.

"God have mercy on them," said Becket piously.

"Amen."

Simon frowned with puzzlement. He had never taken Becket for a religious man, though to be sure such experiences as his had turned more blasphemous men than he to God. Then he saw the way Becket was looking at the recusant lady, who was industriously plying her needle again with a considering expression on her face. Ah, he thought, with a small puff of disappointment, so that's the way of it. Awkward as he was with women, even with his wife, it always amazed him—the easy way so many men could lie when they lusted. Which pun amused him as well.

He thought he would leave Becket to his attempts and wandered back to the spot by the door to the Eightpenny Ward that he had made his own. Soon one came to him who needed a letter to a lawyer drafted and he was kept busy all afternoon.

£]]]

BECKET WAS NOT A man who spent much of his time reminiscing, being generally too busy either avoiding creditors or acquiring them. He was now inclined to bless his memory for hiding away from the Queen's pursuivants like a fox gone to ground, agonising though it had been at the time. He had enough on his conscience without the Queen's ruin on top of it all. What manner of angel had robbed him he could not say, although in a superstitious corner of his fancy he suspected that the ghost of his old friend Tom O'Bedlam had had a hand in it somewhere.

However, this newly reclaimed ability to recall the past, to understand what he had been doing, was a nearly voluptuous pleasure after his weeks of confusion and uncertainty. He spent much of the rest of that day sitting idly whittling a piece of wood with his eating knife while entire cities re-emerged from the clearing internal fog. Some areas of his memory he passed over lightly because they hurt; he saw no reason to think of that earlier time he had spent in the Netherlands as a young man, when Romero and Adam Strangways had tortured and tricked him into betraying the city of Haarlem to the Spaniards. Agnes Fant née Strangways he likewise preferred not to recall. Eliza Fumey was a newer wound, only lightly scabbed over: he knew he had a son he had never met, three years old now, who called a wealthy London burgher his father. When she knew she was with child, Eliza had arranged her own marriage with as cool and calculating an eye as she would have done for her daughters. She had been adamantine in her determination not to marry Becket, despite all his desperate promises: he was a drunk, she said, a roaring boy, a bravo, a fine swordsman, a brave friend and a dear lover, but a husband—no.

Perhaps that was just. He had spent four years under the generous patronage of Sir Philip Sidney, teaching courtiers the right use of backswords and rapiers, and he had done well enough at it, but he had spent every penny he earned and more and he had no idea on what. To marry and settle down . . . it was something he could conceive of, could make attractive little phantasies of a London house, and a wife and children, and that was as far as he got.

Alternatively there was always Kate at the Falcon, and the Dutch girls had been delightful, if only he could remember their names.

His journey to Rheims had been counted out in golden filigree buttons—the others had been put to a more proper use. For vanity Becket had caused a very fine suit to be made for him in Amsterdam, decorated with Sidney's jet buttons, the first time since his father disowned him that he had possessed a first-hand doublet and hose, tailored specifically for him. He was delighted with it and found it greatly improved the way respectable women looked at him.

Now considering what it had been through with him, and considering that unlike himself it did not have the power of healing, it was in good condition. He would pay the little tailor in the Fleet to mend the depredations of the pursuivants.

Rheims had been difficult. The English Seminary was in a small house in a back-street, and they had been welcoming to him. He lied as little as he could; he made no claim to be well-versed in the Catholic faith, only he said he kept to it because it had been his mother's faith. He presented himself as humbly desirous of learning more about it. He said he had gone to the Netherlands with Leicester and then deserted for Parma's side as soon as he could—something done often enough by genuine Papists.

The Jesuits questioned him kindly, as did their chief, the notorious Father Parsons. Why had Parma sent him to help in this secret mission to England? Well, Becket was a man who knew the back alleys of London and had credit with Laurence Pickering, the King of Thieves, and might help to run the old nun to earth. It was logical enough, it hung together, and along with Sidney's artistically forged letter from Parma, it was sufficient for them to trust him. Becket found himself wondering how such unworldly men as these could be so grave a danger to Queen Elizabeth and her kingdom as Walsingham believed.

He ate with them in the refectory, listening to Ignatius Loyola's writings being read aloud, answering "Amen" to prayers he had scarcely any understanding of, and trying not to look at the lurid paintings on the wall which depicted more varieties of martyrdom than even Topcliffe's imagination might encompass. Becket was particularly offended by the sickly expressions of forbearance glorifying the martyrs' painted faces. Blood and broken bodies he could deal with, but sainted anguish put him right off his vittles.

He remembered that Tom Hart and he had joked about it on the way from Calais to Dover. He liked Father Hart, he found regretfully; he was a good companion who behaved like a gentleman and preached no sermons at him. They had more in common than Becket had expected: both younger sons, both disowned, though for different reasons. Both of them were hideously seasick in the four-day crossing as the autumn gales bounded the small packet-boat over the waves, which gave them a bond of shared squalor.

At last on dependable earth again, after answering the questions of the Tonnage and Poundage men and paying their usual bribes, Becket and Hart sat down to eat for the first time in days at a waterside boozing ken in Dover.

They were both too hungry to talk at first, but at last Becket leaned back, let out his belt a notch and lit a pipe.

"Now what do we do?" he asked. "Do we go to London to search for the old nun?"

Father Hart coughed at the smoke and waved it away from him.

"No," he said. "First we find her family."

"How the devil do we do that?"

"She told me she was the Infirmerar of her convent and its name—Father Parsons wrote to the Mother House and they had the records, which named her originally Mary Dormer and gave her family residence."

Becket nodded. "That simple, eh?" he said.

Father Hart smiled at him. "Of course," he said with irritating serenity. "Since we are doing the Lord's work, naturally He will help us do it."

"Hmf."

And at first it had been that simple; Becket could hardly credit it. They bought horses and went to Sussex and on their fourth attempt found the Lady Dowager Dormer, a recusant and sister-in-law, if she had known it, to a witch. Father Hart said Mass for her and all her household, heard confessions, baptised babes and married the Lady Dowager's eldest granddaughter. Ann, her youngest, was ardent for the church and Father Hart confided to Becket that he was in hopes she herself might go to France and become a nun there. Becket pretended to find this a good idea, although privately he thought it a criminal waste of a woman.

They all travelled up to London before Christmas and took lodgings in the Liberties of Whitefriars. Becket was nervous being back in his old haunts, although he had avoided Fleet Street and Eliza Fumey's shop. With Father Hart he investigated the boozing kens and went armed with gold to see Pickering, the King of Thieves. At last they got wind of the witch who was known as the Spoiled Nun and went to the Falcon to speak to her.

She was not there, but her granddaughter Julia was, self-important, busy, agreeing that her grandam certainly had such a Book of the Unicorn, called it her treasure, and sometimes hinted darkly that the Queen would give money for it. Father Hart had been cock-a-hoop at that. Becket had wanted to find the old woman, take her book by whatever means necessary, and then, he said, get out of the country. But no. Father Hart could not countenance such simplicity. He must first offer a Christmas Mass of thanksgiving at the place where the Lady Dowager lodged and what must the Lady Dowager do but invite all her Catholic friends to it.

Here Becket's newly recovered memory came to a dead stop. He remembered the crowded dining-room and Father Hart's reverently laying out his Mass things that he kept in the false bottom of his chest: the folding crucifix, the tiny chalice and paten, the small box of Hosts. He even remembered Father Hart's strong voice beginning to intone the Asperges, the sequence of prayers, some obscurely muttered, which were becoming familiar to him, though he sat and drank next door, worried at this foolishness. Then . . .

And then the hammering of boots and mattocks on the doors, both sides of the house, the congregation looking at one another in fear, Father Hart's voice rising, firmly continuing with his Mass, the locked door crashing open, a glimpse of Ramme and Munday's faces, greedy with triumph, himself drawing blade and charging into the fray and then . . .

Blank. It was the blink of an eye and he was waking in Little Ease, with his hands crippled.

Becket's mind shied away from that, like a horse from a blazing stable. He saw no purpose in pursuing it either. No doubt someone among the people who had been in the crowded room had been a pursuivant or a traitor; such a thing was to be expected in London. And Father Hart had been a fool to say Mass at all, whatever he thought his duty was.

Still, Becket could find a sort of satisfaction in it. At least Father Hart had remained free. At least he had not betrayed the man; the ghosts of Haarlem were still with him, but so far they had no company. God or Tom O'Bedlam or something had hidden his memory and he had been saved from himself. He did not fool himself into thinking he could have remained true without such a miracle, which thought sickened him and shamed him, and he shied away from that too.

As for Simon Ames . . . It took the sun of remembrance behind a pall of blackest cloud to think of him. Becket had mourned for him like a brother, thinking him dead of lung-fever in 1583. It had hurt him more than he could express, when Dr Nunez told him that Simon would be buried privately in accordance with the Jewish rite, not to be able to pay his respects, nor say goodbye. He had toasted Simon every time he got drunk thereafter. And now it seemed the little turd had been tucked away as snug as a bedbug in plaster somewhere out of London, laughing at him no doubt for being such a sentimental booby. And why, for God's sake? Why had he gone through such an elaborate charade of dishonesty? Was he involved in some secret game of Walsingham's and did not trust Becket?

The thought was not to be borne. Becket burned with fury at Ames, could hardly bear to look at him or speak to him and now found it a burden that he must even share a bed with him in the Eightpenny Ward. That night it was hours before he could sleep in the snoring darkness of the ward, with Simon curled trustingly like a cat beside him. Every deep breath the inquisitor took was a continuous unconscious insult.

Once, as a younger, more hasty, more innocent man, Becket might have challenged Ames on it, perhaps struck him and eased his heart, and gained much by Ames's explanation. But knowing Ames for Walsingham's agent against him, alas, he was more subtle. He played the part of himself as he had been before he saw Father Hart, and thought to his satisfaction that he had coney-catched the little inquisitor. Meanwhile, he meditated on revenge.

And also, of course, on escape.

LIV

LETTER TO DR HECTOR Nunez, Anriques at the Fleet, 30th January 1587:

My dear uncle [wrote Ames in a Hebrew cipher], *I am concerned at the behaviour of our friend. After the notable victory of his recalling Zutphen, we have had little further progress, although he seems to sit easier with himself. He has been spending much time upon movement and strengthening his hands in particular, and has prised up a cobblestone from the courtyard to carry about with him and move from hand to hand to improve his grip. He has also taken one of the little beggarmaids under his wing, which is charitable of him, although I think the child is helping to procure him a woman, his lack of which much concerns him. To this end he has had his doublet repaired and his nether-hose darned by one of the recusant women here, although he spent the day complaining that he looked like an Irishman with his legs bare.*

My immediate cause for concern is this: Today he approached me with a slate upon which he had marked out the Pythagoras theorem, for entertainment, so he claimed, although never have I met a man less entertained by the Arts Mathematical. There being a clear and obvious mistake in the calculation, I corrected it for him and explained his misunderstanding with care and in detail, but in retrospect I might have done better to have left it faulty. After all, a ladder might make an hypotenuse as well as anything else.

In case our friend is indeed plotting an escape, I must herewith insist that he be brought forth from the Fleet at once and taken into secure ward privately, preferably at your own house, until we have a better understanding of exactly how much he has recalled.

I am, sir, your affectionate and respectful nephew.

The letter was passed to the turnkey along with two others that Ames had drafted for a short-sighted gentleman, to be carried out of the prison by one of the servants. It would take a day to reach Nunez and another day to be acted upon. Ames began to pray quietly that Becket would make no move until the Wednesday, the eve of Candlemas, if that was what he was up to.

As happened often, that same day a man that Newton believed to be holding out on him was put in the pillory in the corner of the courtyard. They were kept awake half that night by his begging and cursing, until Newton went staggering out with his club. Three parts dead with cold and beating the next morning, the man paid over the money he had hidden and was beaten again and put in the Hole to show, as Newton put it, the benefits of honesty.

Becket was tense that morning. Simon stayed close by him as much as he could, and even played the utterly dull game of dice with him. Eventually Becket muttered something about finding a more entertaining opponent and wandered away.

Simon stayed where he was, in a dream-world of his own made of number and calculation, revolving around his perennial itch of curiosity about the earth's crystal sphere. His eyes fell on the little beggarmaid playing by herself. She had a cup-and-ball toy—a wooden cup on a stick with a ball attached to it by string—but instead of twitching the ball up and trying to catch it in the cup, she was twirling it idly round and round in her loose fingers, so that the ball circled the cup on its string.

Something focussed into a point in Simon Ames's mind then, something shocking and wonderful which made him stop breathing for fully fifteen seconds as the brilliant light of his idea cascaded through him. Why have spheres at all? he asked himself. Surely all that was needful to keep the earth circling about the sun was that the earth move and that there be some kind of string to hold it in the sun's allegiance?

Unaware that he was moving at all, Simon crossed the courtyard to the child and bent to her.

"May I . . ." he asked breathlessly, "may I buy your toy from you, maiden?" He held out the first coin that came to his fingers which was a groat.

Thomasina looked up at him cautiously, clearly thinking he was mad, a grown man wanting a toy. If Simon had been less enchanted by his idea, he might even have recognised her then, but he did not.

She curtseyed and gave him the cup and ball. "Here," she said, taking the money. "I am tired of it, you have it."

He took the toy and began spinning it in his hand likewise. Yes, it was possible, clearly possible. The ball tugged outwards from the cup, but the string held it in place, and the shape it traced out as it went around was a circle.

Simon laughed. What could the earth's string be made of? It must needs be very strong to hold the weight of the earth, and resistant to heat. Perhaps it was love that made the string? And the moon likewise might go about the earth on its own string. Not crystal spheres then but some kind of crystal or silken thread . . .

A terrific commotion in the courtyard woke him from his reverie. By squinting he could make out that Cyclops and Becket were at the heart of it. Cyclops was roaring that Becket had been holding out on him, he had not paid his protection, he was a papistical bastard that lied in his teeth about Zutphen. Becket roared back that Cyclops was a drunk, the get of his grandfather on his whore of a mother, and no soldier neither, but had lost his eye to a woman he had tried to rob.

Cyclops threw a punch at Becket, who dodged it, ran behind a table and upended the lot in the path of the pursuing Cyclops. The trader wailed and protested, Becket hit him; the tailor that had mended Becket's doublet, who had a stall next door, instantly attacked Becket; and one of his customers attacked the tailor.

The courtyard boiled into battle and confusion; stalls flying everywhere, merchandise trampled on the ground and ruined. The ruff-making women swept up all their delicate linens and threads and gathered anxiously together under their awning, with the children peeking from behind their skirts. The little beggarmaid in colourful rags who had attached herself to Becket's affinity squatted near to the ruff-makers and watched critically.

Now the chaos was resolving itself into groups of wildly shouting and punching men. The inner gate slammed open and Newton drove through the mêlée with his full complement of twenty large henchmen, all wielding cudgels and veney sticks, turning everything to chaos once more.

At the height of the mayhem Simon saw the wall of the prison which loomed over an alley-way suddenly sprout two short straight branches, behind its barrier of spikes and glass. All his gut turned to ice as he screwed up his eyes to make it out. Between the ladder poles appeared the face of a man, topped with a hat, peering cautiously at the broil in the yard. To Simon's left the broad figure of Becket crawled from under a broken awning. He sidled towards the place just below where the man was hefting a roll of rope that was certainly a rope-ladder.

Horror made Simon shout aloud. Nobody heard him. He moved to try and stop Becket, but somebody kicked his legs from under him and he rolled, the same somebody kicked his ribs and it was a while before Simon could get himself to his feet. In a dream he saw Becket grip the rope-ladder, start to climb and then fall for the weakness of his hands. Twice more it happened, and on the third time Becket roared with frustration and kicked the wall, then stopped and stared wildly at nothing. Suddenly his back arched and he toppled like a tree, rolled unknowing and unseeing away from the wall, his feet drumming the cobbles and his face turned into a gargoyle.

Simon could not see well enough without his spectacles to make out Becket's helper. The man at the wall's brow paused, puzzled, seemed to shake his head, then swiftly and decisively rolled up the rope-ladder again, disappeared from the top of the wall, and the ladder poles too vanished.

As suddenly as it had started, the fight petered out, leaving Becket wrestling and struggling with thin air on the cobblestones. Two of Newton's servants laid hands on Becket and were thrown off by a convulsion, another had grabbed hold of Cyclops.

Newton was enraged, roaring and stamping and telling Cyclops that he was expected to maintain order, not start riots.

Propelled by a terror that Becket would lose the last shreds of his reason, Simon ran to him and held his shoulders as his face finally slackened into unconsciousness.

It was a mistake. Two of Newton's bully boys twisted his arms behind him and wrenched him away, while another began slapping Becket's face to wake him up.

"Sir, sir," Simon protested, "he has the falling sickness, he must not be wakened . . ."

"He's lying," yelled Cyclops. "Him and that bastard plotted this riot together."

Newton snapped his fingers and his henchmen brought Simon to him.

"I must protest at this ill-treatment, sir," said Simon with as much dignity as he could, given courage by his relief that Becket's escape plan had failed. "Mr B . . . Mr Strangways is a sick man and you should—"

"Shut your mouth," snarled Newton. "Right. You and your bum-boy can spend the night out, understand?"

"This is an outrage!" Simon shouted back, astonished at the fury filling his meagre chest. "He has the falling sickness, he cannot possibly survive—"

Somebody had tossed half a bucket of water over Becket's head and he was slowly coming back to wakefulness, spluttering and coughing and looking as bewildered as a child woken in the night.

"He will catch a lung-fever. This is base injustice and beyond your office. I shall take you to the Star Chamber for your tyranny, sir, be sure of it . . ."

Newton held up his fist with a cudgel in it. "You'll catch more than a lung-fever in the Hole," he hissed. "If you don't shut your fucking mouth, Jew, I'll flog you to the bone."

Becket was staring at the two of them, blinking and shaking his head.

"Quiet, Simon," he said softly. "The pillory is better than the Hole or a flogging."

Simon gaped at this judicious peacemaking from Becket. Newton grinned wolfishly.

They were hauled over to the pillory and stocks, Newton stamping about and roaring orders, Cyclops strutting after him making obscene gestures at the pinioned Becket, who was putty-coloured and still unsteady on his feet. Simon was wishing fervently he had minded his own business. They forced Becket's head and hands into the pillory, on the grounds that he was still the more dangerous of the two as well as the taller, slammed down the upper half. Becket was recovering fast, he swore at them as they bolted it shut, straining his shoulders against it and kicking the post. Simon did not dare resist any more when he was made to sit down on the cobbles and they closed and bolted the stocks on his ankles. He felt sick. Everyone in the courtyard was watching the show, some of them laughing at Becket. Becket started to curse them as well as Newton, which was a mistake: some of the bolder ones picked up bits of mud and vegetable peelings, the timid copied them, and for a few minutes there was a rain of missiles. Simon put his arms over his head to protect it while Becket shouted at the crowd who had listened so reverently to his tales of Zutphen a few days before. Newton laughed as well and threw a couple of stones on his own account.

At last the gaoler and his turnkeys went back to their gatehouse to celebrate and Cyclops moved among the crowd. They stopped throwing stones and dispersed quickly then, going to help the ruff-making women with the injured and then to retrieve what they could of their usual business from the wreckage around them.

"Oh, David," said Simon miserably, "what have you done now?"

Becket turned his head cautiously in its hole to look at Simon, smiled sweetly at him.

"Never fear, Ames," he said. "I have not run mad yet."

Many times the next day Simon asked himself why he did not notice that Becket had finally remembered his real name. It had been a thing he was looking for, one of the keys to Becket's memory—he had been waiting and hoping for Becket to call him by his rightful name so that he could explain, so that Becket would begin to trust him and they could begin probing together for the memories that Becket had lost to Ramme's cosh.

But he did not notice, did not catch the importance of it. He was too horrified at himself for his defiance, horrified to be made so helpless, to be sitting on hard stone cobbles which were already bruising his meagre hams, to be facing a night in the open in winter, when the last time he had done such a thing he very nearly had died of lung-fever. He was also enraged at Becket for his cunning, his near escape and the disaster to Simon's family that would have followed it. But there was nothing he could do without revealing his game to Becket. At least the attempt had been foiled.

And so he sat as he must, staring at his pinned legs, angry and self-pitying and frightened and also, surprisingly, obscurely ashamed. To be publicly punished like a child, like a peasant. He had not suffered such a thing since he was at school and hardly ever then, since he had been painfully obedient and happily diligent. He had done much of his brothers' work for them, grateful to them for their loud and quick-fisted protection in the wildwood of the school. They had all gone bounding out into the world ahead of him, elder and younger alike, all except him being large, and bold and restless, and were scattered across Europe. One was commanding a fort in Ireland, one was living in Portugal in the shadow of the Inquisition, hiding his religion and daring death every time he sent a despatch through divers routes to Nunez, telling of the King of Spain's ships. One was fighting in the Netherlands. He had missed them, especially after his quarrel with his father in 1581 over the futility of backing the Portuguese pretender. Their estrangement had been made worse by Simon's turning out to be completely right that the venture would founder expensively and squalidly. He had been lonely in his work for Sir Francis Walsingham, suffered the ugliness of the strong against the weak in a way he had never known before.

Into that loneliness Becket had come, first bailing him out of a beating as his brothers had done before, then drinking with him, arguing with him, protecting him again. Neither of them was a boy-lover, but there are other kinds of love than Eros. For all the way Becket had soured to him later, Ames had thought of him as a new brother. It had pained him greatly that for the security of Walsingham's game with Honeycutt, he had been forced to lie so grievously to Becket as to lead his friend to think him dead. He had felt it as a dishonour to him, an injury to one who had done him none. He had almost been grateful for the fact that the Queen demanded his help in whatever dark business Becket had entangled himself in. He had rushed thoughtlessly to help Becket when Becket had been betrayed by his own body and left helpless, as he had once or twice astonished everyone by doing long ago for his real brothers at school. But there had been no gratitude, nor even recognition, in Becket's eyes; only a kind of grim humour. It worried him.

The bell rang for supper and the courtyard emptied as the evening came down. Becket shifted his feet and sighed, tried to ease his shoulders which must be aching already from their being held in such a hunched-over position. It was astonishing to think they had only been there for an hour or two. Already Ames was chilled and sore. He put his hands in his armpits to warm them for a while, but found that uncomfortable as well, since he had no support to his back. There was too little play round his ankles for him to bend his knees much and so, if he wanted to hunch up to conserve warmth, he had to stretch his hamstrings and Achilles' tendons until they ached. But if he lay back on his elbows, they ached and so did his shoulders and he got colder. He was starting to shiver. Also he had a pressing need to piss. He shifted as much as he could onto one buttock, fumbled with cold fingers, and aimed as far away as he could. To his frustration some of it trickled back towards him because other men's backsides had worn a dip in the cobbles where he sat. He swore in Portuguese.

"Good God, man, what happened to your cock?" came a rasping demand from beside him.

Ames flushed like a girl. "It is . . . I am a Jew, as you know," he stammered, fumbling again. "We . . . er . . . we are circumcised."

Becket was staring in frank horror. "Is that what it means?"

"Er . . . yes."

"But how could you bear to let them do it?"

"Since I was eight days old when it was done, I do not remember having much choice in the matter."

"Jesus Christ."

"He too was circumcised."

Becket did as much of a double take as possible to a man in the pillory and then laughed. "Ay," he said, "no doubt He was. Good God Almighty. Must make it difficult to hide from the Inquisition in Spain, eh?"

"For that reason it is not always done by Marranos."

Becket laughed again.

"Why is it funny?" Ames demanded, very much annoyed.

To be fair to him, Becket tried to stop. "Well," he said, coughing, "to know a man's religion by his cock . . ."

"Christians may be known similarly," Ames pointed out frostily. "In Turkish lands to be sure, for all the Turks do as we do. And perhaps in other ways. As I understand it, a Christian member ought to be known by its disuse, but rarely is, and I have often thought it curious that the mitres worn by Christian bishops bear such a striking resemblance to . . ."

Becket was laughing again. "Ay, so they do," he agreed, "so they do."

Ames was offended enough to sniff and turn his shoulder to Becket for a boor and an uncivilized gentile.

"Well, but do not huff at me . . . Simon," he said. "I was only surprised."

"How can you laugh when we are . . . we are like this," said Ames.

"What should I do? Pray? Mourn for my sins?"

"Perhaps resolve . . ." Ames stopped himself from admitting that he knew what Becket had been up to. None other seemed to have noticed, or Newton would surely have flogged them then and there. ". . . not to be so quick-tempered next time."

Becket tutted at him and shifted his feet again. "What makes you think there will be a next time?"

"I am glad to hear it," said Ames pompously. "To spend a night in the cold like this for the pointless satisfaction of fighting Cyclops . . ."

"Bah," said Becket. It was too dark by then for Ames to see anything except the occasional flash of eyes and gleam of teeth from Becket when he craned his neck to look at Ames. "Nobody invited you."

Ames fell silent then, because it was true; he had interfered unasked. It seemed also unwelcomed. He was a fool to go seeking brotherhood in a gentile.

Ames always was a chilly mortal although he had been born in England.

The summers were hardly ever warm enough for him, and every winter that he could remember had been a long dark misery of chilblains and head colds. He was wearing no more than two shirts and a padded waistcoat under his doublet and the only times he had been truly warm in the prison had been late at night, curled up under the blankets next to Becket's snoring bulk. Now the cold was striking up through his padded hose from the cobbles and down through the frigid air and he was tired and could find no way to be even slightly comfortable, which was of course the whole purpose of the stocks. When he looked sideways at Becket he could make out that the man had propped himself wearily against the pillory, turned his head so his Adam's apple was not crushed by the wood, and somehow managed to doze off.

Biting back his unreasonable envy of the man's stoicism, Ames hunched over and shivered, clamped his teeth to stop their chattering and wondered how long it would be before dawn. He started to think about chess and from there in easy progression to a problem in Euclid. It had been proven that an equilateral triangle could only have angles of forty-five degrees. Or could it? Instinctively, Ames felt that perhaps it could and that if it could somehow be proved that it could, other interesting consequences would follow.

The stars rolled slowly above them, only a little hazed by the smoke of London. Blurred by his short sight, the Milky Way wisped from horizon to horizon like pipe smoke of the Almighty. Orion strode after it, an archangel of bright sequins. He wished he had his spectacles. The scatter of diamond sparks on velvet was like a meadow filled with beautiful riddles. Why were some stars points and others smudges? What was the Milky Way made of, since plainly it could not be milk as the legend had it? Were there two different kinds of stars? Or were the points stars and the smudges something else? Where did comets come from? Did the Almighty send them to warn sinful men of His vengeance, as everyone said, or were they something else? Why could you not see the spheres that carried the planets? What were they made of? Truth? Or were the planets carried by their ruling Archangels, as the Hermeticists said? Or was there a different mystery going on, something subtler? He had been thinking about it when Becket's riot had started: what was it now? What had he suddenly seen?

Ames had a crick in his neck from looking up and the bony points of his elbows felt as if they were wearing through to the cobbles, but something about the stars drew his soul. Once, as a boy, taken to a lonely beach to meet a smuggler captain of his father's on a warm night in summer, he had gasped at the sea. It was glowing with a strange green-blue light, and at first he had been afraid, thinking that the sea was on fire. His father had been busy talking, had brought him only so that the captain would know his youngest son by sight if their family had to escape from England . . . It had been in Bloody Queen Mary's reign, so he must have been a child of five or so. The adults in the Ames family had been afraid for much of his smallest childhood; perhaps their fear had infected him with a chronic form of that wasting plague. Any Jew, and in particular a Marrano, understood that once the Queen ran out of heretics to burn, without doubt her inquisitors would turn to Jews, as they always had.

The Almighty had been merciful and Queen Mary died, to be succeeded by her riddlesome sister Elizabeth, who chose to take the small colony of Jews in London under her protection. But a soft summer night under the stars had already lit the young Simon Ames with wonder. Seeing the waves shining with pale fire, he had simply paddled out in it, ignoring the damage to his shoes and hose, tried to cup the beautiful water with his hands, glorying at the chance to look at it. Then he realised that close up, the sea was not burning. Stars had come down to swim in it. They darted and flashed in the water, stars perhaps, but certainly animals. He had looked up at the other stars, his head floating and bursting with joy to think that he had learned their secret, that they were tiny burning creatures swimming slowly in the seas above the firmament.

Even as his teeth clattered, Simon smiled at the memory. Joy had not come so often into his life that he was likely to forget its visits. Such happiness had been well-worth the scolding he got from his mother when they came dripping home, he and his father both. It was not so bad an explanation as all that either, and made more sense than the one his nurse had given him, which was that the stars were little holes in God's robe that let you see through to God's glory. This struck the prim small child as unlikely; nobody he knew had holes in their clothes, not even their meanest scullery maid was allowed by his mother to wear anything other than decent livery. Why would the Almighty (Blessed be He) have holes in his clothes then, as if He could afford no better?

Something clattered on the narrow scrap of wall by Fleet Lane. Ames hallucinated a distinct thud as his soul came back to the present, turned his head to look. He had trouble seeing so far and his night-sight was not good enough to make out more than a black indistinct lump that moved at the top of the wall where the spikes and broken glass were.

A different kind of revelation burst upon him. His mouth opened and he turned back to Becket, saw he was fully awake and showing his teeth again.

There was a stealthy scrape, a very soft curse, another scrape and something long and thin rose up against the sky like Jacob's ladder, then fed itself down again. In very truth a ladder. Obviously a ladder. In fact, he himself had helped Becket establish its proper length.

LV

BETHANY DAVISON LAY LIGHTLY on linen only a little whiter than her face and dreamt of being caught in a deep fiery swamp to her waist while the Queen scolded her for being a whore. Then the black fur of her lashes parted a little and she gasped, for she thought the Queen of her dreams was made flesh before her. And then she realised that Her Majesty had honoured her bedfellow by visiting her sick-bed. It was a kindness the Queen bestowed only on her best-loved servants. She had visited Burghley likewise. Guilt and weakness filled Bethany's eyes and overflowed to trickle down her face.

Very gently, like Bethany's mother, the Queen patted away the tears with a soft cloth.

"I'm sorry, Your Majesty," Bethany whispered. "So sorry . . ."

This bed had proper curtains, beautifully embroidered with birds and spring flowers on damask. Framed by them the Queen's face was a thing like a figure from Cipanga, enamelled white and red. Her lips tightened and the lines drew down familiarly with rage. Bethany shrank away.

"Don't be angry with me, please," she said. "I am so sorry, so—"

"Quiet," said the Queen. "Who did this to you?"

"The witch."

"Of course. The name?"

Weakly Bethany shrugged and shut her eyes. She did not see the expression on the Queen's face then, which might have comforted her.

"I meant," said the Queen very softly, "who was the man who got you with child?"

Even muzzy with fever and being bled, Bethany knew what the Queen was offering: revenge for her dishonour, the blame to fall upon her lover. But it had been her fault, after all; she was the fool who believed what John Gage had said of handfasting. She had wanted to believe him, had wanted an excuse for sin.

"He never . . . forced me . . ." she started to explain, breathless and anxious, "It was . . . I loved him . . ."

"Let me tell you how it was," said the Queen, bleakly staring at a point on the headboard, not at Bethany. "He was tall and strong and broad and his beard tickled your ear and his lips made prints of fire all down the side of your neck to your breast. And he said to you, 'Have pity on me, I burn, have pity, great lady, sweet one, glorious beauty,' and you felt how he burnt and you burned yourself so that you could hardly stand. And he told you how all would be well, he would take care and spill his seed and that you were handfasted in the sight of God and moreover he would marry you, and you wished to believe, so you believed. After all, we are creatures made for passion. And in the flurry and glory of the game of the two-backed beast, he forgot and you forgot because when two become one there is a melting and annealing and alloying into one golden instant and why in God's name should either one of you remember? Even the first time, when it hurt you, even then you understood why we are misers with such gold, why we lock up our daughters to keep them pure as we lock the dogs out of the wet-larder, for if once you begin to feed upon desire, it only deepens your hunger."

Bethany gaped at the Queen, whose ruff creaked as she tilted her head to look full in Bethany's eyes.

"But then come the wages of sin," said the Queen. "At first you told yourself your courses were only late and then you convinced yourself they would come at any moment, and then, when your breasts were sore and your belly began to round out, you knew . . ."

"I was afraid," Bethany said.

The Queen nodded. "And you were desperate and so you went to a witch."

"How did you . . ." Of course, the doctor had told her. The Portuguese doctor with the grave angry face and the gentle stubby fingers. "Yes."

"Do you know her name?" Bethany shook her head, slowly and wearily, "Nor where she lives? Where did you go?"

Her breath was coming short. "They were . . . kind."

The Queen snorted. "And your lover?"

Bethany shut her lips. It had not been his fault, truly, she should have known, should have held fast to her virtue; her fault, her fault, her grievous fault.

The silence stretched out. "Yes," said the Queen, answering Bethany's thoughts, "yes, I am angry, of course. You were under my protection and . . . this happened. But I never understood my stepmother's anger, either, so why should you?"

Stark astonishment made Bethany open her heavy eyelids again. The Queen smiled, a very grim and frightening smile.

"That woke you, I see, and no wonder. Do you think I know nothing, child?"

As Bethany had in fact thought precisely that, she only stared.

"Tell me his name."

Obstinately, Bethany closed her lips. She was too tired to explain why, with the wings of fever lying before and behind her. The Queen sighed.

"If you could only see . . . My dear, young men are all alike in this, whatsoever their differences otherwise. When they say they burn, they speak the truth; when they make tragical rhymes of how you have taken them to desperation and beyond, when they say that all they desire is the glory of you, ay, they tell the truth. But when they say they love *you* . . . They might believe it themselves, but they lie. What they love is the treasure under your skirts, and for the owners of the treasure they have very little interest, if any. How else do you think they can go to whores?"

More annoying tears welled up and flowed into Bethany's black hair and the Queen tutted and mopped them up. "They believe they love, my dear, but their desire for your flesh burns too hot for them to see anything but that flesh. I am reliably informed that once married, and their need assuaged, then they can learn to love as well as any woman, but before . . ."

"I do not hate him," Bethany protested.

"No, no, my dear, nor do I. Nor any man. The world without men would be a sorry place, a world without fire or metal, without song, truly without any salt or spice, without meat. Who would live in such a world, willingly?"

A piece of wood in the fireplace cracked and sank. Bethany could feel the waiting waves of fever surging back over her, pounding and crashing in her eyes and ears like the sea, swirling around the real Queen and turning her into another Queen, a Queen of shadows and smoke. Well, I am also the Queen of Hell, as the theologians attest, Queen of the dawn and the day and the dusk.

"What was his name, child?"

Bethany relaxed quite happily into my shadow-waves, relieved she had kept John Gage safe to marry the ward his father had bought for him. Far in the distance she heard the Queen muttering that Bethany had more honour to her than the swinish pillock that had ruined her and smiled to know the Queen thwarted by her. Then she let herself fall into my arms and I carried her until she should be strong enough to go through my portal herself.

She did not hear the door open quietly, nor see the Queen turn upon her stool as the broad Portuguese doctor came in soft-footed.

He bowed. "Your Majesty," he said.

"Nothing," said the Queen. "She told me nothing."

"Not even the name of the evil witch that committed this abortion?"

"No."

Dr Nunez was very angry himself, at the crime that had taken two lives at once.

"She is worse than a murderess," he said to himself in Latin, not remembering the Queen knew Latin as well as he did.

"Oh, indeed?" said the Queen sharply in that language. "We are very quick to condemn, are we not, Doctor?"

"This child has sinned gravely," rumbled the doctor, stern with rectitude, "I pity her, but I cannot condone—"

"Condone? Who asked you to judge her, Doctor?"

He was astonished to find a woman arguing with him on the point, even the Queen. "It is beyond question she has sinned greatly," he intoned, his Latin more fluid than his English. "Firstly in fornication and secondly in doing away with the consequences of her fornication. This is sorrowful, but it is the judgement of the Almighty upon—"

The Queen was standing, facing him now, quite a small woman rigid with a mysterious rage. "Ay," she hissed, "the consequences of her fornication. And what consequences for her lover, eh? Has he suffered for his fornication?"

"He did not commit the wickedness of inducing an abortion, Your Majesty."

"No. Why should he? Was he the one who fell with child? Was he the one who faced shame and misery for it? No, Doctor, depend upon it, he sinned no less, enjoyed himself no less, and then passed on, unmarked, untroubled. All the consequences of sin, of both their sins, fell upon this poor girl-child, as they always do, *as they always do*, Doctor."

Shocked and frightened by this vehemence, which he did not at all understand, the doctor went to the other side of the bed, gently loosened Bethany's fingers from their grip about a trinket on her neck, and felt her pulses. The fleshy folds of his face straightened as he interpreted the news they gave of her humoral balance, which was very bad.

"She fades fast," he rumbled, still in Latin.

For a moment the Queen said nothing, her eyes fixed on the thing Bethany had been holding, a pretty locket of midnight-blue twined with roses and stars.

"She has repented of her sin," she said. "Please fetch a priest to pray for her. I will sit by her until you return."

Thinking better of any further argument, the doctor bowed and left the room again.

LVI

AMES'S HEART BEGAN TO thud as Becket's henchman creaked his way cautiously down the ladder, paused at its foot to inspect the courtyard for guards and then hurried quietly over to the pillory. His first emotion was grateful happiness: they would be freed, he would be able to stand up and stamp his feet and flap his arms and warm up a little and then . . .

He and all his family would be expelled from England, as the Queen had threatened.

The dark shape was inspecting the pillory. Ames could not make out who it was.

"Good evening, Mr Strangways," said the man.

"And good evening to you, Father," said Becket. "What kept you? I'm perishing with cold."

Ames saw the priest's shoulders go up as he spread his hands helplessly.

"What can you do if a party of whores entertains a party of gentlemen in Fleet Lane? Would you have me climb the wall as they watch?"

The priest was unbolting the pillory, lifting the upper half. No need for it to be padlocked, with Newton's authority on it. Becket backed out of the pillory's grip still hunched and then slowly straightened up with a long groan. He rubbed his neck and dug his fingers at the cramped muscles in his shoulders, rotated his head and grimaced.

Then he laughed softly with excitement and slapped the priest on the back.

"I am sorry about . . ."

"Not being able to climb the rope-ladder? Why?" said the priest. "It was my fault for expecting it of you, I should have known better. Now, let me see."

He squatted before Becket and examined the links of his leg-irons. Becket looked about nervously.

"I could make assay at the ladder now . . ."

The priest looked up and grinned. "See here," he said, feeling about in a sack he had swung from his back. "Aqua fortis, as your friend recommended, and a blacksmith's bolt-cutters."

He unstoppered the little glass jar he had wrapped in leather to protect it and poured the alchemical paradox onto the middle link, where it hissed and steamed and made a hot, vinegary smell. A few puffs of sand on the same place and then he tried with the bolt-cutters and the jaws broke the links as if they were cheese.

Becket laughed again, pulled the chain apart and stretched his legs luxuriously. The priest grunted and led the way across the courtyard to the ladder.

"W . . . wait," gasped Ames. "B . . . Mr Strangways, will you not take me?"

The priest started, having missed seeing him entirely, since he sat so still in the shadow of the courtyard wall.

Becket looked at him calmly. "Do you want to come, Mr Anriques?"

"I . . . I . . . yes."

"If you are patient, surely your family will bail you out."

"Y . . . yes, I . . . but Mr Newton will surely beat me and put me in the Hole when he comes in the morning and finds you gone."

Becket nodded at this undeniable truth. "Would you not rather suffer it in patience than risk your life escaping with me?" he said, gravely reasonable.

Ames hung his head. "No," he said, his desperation to keep close to Becket lending wings to his thoughts. "He might even kill me for failing to raise the alarm. He has beaten others to death when they angered him."

Becket and the priest exchanged glances.

"He has not shouted to wake the gaoler," the priest pointed out, "which he could have done and been rewarded."

Becket seemed about to protest but then he nodded and came back to the stocks, unbolted them and lifted off the top.

Ames was so cold and stiff he could hardly move, and when the priest helped him up, he found his feet were completely numb with cold and almost collapsed under him. He rubbed his cramped legs and stamped as quietly as he could while he followed the other two over to the ladder. The priest went first, waited for them on the broad top of the wall, where he had put cloaks to protect their legs from the broken glass. Becket indicated Ames was to follow the priest, and then came up immediately behind him, steadying him occasionally on the rungs. They crouched in a row on the wall, glass pressing through the padding and their shoes to their feet. The priest lifted the ladder, hefted it carefully over the three-foot-high spikes, fed it back down to Fleet Lane. With extreme caution, he climbed over the spikes, creaked down the ladder.

Becket had already climbed over and was looking impatiently at Ames while he started to retrieve the cloaks that had been bundled on top of the glass.

"Can you not climb?" he demanded.

"I . . . m . . . my legs are so numb . . ."

"Fft," said Becket, and without further ado lifted Ames up under the armpits and haulted him over while his numb feet scrabbled at the spikes. "Watch out as you come down the ladder."

Becket went next, a jangling hulk, Ames last, moving painfully slowly. By the time he got to the bottom they were whispering together, almost certainly about him and his slowness.

"We must run," said the priest, putting the ladder back in a yard passage of Fleet Lane. "At least until we get to Holborn Conduit. If Mr Anriques cannot keep up, he will have to stay behind."

"You first, then him, then me," Becket said, taking the sword-belt handed to him by the priest and shrugging the baldric on his right shoulder. He drew the sword, tested its weight in his hands, shook his head regretfully and put it back. The priest took a pair of loose-topped buskin-boots from a sack by the wall and Becket changed into them, coiling the broken ends of his ankle-chains into them.

Then they ran, Ames stumbling and lurching until the blood started to get to his feet again, and soon after that he was panting for breath. So was Becket, but he hardly seemed to care; in fact, he seemed as happy as a boy in a race.

At Holborn Bridge they stopped while Becket caught his breath and Ames leaned against a wall and panted. Then, since Holborn was empty, they ran on down Holborn Hill. The priest jinked left at the square tower of St Andrews, down Shoe Lane, right at the Fleet Street Conduit into Fleet Street, past Salisbury Court where the French ambassador had his house, past Hanging Sword Court where the fire-drake had been born five years before, past the Gatehouse Inn where Ames had first met Becket, and left down Crocker's Lane near where Becket had rescued Ames from his attackers. Thence they slipped between two buildings, into a tiny yard and stopped at a door which still had fragments of carving above it, my statue made headless by the Reformers and the serpent under my heel left whole.

By that time Ames was crowing for breath and close to puking. Even Becket was leaning against the wall and gasping.

"Christ, I'm weak," he panted. "Give me a minute, Hart."

Father Hart was unlocking the wooden door. "No," he said, "up you go. We are in the Liberty of Whitefriars, but Davison has sent pursuivants in here before. Better not to be seen."

Shaking his head and spitting, Becket pushed Ames, wheezing, ahead of him up the stairs after Hart, to the second floor and in at the door.

The room smelt sweet as a meadow after the Eightpenny Ward: there were fresh rushes on the floor, a chest, a table, papers neatly stowed. Ames turned to face Becket with a smile, took breath to congratulate him on a smooth escape.

Becket showed his teeth again, and punched Ames deliberately in the stomach.

LVII

CAREY ROSE SEVERAL HOURS before dawn on the day of his duel with Gage. He had made his will the night before, which essentially amounted to the distribution of his clothes and jewels, instructions for his burial and an appeal to his father to pay a couple of thousand pounds' worth of debt, which he had no doubt his father would ignore. George Clifford, Earl of Cumberland, had agreed to be his second and was snoring in the other bed.

Stepping carefully over the body of Michael, also snoring on a straw-pallet by the door, Carey dressed himself and went down to the lane. He felt almost as if he had a fever, unnaturally clear-headed and alert, his stomach fizzing with anticipation. The sky was spattered with stars, and out of sheer habit Carey counted the Pleiades and smiled up at the North Star and Orion. He was content to think of the sky as the wall of heaven, tapestried with black velvet and spangled with diamonds, as befitted a King's palace. On the other side, he knew, was Paradise. He knew, theoretically, that by the end of the day he might be on the other side of that lordly tapestry, face to face with Judgment, but it did not worry him because in the core of his heart he could not really believe it possible. All evidence to the contrary, even despite making his will, like most healthy young men he believed himself immortal and knew that his God would look after him.

By the time he went back up the stairs of his lodging, Michael had gone to fetch hot water and the Earl of Cumberland was sitting up, scratching his face and muttering to himself about fleas.

"Jesus Christ, Carey, why are you looking so bloody happy?" George grumbled. "What's the time?"

"A few hours before dawn," Carey told him with a smile, used to being hated in the morning. "Are you getting up, my lord?"

"Urrrh. Have you got any beer?"

Good-humouredly Carey poured some into a goblet and gave it to the Earl, then poured some more for himself.

"Where the hell is Michael?"

Michael reappeared, toiling up the stairs with two heavy jugs of hot water from the cookhouse down the lane. Carey told his servant to shave the Earl because he preferred to shave himself and got busy with soap and a small mirror.

Cumberland said nothing until they went down the lane to the water-steps to cross the river.

"Second thoughts?" he asked. "Accept an apology from Gage?"

"No," Carey said. "Gage thinks I owe him an apology for hitting him."

Cumberland yawned and rubbed his eyes. "Oh yes. I had forgotten."

"Wake up, George. Have you got your sword?"

"Urff."

"Who is Gage's second?"

"Drury."

"Any good?"

"For Christ's sake, Carey, I'm not planning to fight the other second."

"You might have to if he tries to help Gage. That's why I asked you to be there."

"He'll not fight." George yawned again mightily. "And this is no way to settle a dispute."

Carey grinned. "How would you do it?"

"The proper way. The old-fashioned way. You gather your servants, your kin and your tenants, he gathers his, you find a field and you all fight it out."

"I have only one servant and I share him."

"Scandalous. Or you ambush him. That's how my father would have dealt with it."

"So would mine," Carey admitted. "But this is more honourable."

There was no need of a boat, which simplified life greatly. They walked to the Stangate Stairs across ice, which creaked ominously, and along the muddy road called Lambeth Marsh.

George had arranged for the duel to be in a small field surrounded by copses on a rise of ground by Lambeth Palace. John Gage was already there waiting with Drury, pacing up and down.

Carey took off his hat and bowed politely, a courtesy barely returned by Gage. Drury and the Earl paced together and talked in low voices while Carey looked with interest at Gage and wondered what he was thinking. He was pale, perhaps he was scared. Carey felt extraordinary: not afraid, not at all, but he was at a pitch of excitement he had rarely experienced in his life before. Perhaps it was something comparable to the way he felt when he was hunting wild boar, or perhaps when he was playing primero with the Queen and gambling more than he could afford on a hand he was not sure of. He felt as if his whole body was full of stars, each one fizzing with life, his mind as cold and sharp as a razor. Unbidden the thought came to him that, unlikely as it might seem to anyone else, he was happy.

Out of pure gratitude to Gage for revealing this to him, he smiled across at him, quite unaware of how wild he looked.

The seconds came back and Cumberland muttered something about Gage being unwilling either to receive or give an apology. Carey began unbuttoning his close-cut doublet to give his shoulders more room to move. Cumberland held his cloak. He took his sword-belt off, along with his doublet, and gave it to the Earl. Sharp feathers of cold air bit through his shirt-sleeves.

They moved into the centre of the grassy patch, which was crunching with frost, hard and slippery underfoot.

"Will either of you gentlemen apologise and so avoid this meeting?" asked Cumberland again ritually.

Carey was afraid he might laugh if he spoke, so he simply shook his head. Gage said, "No," and sounded as if he was speaking through clenched teeth. The light was coming up at last, the frost-sugared eastern end of London taking fire from the still-invisible sun. Carey breathed deeply, tasting air like wine. God, this was glorious.

Drury took Carey's sword and checked it, Cumberland did the same with Gage's. Carey took the sword from Drury, smiled as he felt the weight in his hand. Gage also took his sword. They paced off the proper distance, raised the swords so the blades were parallel. Cumberland exchanged glances with Drury.

"Begin, gentlemen," he said.

Carey stepped back at once, as Sidney's sword-master Mr Becket had taught him to do the previous year. Gage misinterpreted this and instantly came to the attack, swinging his blade crosswise. Neither of them had rapiers, on Cumberland's advice, who felt it was un-English to use Italian pigstickers, and furthermore because Gage had been studying with Rocco Bonetti, who was known to teach all swords as if they were rapiers.

Carey parried, parried again, gave ground and parried, watching Gage to see how he moved. They had fought before, veneys with heavy staves, sword practice with blunt weapons for tournaments. They had even drawn against each other in the last Accession Day tilts, and for the life of him Carey could not remember who had won. Probably it had been a draw, because they were so evenly matched.

But this was different. This time the clanging blades were sharp. Gage was still attacking, not finding a way through. Carey tried a couple of experimental passes, feeling him out, very nearly fell for an old trick to make him overreach himself and had to skip backwards to avoid a nasty belly cut.

It was risky, but worth a try. Invitingly, Carey left the opening again, saw Gage slash at him and knew that the man was not pressing home, had unknowingly pulled his blow.

Ah, thought Carey, as if he were watching the duel from far away, he does not want to kill me. In fact, I do believe he is afraid of killing me.

Do *I* want to kill him? Carey asked himself, as they separated and circled, watching each other and catching their breaths. The answer came that he not only would kill Gage, but he could, he had fewer compunctions. But do I *want* to kill him? Carey thought, parrying a couple of experimental blows and ignoring an obvious feint. No, I do not. What would be the point?

His attention was focussed on Gage the way he had been taught, not looking at his opponent's eyes but straight at the middle of his body, so he could see all movement and all intention. But the excitement that had been almost lifting him off his feet since he woke made the whole world sharp and clear. He felt as if his skull were transparent and he could see right through it in every direction. And so he knew, without consciously registering the fact, that they were no longer alone. Something moved among the trees at the very corner of his vision, and neither Drury nor Cumberland, who were supposed to make sure they were uninterrupted, paid any attention.

The blades clanged and scraped again. For a moment Carey felt real fury with Cumberland, but then he laughed and took a chance. "Come on, Gage," he said loudly and theatrically. "This is foolishness and disrespectful to the Queen. Drop your sword."

Gage snarled at him. "Drop yours first, bastard's get."

No, he does not know, he has noticed nothing. Carey backed again, decided to gamble on his guess in the hope of salvaging something from the farce, dramatically threw down his sword.

"There," he said. "Now you."

Gage came swinging for him with his blade, murderous at last now it was too late. Carey had not expected it, had been certain Gage would be wise enough to copy him. At last he was afraid and angry that Gage would attack him when he was unarmed. The world shrank away to the single intensity of the point of Gage's sword; he saw but didn't register Cumberland's mouth open with horror, felt rather than saw more hurried movement among the trees.

Carey caught the beat, dodged the metal twice, and then threw himself bodily at Gage in a shoulder tackle, as if they were playing football. Gage went backwards, still holding his sword; Carey landed on top of him, holding Gage's right wrist, punched him hard a couple of times in the face.

The men-at-arms were already trampling out of the undergrowth, hands grabbed at Carey's shoulders, caught his arms, twisted them up behind him and pulled him up and off. Gage was dazed and had dropped his sword at last. He was treated the same way by two men-at-arms in the red velvet of the Queen's livery. Carey looked over his shoulder at the young Earl of Cumberland, who was standing back, looking completely unsurprised and very relieved.

"George," he said reproachfully. "You traitor."

Cumberland shrugged. "What did you expect? You can thank me some other time."

There were four other men-at-arms standing around with halberds, some of them looking amused, waiting for somebody. Out from the shadow of an oak tree strode a broad figure, over six feet tall, dark-red hair rusted to grey around the temples, magnificent in black velvet trimmed with gold brocade, the white staff of the Lord Chamberlain in his heavily ringed right hand. He paused and inspected them, standing four-square, looking eerily like the portrait of the Queen's father in the Whitehall Waiting Chamber, his eyes less piggy and his face less puffy, but with just as great authority. He was glowering at Carey.

"Oh my God," Carey said weakly. "Father."

LVIII

LORD HUNSDON MADE ABSOLUTELY no concession to his youngest son, did not even acknowledge him. One of the men-at-arms carried the swords as they marched back to Stangate Stairs, over the frozen river again, and this time up the Privy Stairs that led to the Queen's private apartments. Carey marched with them, the happiness of the duel completely deflated and about twenty years suddenly disappeared from his life. He felt as he had when he had been caught for the hundredth time playing with the dogs in the kennels at Berwick Castle instead of attending to his Latin lessons: hot, embarrassed, resentful, knowing perfectly well he was at fault but completely unrepentant. His tutor had birched him regularly for running away, which he disliked, of course, but you got used to it and he always reckoned a sore arse a price worth paying for a few hours of freedom to throw sticks, play football with the stable-boys and dog-pages, climb on roofs and, naturally, fight.

Well, thought Carey as he and Gage stood side by side in the waiting room outside the Queen's Presence Chamber, elaborately not looking at each other, at least now I am a man Father will not beat me for this. Probably. Lord Hunsdon had gone ahead into the Presence, along with the sergeant-at-arms who had commanded the men. There was a low murmur of voices through the door.

When at last it opened and they went in, the Queen was not there, only maids of honour standing around the walls staring at them morbidly, and one or two courtiers. Sir Walter Raleigh leaned languidly on a windowsill in his pearl-grey damask and conversed with one of the red-and-green parrots in a cage, his surprisingly soft voice burred with Devon.

The Queen swept in at the sound of a trumpet, magnificent in black velvet and pearls. Like Papists at their idolatry, Gage and Carey both knelt, as did Lord Hunsdon.

With Lady Bedford arranging her gown, the Queen stepped up to her throne, sat down and beckoned Lord Hunsdon to her. He brought her the swords Carey and Gage had been using, knelt on the top step and let her feel the edges.

"Well?" said the Queen, nodding for Hunsdon to save his legs and stand again. "What is the meaning of this outrage, Mr Gage?"

Very stupidly Gage tried to lie. "Your gracious Majesty, my lord Chamberlain has made a mistake," he said, "Mr Carey and I were not dwelling but practising our sword-play . . ."

"With edged weapons?"

"For . . . for greater verisimilitude," said Gage.

"In a field in Lambeth?"

"For . . . for privacy."

The silence rang with disbelief. The Queen sniffed disdainfully.

"Mr Carey?"

I owe you nothing, Gage, thought Carey and I'm damned if I am lying to the Queen for your sake. Life is going to be difficult enough without deliberately making it shorter.

"I throw myself on Your Majesty's mercy," said Carey, staring firmly at the Queen's feet in their red-and-gold shoes. "I have nothing to say in explanation and no defence to make. I am entirely at fault." Would it be advisable to kiss a shoe? No. The gesture would be courtly but she might kick him in the mouth.

"What is? Are you admitting that you two were fighting a duel, clean contrary to our express will and statute?"

Carey ignored Gage's desperate sidelong stare. Wake up, John, he thought, this is no game. Lie to the Queen and she will never forgive you.

"Yes, Your Majesty."

She settled herself back on the red velvet cushions, leaned an elbow on the carved and gilded arm and tapped her lower lip with one long ringed finger.

"What was it about?"

The surprised him. He had expected her to start shouting at him at once, telling him what stupidity it was to fight Englishmen when there were Spaniards aplenty over the water, demanding to know how she was supposed to explain to their mothers how they had died, swearing at them and throwing slippers and goblets as usual. This icy calm was far more frightening.

"Y . . . Your Majesty?" he stammered.

"Generally we find that there is some reason for a duel, half-witted though it no doubt was," said the Queen frostily, "We desire to know what was the reason. The *casus belli.*"

Carey cleared his throat.

"As I said, it was my fault," he said, still not daring to look up. "Mr Gage wanted satisfaction of me because I . . . er . . . well, I hit him."

"Why did you hit him?"

"He . . . er . . . he insulted my family."

"And why did you do that, Mr Gage?"

Gage said nothing.

"Well, Mr Gage?"

Gage licked his lips. "I have forgotten," he said lamely.

More silence. The Queen's forefinger continued to tap her lip below the stunning scarlet of her lip-paint.

"Which one of you is the father of Bethany Davison's child?" she asked quietly.

Oh my God, thought Carey, she knows, she's found out. And then: Davison thinks it was me. Oh Christ. I am a dead man.

"When we ask a question of our so-called gentlemen, we expect an answer," rapped the Queen's voice. "Which of you was the father?"

Gage said nothing and Carey found he could not speak. Not one of the maids of honour was whispering. Raleigh was still leaning on the windowsill, watching with dispassionate interest.

The Queen rose and taffeta rustled as she paced down the two steps and stood in front of them.

"We are ashamed," she said, her voice vibrating with fury. "We are *ashamed* to think that one of our women has been dishonoured by some gentleman of ours. And further, *I* am ashamed that Mr Davison has seen fit to tell me it is one of mine own cousins. Well, Mr Carey? Do you admit it was you?"

Mentally Carey said goodbye to any hopes of office from his attendance at court. He would be in the Tower or the Fleet by nightfall, he thought, but his problems would really start when the Queen let him out. She would probably not receive him at Court and he could not evade his creditors for ever. He would have to go and fight in the Netherlands. Vaguely he wondered why that prospect no longer dismayed him quite as much as it had.

She was standing directly in front of him, her hands on her hips.

"Robert Carey!" she roared. "Answer me."

Astounding how much noise a medium-sized middle-aged woman could produce when she wanted. Carey flinched at it. And then he got hold of himself and looked up at her.

"No, Your Majesty," he said steadily. "It was not me. If it had been me, I would have married the maiden."

"Without our permission?" the Queen hissed.

"If necessary, Your Majesty," said Carey. "I would rather face Your Majesty's righteous anger for marrying without permission than face it for getting a bastard. I am not Mistress Bethany's lover and never have been."

"Mr Davison says that you are."

"Mr Davison is not infallible and on this occasion he is mistaken."

She sniffed instead of slapping him as he expected and stared at him. "Who is the father then?"

"I do not know," he said, still steadily. It was true enough. He did not know, not for certain, he only suspected. He tried to return the Queen's gaze as a man with the clearest conscience in the world. Lord, this was a mess. Perhaps he could go north and serve as a captain under his brother, who was Marshal of Berwick Castle. Not such a bad idea. The bailiffs would be expecting him to make for Tilbury. But if he could get hold of a decent horse . . .

"Well, Mr Gage. Was it you?"

"No, Your Majesty," Gage lied boldly.

"Oh? Then why did she say on her deathbed that it was you?"

Carey felt his mouth drop open and shut it quickly, with an audible click of his teeth. He swallowed hard. Bethany? Deathbed? What in God's name had happened?

Gage was as stunned as he was. "Your . . . Your Majesty?"

"Bethany Davison died last night of a childbed fever after miscarrying your bastard, Mr Gage. I saw her before she died because she was a dear child to me, despite her dishonour and incontinence. She spoke of many things in her fever and amongst them was the fact that you, Mr Gage, were the father and that you refused to marry her because your father had bought a valuable ward for you."

Carey risked a sideways look at Gage. He had shut his eyes.

"No doubt this is the true root of your duel, although it seems Mr Carey will not admit it. Bethany never loved any other man but you, Mr Gage, and you betrayed her. Well?"

You are done for, Gage, Carey thought without regret; throw yourself on her mercy, kiss her foot or something, and hope for the best. Another part of his mind, the less cynical part, was struck with sorrow. Bethany, dead. Lord God, what a waste.

Gage stuttered and muttered something about fever dreams.

"I beg your pardon?"

"She must have been dreaming," Gage said, busily digging his grave with his tongue. "If she was sick of a fever, she invented it. Or Mr Davison is right and Carey is the father."

With astonishing calm the Queen tilted her head, considering. "Certainly, that is possible," she said. "However, this trinket says otherwise." She held up Gage's New Year's Gift and opened it. "Last night I had a pursuivant take it to the Cheapside jewellers that serve the Court and found out who ordered it made. And this lock of hair was clearly precious to her. You will note, Mr Gage, that the colour matches your hair, not Mr Carey's, since his is chestnut and this is blond."

Gage shrugged, growing bolder as he began to believe his own denials. "The jeweller was mistaken. I am not the only blond man at this Court, Your Majesty. It could have been any one of half a dozen men, and it certainly was not me . . ." With a tremendous sweep of her arm, the Queen slapped his face, almost knocking him over. The crack rang through the Presence Chamber and one of the maids of honour snorted with nervous giggles.

The Queen marched back to the throne and sat down, breathing hard through her nose.

"Get him out of here," she ordered the sergeant-at-arms. "Put him in the Fleet. I will never receive him again. My lord Chamberlain, he is not to be admitted to Court again under any circumstances and you may write to his father and tell him why."

Gage was marched out, the Queen's handprint livid on his face, still denying he had even met Bethany.

Carey stayed where he was since he had not been dismissed, thinking again of Bethany the last time he had seen her, when she said she was not pregnant any more, when she asked where she could find Kate . . . Why had it not occurred to him to question why a high-born maid of honour would want to find a common trollop? Oh, Lord. Was that what she had done? He had heard whispers about it while he was in Paris as a youth, being very well educated by a high-born Countess twice his age. Had Bethany gone to a witch?

"Mr Carey," said the Queen and he dragged his attention back to her, "you will now tell me the full story."

Naturally he told it to her, not omitting the detail that Davison had been blackmailing Bethany for privy information about the Queen. If he was going down, he would make sure he took at least one man who deserved it with him. The Queen cross-questioned him and took him through the story twice, in detail, with a grasp of forensic inquiry very unsuitable to a woman. He might have admired it if he had not been the sweating object of her dissection.

At last she stopped and sat watching him narrowly, while he surreptitiously moved his weight from one knee to the other.

"We have one more question to ask of you, Mr Carey," she said at last. "Why did you not come to me when Mistress Bethany first told you of her condition?"

For a moment he could not answer because it had never occurred to him that he should. Of all the various things he had considered doing to help Bethany, that one had simply not been present. Tell the Queen? When most of Bethany's terror had been at her likely reaction?

Well, it was a question he dared not answer. If he told the Queen how her favorite bedfellow had feared her anger, there was no predicting how she might react. And his wits were far too battered to come up with a convincing reason other than that.

He opened his mouth to try and excuse himself and then decided that he was damned if he would. In fact, he had answered enough. He shut his mouth again and knelt there, letting the silence stretch around him.

It became a kind of covert battle between them, but Carey held the Queen's stare, silently defying her, resigned to losing all place at Court, resigned to the Tower, but absolutely determined not to say another word unless she resorted to thumbscrews.

And then, astonishingly, after what seemed like an hour or two, the Queen sighed, very heartfelt and heavy, and nodded at him.

"My lord Chamberlain," she said to Hunsdon, who was standing by the throne with his arms crossed and all of Henry VIII's thunder on his brow. Seen side by side with the Queen like that, their shared paternity was almost comically obvious.

Hunsdon went stiffly on one knee to the Queen and bowed his head.

"Apart from the fact that he apparently tried to stop the duel himself, do you have anything to say for your son?" she asked.

Hunsdon harrumphed loudly. "Your Majesty . . ." he began, obviously struggling not to shout, "other than that I think the boy is a half-witted ungrateful numb-skulled popinjay of a pillock, no."

Carey began to feel annoyed with his father.

"Do you think he has acted dishonourably?" the Queen pursued.

Hunsdon shrugged massive shoulders. "Stupidly, yes. Dishonourably, no."

The Queen's mouth curved as if she shared some obscure secret with her half-brother.

"I give him to you then, my lord, to deal with as you think fit. He is in your wardship until I release him. For the moment he is under house arrest in your rooms here in Whitehall. But, he may not attend at Court and he is forbidden my presence."

"Your Majesty is a most wise and merciful Prince," growled Hunsdon. "I shall see to it that the boy does not offend again."

Wait a minute, Carey wanted to say, I am not a boy, I am a man of twenty-six. I will not be put into my father's ward . . . Damn it.

"Have you anything further to say, Mr Carey?"

Well, he did, a very great deal, but some particle of sense and experience at Court told him that it seemed he might get off quite lightly, and this was not a time to push his luck. At least he was not being sent to the Tower.

"I am, as always, at Your Majesty's command," he answered, and when she waited, with her head tilted imperiously, for him to kiss the rod, he managed to add, "And I am grateful for Your Majesty's kindness and mercy to this unworthy subject."

She nodded, his father clicked his fingers at the men-at-arms and Carey creaked to his feet. He bowed, they marched out, led by Lord Hunsdon to the couple of chambers at the end of the Stone Gallery where the Lord Chamberlain had Bouge of Court. Carey was beginning to feel aggrieved as Hunsdon dismissed the men-at-arms. Once they were alone, he glowered back at his father.

"What the hell else did she expect me to do?" he demanded hotly. "How dare she think I would inform on Bethany; does she think I am one of her God-damned pursuivants like—"

His father simply roared incoherently and kicked him in the balls.

LIX

"ARE YOU NOT PERHAPS judging him too harshly?" said Thomas Hart, as he pulled a leg off the spit-roasted chicken he was sharing with Becket. Becket grunted and took the other leg, his mouth full of manchet bread.

"The man is an inquisitor, a pursuivant," he growled indistinctly. "He once admitted to me himself that he was one of the men who questioned Father Campion. Believe me, nothing I have done to him is worse than what he and his like have done to others."

Father Hart said nothing at first, but raised his eyebrows. "Or what was done to you?" he commented.

Becket winced. "I can take no credit for standing firm," he muttered. "By some miracle, God sent His angel to hide away my memory from Davison and his men, may the pox rot them in this life and the Devil take them in the next."

"Amen," said Father Hart.

"As for him"—Becket pointed with his thumb—"that bastard made believe to be my friend when they put me in the Fleet and I have no doubt at all they put me there so that he could better worm his way into my confidence. Pursuivants have often enough done the like before."

"It might have been better to leave him in the stocks then."

Becket smiled wolfishly. "No," he said, "this way is better. This way we have a lever against them. We can find out what the Queen knows of us, and when we have finished with him, why, we ransom him to his family again to give us money to get back to France or we cut his throat, whichever is easier."

"If he lives."

Becket shrugged again. They finished their meal while the sounds of London morning rose from nearby Fleet Street, and then Tom Hart brought out the files and blacksmith's gear and they set to work on Becket's leg-irons.

At last Becket could straighten up and scratch his bruised ankles properly.

"Thank God," he said. "Now, Father, are you ready?"

"Where are we going?"

"The Falcon Inn, picking up where Davison made us leave off. And this time, no saying Mass for your friends, Father."

"You know I am the only priest in London; if they ask me to say Mass for them . . ."

"Not this time, Father. Somebody betrayed us that time and they will again. We do it my way, or not at all." For a moment Father Hart looked as if he would argue it further, but changed his mind.

"Very well. You believe she will be there?"

"There or thereabouts. Are you coming?"

"What about him?" The priest glanced at the bed. "When will you question him?"

"In my own good time, Father. He can spend a while thinking improving thoughts about poetic justice and methods for getting the truth out of a prisoner."

"He might escape."

"Lock the door. He's not the man I take him for if he can escape from those knots."

They put on hats and cloaks, and left Simon Ames bound and gagged in the silence, with the carcass of chicken and no fire. If they thought of the rats, they were not troubled by them.

LX

DAWN HAD LONG SINCE come up like the maiden of the Ancient Greeks, wearing rainbow jewels of thick frost that had grown as ethereal moss on every surface, including the empty pillory and stocks. Moments later Newton came lumbering out of his quarters, wiping breakfast beer off his beard and began veritably howling in anguish. He was like a farmer's wife at a fox-raided hen-house and quite amusing to watch, thought Thomasina. She had been sleeping by the bread-oven in a little nest of rags she had made her own, until the banging and shouting and hurrying hither and yon of the prison servants woke her up. Every prisoner in the Fleet was hustled to the courtyard and the wards were searched and searched again, while Newton marched up and down threatening floggings, the Hole and worse to any who had helped Strangways and Anriques.

Thomasina was amused but also frightened. She had known the riot in the courtyard the day before for the ruse it was and had run to the Strand to leave a message to that effect at the Earl of Leicester's house. She had barely been in time to get in at the gates before they were locked at sunset.

Now she squatted quietly in a corner, watching while Newton shouted and threatened the upright man who really ran the prison. Cyclops could hardly contain his grim amusement, only shrugged and denied that he had had any hand in the escape. Annoyingly, her view was then casually cut off by a woman's skirts. She shifted to try and see until she heard the woman's voice, soft and firm.

"Thomasina, you must get out of the prison."

"Why?" It was the recusant lady Becket/Strangways had spoken to a few days before.

"My dear, think. In a few minutes someone will tell the gaoler that Mr Strangways had a beggarmaid helping him, and then Newton will take you and make you tell him where the man has gone."

That thought made her gasp, though it should not have been news to her. Life at Court has made me soft and slow, she thought to herself; I would have been long gone, once.

Cyclops was gripped by two of Newton's henchmen while Newton raised his cudgel, when there was a ringing and a banging at the outer gate.

All the drama ceased while Newton hurried to answer then reappeared with four of the Queen's Yeomen guarding a blond and exquisite courtier in watchet-blue satin. His pale eyes blinked at the rows of prisoners in the courtyard, stunned at some sudden turn of fate that had flung him like a comet from the stellar spheres of the Court into the more earthly realms of the prison. He was made to stand with the Knight's Ward. Thomasina knew him for one of the Queen's gentlemen, though she had forgotten his name.

But Newton had a confession to make, one Thomasina suspected he otherwise might have spent the day avoiding. The yeomen listened gravely to his whispered explanation, while his wide pocked face worked with anger and fear and his fingers clenched and unclenched on the cudgel.

Moments later the Yeomen had marched out through the double gates again.

"The pursuivants will be here inside the hour," said the recusant lady, smiling and nodding as the white-haired Dowager joined her. "You must go to Father Hart and warn him."

Thomasina said nothing, only gazed up at the lady.

"Where does he live then?" she asked.

The lady hesitated, exchanged glances with the Dowager, who nodded imperceptibly.

"Do you know the door in Whitefriars with Our Lady above it?"

"What's that?" asked Thomasina, genuinely ignorant.

"A lady standing on a serpent, but her head knocked off," explained the Dowager kindly. "It is a figure of Christ's mother."

"Oh." Thomasina thought hard. "Yes, I know it, my lady."

"Up two flights and on the left. Tell him what you have seen and ask him to pray for us."

Thomasina nodded. The two exchanged glances again and the Lady Dowager bent down to her. "Sweeting, you have a wise face, I think I can trust you in this. Here is a letter for the priest; it tells him all I know about my poor lost sister-in-law. Take it to him and tell him that he must protect you as well, since the pursuivants will be looking for you."

Thomasina swallowed hard as she put the paper under her bodice. "You are kind, my lady, but—"

"Hush. Go while no one thinks to stop you. Through the kitchen, out to the woodyard and through the lesser gate. Godspeed." Bony fingers gripped Thomasina's shoulders and propelled her in the right direction.

Holding her breath with fright, she scuttled across to the kitchen door, ran in under a servant stumbling out with a jack of beer for Newton, and the whip, through the greasy-floored kitchen where the boys were shoving each other on tiptoes to peer through a window as Cyclops was triced to the flogging post, never mind the basket, out the back door to the woodyard, mercifully unguarded in all the confusion, and through the woodyard to the little gate in the wall.

For a moment Thomasina stared up at it, heart hammering, believing she could already hear the shouts as the pursuivants came after her. She tried the latch tentatively, but it was bolted and padlocked shut, a waste of time. The wall was smooth and high. She might pile up logs from the woodpile to climb over, but it would take too long. In the distance, beyond the noise of Cyclops's flogging, her fear-sharpened ears heard the great doors of the prison opening at the shout of the Queen's warrant.

There was a six-inch gap under the gate. Could she? She bent down to it, tried her head, her shoulders, got on her stomach and eeled and scrabbled in the frost-rimed mud, sweating with panic at someone coming to fetch wood and finding her, sweating more when a nail caught her kirtle over her hips, shoving and squirming until the ancient velvet of her kirtle ripped in yet another place, and then her hips were through and her knees and she was in a tiny alley at the back of the prison.

She ran blindly, her throat thick with terror, realised she had run the wrong way and ran back, threading westwards by instinct through alleys that had been her old haunts once, towards the Liberties of Whitefriars. Behind her she knew there was a hue and cry for a beggarmaid.

£XI

UNDER THE BARRED WINDOW of Snr Gomes by Fleet Bridge a pile of rags stirred and moved. Dame Mary Dormer, Infirmerar and Mistress of Novices, stepped down from my clouds and shucked her dreaming habit like a moth its chrysalis, to wear once again the withered velvet caterpillar of her waking self. Bitter pain grated all her joints and aqua vitae her head and she heaved herself up, muttering. Snr Gomes was opening the barred gate and he tilted his head at her.

Mary hawked and spat and wiped her nose on her trembling arm.

"Come to do business," she slurred. "Brought my ticket and . . . and the money."

The gold was still in the velvet purse Bethany had brought, not all of it spent on forgetful booze. It was none of Snr Gomes's business where she had got the money, so he let her in and a few minutes later the gold passed one way over his polished counter and a small leather package passed the other. Ever suspicious, my daughter-in-law opened the package and found the book with the unicorn embroidered on its cover, checked inside and smiled. She wrapped it again and put it in the pocket of her petticoat, under her kirtle, and hurried out the door, heading for Westminster.

ℒXII

THOMASINA CLIMBED THE NARROW stairs and knocked on Father Hart's door. It was locked and there was no answer; she could have pushed the letter she was carrying under the door, but decided not to. She sat on the top step and nibbled a meat pie she had stolen in Fleet Street. Occasionally she thought she heard a muffled grunt from inside, but assumed it must be from a pig in the yard.

They came back in the early afternoon, clattering up the stairs, Father Hart in the lead and talking over his shoulder to Becket.

Both men stopped instantly when they saw her.

"What do you want, child?" Hart demanded suspiciously.

Becket peered round Hart and seemed to recognise her.

"She is one of the children in the Fleet," he said. "What's your desire, sweeting?"

Thomasina stood up and put her hands behind her back. "I am sent by my lady Dowager with a message," she said in a high, uncertain voice.

Father Hart pushed past her and opened the door. Becket followed him and Thomasina took her opportunity and followed them both. She had been wondering where the small clerk who had escaped with them had gone, and found out what had been making the grunts as well.

"How did you find us?" Becket wanted to know, as he picked a wing off the chicken and started gnawing it.

"My lady Dowager Dormer has this address, of course," said Father Hart.

"Of course?" echoed Becket. "Well?"

Thomasina handed her letter over to Father Hart, who gave her sixpence. Then she waited.

Father Hart skimmed the letter. "My lady Dowager is the Spoilt Nun's sister-in-law. Since her husband died, she has made her own enquiries, and this is the fruit of them," he explained to Becket, who was craning nosily over his shoulder. "There is a description and the names of the grandchildren, one of which is Julia, whom we know."

Becket shook his head. "Julia was hiding something," he muttered. "She knows where the old witch is, depend upon it."

"It's enough that she has promised to bring her grandam to a meeting."

"Expensively promised."

"But worth the silver if she does it."

"If she hasn't decided to sell us to the pursuivants."

Father Hart shrugged. "Betrayal is always a possibility. Since it is all in God's will, why worry about it?"

Becket snorted and then noticed Thomasina still standing behind him. "Why are you still here?" he demanded rudely.

"Please, sir," said Thomasina as artlessly as she knew how, "why is Mr Anriques tied to the bed?"

Becket swung round and glared at the man.

"Because he is a pox-rotted informer, eh, Ames?"

Ames made no answer because he had been efficiently gagged, only he closed his eyes.

"Is there any more, maiden?" Father Hart asked hintingly.

Thomasina had no intention of asking for his protection against pursuivants as the Lady Dowager had advised. She rather thought Hart needed her protection against them, not the other way about.

She shook her head, then held out her hand cheekily and waited until Hart gave her a further few pennies. Then she trotted down the stairs and into the tiny courtyard.

There she stood for a moment, her hands on her hips, head flung back looking up at the top-floor window, lips moving as she calculated. At last she set off up the Strand at a steady trot.

LXIII

SIMON AMES KNEW MORE than most about how pain could be caused to a man and was not at all grateful for his expertise. But he had not realised before quite how much it hurt simply to spend all day tied to a bed with a wad of cloth in his mouth.

Becket was horribly jolly, loud and full of jokes aimed at Simon, who could not answer back and probably would not have dared even if he could. He had not realised before either how much of the bully there was in Becket, who had always shown him his kindlier face. All men have two faces, he thought to himself, trying to be philosophical while his shoulders thrummed with cramp and his stomach and bladder ached, perhaps more. We show one to our family and friends and another to our enemies. If Becket had been brought to me as an enemy of the state when I was an inquisitor five years ago, I would have shown him as ugly a face as he shows me now.

In loud, false tones Father Hart and Becket discussed methods of torture while they ate salt-beef and bacon from one of the cook-shops on Fleet Street, swapping hair-raising tales of things they had done or seen done in their chequered pasts. They seemed very friendly together, quite heartily intimate. Ames turned his face away, which was all the movement he had available, and tried to let their voices fade to a mere babble. In a way it was funny, because if they would only take out the gag and give him something to moisten his swollen mouth, he would tell them whatever they wanted to know without any effort or blood at all. He had been planning to tell Becket everything in any case, as soon as Becket showed he had recovered his memory.

He now knew when Becket had done that and could have kicked himself for being so slow. He could see how his actions would appear to Becket, could understand why Becket thought him an informer and would himself have thought the same thing in the same circumstances. It gave him no satisfaction to understand Becket so well. He could not even bring himself to hate Becket, which might have helped him bear the treason of his muscles, which demanded movement so uselessly, which so busily knotted themselves into hot lumps unexpectedly and in strange places. To be sure, seen from another point of view, the situation was laughably frustrating. His motives had been of the purest, he had been acting only in friendship, and here was Becket arguing that setting light to his balls would certainly fetch the truth out of him if shoving a dagger up his arse did not work first.

Why does he not take the gag out before my jaw breaks? Ames wondered in misery; why will he not give me a chance to explain?

Father Hart expressed regret that the witch had once been a nun. Becket snorted with laughter that had an ugly cynical sound.

"Well, but she is only a woman," he said. "What can you expect if she has no husband to rule her? Of course she will turn to whoring; her hot nature demands it."

"She had a husband. Christ was her husband."

"He should have beaten her when she first went astray then."

Father Hart gave him an odd sideways look. "Do you think Christ no more than a man?"

Becket had stumbled carelessly into honesty and now tried to recover himself.

"Of course not. Only it seems to me hard to give a maiden to a husband that cannot caress her and then blame her when she turns to stronger meat."

"Do you think Christ cannot caress us?"

Becket shrugged, embarrassed. There was a silence. Father Hart found his tobacco pouch and began filling a pipe.

"I am sorry to see that the evil that was done to you has made you so cynical against God," he said. "Surely you were in His Hand when your memory hid itself away?"

Becket shrugged again and started filling his own pipe to have something to do with his hands.

"That's not how it seemed at the time," he muttered.

Father Hart accepted this by dipping his chin and sucking on his pipe-stem to light it from the watch-light they had between them on the table.

"What was it turned you back to the True Religion, Mr Strangways?"

"Various deaths."

"Why? Were they edifying?"

Becket laughed a short sharp bark. "No."

"What then?"

Becket made a complex business out of lighting his pipe and would not answer.

"If you wish, I could hear your confession and give you absolution," said Father Hart tentatively.

"So simply, Father?"

"Forgiveness *is* simple, Mr Strangways. You know the story of the lost sheep and the shepherd who searched all night for it?"

Becket nodded.

"I come from the north, where we keep sheep out on the moors. They are extraordinarily stupid creatures, forever getting lost, particularly in winter. The shepherds go out in the blizzards to find them, poking in snow-drifts, looking under bushes. Generally, though, they find them because the sheep cry to them."

Becket laughed. "Is that what you mean? That I should baa for help?"

Father Hart smiled. "Only metaphorically. We are not sheep but men, and our Shepherd has no need of a crook to probe the drifts of this world for our souls, unless perhaps we extend the likeness and take that to mean the pastoral work of the True Church. But God is no thief. The Protestants say, or at least the Calvinists say, that all are either sheep or goats, elect or damned, now and forever. We say that things are more complex and yet simpler. God gives us free will, that we may better grow to be like Him who has the freest will of all, and so paradoxically limits His own omnipotence; we need not turn to Him unless we choose to. We might be comfortable in our snow-drift, though the cold kill us in the end. He will not rescue us unwilling. But if we hear His footsteps and call to Him, He will come."

Father Hart was leaning forward, seeming anxious to say something that was not in his words.

"It may seem very strange how He treats us, Mr Strangways. I cannot deny that sometimes His works are mysterious to me beyond my poor understanding. But He sees us struggle, He knows our hearts and the truth therein, we may turn to Him and call and He will come. We may afterwards turn away and sin once more, we may deny Him, and yet, if we turn again and call again, He will assuredly come again. Christ bade us forgive our enemies seventy times seven times, and God will outforgive us every time."

Becket's face flickered as if this talk was painful to him. To Ames, listening through a haze of weariness, it seemed very comfortable, although he did not understand the priest's urgency.

"We should," said the priest slowly, as if picking over the words in a market stall, "we should also forgive each other, and ourselves."

"Hah," said Becket. "You want me to forgive Davison, no doubt."

"Yes. Our Saviour hung from nails and forgave."

"He also asked God why He had been abandoned."

Pipe smoke was filling the room. "Do you ask that?" said Father Hart shrewdly.

Becket shrugged and would not answer. He got up, paced to the little window and looked out into the courtyard below.

"When we have her book, what shall we do with the witch? Kill her?" This change of subject seemed like a deliberate blow in the face of the priest, a rejection of his delicate pursuit.

"No," said the priest evenly. "She might still repent."

Becket nodded. The room was darkening with the onset of dusk, and the priest was lighting a couple of rush-dips from the watch-light candle. Becket brought one over and stood beside Ames with it, lighting his face from below and turning himself into a gargoyle. Hot fat dripped onto one of Ames's hands and his wrist jerked uselessly against the bedpost.

"Ralph," said Father Hart. Becket was deep in thought, staring down at Ames. "Ralph Strangways," said the priest more loudly.

"Hm?" Becket looked over his shoulder.

"Do you want to question him now?"

Becket shook his head slowly. "Let us finish our business with the witch," he said. "When we have the book we will have some time to make him talk. Not now."

"Well, then, for God's sake, let him up to piss," said the priest. "That's my bed he is lying on."

Becket nodded, fished the pot out from under the bed and untied Ames's feet and his left hand so he could swing himself round to a sitting position. He kept a dagger at Ames's neck all the while, though Ames was shaking too hard with fear and cramp to do more than what he was ordered. When he put his free hand up to his face to try and make the gag more comfortable, Becket growled and cuffed him.

Docilely he lay down, to be fastened to the bed's four corners again, every muscle shrieking in protest. Despite his blinding headache from hunger and thirst and cramps in his jaw muscles, Ames had suddenly understood one reason for Becket's lack of urgency to hear what he had to say. The priest knew him as Ralph Strangways. Ames knew him as David Becket. In the half-world of fear and betrayal where they were all living, that was enough to keep a man's mouth wadded with shirting. Becket was playing some complicated double game with the Catholic priest which he had no reason to think that Ames would support. Ergo, Ames must remain speechless until it suited Becket to release him.

It is all talk, Ames thought with pathetic relief; he has no intention of putting me to the question, he cannot afford to. If he were planning to slit my throat, he would have done it by now. He has some other plan, the Almighty send he has some other plan. Perhaps he is still my friend.

Becket was still looking down at him, shadowed now because the taper was on the shelf over the bed. His long-lashed grey eyes were incongruous in his square black-bearded face. On a woman they would have been her greatest weapon, she would have darkened the rims with kohl, hidden any burgeoning circles of shadow with a cream of white lead. On Becket they made the upper and lower halves of his face disagree, and the Almighty knew he was no oil painting to start with.

Wishing that eyes could speak as the poets said they did, Ames tried to communicate by the intensity of his stare, tried to reassure Becket that he would be very careful always to call him by mad Tom's old name; he would not break his cover with the priest.

Becket looked over his shoulder. The priest had brought out a little folding metal crucifix and a breviary, was saying his evening prayers as he knelt before the figure of my Son in His agony. Becket squatted down so that his face was close to Ames, his breath garlic-laden.

Perhaps something had been transferred from one pair of eyes to the other. Ames stayed still as Becket's face became huge, his lips brushed his ear.

"I wept for you," Becket said, very softly. "I wept for you like a brother, because I thought you dead four years gone."

I had no choice, Ames wanted to say in his defence, feeling Becket was right to be angry. No one could know I was alive save Walsingham and my family, if the operation was to work. Certainly I dared not tell you; how soon would you have let it out in some drunken boast? You had to think me dead. But he could say none of it; he no longer knew where the cloth stuffed in his mouth ended and his dry tongue began. He turned his face away, but Becket turned it back, fingers digging painfully in Simon's neck. "You fooled me once, bastard, but not twice," Becket hissed. "Not twice."

The fingers gripped tighter until Ames could not breathe, until blood roared in his eyes and ears. He jerked and threshed helplessly, trying to writhe away until Father Hart came and pulled Becket's hands off and he could gasp air through his nose and see again.

"No," said the priest. "Do you truly want him dead?"

Becket seemed to be considering this seriously. "No," he said at last. "I want to talk to him."

The priest nodded. "Christ also forgave Judas," he said cryptically. "Be very sure he cannot escape." Becket checked the ropes, retied one where it had been loosened by Ames's struggles.

Again they put hats and cloaks on, preparing to leave him alone. Ames hoped they would leave him at least one light; he was afraid of the rats who had feasted on the chicken during the day, but Father Hart thriftily blew out all the taper flames. The key turned in the lock behind them.

LXIV

FOR A WHILE AMES lay listening in the tantalising smell of mutton fat, his heart still hammering for lack of air and fear and helplessness. And then he lost the calmness that had preserved him during the day. Panic was a hot flood inside him, blotting out pain and thirst. If he had been able he would have screamed. He wrenched angrily at the ropes, wrenched again, stupidly, uselessly, hurting himself like an animal in a trap and then moaned when cramp conquered rage again.

There was a sound on the window shutters. Ames lay like a stone, listening to the rats and his own muffled gasping. Another soft rattle. Ames rolled his eyes, craned his head sideways to peer at the shuttered window. There was a knife poking between them, jiggling patiently at the hook holding them shut. Slowly it pushed the hook out of its eye, the shutters swung quietly open.

Expecting anything—Becket, a thief, even Francis, who was the boldest and wildest of his brothers—Ames gasped to see a child in a dirty biggin cap and indistinct rags swing herself over the sill and drop inside. She breathed hard as she checked all round the room. The last rat squeaked defiantly at her and then skittered away down its hole. She came over to the bed.

Ames lifted his head and shouted at her through the gag, but she put her finger on her lips.

"Mr Ames, I am come to free you, but you must swear to keep quiet, please."

He nodded frantically, willing to promise her the world, his body, his fortune, comic in his desperation. Her small cold fingers worked busily at the knots behind his head, she tutted and told him to hold still and then she slipped her knife carefully between his cheek and the cloth, slit through, pulled out the wad. Ames could still not speak, his mouth would not close, he could not move his tongue.

She was cutting the ropes holding him down; quietly efficient, she fetched beer from the flagon on the table, poured him a beaker. His hands were too numb to hold it, she did that for him, he gulped greedily, slopping it because his jaw was still frozen open.

"I could not come earlier because I was fetching this," she said coolly, and found the tinder-box by the fireplace, lit one of the tapers. Ames was contorting himself to stretch his muscles, pull against the cramps of release. She unfolded a piece of thick official paper with two seals on it, spread it on the table. Ames put a useless paw on it to hold it down, digging and circling his knuckles into the angle of his jaw and squinting to read the italic.

It was a Royal warrant, a general warrant, signed by the Queen, identifying him as her servant and giving him all of her Royal power that could be held by a single man.

Ames stared from it to the child in the taper-light. Astonishing that one so young could be so . . . His eyes narrowed and he stared harder at her, still speechless. He reached out and clumsily untied the strings of her biggin cap so it slipped back, then turned her face one way and that so that the pale smoky light fell on it. She let him do it. The lines were faint, crinkling the corners of her eyes and her mouth.

"You are the Queen's muliercula," he croaked flatly, after another gulp of beer. "The Queen's Fool."

She curtseyed to him and smiled. "And you are the first man with eyes to see that I am no child."

Staggering like a drunk, Ames went to the window and looked out. She had come along a narrow ledge from a meeting of roofs farther along. To be sure, mad Tom had stepped along such ledges and from roof to roof with confidence, knowing his angels would bear him up. Ames had not the madness nor the courage. Even looking out made him dizzy; he was too short-sighted to see more than a blur where the little courtyard lay below.

"Key," he said to himself. "Perhaps there is a key."

He searched the room methodically, his stomach too clenched with fear and excitement to consider the remains of Becket's and Hart's meal. Besides, he could not bring himself to eat what the rats had left. There was a small chest under the bed that was locked. Ames found the file that had broken Becket's leg-irons and used it to break the lock, opened it up. Inside, under a false bottom, were Mass things—a chalice, a paten, a little metal box to carry the Eucharist. Underneath them was a surprising quantity of gold, a bottle of excellent aqua vitae, from which Ames took a much-needed gulp. Next to it was a little leather-bound notebook. From sheer habit, he picked it up and flipped through the pages, then froze. Perhaps no other man could have understood what he saw.

"What is it?" asked Thomasina, busy checking for key hooks by the door. "What's wrong?"

"This . . . This is Phelippes's writing," Ames stuttered, staring down at the code book.

"Phelippes?"

"Sir Francis Walsingham's code-breaker."

"But it was in the priest's box."

They exchanged a long slow look and then something snapped inside Ames. He sat down on the bed with the book in his hands and giggled helplessly, hooted with spreading hysteria and had to wipe tears from his eyes with his sleeve.

Thomasina brought him another cup of beer.

"Here," she said drily. "It is said to be good for madness also."

"No, I am . . . I am certainly not mad." Ames had an attack of the hiccups and sniggered again. "I am only thinking of poetic justice."

"Hm," said Thomasina, looking comically wise. "In my experience there is no such thing."

"Oh, but there is, there is," Ames assured her, struggling with hilarity. "You could make a whole heretical theology of it."

"Mr Ames," said Thomasina witheringly. "When you have finished, shall we consider what to do?"

Ames ducked his head and got a grip on himself. "Forgive me," he said more quietly. "I am tired and overwrought and not used to all this. Give me a moment."

"How long do we have before Mr Becket and his friend come back?"

"All night," said Ames. "And longer, I think."

He stood up, went to the window and looked out again. The beer was working on him now, clarifying his mind, giving him some counterfeit boldness. If I got drunk enough, could I be a soldier? some part of him wondered, and then he shook his head at the idiocy of the thought. He looked at the door, at the hinges of it. They had found no key.

"Mistress Thomasina," he said politely to her. "It must be a great burden to you to be so wise and yet so small."

Her little neat head came up and she looked shocked. "Yes," she said, truth surprised out of her, "it is."

He picked up the warrant, folded it hid it in the front of his doublet, and put on his hat.

"The Queen knows you, though," he said. "She has sent you to find the Book of the Unicorn as well."

She nodded. "And to watch you," she added.

"Of course. Well, Becket and his cunning friend Father Hart are even now paying gold to an old witch for the book. Knowing Becket, I expect he plans to cut Hart's throat once they are clear of the Falcon Inn."

"And Hart?"

"Hart knows it and has certainly laid plans. I make no doubt he is a true priest, but I suspect he hardly cares if Davison lays hands on the book and it is quite possible he knows Becket for a double-dealer as well. Sometime while Becket was in the Tower, the pursuivants must have caught Hart and turned him."

She nodded. "What shall we do?"

"Do you think the ledge will support my weight?"

She nodded again hesitantly. "It is not an easy climb, even for me."

Ames smiled, suddenly buoyed up with strange confidence. The priest had talked of Becket's being in the hands of the Almighty. Well, that applied to him as well. Even a traitor could speak the truth. Either what he was doing was the Almighty's will or it was not: if it was, he would not fall; if it was not, then he would not succeed anyway. "If I fall, take the warrant to Dr Nunez in Poor Jewry. Tell him what happened to me, what is happening now and ask him to use it as he sees fit."

Becket had hung Ames's knife-belt on a nail by the door. Ames retrieved it, strapped it on and wished he had a sword and better clothes. Curiously, it was the weight of his penner on his hip that comforted him, not his dagger.

"You go ahead," he told the muliercula. "Show me which way to go."

She climbed out onto the ledge, began moving slowly along it, facing outwards. Ames peered down into the street. I am not a brave man, he thought to himself; I am nothing like Becket and yet I do these things. For a moment he was frozen with fear again, thinking of the long way down, the stiffness and unreadiness of his joints. In his mind's eye were his brothers—tall, handsome, effective, outmatching him in everything bodily that he did, somehow making him more clumsy by their aptitude.

One way or another I have to do it, he thought. I have done it before, when the fire burnt us out of Becket's lodgings. The Almighty held me up then and also later, under London Bridge. He will do so again if I call, as the priest said.

Praying incoherently under his breath, he climbed slowly through the narrow window, barely big enough even for his meagre shoulders, and stood on the ledge. Sickness rushed spit to his mouth, and the ground seemed to be swooping up to catch him. Gasping, he turned and faced the wall with its cracked plaster and faint iron smell, inched shakily along it, guided by Thomasina, who was sitting like a small gargoyle by a chimney whispering instructions to him.

He reached the other roof, clung to it and vibrated there for a few moments, blinking sweat out of his eyes. The thatch was cold and slick, as if the house had wet hair.

Thomasina was lying full-length on it and she slid and slithered around the curve of the roof, to another roof, this one made of shingles. There was lead guttering; she reached down and caught hold of it, shinned down and stood in Hanging Sword Court, her head tilted to look up at him.

Simon followed, reached the lead guttering, began climbing down it painfully.

A squeak of alarm made him look up. The staples holding it to the wall were coming out, the whole lead pipe was pulling away.

Simon slid the rest of the way, bruising his hands, and jumped to the ground. Above them the guttering quivered but stayed where it was, frozen in mid-disaster. He had to bite the inside of his cheek to stop himself giggling again.

They were in a woodyard, Hanging Sword Court Woodyard, where Richard Broom's son-in-law carried on his carpentry trade. The gate was locked, but there was plenty of wood and a ladder stood by some scaffolding.

In the street Ames took Thomasina's hand.

"Mistress Thomasina," he said, "I am clumsy and unhandy and you are very patient. Do you know where the Falcon Inn is?"

Something old and ugly crossed her face. She nodded.

"We will go there across the river, not by Paris Garden Stairs but by Barge House Stairs and then along Upper Ground. I want you to go ahead and see what is there. I'll wait for you in the alley by Pudding Mill."

Again she nodded and led the way through the narrow alley, past the sorrowing Christ in the whore's beautiful salvaged window, still there against all the odds, through the tiny gate and into Temple Lane.

They stood a few minutes later on Whitefriars Steps where there were no boats, only the roughly frozen Thames.

It took as much courage to do it as it had taken him to dare the roof-tops, but Ames went down the steps and trod the ice. It creaked a little but held firm. Surely the thaw would come soon; London had tired of the Frost Fair; they had stopped lighting bonfires on the ice.

He felt naked and strange on the ice, could almost see himself from afar, a solitary figure crossing a false river dry-shod with a strange false child at his side.

Tension broke inside him. He ran the last few hundred yards, climbed the Barge House Steps and crept along Upper Ground, past the fair bawdy-houses and their gardens, and then ducked into the alley by Pudding Mill. Thence Thomasina crept on ahead of him, flitting from shadow to shadow with a sure-footedness he envied.

A few moments later she was back, her face monkey-like in its fury.

"Yes," she breathed in his ear, "Davison's pursuivants are there. I saw a dozen men around the inn, four to each doorway, commanded by a short round man and a tall elegant one."

"Munday and Ramme. Where is Ramme, the tall elegant one?"

"Next to the Falcon Stairs."

"What about Becket and Hart? They have not come out yet?"

Thomasina looked prim. "From the sound of it, they are enjoying the Falcon Inn's hospitality."

Ames grinned; it was endearingly typical of Becket that in the middle of a dangerous piece of business he would stop to get drunk and whore. Certainly the house was rocking with music and a frantic number of lights. "Both of them?"

Thomasina shrugged.

"Where is Munday, the other one?"

She gestured. Ames squatted down in the shadows, frightened at what he planned to do, and yet oddly exhilarated. The Almighty had held him up, kept him from falling off the ledge, brought him here. Perhaps it would work . . . Thomasina slipped away again. He took the warrant out from under his shirt, read it to give him courage.

LXV

A T THE TOP OF the Falcon is a room rarely used except by the courtiers who can afford to pay for it and who like the effect of it, being as near to a metaphor of the Court as a physical thing could be. Upon the floor are decent rush-mats, which are covered by Turkey rugs and cushions for festivals, and there is a sideboard which can be arrayed with newly redeemed plate if necessary, to give an illusion of gracious living.

But to walk into the place is like entering a crystal, like becoming the flaw in a diamond. Its walls and ceiling are crusted and crowded with mirrors, giving back in multiplicities of blue reflections whatsoever enters. When not in use it is a storage place for benches and tables and old broken beds and the out-of-fashion finery of long-poxed whores, waiting to be remodelled. So to walk into the room and pick your way among the furniture is to enter upon a kind of dusty, cluttered infinity.

They say magic may be done in such a place. To be sure, if Becket and Hart had been able to look with the right eyes, they would have seen me watching them from within the congruence of light made in the corners, but they could not, and besides the light of the rush-dips they carried was too little.

Sister Mary was waiting for them there, sitting on a scorched bench, staring at the reflected wreck of herself. The cruellest pain of becoming old is to look in the glass and always to be surprised at the time-slashed face of a stranger that looks back.

It had been a fearful wait for Mary, small ghosts and great regrets had whispered to her out of the fumes of aqua vitae, the contraband she carried in her petticoat seemed to be burning through her skirts. Only her determination to gain Pentecost's dowry kept her there. Worst for her, she could see me where I watched from the mirror-maze, but could not meet my eyes. Once again she was horror-struck at what she had done.

"Father," she mumbled when she saw him and she swayed on the bench. "Father, I am . . . I am evil . . ."

Tears glittered on her cheeks like glass beads.

"Have you got . . ." Becket began and stopped when Hart trod on his foot.

"Sister," said Tom Hart, went to her and embraced her. Mary shook her head and tried to pull away, but he held her firm while she muttered and the tears fell.

"Bless me, Father, for I have sinned . . ."

"Do you want to make your confession again, Sister?"

She nodded. Hart looked over his shoulder at Becket.

"Excuse us for a moment," he said.

Becket's face worked with irritation and impatience. "For Christ's sake," he protested, "she's drunk. For all we know the pursuivants are on their way, can it not wait—"

"For Christ's sake," said Hart. "Out."

Becket sighed through his teeth, took his rush-light and stamped out the door, where he stood on the narrow landing and stared at the moonlight slanting through a tiny window high under the eaves. By standing on tiptoe he could look through, though it was too high for him to see anything useful, such as the pursuivants. Instead he stared beyond the Falcon water-steps at poured silver, carved and chased by feet and fire, flowing unmovingly through the litter of London, the Thames turned to metaphor by frost. As he watched, clouds came walking from the west, hunting the moon and outing the stars one by one.

Within the upper room, unconfused by his multiple reflections, Tom Hart listened with his head bowed to the witch's new litany of sins, great and less, of theft and greed and the ugly killing of Bethany's babe and the incidental killing of Bethany herself.

At the end of it he sighed and closed his eyes in prayer. Anxiously Mary awaited the *Ego te absolvo.* "I do not know what penance to give you, Sister," said Hart at last. "I believed you had truly repented before, but . . ."

She clasped her hands until the arthritis burnt. "I did. Only, I am weak . . ."

"Do you think so? I think not. Most women would have been killed many times over by all that has befallen you, Sister; most men would hardly have survived. I think you are not weak at all, but very, very strong. So strong, your greatest sin is pride."

That cut through the aqua vitae. "Pride?" Mary demanded, cold and furious. "How could I be more humbled than I am? Look at me, Father, how could I be proud . . ."

"Nevertheless. We recognise our own worst sins in others, I think. Now you gave me a great gift last summer."

"I?"

"Yes. In my pride, when I was being hunted, I thought it was mine own effort and intelligence that would bring me safely away, and I was desperate, for I knew myself inadequate. And then you helped me, poor as you are, you led me away from capture and you told me that if it was God's will I should be taken, I would be; and if not, then the Blessed Virgin would protect me. I was shocked at such a truth coming from so . . ."

"Old and ugly a mouth?"

Hart nodded. "Yes," he admitted simply. "And then you demanded that I hear your confession, that I perform what I was ordained to do, in the teeth of all Walsingham's pursuit. It was . . . it was salutary. I have been near death many times since then, but I have never been so afraid nor desperate, because of your teaching."

She nodded, pleased at this.

"Perhaps I do have some wisdom," she said complacently.

"Then it is a pity you do not use it for yourself," said Hart, his voice like a whip. "You bade me trust myself to God, to hear His Voice. Why can you not do the like yourself?"

Her face folded into shadow again. "I try . . ."

"Sister, I believe that with the power of will you have, if you had ever truly attempted it, you would have succeeded. There were things you could have done to help the poor maiden you killed, but for greed and for pride you did not so much as think of them. Do you think God has no plan in this matter of the Book of the Unicorn? Do you think He has no interest in you?"

After a moment she lifted her head again and was much changed. "Why, yes," she said, the ice in her voice grating the air. "I do think that. What interest has He ever shown in me? His Son was my bridegroom and He threw me out of the house where I was happy and made me what I am now, and all the comfort I have is the booze and my little girl Pentecost . . ."

"Enough!" snapped Hart. "Lord above, Sister, listen to yourself. Do you think like the Puritans that a man beloved of God shall be happy and rich in this life? Was that our Saviour's life? Do you think that because you were a good nun, which I do not doubt, then God would hold you harmless from all travail and hardship? Think again. The harder your life, the more greatly has God favoured you."

Mouth open with shock, Mary said nothing.

"I would like to absolve you, but I dare not. I do not know what penance to prescribe except to ask that you run counter to your pride, that you trust in God as you told me to do."

"B . . . but you must shrive me, I may die at any . . ."

"So may we all. Do you think this sacrament of confession is a spiritual wash-house, Madam? Do you think the *Ego te absolvo* is soap for your soul? Think again. God forgives, not I. The power to bind and release sins was given to Saint Peter by Christ, and Christ knows your heart and your pride. Christ is not fooled by boozy tears, Madam, nor is He unmerciful to true repentance. I will pray with you for grace to leave your sins behind, but absolve you I will not."

"Our Lady forgives me. The Queen of Heaven loves me."

Hart rubbed at his eyes, which were growing sandy with weariness. "So she does, Sister. Ask her for help."

"She is more faithful than her Son."

The priest shook his head. "I pray that you will soon understand that all faithfulness comes from Christ."

Mary spat in fury. "You are no priest, you proud pompous little man. I hope Walsingham catches you and racks you until your joints burst . . ."

"Maybe he will, Sister . . ."

Becket's head poked round the door. "Have you finished?" he demanded pointedly. "I have been waiting above an hour."

"Yes," said Tom Hart. "Come in."

I watched them from my mirrors, seeing the rage burning in Mary's soul, all the hotter because she knew that from Tom Hart she had heard the truth spoken to her for the first time in many years; seeing the fear and doubt of himself writhing like Leviathan in the depths within Becket, which he strove so hard and successfully to hide; seeing the priest, heavy with sorrow and doubt at what he had done.

To see clearly is not always a blessing. I would have spoken to them, warned them, if I could. Do not mothers always wish to preserve their children from pain?

Becket sat beside the priest and Hart unbuttoned his doublet and took off the heavy money belt he had been carrying. Mary brought out her book with trembling fingers and gave it to them and each opened it, leafed through it to the right place and read quickly what was written there in a firm childish italic.

Then Mary snatched it back from them and clutched it amongst her skirts.

"Count the money for me."

Singing filtered up from the common room below, singing and the music of lutes and tambours and rebecs, much cheering and laughter. Exchanging glances with Becket, Hart poured the gold on the table and he and Becket counted through it carefully. As Mary had demanded earlier, there was silver among it, to be spent more easily.

It clinked and shone as the two men counted through it, too impatient to pay it the proper worship that Mammon prefers.

Mary's eyes watched them, blinking and hard as onyx, and every mirror showed a different view of her stealthy duplicity, if the men had raised their eyes from counting to see it.

At last they finished. They put it back carefully into the money belt and Becket pushed it over the table to the witch. She took it, her hands still shaking, pulled up her skirts uncaring of any modesty, and strapped it on about her bony hips.

"The book, Sister," Hart reminded her.

She was already at the door. She turned and tossed it to Becket, and then was out on the landing and scuttling down the stairs. Hart strode after her, called softly.

"I will hear you at any time, Sister, only consider my words . . ."

She paused a second and looked up at him briefly, then she shook her head and laughed, trotted to the ground floor and slid into the noise and light of the common room.

Becket was behind Hart. "Where is she?" he demanded. "Where has she gone?"

Hart shrugged, weary again with sadness and an inevitable gnawing fear of what he had done. "Will you give me the book?" he asked.

Becket paused fractionally and in that shard of time came a number of possibilities that Hart could see very clearly, perhaps even the necessity of fighting Becket. A little to his surprise, Becket only handed the book over in its leather covering. Hart checked the front to see the battered horned horse and put it inside his doublet.

"Let's go," he said, his voice harsh.

Their boots thundered on the stairs, but Becket paused again by the door to the common room.

"Wait on me for five minutes," he said. "I must go to the jakes."

Moments later, Thomasina saw him plunge into the Falcon's yard, check the woodpile, open the door of the goat-shed, the jakes, the wash-house, where he checked the bucks, and even opened a cupboard used for storing soap, then came hurrying back through the revelry to where Hart was tapping his fingers by the door to the water-steps. Thomasina would have called from her perch on the wash-house roof to warn him, but dared not reveal herself to the men waiting by the yard's back gate.

LXVI

A MES HEARD A MUTTER of men's voices, the bang of a door. Boots sounded on the gravel of the road.

"Halt in the name of the Queen!" boomed Ramme's voice, sharp with triumph. Gravel scraped and spurted under the boots of the men-at-arms, dark lanterns spilled light. Ames could see Becket and Hart in the midst of a crowd of men, all armed with cudgels and halberds. The whites of Becket's eyes were showing as he looked about, searching for an escape; Father Hart seemed relaxed, unsurprised.

Ames froze there, sabotaged by indecision. Becket believed him to be a traitor, whispered an ugly voice within his breast, Becket had gagged him and tied him to a bed all day, Becket had nearly throttled him a few hours before—why should Ames risk his life to help?

Ramme was grinning as he came up to Becket to take his sword and Becket flinched back from him. There was something creepy in so large a man being so instantly cowed. Ames could read the torment on Becket's square ugly face and briefly his heart was wrung with pity for the man, that he had been thus reduced.

Ames stood up and marched forwards between the men-at-arms. Ramme was prodding at Becket's jerkin, feeling for the book that had cost everyone so much blood.

"Mr James Ramme," said Ames as he came close, putting every ounce he could find of frosty command into his voice. "You are relieved of your office."

It was astonishing enough for Becket, who simply stood for a few seconds and goggled at him. Ames did not deign to acknowledge him, entirely focussed on the pursuivants.

Ramme knew Ames, of course, but thought him dead. He stared, blinking, as his mind struggled to put a name to the face he knew but could not place. Anthony Munday, whom Ames had never met, stepped busily between them.

"How may we help you, sir?" he asked with a threatening courtesy.

Ames took out the warrant and flourished it. "This is from the Queen," he said. "It gives me full authority to take charge here. Read it, by all means."

Munday nipped the paper from his fingers, squinted at it in the lantern-light, held it up to look at the watermark, fingered the seals.

"B . . . but you are . . . you are dead," Ramme stuttered.

Munday was scratching his head. "This is ridiculous," he said. "Our authority comes from Mr Secretary Davison."

"Mine comes from Her Majesty the Queen," said Ames. "You will please to bring Mr Becket and Mr Hart with me to . . . to my lord Earl of Leicester's residence."

Ramme's face twisted with rage. "No," he said. "No! This is a forgery."

"It looks straight enough," said Munday cautiously.

"It's a forgery. And you, sir, whoever you are, you are not Simon Ames. Sergeant-at-arms, arrest this impostor; we will take them all to the Tower."

When all was said and done, it was only a piece of paper. Ramme put his cudgel under his arm, snatched the warrant from Munday. "A forgery!" he sneered, tearing it in half and then in quarters. "It's treason to take the Queen's name in vain."

"Mr Ramme," Ames said between his teeth, "I will not argue with you and we can settle this in the Queen's own presence if you wish, but in the meantime I will take the prisoners to the Strand."

At first he could not understand what happened next. Ramme had swung his cudgel out from under his arm and prodded him with it; the end poked into Ames's stomach, accurately under his breast-bone, where Becket's fist had left a large bruise, and suddenly his ability to breathe was absent again. He was hunched over, tears in his eyes, struggling and straining with the air around him, which had somehow become as solid as the Thames. All the men-at-arms were watching him and Ramme, Munday as well.

That was when Father Hart moved decisively. Not Becket, who was still staring at Ramme like a rabbit at a fox. Soft-footed, almost daintily, the priest drove his elbow into the ribs of the man-at-arms standing gawping beside him, snatched the man's sword from its scabbard and slashed thrice before anyone had turned their attention back to him. There was pandemonium. Two men-at-arms were felled by the blows, a third flinched back, Becket woke from his trance of fear and charged through the crowd like a bull through mastiffs, the lanterns fell to the ground, one went out, the other flickered and cast confusing shadow monsters all about. Becket was grappling with Ramme. Another man-at-arms swung a halberd at his head, missed and looked down in astonishment to where Simon Ames, still crowing and weeping, had managed to stab him with his dagger.

The second lantern was doused, there were shouts, the sounds of window shutters being flung open. Ames hauled his dagger out of the man-at-arms's ribs, punched wildly around him.

"Run, Becket!" he shouted. "For God's sake, run! I can hold them." Please let him do it, he thought desperately, remembering that for Becket it was always easier to fight, wondering even then at Hart's actions.

Fists, halberds, boots, deep-voiced grunts and shouts of command; Ames tripped and fell on his face, there was the bellowing boom of a pistol, something punched his shoulder, he rolled, got his feet under him, felt cloth and hit out. Somebody gripped the collar of his doublet.

"This way," hissed Becket's voice, and Ames found himself being pulled almost off his feet, running with his legs all astray, gravel under his boots, something horrible and sour at the back of his throat, his shoulder freezing cold.

He rammed against a low wall, jumped over it and they were among trees. Brambles and dead bracken snatched at his legs, ripped his skin, he mewed because he still could not breathe properly and Becket was dragging him on, bearing right, somehow knowing where he was and where he was going.

They broke from the trees, heard shouts behind them; Becket pulled him, half-sitting, down the bank of a stream. Their feet crunched through the ice into the water, they stepped hugely, ice blades cutting them, up the other bank, running again. Another stream, another icy bank, through a hedge and then more trees. Something was wrong with Ames's back, he had got icy water on it, there was ice dripping down his arm.

Another stream, also frozen but this time the ice held; another bank, more tussocks of razor grass to cut Ames's hands, and all the time he was wondering where the water on his back was coming from.

And then Becket thrust him down through a tangle of thorns and old convolvulus, crawled in afterwards and they lay side by side, panting in the musty smell of animals and the mushroom scent of damp frozen earth, the gust of aqua vitae and bad teeth on Becket's breath coming and going.

Darkness reached out of the trees for Simon's head. Why am I cold? he wondered. I should be hot from running.

Becket rustled in the leaves and laughed softly, without a trace of humour.

"By God, Simon," he rumbled. "That was a pretty piece of work."

"I . . . I think I remembered s . . . some of your l . . . lessons," Ames croaked, his teeth chattering, sickened with the cold. Why was he so cold? "B . . . but y . . . you should have run at once," he muttered. "Saved yourself."

"What?" Becket's voice was now rich with amusement. "And die of curiosity? Last time I saw you, you were trussed to a bed. How did you get free? Why are you not working with Ramme and Munday? Whence came the warrant?"

Where is Thomasina? Simon wondered muzzily. Why is my shoulder so cold?

"I . . . I am not your enemy," he managed to say. "I wish you had . . . run and left me."

"Well, read me the riddle then. Explain yourself."

"N . . . now?"

"Certainly now. They will look for us for a little, but then they will go to fetch dogs, and by that time I must know what in Christ's name is going on here."

Ames was shaking so hard he could hardly think and he could not move his lips properly, they suddenly felt swollen again.

"C . . . can't," he managed to whisper. "T . . . too cold."

"What?" Leaves rustled again, something ripped, Becket was sitting up on his elbow, passing one hand lightly over Simon's body. When he came to the cold place in Simon's shoulder, his finger snagged on something and the sickness turned suddenly to fire.

"Oh, Lord," Becket said wearily. "Why did you not say you were hit?"

"D . . . didn't know," Simon said, shutting his eyes. That was it, that was what the cold was. A claw was ripping into his shoulder, of course there was; why had he not noticed before?

"Hold still."

Becket's hands moved and prodded; Simon fought back a cry.

"Well, you are in luck," he said, "some luck, anyway. It's not a bullet wound. I think a halberd must have caught you in the scuffle."

"Oh." There was a strange split inside Simon, stemming from the icy claw in his shoulder, one part overwhelmed with pain, the other part standing somewhere quiet and far off, observing. I have been wounded, said the distant part; how strange, this has never happened before. Simon was familiar with all sorts of illness, with the confused vividness of fever, the frightening treasonous pain of infected lungs, the weariness and cramping thirst of the flux. Occasionally he had suffered a beating, but never had there been an actual hole made in his flesh. It was terrifyingly unfamiliar to have such a burning pain running through him, to be shaking so hard with the cold. His teeth chattered and clacked and it took all his strength to hold them together, to keep quiet.

Becket was swearing softly under his breath, making complicated stealthy movements and hampered at every one by the grabbing brambles around them. Simon lay with his face in the frozen leaves, wheezing, wondering what the Almighty thought He was doing and in what ineffable way He thought this was funny.

"If I had light and a needle and thread I could do better than this," Becket said, cutting and ripping with his teeth at the bottom half of his shirt, "but it will have to do. Take your doublet off."

The struggle seemed endless—to undo a multiplicity of buttons, to pull his arms free. Becket helped him, freed him when he snagged cloth on thorns.

Becket's square fingers were gentle as they probed to find the ends of the slash, wadded up his bits of shirt and tied it tightly to Ames's shoulder with strips he had torn from the tail. A little bottle of rough spirits clinked against his teeth and Ames gulped gratefully, felt fire answer fire and warm him a little.

Becket was peering out of the thicket, squinting around in the starlight.

"Come on," he said.

"Why?" Ames was querulous, he wanted no more blundering about in brambles.

"I told you. The pursuivants have gone for dogs. If you want to play the part of a stag in Lambeth Marsh, I do not."

Meekly Ames climbed out of the brambles and followed him, his body divided into three, with a head made of clouds, a shoulder made of fire and legs of butter.

Again Becket seemed full of certainty and knew which way to go. Ames wondered how he could tell, with the trees and streams. Or no—rather these were drainage ditches, all frozen.

Becket looked down at the icy ditch and cursed.

"Generally I would walk up the ditch for a mile or so," he said to himself. "Damn the weather."

They walked beside it for a little to a hedge and even Ames could have followed the trail they left in the frosty leaves.

Becket scouted for a bit, found a weaker spot in the hedge and climbed through, helped Ames in after him.

"Where are we?"

"Hush."

They passed through an orchard, watched warily by a donkey in the corner, came to a little foot-bridge over the drainage ditch. Ames blinked around at the starlit silent houses and the light spilling from around the shutters.

"B . . . but this is where we started, that is Pudding Mill."

"Certainly it is," said Becket, with a grin. "I had a bet with myself that Ramme would not have the sense to leave a watch, and it seems he did not."

"He must have," Ames said. "Not even Ramme could be so foolish."

A small neat shadow detached itself from other shadows and came towards them. Becket had his hand on his knife, but Ames put an arm out reassuringly.

"Mrs Thomasina?" he called softly.

Becket frowned at the sight of a child, looked doubtfully at Ames and back at the muliercula.

"Ames, what is going—"

"Quiet." Ames wedged his clumsy feet against the cobbles, took deep breaths to steady himself. "Mistress Thomasina, can you bring us to the Queen?"

There was a soft snort. "Not tonight. This way."

"But—"

"Quiet," Ames said again. "I will explain later. Where are we going?"

"The water-steps. Come on."

"Ramme . . ."

"There was a man waiting here, but he is safe now."

"Drinking?"

"No," said Thomasina, showing her teeth in exactly the way Becket did. "Dead."

Becket was shaking his head, laughing softly. Ames understood how he felt. Under the starlight it was all too strange, as if they were in a play. Only the fire in Ames's shoulder and the palsy in all his flesh nailed him to reality.

The moon had been buried in cloud, with only a patch of silver to show where it burned cold. They crept softly to the water-steps and saw the men-at-arms waiting there patiently, two at the steps and four on the ice, tried for Upper Ground and saw more men standing in shadow, waiting for them.

Becket had lost his serenity now he had time to think. His voice shook with frustration and fear.

"They know we are in this part of the South Bank," he whispered. "When they bring their dogs, we'll be taken." Ames was too weary and cold to argue, though he watched Becket's hands clasp and unclasp about each other, as if they were pale animals seeking comfort. Thomasina's little black eyes narrowed and her mouth tightened at such a crumbling pillar of a man.

"This way," she hissed and led them, creeping one behind the other, into an alley between houses, then into the millstream, which the miller had broken many times to keep his mill working. More cold water, Ames thought sadly as he put his legs into it, and shivered across.

Here at least there were no men-at-arms. Thomasina opened a door, then shut it behind them. They were surrounded by the choking smell of grain and flour, the mill store-room. Ames sat down on a sack and shivered. Matter-of-factly Becket put his own dank cloak around him and squatted down nearby. Thomasina's voice came out of the darkness, soft, self-possessed and marked with London.

"I am Thomasina de Paris, the Queen's Fool and muliercula." The soft dusty darkness flowed back around her words and Ames coughed. "I am Her Majesty's most private informer in this matter."

"You both know me," Ames said in turn, hearing his own voice flattened with weariness. When had he last had a night's sleep? The night before yesterday. He had been in the stocks last night, had managed to doze off a couple of times during the hideous day tied to the bed, and now had a slash in his shoulder to keep him awake.

"You are not a child?" Becket said.

"No." Thomasina's voice was forbidding.

"Forgive me," Becket said, "I thought . . ."

"No reason why you should think anything else, Mr Becket; others have made the same mistake and with less cause."

We are voices in darkness, Simon thought; how strange. Is this how we shall be in the grave?

Becket sighed gustily and swallowed a cough from the flour dust. "Did you know Mr Ames was wounded rescuing me from being arrested?" he rumbled.

"No." Thomasina spoke sharply. "Badly?"

"Not too . . ."

"It feels bad enough to me," Ames said, aggrieved.

"There is no reason in the world why that slash should kill you," Becket told him. "It is down to the bone in one place, but if you can find a surgeon to sew it up, you will be better in a week or so." Simon felt himself bridling inwardly at this dismissing of the terrible hole in his body, and then reminded himself that to Becket it was no very great thing. Becket dealt in a world where such things were as much a hazard of living as catching cold.

"We must consider what we are to do," said Thomasina.

Ames found his voice dammed by a complete lack of inspiration. After a moment, Becket's voice came muffled and utterly exhausted. "Why, what can we do? They have us stopped up like game. When they come to search the mill, we will be taken . . ." His words trailed away and the darkness and silence pressed down on their heads. Ames blinked at Becket: this was not the man he had known, to despair so quickly.

Becket coughed again, seemed to be making some mighty effort. "In the meantime, I desire to know some answers."

"Why?" demanded Thomasina.

"So that when Davison puts me to the question again, I shall have something to tell him!"

Eyes glinted in the darkness; Ames and Thomasina exchanged looks. Instinctively, Ames felt that Becket's despair was the worse danger to them. As he had been once, he would be capable of finding a way out; as he was now . . . he might even surrender to Ramme and Munday.

Where to begin? "It concerns the Book of the Unicorn . . ." Ames began, heard the echo and realised Thomasina was saying the same thing.

"Oh ay, the Queen's book," said Becket dully, "I know that. The thing with her will and testament in it, and a confession also, from the time when she was a fourteen-year-old slut and thought she was dying of childbed fever."

Thomasina gasped.

"Did you not know that was what was in it?" Becket asked, a little roused by her surprise. "To be sure, that is why she cannot have Walsingham search for it. Even Sidney could understand that. She was with child of the Lord Admiral Thomas Seymour in her fifteenth year and brought on a miscarriage. She thought she was dying and wrote a will and also, I think, a confession to assoil her soul."

"Never," said Thomasina positively. "She would never do that."

"She did," said Becket as positively, "I have read it. She was a girl, frightened, vengeful and also feverish, not the politic Queen you know now. The witch that attended her, must have stolen it from her and kept it all this time."

"Good God," said Thomasina, clearly shaken to the core. "No wonder . . ." No wonder what, she did not say. Sitting in the thick darkness as they were, Thomasina's voice was high but mature, Ames thought. You would not mistake her for a child if you only listened to her voice.

"Now your turn, Ames."

"Where shall I begin?"

"With your death." Becket's voice was cold and hard.

Ames swallowed and put his freezing hands under his armpits. He could not get warm, though the shaking had eased.

"David," he said, "I . . . I cannot say how sorry I am to have fooled you. It was done for policy, for reasons of state, and when we have more time I will break the whole matter to you, but not now. I did not realise . . . I had no idea you would be so grieved by it."

Becket sniffed.

"Will you accept my apology?" Simon said humbly, "I wronged you by not trusting you and it was ill-done, but . . ."

"You pretended to be my friend in the Fleet when I was still wounded in my wits." Harshness still crackled in Becket's voice. "That was why I was so angry. That you should play the informer against me."

"Yes," said Simon, "though there I think I am less at fault. After my Uncle Hector attended you in the Tower, he sent for me and I came back to London from Bristol where I have been living, and my whole intent was to see you released from there. But when I spoke to the Queen, it turned out that you were engaged on a quest for her Book of the Unicorn and she forced me to work upon you as I did in the Fleet."

"How?"

"She threatened to expel us from England."

"Your family?"

"All of us, all the Jews here. My intention was to stay close to you and as soon as you showed signs that you were remembering your past, I would have revealed myself to you and we would have conceived a plan to pursue the matter."

"Why did you not do it?"

"David, you were very careful to keep it secret that you had remembered. I know now it was after you saw Father Hart, but I did not know it then or I would have spoken to you at once."

There was a small sound of acknowledgement from Becket.

"The Queen set me to watch you also," said Thomasina. "She asked me because I am her Fool and answer only to her, because I am no creature of Burghley's or Walsingham's, and because I can pass as a child and so be more secret. She wanted me to watch both you, Mr Becket, and Mr Ames, since she did not entirely trust him either."

"Despite holding so many hostages against his good behaviour?" Becket asked.

"Certainly, Mr Becket." Thomasina's voice held the ghost of amusement along with its worldliness. "If you were the Queen and placed as she is, would you trust anyone at all?"

Becket snorted. "No."

"She could hardly search for the witch herself, she could trust none of her usual intelligencers, and so here we are—a dead man, a midget and yourself, Mr Becket, and yet it seems we have succeeded. Will you give me the book now, or would you prefer to present it to the Queen yourself?"

There was a short regretful pause. Becket sighed.

"To be sure, Mistress Thomasina, I do not have it. Father Hart had it."

If the darkness had been a lake, Becket's words would have crashed into it and made it fountain. There was a rippling of silence, in which Ames could hear faint bubbles of sharp sound in the distance.

"What?" Thomasina's voice was strangled down to a croak.

"Well, what could I do? After all, he had the Spanish gold. My plan was to . . . er . . . take it off him afterwards."

"And Father Hart is . . ." Thomasina asked, still breathless with dismay.

"Who knows? He fought when I was struck to stone, he made the chance for us to get away when I could not. God knows, I had thought him no more than an ordinary traitor, but . . . perhaps he is dead, perhaps captured, perhaps he escaped. I have no idea . . ."

"And you left the book with him."

"I had no choice." Becket's voice was as icy as the drainage ditches. "I was more concerned to keep out of Ramme's clutches myself, having been in them once too often, and Ames and Hart between them had made me a little tiny chance which I had needs take at once, without sparing time to go searching about in any man's doublet for some God-damned Book of the Unicorn. What would you have me do, woman, say to Ramme, 'Ah, excuse me, your honour, give me a minute before I run like a rabbit; let me just take this book from the priest who is fighting three men at once in my behalf . . . ' "

Thomasina did not answer his sarcasm. And Ames could bear to listen to Becket's self-contempt no longer.

"Shh. I know what we can do. Listen."

The calling of dogs sounded in the distance, deer-hounds giving tongue.

LXVII

DAVISON SAT ON A stool and looked down at the book in his hands. The velvet was worn down to the nap from being carried, with a long scrape scarring it on the back. The embroidered unicorn had partly come unravelled so that the padding drooled out, the ruby for its eye and the golden thread of its horn had long ago been sold, some of the pages were stained and others stuck together. Others had been cut out.

He looked at the man on the bed whose breath bubbled and caught harshly in his throat.

"Well, Mr Hart," he said softly. "What have we here?"

"You know I am a priest," said the Papist.

Davison inclined his head. "I know," he said. "I do not regard you as my father."

There was a flicker of humour in the priest's eyes.

"Nevertheless," he whispered, "I regard you as my son, prodigal though you are."

Davison's lip lifted with distaste. The priest was going to die because no man can survive a halberd thrust squarely through the middle of his back. They had had to saw off the shaft to let him lie down, and the end of the blade poked out through his belly where his fingers plucked at it unconsciously. He could not live long enough to betray any of his associates, nor could he meet his death properly in public, as an edification to the foolish multitudes. Davison would not be taken in by him again.

"Tell me what is in the book," suggested Davison.

"Read it yourself."

"Some of the writing is . . . damaged. Tell me."

The priest's eyes considered him for a moment, and he smiled.

"Recommendations to the holy state of virginity."

"And?"

"And? The Queen's sin. Your precious Virgin Queen is no such thing."

Davison's face remained as smooth and calm as an effigy.

"Do *you* believe it?"

"Her own hand. Her . . . will when she was a chit of a girl . . . her confession."

"Confession?"

"Her admission that she was dying . . . or thought she was . . . because she fell with child by . . . Thomas Seymour and did away with . . . the babe herself."

Davison was silent for a long time.

"*I* have it now," he said.

"Of course," said the priest. "As . . . I intended."

"Why? Why have you helped me lay hands on it?"

"Nothing . . . I could do . . . with a spear in my back."

"No, Mr Hart. Without your message, we might not have been at the Falcon at all. Why did you help us?"

"Why does . . . it matter?"

"I am curious." Davison was also uneasy. If the Queen's reaction had not made it so obvious the bill was true, he might have suspected the Jesuits of cooking the whole thing up and forging the book, the better to turn the Queen's men from their allegiance. The priest shifted. Like many clever men, he liked to boast of his cleverness, even if it hurt him.

"Think about it. We of the True Faith know the Queen is a wicked immoral Jezebel . . . but she has enchanted all of you with her witchcraft. Yes . . . I could have taken the book . . . to Rheims and printed it and made it public, and . . . you would have ignored it as a manifest forgery."

Davison tilted his head because this was incontrovertibly true.

"Now . . . you, Mr Davison, and Walsingham and Burghley . . . are misguided Protestants, but even at Rheims we know you are honest men. I knew that . . . if you could but see what a . . . whited sepulchre she is . . . how she is a witch on a throne of lies, you would take steps to control her. Also I was sure Becket, bless his heart, would . . . cut my throat once we had it. A recusant told me that he is the Queen's man, through and through . . . He was working, I believe . . . originally for Sidney. He would have burnt it or returned it . . . to the Queen. I was happy for you or Walsingham to have the book . . . I had not expected a halberd." The priest sighed.

"Sad, eh?" he whispered with an ugly grin, the strength that was fuelling his words ebbing. "No wonder she has made such a point . . . of her virgin state. Well, no doubt you will burn the book."

"No doubt," echoed Davison, staring into space.

"The truth is a hard thing, eh?"

Davison did not answer and the priest shifted again, vainly trying to find some less uncomfortable way to lie. He let out a soft cough, his face crumpled with pain. Davison switched his attention away from the book between his hands.

"Would you like a doctor to attend you?" he asked.

They were not coughs, but truncated gusts of laughter.

"Should you not be trying to turn me to your . . . heresy, Mr Davison?" said the priest. "This is your last chance to save . . . my soul, eh? Where's your zeal, eh?"

Davison shook his head. "I am sorry for you, Mr Hart," he said, "but I am afraid there is no question but that you are damned for all eternity because you cleaved to superstition and idolatry when you could have followed the True and Pure Religion."

Hart rolled his eyes. "Is it not . . . also idolatry to worship a fleshly Queen?"

"Perhaps it is. I do not do so, myself."

"Poor Mr Davison," said the priest. "He knows nothing of worship. I cannot make my confession . . . No last rites . . . But Christ Jesus will have mercy on me and perhaps even on you. I forgive you, Mr Davison, for killing me . . ."

"I do not require your forgiveness."

"Thank God you were not . . . in the crowd with our Saviour, Mr Davison, or . . . the woman caught in adultery would assuredly have died. I forgive you and pray that . . . Christ will forgive you your many offences, particularly the deadly sin of spiritual pride, as I have no doubt He will forgive mine . . ."

With enormous effort the priest lifted his hand and made the sign of blessing, but it was to an empty room. Davison had left while he was talking, leaving him alone and unattended.

If he had indeed been solitary in the small panelled room, no doubt Tom Hart would have been distressed by it. Fortunately he knew he was not alone, for he could see me step from the moon to lay my hand on his brow and my mantle over his body. He smiled to see me and called me Mother, which pleased me, and stopped trying to fight his pain, which eased it a little. I am also the Comforter of the Afflicted, the Gate of Heaven, but his work was not yet done.

LXVIII

AMES STUMBLED THROUGH YET more muddy icy water of a drainage ditch and heaved himself up onto Gravel Lane, ran north along it and then dodged right, piled through a hedge and rolled among trees and dead undergrowth again. His shoulder was burning at him and the cold told him that the soft scabs which had formed had burst apart, so his blood left a clear trail behind him. He lay gasping for breath on his back, looking up at the stars and squinted to form the blurs and find the Great Bear, providentially in a part of the sky not quite covered by cloud. There it was, Polaris. If he stood and faced Polaris, he should turn right and go straight; Becket had said he would come to a series of gardens bounded with hedges which he should be able to slip through, considering how small and skinny he was.

Weaving between the trees he found the first hedge, flapped at it with his hands and then shoved at a place between trees where the hedgers had not woven the branches securely enough. If he had tried it in summer, he could not have got through, but in winter and not caring what he did to his clothes or his skin, he could manage.

Why am I doing this? he wondered briefly to himself and then decided that it was no longer important why.

Beyond the hedge was a neat vegetable garden laid out in rows, already dug and dunged for the spring planting, through which he ran careless of the gardeners' work. There was another hedge and the hounds were yelping among the trees. As he pushed through beside a tall beech tree, one found the scent again and gave tongue. His breath came raw, his head hammered and he was so sick with fear he could not feel the tearing of thorns. This is what it must feel like to be a hunted hare, he thought, and it had never occurred to him before, when he had gone hunting with his brothers, that the hare might suffer so.

The next garden had been planted with something, and through it he left a broad trail of footprints, hopping and stepping several times to leave more of them, feeling quite proud of himself that he was able to think so coolly with the maddening crying of dogs behind him.

Another hedge, this one too firmly plashed and interwoven to be broken. He followed it down to the lower end to a gate from the garden onto the broad common where cows lowed nervously at the sound of dogs. An amusing idea struck him. He ran to where the cows had been lying, as they clumsily got up, mooing and turning their horned heads. Generally speaking he was afraid of cows, but now he was more afraid of the dogs and so he ran among them and stood for a moment catching his breath, then shoved aside a few bony rumps and headed for a pollarded tree beside the gate to the Pike Garden.

The gate was iron and had spikes on the top, but the hedge beside it looked as if it could be climbed. He began to climb, hands wet with something other than sweat, cold air clammying his ripped shirt and doublet, the hair on his head stark upright as the hounds ran to the cows and began yelping and barking at them and trying to round them up.

Men's voices joined the noise, cursing and whipping the hounds away from the cows, who added to the bedlam with their distressed lowing. Ahead of him he could hear deeper, more threatening baying as the dogs in the kennels behind the bull-baiting ring awoke and gave tongue. Shutters were being flung open, women were screeching and babies crying.

He climbed over the top, very careful of the nearest spike since he was shaking with weariness, and dropped into the relative peace of the Pike Garden. In front of him were four large square tanks of water, assiduously kept free of ice by the fish farmers, like pools of ink, here and there giving back distorted stars to the sky.

He could run no more. He spat an ugly accumulation of phlegm and walked, still wheezing, unsteadily past the fish tanks, which fed Londoners on Fridays, and looked at the last hedge. Becket had given him very strict instructions here, being well-acquainted with bull-and bear-baiting lore.

"They leave a couple of the older mastiffs off their chains at night to be sure no one creeps in and tries to harm the dogs or drug them. Climb the hedge, but for God's sake, do not go on the ground."

He climbed, branches thrusting themselves in his face, where he could see the wooden backs of the dog kennels. As he lifted himself over the top he heard a couple of soul-satisfying splashes as the leading hounds hunting him fell into the pike tanks, followed by anguished yelping.

The roofs of the kennels sloped downwards and were slick with ice. There was no chance that he could do more than perch unsteadily on the roof-ridge, holding on to the hedge to keep himself from falling.

He squatted there, at last catching his breath, while the mastiffs who were roaming the yard discovered his rank smell and came running over. They barked and bayed and growled at him and tried to leap up to tear his throat out, falling back ungainly in a clatter of nails as their paws slipped on the icy kennel roofs. Every dog in the place was awake, straining on its chain, baying and yelping and growling. Behind, in the field beyond the hedge, the hunting hounds milled about, also giving tongue, hackles up, growling back at the mastiffs they could smell and hear beyond the hedge and wisely refusing to go any farther.

The noise was miraculous, and more was being added as the men behind the hounds came to the hedge and realised where they were, as the men who looked after the bulldogs found candles and torches and hose and came out of their houses to find what was causing the riot, as the cows in the field continued their offended lowing and as every soul on the South Bank put his head out of the window and bellowed to know what the hell was going on.

Ames squatted where he was and looked up at the Milky Way. His shoulder hurt him badly but his head was clear and he could breathe properly again, and above him as always was the crystal objectivity of the stars. Their riddle was the same as ever, but he had a new, less philosophical one, to contend with.

Why in the name of the Almighty am I smiling? he wondered.

It was stalemate, as Becket had predicted. The hounds would go no farther, and anyone climbing up the way Ames had done could be easily kicked off by him. And so Ramme and Munday must tramp round to the road, passing through an aggrieved householder's kitchen and hall, fending off demands for compensation for destroyed seedlings and the threat of a lawsuit that would make them sorry they were born, since the householder's cousin's wife's brother-in-law was a notable barrister . . . Once on Molestrand Dock, they must further march to the Bank and hammer on the gate of the bull-baiting ring and then persuade the owner to let them through, explain their business, show their Privy Council warrants, explain again to his brothers and a third time to his indignant wife.

And then the bull-baiting owner must call out the dog wardens. They must go into the broad yard behind the bull-baiting ring, call and chain up the two bulldogs, named Bessy and True, feed them to calm them down, tell them they were good dogs and had guarded well, tell every single hysterical dog in the place individually that it too was a good dog, and for God's sake, be quiet. Finally they could conduct their honours, the Queen's pursuivants, through the bull-baiting ring, past the dogs who were barking again and past more tanks full of fish to where Simon Ames sat now shivering and shaking on his kennel roof like an escaped monkey at a fair.

Both Ramme and Munday were dishevelled from their wild hunt, and Munday was walking with a limp. Both were grim and furious and then, when they saw Simon Ames, evidently and triumphantly alone, horrified.

"Where is Becket?" demanded James Ramme.

Ames grinned at them. "I have no idea, Mr Ramme," he said. "Have you seen him?"

Ramme's fists bunched uncontrollably and he stepped towards the kennel. "Come down from there!" he roared. The brown bulldog growled back and launched itself at him, to be jerked to a stop by its chain.

"Certainly not," said Ames fussily. "The dog might bite me."

It stood there pulling its chain almost off the staple, baying and howling while the dog warden came hurrying up to pull it back and be snapped at for his pains.

They managed to calm the dog with some meat and curses and dragged him away, still baying.

"Now come down, Mr Ames, or I will knock you down," hissed Ramme. Munday's head jerked as he turned to look.

"I congratulate you on your returned memory," said Ames complacently. "I would like to come down, but I fear I cannot. I might slip and hurt myself. Also my shoulder is wounded. Can you not find a ladder?"

"You know him?" Munday asked Ramme anxiously.

Ramme shrugged and beckoned a dog warden over to order him to fetch a ladder.

"You said you did not know him." Munday's voice was full of accusation.

The dog warden hesitated, eavesdropping in fascination until Ramme gestured angrily for him to be off after the ladder. Munday was dry-washing his hands.

"But if you know him, if he is in truth Mr Ames, then his warrant might have been real, it might have been from the Queen herself."

"Depend upon it, Mr Munday, he forged it."

"Never heard of anyone could forge the Privy seal. And the Queen's signature is—"

"The best judge of that will be the Queen's Majesty herself," interrupted Ames. "I desire you to take me to her immediately."

The dog warden came back with the ladder, beginning to forget his lost sleep and enjoy himself.

They placed the ladder on the angle of the roof so there was a smooth path to the ground.

"Now come down, or I come up and get you," said Ramme.

"Certainly, gentlemen."

All the temporary physical boldness born of fear had gone. Ames inched his way painfully down the slippery ladder and faced the two pursuivants, who were looking almost as battered and dirty as he must have been. Ramme had twigs caught in his hair; he had lost his hat and there was a wide rip in some expensive-looking damask. Munday's sober grey wool looked to have survived better, though it was darkened with splashed water.

Ramme grabbed Ames and tied his hands behind him, making him cry out with the pain to his shoulder. Munday looked and tutted.

"Best find a surgeon for him before he sees the Queen," he said, but Ramme only showed his teeth.

Ames had assured Becket repeatedly that if only he could avoid being ripped apart by the dogs, the pursuivants would surely treat him well and take him to the Queen, if for no other reason than to protect themselves in case he should turn out to be genuinely her servant. Now seeing the feral look on Ramme's face, he was not so sure. The cold winds of fear started blowing through his heart again and he was dizzy.

It was not exactly that he wanted to pass out, it was only that he saw no reason to resist as the world turned black and he fainted. His last conscious thought was the hope that Becket had turned his desperate performance as a decoy hare to good account, or he would want to know the reason why.

LXIX

THE PRIVY COUNCIL MEETING was as sterile as ever; matters to do with the Scottish envoys and the funeral of Sir Philip Sidney, set for the sixteenth of February, were dealt with quickly. The rest of the time was wasted in veiled beseechings that she sign the warrant for the execution of the Queen of Scots. Walsingham was absent, being sick of the stone; Davison had sent his excuses, being busy in a matter of a Papist priest. Only Burghley, Leicester and Hatton remained to plague her.

The Queen had a splitting headache. She had heard nothing from Thomasina, nothing from Mr Ames, and the uncertainty was wearing at her nerves like sandpaper. She dismissed her loyal councillors impatiently, wanting time to sit alone and think in the Privy Chamber, as she often did. As she sat, Mr Davison came in and bowed low to her, then knelt.

"What do you want, Mr Davison?" she demanded.

"This is a confidential matter," he said smoothly, glancing at her two gentlemen behind her chair.

She clicked her fingers and gestured that they should wait outside. They went resignedly, Drury leaving a goblet of spiced wine at her elbow in case she should need it.

"I have come to report complete success in the matter of the Book of the Unicorn," said Mr Davison in a soft harsh voice.

The pit of her stomach fell away into her red leather boots. But worse things had been said to her in her life and the red paint would hide the green pallor of her cheeks. She steadied herself, not noticing that the grip of her left hand on the table edge was driving all the blood from it.

"Oh?"

"Yes, Your Majesty," said Mr Davison. "We arrested a Father Tom Hart last night in Southwark, and expect momently to arrest his confederates. He had on him the Book of the Unicorn, which is now in my possession."

"How do you know what it is?"

"It has the remains of a unicorn embroidered on the cover, very finely worked. And inside is Your Majesty's own last will and testament."

She could not help it. Her breath wheezed out of her rib-cage as if she had been punched in the pit of her stomach. So this was how her reign ended.

"A forgery?" she said, trying a last throw.

"I think not."

Davison knelt before her, bodily humble but spiritually triumphant, as proud as Lucifer, condemnation of her childish looseness in every inch of his black-clad form. What did he know? What did any of them know? Just so had those who hungered for purity in all things driven her cousin Mary from the throne of Scotland. Just so would they treat her. Perhaps they would not drive her from the throne; perhaps, if she proved co-operative. But they would rule her and she would have to let them, for expediency. She would no longer be a regnant Queen, it would be worse than if she had risked taking a husband; she would be ruled by these men who could only think in black and white, and ruin would be at the end of it.

For a moment she almost lost control and would have screamed and wept and struck at Davison who had defeated her. She sat, turned to salt like Lot's wife, but this time for not looking back. "Be sure your sins will find you out," came the voice in her mind, echoing and whirling in the devastation within.

Damn him; Davison knew what he had. Beneath his respectful veneer his face was flushed and his eyes sparkled. She could almost see his thoughts spinning and clicking there, like an over-complex astrological clock; how he would have power, how he would be her Lord Treasurer instead of the old goat Burghley, how he would direct the kingdom from her shadow, how he would jerk her puppet strings and she would dance for him.

Or he would publish it and shame her before all the world. That was the unspoken threat, wrapped in self-righteousness. Lord God, how the Papists would sneer and enjoy it. How her people would be angered at the way she had fooled them with her virginity. They had respected and loved her for it, cheered when she had proclaimed that, nun-like, she was wedded to her kingdom, and now it turned out she was no better than a trull from the South Bank bawdy-houses by the fish-stews.

Whichever way it went, she was done for. She doubted many things and knew well how to hide her doubts behind a smoke-screen of verbiage and subtlety, but of this she had no doubt. Under the rule of these simple-minded God-besotted Puritans, her treasure would be poured out uselessly to aid the Netherlanders, and when King Philip sent his fleet, they would have neither money nor men to meet it.

By the year of Our Lord 1590, Philip will sit in what remains of London and England will be Catholic again, she thought bleakly. I will be dead, at least; but God's blood, the ruin of it, the ruin to my people . . .

Pity for the commoners who would die pointlessly fighting the veteran Spanish troops of the tercios and pity for herself welled up behind her nose, making it prickle and burn and bringing tears into her eyes.

She bit her lip and swallowed it all down mightily. Temporise, play for time, see what you can do, she told herself, there may be a way . . . What? She had no idea, only Time had always been her friend. She had won many battles simply by refusing to act, by refusing to choose sides, by deciding only when it was forced on her and the choice had narrowed down to no more than two options. Time will be my friend again, she thought.

So she would admit nothing. She waited until she could speak calmly, until the treasonous flood of tears had subsided again, and Davison waited with her, smug and confident with his lever to move the world.

"Well?" she said haughtily, challenging him to name his price.

"The Queen of Scots, Your Majesty," murmured Davison, complacently and predictably. "When shall I bring the warrant for her execution?"

So it began. First they would knock down the citadel gate, the better to send out troops to their co-religionists in the Netherlands. Very well. She would buy time with her cousin's life.

"Bring it to me with my other papers."

"Your Majesty will sign?"

"I will decide what to do when you bring it," she almost screamed at him. "Get out!"

She picked up the goblet to throw at him, but then thought better of it. If Davison planned to be her secret master, let him think she was more cowed than she was. Let him continue to underestimate her. Davison rose, bowed and backed from the Privy Chamber as she drained the spiced wine to the last drop. Its heat did not make any impression on the sick wilderness inside her.

Drury poked his head round the door.

"Your Majesty, will you—"

With an incoherent shriek of rage she threw the goblet straight and true for his head. It rapped his skull and bounced to the ground and he yelped and grabbed at the place, then disappeared behind the door again.

She got up, paced furiously past the stools by the council table, paced back again. The silver goblet was lying there, dented. She kicked it and it rang satisfyingly against the door panels.

"Bastard. Bastard Puritan."

By the time the door opened and Davison reappeared she had carefully mopped the tears that had welled up as she thought out the ramifications, dabbing with the corner of her handkerchief so as not to disarrange her face-paint, and was standing by the window, looking out on the cobbles of the Preaching Place.

She turned as he came in, bowed with exaggerated and ironic respect, laid a sheaf of papers on the table and then put out a selection of pens, an ink-pot, a sand shaker.

In grim silence, she came and sat down. He moved her chair for her. She did not thank him. She took the papers; most of them concerned the public order preparations for the funeral of Sir Philip Sidney. A couple were for minor offices at Court, and one for a contract for composition of purveyance with Cornwall. Amongst them was the warrant for the execution of Mary Stuart, once Queen of Scotland.

Her pen caught its drops of ink out of the ink-pot, she made the intricate flourishes, turning and turning again, forming the letters carefully as an exercise against internal dissolution. She could hear Davison breathing through his mouth beside her, excited, impatient, nervous. There it was, three papers down. No, she would not allow her hand to tremble. She was killing her cousin, executing an anointed Queen, instead of following sensible tradition and having her assassinated. This formal legalistic removal of a crowned head with an axe was in the way of a door opening; any fool who read history could tell that. Who else would they end by executing, if they could execute a monarch? Perhaps they would eventually execute her for the crimes of fornication and abortion; why not?

The pen swept on, forming its loops automatically, steadily. I have killed before, the Queen thought; certainly I have killed many times by proxy—by signing warrants for execution, by sending men to fight. Any monarch's hands are soiled wet with blood, but our anointing gives us dispensation from God. This is none so ill a death I am sending her to: she may be a martyr and wipe out her former sins and to die by the axe is not so very bad; you have warning, you may settle your affairs. To be sure there is the fear of it before . . .

She had not seen her mother die, had not been old enough to know anything but whispers and looks and the rumour of disaster. Her mind could form things she had not seen, though, and the picture of Tower Green and the swordsman hacking at her mother's neck had ripped her from her sleep many times until she became Queen. At least as a regnant Queen, she had thought she would be safe from it. But now no more. What they could do to Mary Stuart, they could do to her. She could only pray the silly cautious lawyers on her council did not realise it. Now Davison moved restlessly, unable to bear the tension as her pen swept through its ceremonial loops.

"Your Majesty has a great many calls upon your time," he murmured, watching greedily. "It may be worth considering the making of a signature stamp, as the Scots King does."

Pure rage made the pen wobble in her hand. Oh yes, she thought, a signing stamp, for you to hold, Mr Davison, and use to destroy your enemies; yes, I am sure you would like that very much indeed. Over my dead body, Mr Davison. She said nothing aloud. Let the ambitious weevil dream his dreams of power.

There, it was done, fully formed, a triumphal expression of the power of her name. Davison let out a soft sigh of triumph. She looked up at him steadily, comforting herself with the image of him screaming for mercy as the executioner disembowelled and castrated him. It was a pleasant thought but she was too realistic to think it could ever be true. He was not, strictly speaking, a traitor, but something more subtle and more dangerous.

"There you are, Mr Davison," she said. "Take that to Walsingham. No doubt the joy of it will go near to killing him outright."

LXX

LORD BURGHLEY WAITED FOR Davison at the end of the Privy Gallery, looking out of the diamond-paned window on the graceful curves of the Holbein Gate. He was lame with gout again, but had hopes that summer weather would ameliorate it.

A door banged farther down and Burghley turned to look. There was Davison, an extraordinary sight, one fist high above his head in victory, the other fist clutching a sheaf of papers, and his legs doing a quick clumsy jig on the matting.

Burghley smiled at the sight and then became grave again. It would not do to laugh at the man when he was happy. Davison came towards him, pacing fast, face shining.

"Hm?" Burghley asked.

"*Habeo.*" said Davison. "I have it. Look."

He held out one of the papers, formally written over in secretary hand except for the commanding flourish of italic at the bottom. It gave orders for the execution of a Queen.

"Thank God," said Burghley fervently, "you did it. Mr Davison, you are a marvel. My congratulations, a coup indeed, a veritable coup." He pounded Davison on the back, and Davison for once in his life accepted the familiarity without bridling. Then, remembering who he was and where they were, Burghley coughed and stopped.

"We must set it all in train at once," he said. "Lord knows how soon Her Majesty will change her mind . . ."

"This time I think she will not."

"She might. She might well. You do not know her as I do, Mr Davison; it has been a veritable cross to my back. How did you manage it, how did you persuade . . ."

"I brought her stronger arguments and in the end she yielded, as all women must," said Davison sententiously.

"Quite so, quite so," said Burghley. "And these arguments were . . . ?"

"Forgive me," said Davison. "I had rather not run through them again just yet, my voice is hoarse with it."

"Hm," said Burghley, wondering a little. There had been none of the dramatic sounds he had come to expect from the Queen's being persuaded to do something against her will, only Drury retiring with blood on his head from something she had thrown. Davison himself seemed completely unscathed, not a drop of ink on him anywhere.

Never mind. It was done. They had the warrant and could extirpate the serpent.

"I will send Beale with it at once, and we must go immediately to Seething Lane to consult with Sir Francis," he said. "He will be delighted. Truly, Mr Davison, you are a valuable addition to Her Majesty's councillors; any man who can persuade her to make a decision, any decision, never mind such a one as this, is valuable beyond pearls. I believe Sir Francis has found a man who is willing to do the office of executioner, and if we move quickly we may see the serpent dead by next week."

"Not sooner?"

"Certainly sooner if we can, but the thaw has begun and the roads to Fotheringhay will be very bad. I doubt anyone can reach the place in less than two days, though he ride like the wind; it is off the route of the regular couriers and very isolated. Yes, certainly, we shall send Beale, and perhaps Shrewsbury and Kent can be witnesses. The local gentry must be alerted so they can witness it also, and perhaps you would care to go north too . . . Well, well, so you persuaded her . . . I would never have thought it; I had made up my mind she was intending to wait it out until the woman dropped dead naturally."

Davison simpered as they walked back along the Privy Gallery and turned to go through the Privy Chamber and out of the Queen's apartments.

LXXI

THE WEATHER HAD SUDDENLY turned warmer with the clouds from the west. Not, to be sure, exactly warm, in fact it felt colder because of the rain, but the hard grip of frost on London was broken. Thomasina and David Becket were the last to be able to cross the Thames dry-shod, and they had to skip lightly and quickly while the ice groaned and cracked under them. Neither of them spoke while they crossed, needing to concentrate on keeping their feet, and unwilling to mention to each other the sounds of hunting and dogs from Southwark where Ames was playing his part of decoy. The sound of a hunt is hard to resist; as they had hoped, the men-at-arms set to bar the Thames to them had come excitedly up the steps and plunged southwards into the Lambeth Marsh, eager to be in at the kill. In a couple of minutes the coast was clear and they had hurried down the steps. Endearingly, Becket put out his hand to hold hers, to reassure her, and then coughed and looked embarrassed when he remembered she was not really a child.

"Do you have children, Mr Becket?" she asked him as they climbed the Whitefriars Steps.

"As far as I know, only one."

The cautious answer made her grin. "Not married?"

Becket's voice had a single-noted dole to it. "No."

"And the mother of your child?"

"Married someone else who could better support her."

"I am sorry to hear it."

"Well, I am not a very good catch, as Eliza pointed out, and the man who offered for her was a rich merchant who was also sick with the stone and unlikely to trouble her much."

"Ah," said Thomasina wisely, and nodded. They walked up Temple Lane companionably enough, past the cloisters of the old Dominican monastery, through the little gate to the yard at the back of Crocker's Lane. There Thomasina left Becket to hide by the jakes while she trotted softly up the stairs to check for pursuivants. Moments later she came down, smiling, and they climbed the stairs to Father Hart's lodging.

Becket produced a key and opened the door and they went in. Thomasina turned and looked warily at him.

"What did you want to tell me?"

Becket poured himself some aqua vitae, then looked at her, and poured her some as well. She took it with a grateful smile.

"How long shall we wait for Father Hart?" she asked.

"No time at all," said Becket, sighing yet again and making a stool creak under his bulk. "I only wanted to speak to you in private."

Thomasina climbed onto the bed and sat there cross-legged, sipping occasionally.

"Mistress Thomasina," he said, taking the deep breath that betokens bad news unwillingly delivered. "Mistress Thomasina . . . I am sorry, I lied to Ames at the mill."

"Oh?"

"In the fight by the Falcon, I am certain sure I saw Father Hart take a halberd in the back. At the very least, Davison has him and also the Book of the Unicorn."

She almost dropped her little horn-cup, then put her face in her free hand and wailed, "Oh no."

"Wait, mistress, this is not so very bad—"

"Oh, but it is, Mr Becket, it is. Oh, poor lady, poor lady . . . If it's true what you say is in it . . . My God, they will crucify her."

"Wait . . . Listen to me."

She was crying and rocking herself. "They will depose her like they did the Queen of Scots . . . Oh my God, what will she say to me . . ."

"Mistress Thomasina," bellowed Becket, too tired to be patient. "Act your age and listen to me."

Thomasina's head jerked up and she glared at him. Nobody had ever said that to her before.

"Now," Becket continued quietly, pouring more aqua vitae, "it is true that Davison has the Book of the Unicorn. However, we did not buy it sight unseen. The first time we saw it, there was the Queen's will and confession in it. The second time, after we bought it, I checked again and both the pages had been cut out."

Thomasina's mouth dropped open. "You mean . . . ?"

Becket was smiling cynically. "Yes, mistress, the old hag coney-catched us. She still has the will and the confession with her somewhere. It suited me that Father Hart should have the book and not the confession, so I said nothing about it and let him think it was complete."

"So then . . ." Thomasina was laughing with relief. "So then, all Davison has is a book of recommendations to the—"

"State of virginity, yes." Becket laughed with her. "I am sure he will find it very edifying. But he has not gotten the Queen's confession of fornication, adultery and abortion."

Thomasina reached out and touched his arm.

"Do not judge her too harshly," she said softly, recognising the condemnation in Becket's tone. "To be sure, she sinned, but I think she has paid for it since."

Becket moved his bulk on the stool. "I'll say nothing of it," he rumbled. "Lord knows, I am not one to sit in judgement of mortal sin."

Thomasina finished her drink and jumped off the bed.

"Where are you going, mistress?"

"Back to the Falcon, to find the witch."

Becket shook his head. "She is gone. I looked for her, under cover of finding the jakes; she must have scuttled off as soon as she had the money and the cut pages with her."

Sheer dismay made Thomasina sit down again. "She did. I saw her go. Why in God's name did I not . . . Pffft. It is all to do again."

Becket nodded ruefully. "We must find one old woman among all the old women in London."

"But . . . but where shall we start?"

Becket shrugged and poured more aqua vitae. "God knows, mistress, only I think we wait for a while."

"Why?"

"Davison will know the important pages went missing. He will look for her as well."

"So we should move faster, before he discovers her."

Becket shook his head. "No," he said, "because his pursuivants will be out in force, ripping London apart to find her. And us. She knows it too. Depend on it, she will go to ground somewhere, avoid the Falcon like a plague-house, stay away from her usual haunts and hide. Let Davison's search cool, and then she might come out to spend her money and then we might catch her."

"What if Davison finds her first?"

"I doubt that he will. One old woman in London town? No. Even if he does, what can we do about it?"

Thomasina nodded and put her horn-cup down on the floor.

"Well, certainly, I can do something about it," she said. "I think it is time to talk to the Queen. Once she knows that Davison has the book but not the confession, she can take steps herself. Will you stay here?"

"No," said Becket wearily, rubbing his eyes. "Father Hart will tell Davison where his base is. If he has not done so already. In fact, we should move at once, before the pursuivants arrive to search the place."

"There is gold in the chest that Ames broke open."

Becket grinned. "Excellent." He opened it, took the bags and hid them under his shirt. "Once the search dies down, I will find the hag," he said.

"Why could you do it when Davison cannot?"

"Because I know where old witches are likely to go to get drunk on their ill-gotten gains."

"How will I contact you?" Thomasina asked.

"While you are talking to the Queen," Becket said, speaking across her words, "make sure she finds Ames and gets him out of whatever dungeon Davison throws him into. I think he could not survive an interrogation."

"No, indeed. Of course I will. How will we pass messages?"

"Do you know Dr Nunez?"

"Yes."

"Through him then. He is trustworthy, and Simon's uncle."

"If you want to find me, you must ask my lord the Earl of Leicester's major-domo, Mr Benson."

"And he will have me thrown out for troubling my lord's household."

"Mmm." She went to Hart's chest, found paper and pen and ink, wrote swiftly for a while. For all his misery at the return of the black mountain of fear in his heart, Becket hid a half-smile to see her childish head in its grubby biggin cap bent over paper, and the woman's writing flowing from her pen. But he took the paper without unseemly comment, found it to be a letter of introduction proudly signed "Thomasina de Paris, muliercula, the Queen's Fool."

"Are you French then?" he asked, tapping the name.

Thomasina laughed. "No, Paris as in Paris Garden. I was one of the tumblers there before I came to the Queen."

"And found your fortune."

"Certainly," she said, her chin tilted with pride. "The Queen has been my most kind and loving mistress."

"Is it true she throws things at courtiers when they annoy her?"

Thomasina grinned impishly. "Certainly. I myself have seen my lord Burghley with an ink-pot upended on his head."

Becket shook his head in wonder. "Sidney told me she did, but I did not believe him. Well, well. We had best be going."

They went down the stairs and through Crocker's Lane to the morning bustle of Fleet Street.

"Farewell, Mistress Thomasina," Becket said. She nodded brightly and skipped into the street, then turned back and gravely shook his hand. He bowed to her as if she had been a great lady of the Court. It touched her heart and she said impulsively, "Mr Becket, the Queen will be sure not to forget your faithfulness in this matter. I am sure you will be rewarded."

"No, mistress," said Becket heavily. "I think you mistake Her Majesty. Knowing what I know, I think she will never forgive me."

Thomasina bit her lip because this was true, and then ran off down Fleet Street to Leicester's palace on the Strand. Becket set his shoulders, turned and walked the other way to the City and the goldsmiths along Cheapside, his broad back prickling for fear of pursuivants.

LXXII

NOW MARK HOW THE affairs of men and princes may be turned by the very tiniest of events. You convince yourselves that you are masters of your fate, and so you are, somewhat. But at any time your plans are no steadier than walnut-shell boats, with a sail of paper and a mast of a toothpick bobbing on the ocean swell.

The Earl of Leicester is a puissant lord who has a hundred servants to do his bidding in his palace on the Strand. The man in charge of them, his majordomo, had been introduced to Thomasina in her new guise as a beggarmaid.

Alas, for Mr Benson. Being in his cups on the night that Ames and Becket escaped from the Fleet, he fell down three pair of stairs and broke his leg and his head. As Thomasina skipped down Fleet Street, through Temple Bar and along the Strand, Leicester's household was being ruled by the major-domo's deputy, a plump, efficient fellow who had never met her, and the whole place was in uproar.

"No," snapped the cook at the child who was standing at the kitchen door, fury blazing in her eyes. "I'll not disturb Mr Benson, certainly not. How dare you, you little kinchin mort; now get out."

"I have a very important message for him," insisted the beggarmaid. "I must see him."

"You may see Mr Howard and content yourself, it's more than you're worthy of."

"No," said the beggarmaid. "I do not want to see Mr Howard, I want to see Mr Benson . . ."

The cook pushed her away from the door and picked up a basket of wizened pot herbs.

"Sam, come here and peel these. I want two pounds of breadcrumbs and the lard in the green pot."

"It is extremely urgent that I see Mr Benson," repeated the beggarmaid in a high, insistent voice. "This concerns the Queen's Majesty, it is very very important—"

"Important to get yourself a chance at the silver plate," sneered the cook. "I know your kind. Get out."

"No, you fool!" shouted the beggarmaid. "I have a message for Mr Benson, he knows me—"

The cook strode over to her and cuffed her ear hard enough to knock her into a pile of kindling. He threw a stale penny loaf at her.

"There's some food for you, you little bitch; now get out."

Unwisely the cook turned his back on her, and was hit on the head by the bread-roll, shrewdly thrown. The beggarmaid was standing up, red with rage.

"How dare you!" she shouted. "How dare you touch me! I must see Mr Benson—"

The cook picked her up by the back of her ragged kirtle and threw her bodily through the kitchen door so she landed on the midden.

"If you come back, you'll get a whipping. Go and beg somewhere else."

A couple of hours later, the Earl of Leicester's still-room woman went bustling into Mr Benson's sick-room with a posset and found a beggarmaid climbing breathlessly onto the window-ledge. She stank of vegetable peelings and animal guts and was scratched with hedge twigs from her climb up the side of the house.

The still-room woman knew what to do with thieves. She caught the child deftly after a certain amount of dodging about the room and shrieking, twisted her arm behind her and brought her to Mr Howard. Mr Benson was too deeply drugged with laudanum to wake up.

"She was trying to steal from Mr Benson's room," reported the still-room woman, "but I caught her at it."

The beggarmaid's face was ugly with fury as she writhed in the woman's maternal grip. "I am not a child . . ." she hissed. "I have a message for Mr Benson . . . He knows me."

"No doubt," said Mr Howard, looking at her with disgust.

"Will you call the magistrates?" asked the woman.

"No," said Mr Howard. "I am far too busy to go through that. Besides, the child is undoubtedly working for some upright man to bring him what she steals. I expect she is hungry."

"She seems plump enough."

"Listen to me. I tell you I have an important message—"

"No, child, you listen to me. It is a very wicked thing to go climbing into men's bedrooms to steal their belongings, especially when they are gravely ill with a broken leg. God sees all you do and knows when you sin, and stealing is a sin. We are Christian folk here and we will not give you to the magistrates if you tell us the name of the upright man that is your master."

"There's no upright man, you fat half-wit. I am not a child at all, damn you, I am the Queen's muliercula—"

The still-room woman fetched her a ringing slap on the cheek. "How dare you swear at Mr Howard when he is being kind to you, bad girl!" she scolded.

"Let me see my lord of Leicester; he knows me too."

Both of them laughed at the child's delusion. "My lord is a very great man," said Mr Howard. "Being a good, charitable nobleman, he may have given you money in the street, but that does not mean he knows you. Now tell us who ordered you to steal from here."

"I was not stealing. I was trying to deliver a message."

"And the message was?"

"To admit me to the house so I can change and to hitch up my carriage so I can return to Court and speak to the Queen, my mistress."

Mr Howard exchanged glances with the still-room woman and both shook their heads. The little maid was clearly wandering in her wits.

"Child," said Mr Howard, not unkindly, "to your previous sin of attempted theft you are now adding the further sin of lying. Now come, sweeting, admit your fault and we might even give you a penny."

The child's shriek skewered his ears and quite shocked him. Nobody had ever suggested he put a penny in such a place before. Over the shrieking, he said quietly to the still-room woman,

"She is obdurate in her wickedness, but we shall still be kind to her. Birch her to teach her to mend her ways and follow God's law, lock her in the woodshed overnight and then give her some food and let her go. If she comes back here, we will certainly give her to the magistrates, who will treat her much less gently."

True, the child's stony glare as the still-room woman hauled her away did give him pause. So did her quiet parting shot that she would see him apologise to her grovelling on his knees, dismissed from his place and barred from any other. But so many of the street children had a battered maturity beyond their calendar years, corrupted and aged by their immoral lives. Certainly he had never met one so insolent nor so persistent; most were happy enough to use flattery and humility to escape if they were caught. Perhaps the child was touched with madness as well as being a beggar, perhaps that was why she was a beggar. Truly he pitied rather than condemned her, and forgave her foul language and the time he had wasted on her.

LXXIII

AMID ALL THESE COMPLEXITIES and heroics, where was my daughter-in-law? If she had known then what I know, she would of course have acted differently, but she was still meshed in the web of reality. Her soul still wore its tattered carcass, her bones still ached, her hands were still stiff and swollen, her guts were still disordered and her head still full of tobacco smoke and the fumes of aqua vitae.

At least she was warm. Cold was familiar to her from her earliest days in the nunnery. The nuns' cells could never be warmed properly in the winter and they were enjoined to offer up the discomfort of breaking the ice on the water in their bowls in the morning to the glory of God and the subduing of flesh. Which was economical of firewood.

She thought of the mirrored room at the Falcon as she sat by a roaring fire, thought of the men and their gold. To my sight then they were children, and she saw them likewise. Large, loud, dangerous children. The one called Father Hart was short and neatly made, with bright knowing eyes; the other a hulk, tall and heavy with a brooding face and black curls, whose eyes found her as invisible and discountable for lack of interest in her wrinkled flesh as any other man. Mary was neither a man nor yet a bonny girl he could imagine lying with; therefore she was nothing.

To be nothing is very painful. I too have been old, although you would never know it from men's pictures of me. I was in my middle years when I held my Son on my knees and marvelled at the dead weight of Him, at the ugliness of his wax flesh, at the smell of death on Him, when the babe that He was and the man He became melted together in a corpse that stabbed my heart with a sword. So it is with any woman misfortunate enough to live to bury her child. They never show this; all the artists paint me or carve me as a young creature, such as they prefer being men, slender and smooth-faced and virginal. They never show that I had thickened at the waist, as you do, that my face was tired, that my hands were hard with work. Do you think they honour me to show me as a young miss with a bovine expression on her face? No, for I had become something very different, less delicious to an artist but far more honourable. Perhaps I looked as they picture me only once, when I stood bewildered in a garden with Mary Magdalen and recognised the gardener.

After the hurry of that time, even after the flames that came on the wind from heaven, I aged as all flesh must if it live. My hair whitened, my teeth loosened and yellowed, and every pool of water was an ambush of truth, every man's expression a revelation. Do you think some reversed alchemy aged my inward thoughts as Time's rape changed my face? No, for our inward thoughts stem from our souls, which are immortal and therefore ageless. Within my battlements of age spots and wrinkles I was still a girl, still surprised at men's dismissal, when once they had paid tribute. So Mary was also, and so she despised the men she had decided to coney-catch.

As they counted out the gold, Mary laughed to herself, because within the broad compass of each golden crown and angel she saw the barrels of aqua vitae lining up, and also her darling girl Pentecost's dowry, to match her to a man who would not beat her too badly and free her of the bawdy-house where she was born. Would such a man have her? Certainly he would, if the dowry was big enough. Mary would take care in her choice. She would find her a man old enough and sick enough that soon Pentecost would be a widow and could please herself.

Also she laughed because she had cut out the meat of the matter. When making the deal she had felt no compunction at ruining the Queen—what had the heretical bitch ever done for her?

But then she took thought, and in her anger with Father Hart's refusal to absolve her it seemed to Mary's fuddled mind that she might make them pay twice. And so, surrounded as she was by multiple truthful mirrors, she hid the Book of the Unicorn among the tattered blue and green velvet patches of her skirts. Her thumbnail she grew long and sharp, the better to cut purses with when she could and also for breaking women's waters. It was the work of a couple of heartbeats to draw the sharp talon down the gutter between the pages and so cut out the last two pages out, fold them and stow them in the pocket of her petticoat. Then she wrapped the gold round her loins, gave the overgrown boys their book and hurried out of the room, down the stairs one at a time to favour her bad knee, along the back passage, into the yard and scuttled as fast as her poor legs could go to Paris Garden Stairs.

Well, no, it was not quite so simple as that. There were men waiting by the back door as well, who moved when Mary first appeared. Then they saw her in their lantern-light: hunched over, ugly, grey wisps of hair starting from her cap, muttering toothlessly to herself and cackling. Had they thought to stop her they could have made a mighty gain for their master Davison. But they did not. They were there to arrest two men who might well fight them and were nerving themselves to do that. To be invisible, to be of less importance than a louse is not always a burden.

It would have been a harder matter usually to cross the Thames, but with the ice, Mary could step down from the jetty and walk across. Even then she was not fool enough to run, for Time rots your bones as well as your face and she was afraid she might break her hip.

However, she did not go to the Whitefriars Steps, nor the City. I had conceived a plan even as it occurred to her to keep the Queen's testament and confession. It was a frightening plan, now she saw the state of the Thames ice, for the ice seemed worn and there were black patches where it had gone thin; it creaked and bounced under her. She stepped as lightly as she could, prancing like a pony sometimes as she heard it groan. When she was at the other side, in the shadow of the walls, she turned left, heading westwards and past the gardens of the great men's houses on the Strand. For all her fears, I bade her stay on the ice which would not hold a trail. She muttered at me, complaining as the cold broke through the thin soles of her turn-shoes and numbed her bare feet and ankles within. It took a long time. Once she hid in a booth of the Frost Fair, to rest her poor bones and finish her bottle of aqua vitae, and must have slept. When I jerked her awake at the far-off sound of dogs, she was stiff and numb with cold. But she got up and shuffled on, talking to me as I encouraged her, flapping her arms to move the sluggish blood about her blue veins.

She was in terror that there would be a hue and cry for her. The heavy man who called himself Strangways had not borne the look of someone who would be lightly coney-catched. She kept close in to the wall, passing by York Stairs and Hungerford House, panting and feeling the burning pain in her chest that came often when she was carrying heavy pails, past the kilns of Scotland Yard where the workmen were already piling in the firewood to heat them up, and at last she came to Mrs Twiste's laundry. It has a door that gives straight onto the river, so they can draw water direct from the Thames, although there is water piped in from the Whitehall conduit. Mostly the door is rarely used save in a summer drought, but Mary had gone through it to come to the Falcon earlier that day, and left it unlocked.

She passed through into the boiling-room where they were working at the fire under the coppers, to build it up and start the water in its day-long boil. She slipped past, bearing some bolts of wood she had stored just within the door, for nobody questions an old woman carrying firewood.

Of course they were no longer living at the Falcon. In the little cubby where the children keep their cloaks Mary found Pentecost, curled like a puppy, shook her awake and took her blinking and yawning down to Mary's own kingdom in the basement, where the barrels of piss wait to mature as if they were beer. She did not show the child what she had. She sent her to fetch aqua vitae with a shilling that Mary had saved for celebration, and then she wrapped her great-granddaughter's dowry in a bag made of a shirt she had stolen and put it in the freshest barrel, hanging on a string. That made her laugh too, though the stink of the place always lifts her head off, and taking the lid off a barrel is something no one would do willingly.

Pentecost came back with the bottle and some bread and cheese. She had a jug of beer as well. They broke their fast companionably among the barrels while Pentecost chattered on about the doings of the little daughters of the laundry women; how Susanna had said this, how Kate had pinched Anna, and was it possible that Lizzy had her own white pony with a golden bridle, as she claimed? She spoke wistfully of the child-woman that was a Court tumbler and hoped she would come back and show them more somersaults and she complained that she had hurt her knuckles grating soap and Mrs Stevens had shouted at her for getting blood in it.

Then Mary must get up and put on the yoke to carry her pails. Pentecost turned to go back to her work amongst the laundry women, but her grandam stopped her.

"You come with me today," Mary told her as she counted the pails on her little wheelbarrow, took up the handles and set off.

It was exciting for Pentecost. She had helped wash the underlinen of numerous courtiers but had never seen the Court itself. So she trotted alongside my liegewoman proudly in her blue kirtle and white cap and little apron and Mary's heart ached to see her so eager and dainty. Pentecost's grandmother, little Magdalen, child of her whoredom, that Mary carried strapped to her back along endless hostile roads, had looked just so when she was a child. But Magdalen was a whore by the time she was thirteen and a mother at the age of fifteen. She had five children that she carried to term, one boy who went completely to the bad and two girls who survived to bear children. One was the under-madam at the Falcon, and one was herself a drunken whore, and bore twice, leaving only little Pentecost alive, who killed her. To think of it: so many children in the babe Mary carried and this the last of them that she knew of. Pentecost must have a dowry, Pentecost would have a dowry; this had been all Mary's thinking for a year, once she began to feel the hot burning pain in her chest and knew she would die soon. At least, if Mary slipped through my Blessed fingers and ended in Hell, she would know she had done her best for the child; her mother and grandmother Mary had killed through her incontinence and drunkenness, but Pentecost she would save, come all the world in arms against her. I, the Blessed Virgin, had promised it to my daughter-in-law, I had sworn on my Immaculacy that she would do it.

Mary had planned out her rounds in the Court to save her back. She went first to the farthest chambers, all the way down to Cannon Row, almost in Westminster Hall. In and out of the chambers went Pentecost and her grandam, every one of them crowded with beds, clothes and jewels, although by that time in the morning most of the courtiers were out of their rooms, out trying to gain an office or a wardship, oiling their way through the many layers of the Court.

She never stole. Yes, there was temptation wherever she looked; jewels and costly wrought doublets and bodices and billaments left lying carelessly; gowns and kirtles hanging on walls and folded in open chests that could feed her for a year; plate in plenty wherever she turned. With my help she touched none of it. As I told Mary when first she thought of thieving, if anything went missing after her round, then she would lose her invisibility and become the first they would accuse. Papers are different; papers may be misplaced—and why would an old hag want papers?—but jewels, well, even hags may desire jewels. Sometimes Mary would finish up scraps of food left on plates by lazy servants, and once she found a nibbled marchpane fancy under a bed which she brought back for Pentecost; but that was not stealing, that was preventing waste. She took perks from the laundry, of course, everyone takes perks; shirts that have lost their marks, candle ends, firewood, rose-water and purveyance soap, to give to her granddaughter at the Falcon. Julia showed no gratitude for her gifts, though.

In and out they went, leaving the wheelbarrow at the end of the Stone Gallery, where there is too great a flight of steps to bring it down. She had gone to it to change the pails once before she went into my lord Chamberlain's rooms in the part of the palace called the Prince's lodgings. There she saw a young gentleman pacing about by the window that looked on the Court Orchard. Robin Carey was still under house arrest and confined to his father's apartments, where he was bored witless. He looked up at the noise of Pentecost's prattle, smiled and then went back to his caged pacing. Both Pentecost and Mary thought he was a handsome gentleman with good legs, but Mary was as invisible to him as to all of them. His lute lay abandoned on the window-seat and from the number of screwed-up pieces of paper lying about, he was trying to write a letter, no doubt to the Queen, abasing himself and begging for forgiveness. These things are necessary at Court.

Mary curtseyed to him and pushed Pentecost's shoulder so she did the same; he nodded politely and turned his back as they did their business and shuffled out.

At last they came by the Privy Gallery, where the Queen lives with her women. Mary was supposed to go down to the door of the Queen's own bed-chamber and scratch softly on it, so that the Queen's chamberer could bring out

Her Majesty's slops. Yes, they go in the common bucket, although perhaps if Mary had thought to bottle them separately, she could have sold them to the besotted populace like saints' relics or the once-numerous Sacred Drops of my Milk. Perhaps she should have done so, although that would have been to risk an accusation of witchcraft and necromancy against the Queen. "Who knows how powerful a poison could be made against her from her own waste?" the physicians would have said. Unicorn's horn would scarcely prevail against it, they would agree, rubbing their beards importantly.

On this morning Mary hurried, pails and all, down the sacred Privy Gallery, past the red-clad men-at-arms who nodded her through. Courtiers pay fortunes to be allowed therein; Mary went there every morning and sometimes ventured farther than her remit. Beyond the Queen's bedchamber were record rooms and the Library, and it was to the Library that Mary took Pentecost, praying devoutly to me that there would be no one in it.

There was not, other than myself, the Blessed Virgin, standing smiling by the shelves, to show my approval. Mary put the pails by the door, so she would have warning if anyone came in, and took Pentecost by the hand. She knew her way in there. Occasionally she borrowed books—no, sir, not stole, for she brought them back after she had read them. Reading is a hard habit to shake, once learned.

Pentecost and she went along the shelves looking for a book that was dusty enough from disuse and low enough that Pentecost could find it. I pointed with my silver finger to help them. There was one, beautifully bound in red leather, with craggy old-fashioned letters that in Latin proclaimed it a Dissertation upon the Blessed Sacrament, by Henricus Rex. That made me smile; it could not have been a better choice if she had searched the whole library for it. The nuns of Mary's girlhood had loyally bought one of those books for their convent library early in the Queen's father's reign, though I doubt a single one of them had taken the trouble to read it. To own one was enough then, for King Henry wrote his Defense of the Blessed Sacrament in contraversion of the heretic Luther, and in gratitude was made Fidei Defensor, Defender of the Faith, by the Pope.

Mary took the folded sheets of paper she had cut from the Book of the Unicorn, slipped them between the pages of argument, and put the book back in its gap. Where to hide paper? In a library, of course. Mary knew there would be men combing London for her and if they caught her they would find anything she had on her and no doubt could make her tell where she had hidden everything else, including the gold of Pentecost's dowry. This was the best place she could think of; a place impossible for a mere man to enter unless he were a councillor of the Queen, but clear and open to a mere night-soil woman.

Why should she know that it was a Queen's Privy Councillor who was her worst enemy? I had said nothing of it. She was in terror of pursuivants, and also afraid of the men she had coney-catched and could think of nowhere else that could not be searched. For if pursuivants search, be quite sure they will find what they seek.

"Do you see it?" she asked Pentecost. "Can you remember the book?"

The little girl's eyes were round and wide, her mouth an O. She nodded, reverent at being in such a place with so many books. As pointlessly as she had with Magdalen and her children, Mary had taught the child her alphabeta and she could spell out words, but was not a reader and certainly did not know Latin.

"Those papers carry the Queen's honour, like a chick in an egg," Mary said to her. "Remember where they are. If I should die you must find a way to come back here and fetch the papers. Then keep them until you can find a Catholic priest and sell them to him for the most you can get. They are worth thousands of pounds. Do you understand?"

Pentecost nodded again, wonder stopping her usual mill-race of words. Mary told her the name of the book and made her repeat it, then she made the child look at the shelf where it was and pinched her arm hard enough to hurt, so she would remember it well.

They hurried out and back along the corridor, where they found the Queen's chamberer waiting impatiently with her silver pot. Mary mumbled incoherently when she wanted to know where they had been and after she had lifted her skirts to reassure the woman that she had nothing stolen under them, they hurried on, careful with the pails, always careful with the pails, although God knows the lazy young gentlemen sneak into corners and water them plentifully like dogs. Mary finished her round as swiftly as she could, afraid that the Queen would be back from chapel before she ended and might even recognise her across the decades.

And then there was the hardest part: to trundle the heavy wheelbarrow back down steps and up steps and along through the Preaching Place, around the kitchens, through the woodyard and so in at the back of the laundry, and there Mary could catch her breath and sit down while the burning in her chest settled, before the work of emptying out the pails into the strainers.

She longed to sleep, had been up all night. But she showed Pentecost the packet in its wet hiding place and told her it was hers, to take when her grandam was dead.

The child's eyes filled with tears, though it cannot be a blessing to have an old witch for a grandam, and she asked tremulously why Mary might die. So she told her what she already knew, that we all must die and Mary's time was surely near, seeing how long she had lived and how old she was. Pentecost came to put her arms around Mary and declare that she loved her.

How could Mary tell her that she loved a cesspit of wickedness, a witch damned by her sins, one so evil a priest had refused her absolution? No, she was a coward and let her continue to love, asking me for forgiveness for it.

When Pentecost had gone skipping to see what job Mrs Twiste might have for her, Mary sat a long while and drank. Then she went on her knees to pray to the Queen of Heaven that Pentecost might live, that she might find all the things Mary had hidden for her, that she might prosper, that her children might be raised up to be virtuous and not whores and footpads like her own. If only Pentecost could climb out of the gutter, Mary's life would not be a complete ruin. Mary did not pray to Almighty God, nor yet to her wayward husband, Christ Jesus my Son, for she felt both were too great to hear her prayers. Certainly, they had shown no signs of hearing them before. She prayed to me, the Queen of Heaven, as she always did, and Saint Mary Magdalen, who might better understand her, that we intercede with Our Lord. Perhaps we heard her. She began saying a rosary, from the string of beads she kept round her neck, all that remained to her of her former marriage, her jointure, if you like. I have many faces, many guises: as the Queen of Heaven, and as Theotokos and Saint Sophia, the God-Bearer and Holy Wisdom. Since the Protestants rose up and drove me from religion, they have had a less kindly belief, I think, a more intemperate and demanding God. When Mary was a child, barren women and women whose babies forever died at birth could go on pilgrimage to the shrine at Walsingham and leave gifts for me, pointless pretty things such as bracelets and rings and necklaces, lengths of blue and white cloth, whatever they could afford. Now the Divines laugh at it and call it superstition. So? Some of those women bore children that lived—who cares what they did to gain them, and who are the Divines to laugh at them? Once there was a time when men too reverenced the Queen of Heaven and were gentler for it, I think. Is it so very ill to pray to Holy Wisdom? What they call the reformed religion, besides being a wicked heresy, is also bereft of humanity in its black-and-white simplicity. They approve of simplicity in faith. Why?

Well, Mary was also drunk on aqua vitae, which always makes her mutter to myself, and pray, sometimes entire offices at the wrong time, and in Latin, so the women in the laundry believe she is making spells. Eventually she forgot where she was in her rosary and lay down on the sawdust, huddled in my mantle, and went to sleep.

LXXIV

BECKET MEANWHILE LEFT MUCH of his gold at a goldsmith's in Cheapside. He kept back some, and bought a new sword at an armourer's. Then he walked brazenly through the City to Old Jewry. Dr Nunez found him waiting in his hall and examining the costly hangings that told the story of King David's life from the killing of Goliath to his problems with Absalom.

"Mr Becket," croaked Nunez, awful suspicion instantly flying to his breast. "How . . . how are you? And . . . where is Simon?"

"I am completely recovered, Doctor," Becket said with a polite bow. "Simon, however, is in desperate danger."

Nunez hurried him into his study and sent the servant for wine and wafers. There Becket told him most of what had happened, and in particular what Simon Ames had done for him.

"You do not know whether he survived the chase?" Nunez asked him, appalled at his nephew's foolhardiness and also proud of his courage.

Becket shook his head. "If he did as I advised him, he should have been living at the end of it," he said. "Whether he still is . . ." He shrugged massively.

"Why in the Almighty's name did he not stay with you . . . ?"

"He was wounded in the shoulder, Doctor, by a halberd. Not badly, but enough to bleed copiously and bring the dogs after him. He it was who thought he should play the decoy, not I. I did not force him, indeed I was against it for I should be sorry to have his death on my conscience as well. But he insisted it was the only rational choice."

Nunez nodded, a faraway expression on his face. He sat at his desk, cleared away a pig's thigh-bone, a dead pigeon and a scalpel, and drew paper and pen towards him.

"You do not know where Ramme and Munday might have taken him?"

"At a guess, to the Tower."

Nunez nodded again, and his left hand rubbed his beard. He was looking very worried. "And his mission?"

Becket spread his hands. "We are at a stand," he said. "I know the witch must still have the papers, but where she might have gone with them, God only knows."

"She must have a good bolt-hole to be so elusive."

"Certainly. I believe I should start at the Falcon, but I dare not go there now, for there might be men watching the place to see if I do precisely that. The pursuivants are out in force to search the City; I saw them turning out the Fant household as I passed by. Davison wants me, no doubt believing that I was the one who cut out Her Majesty's confession."

"Confession?"

Becket explained and Nunez showed no sign of shock, only nodded again.

"I knew that all was not as it seemed," he said distantly, "when I examined her with the other doctors during the Alençon courtship."

"Good God," said Becket, shocked and a little sickened to think that Dr Nunez had seen the Queen's privy parts.

"We reported that she was intact and had all that pertained to a woman, that was all. It was sufficient. I have never mentioned it. But this explains a great deal, a great deal. I shall be better able to treat her, knowing that it is an old wound that causes her stomach cramps." He wrote some notes to himself, not in Latin but in Hebrew which would be better hidden from prying eyes. Then he began writing a letter. Becket shifted restlessly.

"I had best be going," he said.

"Why can you not stay here?" Nunez asked. "You need a place to sleep, and as ever my house is your house."

"You honour me, sir, but I dare not stay. Think on it. When Mr Davison knows Simon's name, he will immediately search here."

"Ah. Yes. Yes, he will." Nunez rang a silver bell on his desk, and wrote faster. He seemed to be encrypting from memory as he went. "We had best prepare for him."

When the servant came, he was told to fetch Mrs Nunez and their steward. Becket stood decisively. "I shall return tomorrow," he said. "If a child that is not a child, but a tiny woman, comes here, let her in and ask her to wait for me. If it is safe for me to enter when I come, put a candle in the window by your door, as you do on Saturdays."

Dr Nunez nodded abstractedly. As Becket went to the door, he saw Mrs Nunez and the steward going into Nunez's study and heard the rapid fire of urgent Portuguese. By the time he had passed through Aldgate, the Nunez household was boiling like a copper. He walked swiftly along Houndsditch, by the long wall where the London fullers have their tenter-frames for stretching new cloth in the summer. At the Dolphin Inn on Bishopsgate he hired a horse and joined the people faring out of London into the countryside: messengers and merchants, pack-trains, coaches, common carriers, men with their arquebuses going out to Artillery Yard to practise shooting, men with bows going to the Spital Field to do the same, women with dogs; and, against the flow for a mile, a large baaing herd of sheep coming into the City to be eaten. Becket is stronger than many, but he had not slept for two nights and he noticed hardly any of this, dozing on his horse as he rode. As is often the way, if he had skulked out of the City on foot, the two pursuivants set to watch Aldgate for him would have seen him. Being as he was on horseback and half asleep, they let him through. Mary would say that it was the protection of my mantle again.

Behind him, letters flowed out of Dr Nunez's study like autumn leaves on a stream: to Sir Francis Walsingham, to Mr Davison, to Sir Horatio Palavicino in the Netherlands, to the Earl of Leicester, to the Queen; the physician mustering his very considerable influence to find his nephew in the clutches of the State. Half-way through, the pursuivants arrived, Mr Ramme commanding and looking harassed and exhausted, with rings around his eyes.

It was typical of Nunez that he invited Mr Ramme into his house courteously, offered him food which Ramme refused, gave him spiced wine which Ramme only drank after Dr Nunez had tasted it. The pursuivants worked methodically through the house, while Leonora Nunez fluttered after them wringing her hands and beseeching them to be careful.

They found nothing, of course. Nothing of Nunez's correspondence with half of Europe, nothing of his merchant ventures, nothing of the Queen's Great Matter, only many evidences of the Queen's high respect for Dr Nunez, and letters from Sir Francis Walsingham thanking Nunez for his assistance in the Queen's defence. Even Ramme, who had been certain he would find evidence of treason, began to wonder if it had been quite politic to search the house of so prominent a servant of the Queen, even if he was only a Jew and in England on sufferance. When the Purveyor of Her Majesty's Grocery, Mr Dunstan Ames, arrived with a retinue of six servants and began to question him as to his son Simon's health and whereabouts, Ramme became even more worried. Davison seemed not to be concerned about how he offended powerful men about the Court, saying he was as sure of the Queen's favour as the Earl of Leicester—had he not persuaded her to sign the Queen of Scots' death warrant?—but Ramme knew only too well how fickle was Her Majesty's fancy.

The pursuivants left late in the afternoon. By evening the servants, supervised by a furious Leonora, were cleaning and scrubbing every inch of the house to remove their traces, while Nunez and his brother-in-law wrote more letters and considered how they would approach the Queen.

That was when a beggarmaid with a grim dirty face approached the back door and asked humbly if she could speak to Dr Nunez. Nunez went out to her, preoccupied with something else, stopped and stared.

"Mistress Thomasina?" he asked. "Is it you?"

She looked up at him and her face screwed up in a monkey-like squint, which was the outward sign of her longing and refusal to burst into tears.

"Yes," she said.

"Aha, the child that is not a child. Please, mistress, come in, we have been waiting for you."

She came and although she refused to sit down, she drank two gobletfuls of spiced wine and ate some pheasant pie. She seemed very weary, and so Leonora Nunez put her to bed in the best guest-room, after she had washed in a hip-bath and shucked her gaudy rags. Leonora had no children, to her bitter sorrow and regret, but her brother Dunstan had fourteen, five of them maidens. A servant was sent running to the Ames household and came back with a fine smock and embroidered velvet bodice and blue embroidered kirtle so Thomasina could dress herself as more befitted her station.

She slept until Becket arrived refreshed at noon the next day, having lain at the Angel Inn at Islington overnight and slept solidly from before sun-down.

They conferred in her bedroom once she was properly dressed and then went purposefully to Dr Nunez in his study.

"Doctor," said Thomasina, sitting down very gently on a cushion, "whence come the soap-cakes you use?"

"The soap?" repeated Nunez. Thomasina was a woman, but he had not expected interest in huswifery from the Queen's Fool.

"Yes," said Thomasina flintily, evidently enraged at someone and having trouble being civil, "the soap."

Nunez was also having trouble, being more concerned about his nephew than he liked to admit. Walsingham had not yet responded to his letters, neither had the Earl, whereas Davison had written only to deny he had any such man in his keeping.

"Er . . . from Seville," he said, willing to humour her. "I import from Spain, where they make the finest soap."

"What does this stamp upon it mean?" She produced the bar of soap that Leonora had given her for her toilet, rose-scented and now well-used. Nunez blinked at the stamp and then coughed.

"Ah," he said, "well, the stamp indicates that these are . . . er . . . intended for purveyance to the Court. My brother-in-law supplies the Court with grocery."

"And soap?"

"Yes."

"All the soap?"

What was this with soap, in the name of the Almighty (Blessed be He)? How could it possibly be important?

"Yes."

Thomasina put down the bar on his desk and looked significantly at Becket, who seemed embarrassed, as if he agreed with Nunez, not Thomasina. He did not seem inclined to speak and so Thomasina made an irritable *tchah* noise and continued.

"Forgive me, Doctor, all will be clear in a minute. Does your brother-in-law supply the Falcon Inn at Southwark as well?"

Nunez frowned. "No, why should he? He supplies the Court."

She smiled in triumph, the first he had seen from her.

"Tell the Doctor what you saw at the Falcon, Mr Becket."

Becket shrugged. "Only the same stamp on the soap there, in the whores' wash-house when I was looking for the witch. It was coarser than this, though, grey and grained and smelling less sweet."

Nunez still had no idea why they were interested.

"The Falcon Inn has been buying embezzled purveyance soap," he said, "wherefore is this . . ."

"Where would they be getting it from?" asked Thomasina.

Nunez shook his head, bewildered. "I am not a woman, I know nothing of varieties of . . . soap."

"Nor do I, for before I was the Queen's Fool I knew nothing of the stuff, and since then I have needed to know only that it cleanses," said Thomasina. "May we ask your wife?"

Leonora came when she was sent for, looked as puzzled as her husband, and pronounced that she thought it must be laundry soap from the description and that it was a scandal and a shame how the Queen was cheated throughout the Court by dishonest servants and—

"By God, that's it!" shouted Thomasina.

Leonora gave her an old-fashioned look that implied a person who looked like a child should not blaspheme in her house. Nunez swore under his breath in Portuguese and received the same look.

Thomasina was on her feet, waving a small fist over her head.

"That's it, that's where I saw her. She's the old hag at the laundry, Pentecost's grandam. I knew I had seen her."

By the time she had calmed down enough to explain, Leonora had left to oversee her grumbling maidservants at their pre-Sabbath cleaning.

"You say," Becket rumbled slowly, "that the old hag who had the Book of the Unicorn and who coney-catched us the other night, she works at the Court laundry? Good . . . good heavens." He thought for a moment and then grinned. "Ay, it would make a fine bolt-hole. Where better? I think Davison and his precious pursuivants would scarcely dare to search within the Virge of the Court."

"The old woman that you have been seeking has been all this time at Court?" asked Nunez, catching up fast. "I thought she was a witch at the Falcon?"

"Ay, why not both? She is a witch, to be sure, and we met her at the Falcon, but she scuttled off away from there once she had her money. I have been racking my brains where she could have gone to hide. It makes sense. And certainly the whores at the Falcon wash in the same soap as the Queen, near enough."

He grinned again. "So we have her," he said. "Now all we need is to catch her and talk to her."

"You do so," said Thomasina. "I must go back to the Queen at once."

It was only Leonora Nunez's hospitality that prevented disaster then, for she insisted she could not allow friends of her dear nephew (may the Almighty preserve him as Daniel was preserved in the lion's den) to leave her house still hungry, and so they sat down to a dinner of bread and rabbit and beef and saltfish and pheasant and a sparrow pie, and a tart of preserved gooseberries and wafers made with honey.

Just as they rose, the Queen's Grocer, Dunstan Ames, arrived in haste with news of the Court. The Queen, he said, had retired to bed with her old complaint in her stomach, but when he had enquired if Dr Nunez would be needed, he had been told roundly that they would bring in a doctor who was not a Jew. Burghley was suffering another attack of gout and had retired to his own house. There had been a generalised remove to Fotheringay now that the Queen of Scots' death warrant was signed. Walsingham had not been seen for days, but his deputy, Mr William Davison, was very busy about the place, as were his servants. Oddly enough, since he had been one of the Queen of Scots' worst enemies, Davison was not going to gloat at her beheading. He had made changes in the gentlemen guarding the Queen. Further, the rumours were flying that the Queen's Fool Mistress Thomasina de Paris, had been plotting against her life and that there was a warrant for her arrest.

Nunez sighed, stroked his beard and sat down heavily.

"So it has begun," he said.

Becket sat down as well, looking at his hands which were now only braceleted with purple scars, and chafed them as if they had suddenly turned to ice.

"Christ have mercy," he whispered. "Poor Simon."

"Mr Ames has told Davison about me?" Thomasina asked, not following their sudden depression, being too angry and distressed for herself. "Why did he betray me?"

She felt ashamed of her naïvety when Becket looked at her as if she were mad.

"Davison has had time to break him by now," he said. "God knows, I had hoped we could bail him before then, but on a charge of treason . . ."

Dunstan Ames had his head in his hands. Nunez went to him and patted his shoulder, spoke in rumbling Portuguese. After a moment Dunstan lifted his head and nodded.

Nunez cleared his throat. "I was saying, Mr Becket, that it seems likely the Queen will order our expulsion within a few days," he said. "We will prepare for this, of course, and we will send to Simon's wife that she should remove immediately with the children to the Netherlands."

"In the meantime," put in Dunstan, "it seems that the only hope of saving my son and all of us is for you to find the pages that were cut from the Book of the Unicorn."

"Yes, but I do not understand," Becket protested. "To be sure, Davison has the book, but it contains nothing incriminating. Why is the Queen obeying him?"

"He does not need to show it to her, does he?" said Dunstan. "If he knows what is in it, that is all he needs."

"Oh, poor lady," said Thomasina, with her hand to her mouth. "This is terrible. Terrible. God rot Davison's bowels, God curse him with the pox and the plague and leprosy; may his cock bleed and his—"

"My dear Mistress Thomasina," said Nunez, "please. Do not curse in my house."

Thomasina fell silent, abashed.

"It is clear to me," Nunez continued, "that we are at the cusp of power here. Davison is bidding to be the Queen's First Councillor, her puppet-master, and it is a gamble in which there is no going back. For as long as either one of you is loose, he is not secure in his hold on the Queen. He is not secure in any case because she is not at all the foolish woman he thinks her, but while he makes his base stable, he is liable to kill all that are not his creatures."

"I must warn her, but how can I do it?" said Thomasina.

"How had you planned to do it?"

"I would go to the Earl of Leicester's palace and fetch my carriage and return to the Court as I left it."

"I think you would not go further than the Court gate," said Simon's father soberly. "After that you would be in the Tower."

"How did you get in to fetch Simon's warrant, the one that Ramme tore up?" asked Becket.

"Through the Lord Chamberlain's lodgings, my lord Hunsdon. He is her half-brother and he knows me."

Becket and Nunez looked at each other significantly. Thomasina was not slower than they.

"Ah," she said, "yes, indeed. But if he is her brother, will Davison not remove him?"

"My lord Hunsdon is not a councillor but a courtier, a well-known Knight of the Carpet," said Nunez. "I suspect Davison will not think him dangerous immediately."

"Well then, that is what I must do. Not now, not in daylight, but as soon as night falls."

"What about the hag that caused all this trouble?" said Dunstan. "Will you find her, Becket?"

"Oh ay," said Becket. "Certainly I will find her now."

LXXV

ROBERT CAREY WAS HAVING trouble sleeping well. His father, deliberately, he thought, had given him a truckle-bed in his own Court bedchamber, and relegated the manservant to a straw palliasse. The three of them trumpeted through the night, but Robert Carey could not be comfortable since his legs stuck out over the end of the bed. Even now that Lord Hunsdon had gone north, leaving dire warnings of what he would do to his youngest son if he got into any further trouble while he was away, Robert spent hours each night watching moonlight stripes slide across the wall. Every four hours he heard the men-at-arms standing guard at the Queen's door into the Privy Garden change over with a cautious scrape of boots and grounding of halberds, muffled by the intervening Stone Gallery.

He was lonely and bored and worried by reports brought him by his father's servant of changes at Court. They had not been obvious until many of the most important men had gone north to the Queen of Scots's execution. He wished with all his heart that his father had stayed, for his father could speak to the Queen whenever he wished and the word was that it was hard to come near her now without Mr Davison's favour. The manservants that Hunsdon had ordered to guard Carey and keep him out of trouble were openly considering taking horse north to bring back the Lord Chamberlain, in case the Queen had urgent need of him. But as was commonly the case at Court, everything was shadowy, a great deal of rumour and movement and no hard facts.

There was a very soft scratching sound at the end of the room, where the windows looked on the Whitehall orchard. A soft puffing noise, another scrape.

He got up and went to open the window-shutter to look out, his poignard in his hand, wondering at an assassin who would choose so very roundabout a way of reaching the Queen, but cynically suspecting a roving courtier.

Below him, clinging to a drain-pipe, was what looked like a child, her kirtle kilted up in her belt.

"Good God, Mistress Thomasina," he blurted. She looked up at him, scowled and nearly slipped.

"Help me up," she hissed. "Quick, before I fall. And shut up."

He had heard that Thomasina had fallen from favour for desertion, but . . . He could not resist his desire to know what was happening, and further he thought he could cope with Thomasina if she had suddenly run wood-wild and come to kill the Queen.

He opened the shutter cautiously, and the window, and leaned down to clasp her hand. She was heavier than she looked but he gripped her and she walked up the wall and eeled through the window to land gasping softly on the floor.

"I am out of practice at this," she said. "Where is my lord Hunsdon?"

"Gone to watch the Queen of Scots' beheading . . ."

"Damn him," said Thomasina, very unladylike, standing straight and un-kilting her kirtle, which was a pretty velvet. "Is there no one loyal in all the Court?"

Carey frowned. "Why, what's afoot?"

"There is a bloody palace revolution afoot, you ninny; how can you live here and not know it?"

"Mistress, I have been in disgrace and under arrest in these rooms for a week; I know only what my servant tells me. Hush."

He looked cautiously at his man, who had turned on his back and was rattling the painted rafters.

In a fast, ferocious whisper, Thomasina told him exactly what was happening, leaving out the precise nature of Davison's hold on the Queen.

"Now, get me in to see the Queen," she said.

Carey was appalled. "But Mistress Thomasina, I have been forbidden her Presence for days. She would never admit me."

"Who is guarding her tonight?"

"How should I know? I have not left these rooms. If it was Drury or the Earl of Cumberland or another of my friends, I could likely talk my way through, but if Davison is taking power as you say he is, I have no doubt he has put his own men about her."

"Get me through them."

"But—"

"Can you not see what is happening? What I tell the Queen will stop Davison in his tracks, but I must tell her face to face. If I go there openly, Davison will arrest me. I must break in secretly."

Carey blew his cheeks out. "Break into the Queen's chamber . . . Good God, woman, do you know what you're asking?"

"Yes," she said, staring him straight in the eyes. "If it goes wrong badly enough, they will hang, draw and quarter you, and me they will burn."

Carey swallowed hard. "Well, but . . . in God's name, can we not wait until Father returns . . . ?"

"In God's name," sneered Thomasina, "do you think once Davison has entrenched himself, do you think he will let the Queen see any one of her relatives, any one of her former friends again? Your family will be out on its ear, and no doubt winnowed with treason trials as well. I expect Davison has a troop of hungry relatives he wishes to enrich for all his bloody virtue."

Carey blinked. He had served at Court for seven years and learnt to keep his feet as all about him men moved and counter-moved against each other, swirling in the feverish glittering greed of the place, where the Queen's smile weighs as heavy as gold and a great fortune may be made in an instant from nothing more substantial than charm and elegance and intelligence, as Sir Walter Raleigh had proved. But through it all sailed the Queen, a galleon among wherries, the undisputed mistress of all and as biddable as the wind. The thought of one man being able to force her to do his will . . . it was so alien, he was having a hard time making his mind encompass it.

"Are you sure this is no game of the Queen's, to give him enough rope to hang himself?" he asked.

"If it is a game, I doubt the Queen is enjoying it. He has her in a vice. That is why she signed the Queen of Scots' death warrant, when she had determined not to do so."

"How do you know she was determined?"

"She told me. She has many politic reasons for keeping her cousin alive. If he had not coerced her, she would never have signed."

Carey was silent again, trying to think how he should decide.

Thomasina mistook him. She stood up and kilted her kirtle again. "I was truly a Fool," she said wearily. "I thought the Queen's own family would help me in this quest, but I had hoped to find her brother, not a popinjay cousin with a sword as soft as a boiled bean-pod. If you are too frightened to help me, at least give me an hour before you call Davison's guard."

She was half-way to the door when he caught up with her in long strides and turned her, with his fingers nipping her shoulder more tightly than he meant.

For a moment he was too choked with anger to say anything, but at last he managed to whisper, "Give me a chance to dress. If I break into the Queen's chamber barelegged in my shirt, she *will* hang me."

Thomasina shook his fingers off her shoulder and stood with her fists on her small hips as he scrambled into his black velvet doublet and hose. It amused her that he took the time to put on a small ruff and his rings, and to run a comb through his curly dark-red hair. By the time he had finished he looked as trim as if he were going to attend upon her as a Gentleman of the Bedchamber, rather than to try a desperate break-in.

He hesitated over his sword-belt, then shrugged it on with an angry growl.

"If it comes to swords, we may as well surrender," she said sourly.

"I know that, mistress," he said. "But you may need time to speak to her, which a sword can provide."

And then he grinned like a boy on an apple-scrumping expedition. "Lord, mistress, this is a fine night," he said. "Will you be guided by me?"

For a moment she hesitated and then nodded.

LXXVI

IN ALL HIS MANY affairs, Mr William Davison had a very keen eye for the niceties of life. His sinful young cousin had not been buried yet, but was lying in the crypt of St Mary Rounceval by Charing Cross. Her parents and uncle had not yet arrived from the countryside. Despite his overpress of business, he made time to go and pay his respects to her corpse, although of course he had no intention of praying for her soul, because he believed she had already been judged and sent to Hell. Poor child, I would have shown her some mercy, but Davison's stern God knew nothing of the term. However, he could bend his head and offer praise to God for His justice and thank God likewise, as did the Pharisee in the Temple, that he himself was not so sinful and foolish.

The coffin was closed because the manner of her death had taken most of her beauty and her skin was no longer the velvet cream that had once enchanted the Queen.

In the crypt Mr Davison found one of her room-mates, another maid of honour, crying softly by a mourning candle. She was a pretty little thing, with pale-yellow hair and pink-and-white skin. Davison had need of a new spy among Her Majesty's women if he was to be sure of his power over her, and so he smiled at the girl with as much sympathy as he could muster.

"Can I help you, sir?" she asked politely.

"Do you know who I am?" Davison asked.

"Yes, sir, I think you are Mr Davison, Sir Francis Walsingham's deputy." She curtseyed to him prettily. "I am Alicia Bradbelt."

"Just so. Also I am Mistress Bethany's cousin."

The tears began spouting anew and Alicia twisted her hands together.

"Oh, it is a tragedy, sir, it is so sad. Poor Bethany. If only we had known."

"Hm. I am at a loss to know how she took the fever that killed her," lied Mr Davison. "Was it the plague?"

Alicia blushed beet root and looked at the worn painted tiles on the floor. "No, sir," she muttered.

"What was it? I heard a rumour she was with child; was that the trouble?"

"Oh, sir, she went to a witch."

"And how do you know that, Mistress Alicia?" said Davison severely. "Surely any unfortunate sinful girl that is with child may lose it and die of it."

"No, sir, it was the paper, the message we found when we came back from helping the Queen to dress for meeting the Scottish ambassadors."

"What message?"

"I have it here, sir. I was going to put it in the coffin with her, so she could explain it to God at Judgement Day, but the lid is on, sir, and I was going to burn it in the candle."

"Give it to me," said Davison instantly, out of mere curiosity, for he had no reason to think it was anything more than a simple message. Perhaps he thought it might be Bethany's will.

Reluctant but accustomed to obey, Alicia handed over the message Mary had left under the goblet on Bethany's bedside chest. Davison read it, his chin folded to his ruff and his mouth drawn into a tight line of disapproval.

On it Mary had written, "This child has been lightened of her burden by a witch that has bungled it. Fetch a doctor."

"Whence came this?" he rapped at Alicia.

She began clasping and unclasping her hands. "Sir, I am sorry, I do not know, I know nothing of it. It was by her bed."

"Who could have been in her chamber? One of the gentlemen?"

"No, sir, of course not; none of them would dare."

"So it was a woman. The Mistress of the Maids?"

"No, sir, she would have called the doctor herself, not left a message about it. Any one of us would, if we had known; we did call a doctor once we understood and he was very angry; he said the message was right and he wanted to know who left it for he said it takes a witch to know what a witch has done. But he could not save her, though he bled her and put a dead pigeon on her feet and everything."

"It takes a witch to know what a witch has done," muttered Davison. "Hm." Mary had left a dirty thumbprint on the edge of the paper and Davison examined it carefully, held it up to the light, turned it over, then sniffed delicately at the print. His nose wrinkled at the smell, and he frowned in puzzlement.

"Who else could have been in her chamber? Her servant?"

"No, sir, we all three share Kitty for our tiring-woman and she was fetching our ruffs from the laundry. That was why Bethany was all alone, poor thing, poor baby, all alone and—"

"Control yourself, Mistress Alicia. Think. If there is a witch at Court, that is a serious thing. Do you know what it says in Scripture: 'thou shalt not suffer a witch to live'? She could enchant the Queen, or poison her."

"Oh, sir, I never thought of that."

"Well, think of it now. Who else could have come into Bethany's chamber?"

Alicia's smooth white brow wrinkled as she forced her mind into unaccustomed exercise. The Queen treated most of her maids of honour with contempt because they were, in fact, foolish feather-headed girls who only served her to catch a husband.

"Well, only the night-soil woman . . ."

Davison let his breath out. "Ahhh," he said. "What does she look like?"

Alicia's wrinkles furrowed deeper. "I do not remember. She comes muttering round with her pails in the morning."

"Is she old, young?"

"Old, sir. Very old. Old and dirty, she looks like an empty leather bag."

Davison smiled in satisfaction. "And where does she live?"

Alicia shook her head. "Well, sir, I do not know. She is only the night-soil woman."

"Then where does she come from? Where does she take the pails?"

As it had never in her life occurred to Alicia to wonder what happened to the gallons of waste produced by the Court, she could only shake her head again in bewilderment.

"Never mind," said Davison with unwonted patience. "You have helped me greatly, mistress; I am indebted to you."

"Yes, but what does an old woman matter, sir?"

"Think of what the doctor said. That it takes a witch to know a witch's work? Surely the night-soil woman is the witch that left the message about Bethany."

"Oh." Alicia's eyes and mouth were three round Os, as if she were singing in chapel. "Ohh. Yes, I see. She certainly looks very evil and she mutters all the time, not words but spells."

"Quite. Any witch is a danger to all our souls."

"Yes, sir."

"Do not trouble yourself with this any more, Mistress Alicia. You have unburdened yourself very properly to me, and that is all you need do. I will see to it that the witch does not come to Court any more."

"Yes, sir. Will you burn her, sir?"

"Unfortunately she is more likely to hang in these irreligious times."

Alicia nodded, her eyes still very wide. "How terrible," she said.

Davison walked swiftly to his lodgings, which were in Whitehall. To be sure, he had not made the leap that connected Mary with the Book of the Unicorn; only he found the idea of a night-soil woman who knew how to read and write an interesting anomaly. He desired to question her. Perhaps he thought her a spy as well as a witch. In any case, his men were quartering London in search of an old woman that had slipped away from the Falcon two nights before and this one would not escape him, if he could find out where she went. He could do nothing that night, but he was patient. He would find out from the Clerk of the Board of Greencloth where the night-soil went and then he would arrest her and question her about her activities. He had no doubt that Mary would tell him all he wished to know.

He was also searching for Becket and had likewise drawn a blank, since Becket was clearly keeping well away from his former haunts. Not even Laurence Pickering, the King of London, knew where he was. But Davison had faith that his God would bring Becket to him.

LXXVII

CAREY PUT HIS HEAD round the door of the bedchamber and whispered urgently to the two men his father had left to guard him who were sleeping in the outer chamber. By that time his manservant was also blinking awake and demanding to know what was happening.

All four of them crowded into the bedchamber where Carey spoke rapidly, in a voice tinged with Berwick, telling them that although the Queen had ordered him banned from her Presence, he had got wind of a deadly plot against her, and as her loyal subject he could not sit back and let her be assassinated. Therefore he proposed to break into her bedchamber that night.

The two men-at-arms exchanged glances and looked deeply unhappy.

"Well, but sir," said one, "my lord said you was to stay here and we was tae keep ye here and not let ye get in any more trouble."

"For God's sake, Selby," Carey snapped, "you know I would never take a risk like this for anything less than the Queen's life. You know that."

"Ay, sir, but—"

"Ye'll get in no trouble yourself. I'll make it clear I ordered you to help me."

"Ay sir, but—"

"But what, Heron?"

"How are we tae get in tae see her, sir?"

"You're not, and nor am I. We are going to clear Davison's men away from her door and then Mistress Thomasina here is going to talk to her. We hold the door to stop anyone interrupting them. That is all. Do you think Mistress Thomasina could hurt the Queen?"

The men looked at her uneasily, and probably understood for the first time that she was not a child.

"Nay, sir, but—"

"But what, Selby?"

"How are we to dae it, sir? Ah mean, clear the guards away? Cut their throats, d'ye mean, sir?"

Carey winced. "No," he said forcibly. "Under no circumstances are you to cut their throats. Understand? No blood is to be shed."

"Ay, but they may not be sae nice about ourn, sir."

"Are you scared, Heron?"

"Nay, sir, not me, sir."

"If you are you can stay here and deny you knew aught about it."

"Nay, sir, Ah'm no' scared, only a bit canny."

"Nothing wrong with that, so long as you do as you're told. Now Mistress Thomasina, is there not a door from the Lesser Withdrawing Room into the Queen's bedchamber?"

Thomasina thought. "There is, but it's locked and bolted from inside her chamber at night. Also there is a lock on the Lesser Withdrawing Room's door to the Privy Gallery. It's very solid, we could never knock it down in time."

Carey sucked his teeth. "A pity. Oh well, it was not likely we could do it the easy way. Right, unless Davison has changed the pattern of the guard, there will be two men here at the junction of the Stone Gallery with the Privy Gallery. Another two at the other end of the Privy Gallery and then two gentlemen on truckle-beds in the alcove by her door."

Heron and Selby nodded, their eyes narrowing in a businesslike manner.

"Sir, sir," said Carey's manservant. "What am I to do, sir?"

"You lie low, Michael. Stay out of trouble. If you hear a lot of shouting and clattering, hide somewhere. The same if you hear I've been arrested. Whatever happens, if I don't come back, in the morning you get out of the Court, ride to Fotheringay and fetch my father."

"What can he do?" asked Thomasina.

Carey smiled at her under hooded eyes. "Call out his tenants and deal with Davison that way. He will have help. I think the Council will not like Davison's way of proceeding."

"But that is civil war."

Nobody answered her for a moment.

"Best of all is if we stop Davison now," said Carey. "Which we are going to do, just as soon as we have devised the means. Right. So, the main problem are these two at the entrance of the Privy Gallery. Once past them, I suspect I can manage the two at Her Majesty's door, especially with the Queen's Fool at my side. With luck, if it all goes smoothly, the men up the other and of the Privy Gallery won't have time to do anything. Trouble is, the ones at the Stone Gallery entrance are standing up, they will be awake. We need some kind of distraction."

Thomasina smiled secretly and tugged at one of the panes of his hose.

"Now, Mr Carey," she said impishly, "you are forgetting me."

A little while later a strange procession marched down the Stone Gallery, lit by the half-moonlight coming through the diamond panes on one side. On either side were the painted cloths of the Trojan War and the tale of Achilles, bought at hideous expense by the Queen's father. They were not as costly as the tapestries put up for important foreign embassies, which shone with gold and silver thread and twisted with allegorical meaning, each one the worth of a galleon fully fitted and armed. But even so there were concentrated in that gallery at least two or three monasteries' worth of woven and painted cloth.

Those who have designed entrance and egress from the Queen's apartments have thought much like fortress engineers, for the Queen must live, as it were, in a subtle fortress. And so the passage that led from the Stone Gallery to the Privy Gallery was too narrow for more than one man to pass at a time. It was formed by boarding up part of the Withdrawing Room, from one door to another.

Carey had decided that stealth was pointless if the two men guarding the lower end of the Privy Gallery were awake and unnecessary if they were asleep. And so he strode ahead, carrying a candle in one hand and a silver plate with a covered silver goblet on it in the other. Just behind him trotted Thomasina, trying not to look terrified.

The two men were awake, but they were not Her Majesty's usual men-at-arms. Carey wished they had been, for Sir Walter Raleigh was above all else loyal to the Queen, which was why she had so promptly made him Captain of her Guard. He too had scurried north to Fotheringay to gawk like a streetchild at the Queen of Scots' beheading.

However, this meant that the men were not familiar with the routine of the Court, nor were they sure what was normal and what was not. They saw a gentleman and a child coming towards them, the gentleman's clothes and bearing shrieking that he was a courtier with every stitch and button. How could a man carrying a candle and a goblet and a towel over his arm be up to no good?

They looked towards him, had their halberds ready crossed to bar his path. The child slipped under the staffs and began slowly somersaulting and flip-flopping down the Privy Gallery.

"What's your business, sir?" asked one, civilly enough.

"Hey, you," hissed the other. "Stop there."

Thomasina ignored him and carried on tumbling.

"I am bringing Her Majesty's night-time posset," said Carey, putting all his considerable acting ability into looking dense and aggrieved, a functionary prevented from doing a perfectly normal duty. Perhaps he pitched his voice a little higher than normal, gave it a stronger University accent.

"Nobody said anything to us about it," said the man-at-arms.

"Why would they?" said Carey. "Her Majesty always has a posset at this time."

"She didn't before."

Carey looked daintily appalled. "Do you mean to tell me no one has been bringing it to her while I have been sick?"

"Hey," said the other man in the strangled tones of someone trying to shout in a whisper, "you, little girl, stop that."

Thomasina stopped and stood straight, looking down half the length of the Privy Gallery.

"She never asked for it," said the first to Carey, plainly worried now.

Carey shook his head and tutted. "You had best let me through quickly, before she puts you in the Tower."

"Might be poison," pointed out the man-at-arms who had called to Thomasina.

"You are a loyal subject, I see," said Carey with a smile. "And a quick-thinking man. Of course it is not poison, but look, I will prove it to you." He gave the man-at-arms the candle to hold and, after taking a sip from the goblet, offered it to him to taste.

The man-at-arms watched critically for signs of collapse, then shook his head. "Ay well. If you drank from it, I believe you. Go on."

Carey took back his candle and marched between the halberds, back stiff and straight and prickling with the urge to turn round, knowing they were turned to watch him. There were two soft thuds, a muffled clatter. He looked back at last to see Selby and Heron grinning at him and giving him the thumbs-up sign from over the prone bodies of the men-at-arms. Selby dragged each one into the Withdrawing Room and then the two of them took up the halberds and stood to attention.

Carey expected more trouble from the gentlemen sleeping at the Queen's door. He hoped very much that at least one would be someone he knew, like Drury or the Earl of Cumberland. One of them had woken up already and was sitting up on his truckle-bed across the Queen's bedroom door, blinking in Carey's candle-light.

Unfortunately, it was a gentleman who knew Carey but was not a friend.

"What the devil are you doing here, you're not supposed—?"

Thomasina moved like a little cat pouncing on a dog. She jumped up by his head, put her hand over his mouth and let him feel the little knife she was pressing to his neck artery.

"Stay still, or I'll cut your throat," she hissed, in the accents of a London footpad. The man froze, his eyes showing white all around the pupils.

The other sleeping gentleman grunted and turned over. Carey put down the candle and the tray and goblet on the floor, stepped to his bed, turned him on his stomach with his face in the pillow and put his knee in the man's back, then tied his hands with ropes cut from the Lord Chamberlain's curtains. As the man was beginning to buck from suffocation, he lifted him off the pillow by his hair, stuffed a handkerchief in his open mouth, twitched the pillow out from under him and let him fall back again on the mattress.

The other gentleman's eyes were rolling wildly. Thomasina could feel him juddering under her hand, which was slick from his spit. Suddenly he bit her, and when her grip loosened, managed to let out a half-strangulated yell. One of the Queen's lap-dogs began barking from somewhere near.

Carey grabbed him, punched him hard in the gut to quieten him, then shoved another handkerchief in his mouth. A moment later he too was trussed and lying on his stomach, pillowless, gasping through his nose.

"I apologise to both of you gentlemen, truly I do," said Carey formally. "You may both demand satisfaction of me afterwards . . ."

Thomasina hissed at him. All three of the Queen's dogs were barking like miniature Cerberuses. The two men-at-arms at the Holbein Gate end of the Privy Gallery were running towards them with their halberds.

Carey gave Thomasina the candle and pushed the two truckle-beds with their helpless passengers so they wheeled down the Privy Gallery into the men-at-arms' path.

"Get in. Now. I'll hold them," he told her.

Thomasina nodded. She knew the door would be bolted from the inside. She banged on it with her small fist and shouted, "Lady Bedford, let me in, quickly, *let me in . . .*"

Down the Privy Gallery shadows leapt. The two truckle-beds trundled to a stop and one fell over, dropping its gentleman on the floor with a despairing muffled wail. The men-at-arms swung their halberds, Carey danced between them, sword and poignard out and crossed, deflecting one, dodging the other.

"Let me in!" Thomasina's voice rose to a shriek over the yelping of the dogs. "Let me in or the Queen will DIE . . ."

Where the Privy Gallery joined with the Stone Gallery, Heron and Selby looked anxiously into the darkness, not quite able to make out what was going on. They had been given strict orders by Carey not to interfere with any fighting they saw but to concentrate on stopping anyone else coming through from the Presence Chamber.

Carey was ducking and weaving, using his weapons defensively, always aiming to be farther up the Privy Chamber, farther away from the Queen's bedroom door. Sooner or later, Thomasina thought, her guts twisted with fear, one of them will understand what he is at and come back this way. Please, God, let the door open . . .

Carey kicked one of the men-at-arms in the balls and missed by a hair's breadth having his head cut off by the swishing halberd blade of the other. The man he had kicked sank slowly to his knees, supported by his halberd-staff, gripping on to it while his face worked, like a knight of old at prayer.

Thomasina lifted her fist to bang again, and then refocussed her mind to accept that the door was open a crack and a woman's face was looking out, wild under its curling papers and skewed nightcap.

"Oh, my lady Bedford," she said. "Please, please, let me in. I must see the Queen."

"What in the name of God is going on? Who is that down the gallery?"

"It's Robin Carey, ma'am, your youngest brother." They were both shouting over the noise of the dogs.

"Why is he fighting the Queen's Guard?"

"To give me time to see Her Majesty. Please let me in, please. You can arrest me later, you can send me to the Tower later, or beat me or whatever you like; but please, you must let me in, I must speak to her . . ."

The words were tumbling out without any conscious thought from Thomasina, who was also wondering what was making her face so wet.

The Countess of Bedford's eyes narrowed. She was the most intelligent of the Queen's women, in many ways very like her, and had served her for decades.

"Come in," she said, and opened the door.

Thomasina rushed through the door, shut it and bolted it again, then tried to get her breath so she could greet the Queen properly.

An extraordinary sight met her eyes. The Queen was standing up by her bed, short grey-and-red hair standing on end, wearing only her smock and the most ferocious expression Thomasina had ever seen on any face. In her fist was a short jewelled dagger. Between her and the door stood Alicia, the maid of honour who now slept in her bed with her, shivering with fright, holding a goblet in each hand. Lady Bedford had her eating knife out. Felipe and Eric were guarding the Queen too, yapping and growling, their ridiculous hackles up, while Francis lunged in and out from behind a bedcurtain.

It was like a scene at the playhouse. For a moment Thomasina simply stood and gaped as she realised that though they knew nothing of the art, all of those in the Queen's chamber had been willing to fight for her, women and dogs alike. It was both pathetic and magnificent and it made Thomasina's throat swell with pride for them.

At last Felipe recognised Thomasina and stopped growling, began wagging his tail. Eric continued until Alicia dropped her goblet-weaponry and picked him up.

It was the Queen who spoke first.

"What is the meaning of this, Mistress Thomasina?" Her voice was dry and cold and betraying not the smallest trace of fear. She looked more like an old she-wolf at bay than a woman.

Thomasina instantly went down on her knees and gulped hard before she could answer.

"It is the Book of the Unicorn, Your Majesty. I came to tell you of it."

"That you had failed?"

"No, Your Majesty."

"Davison has it. Is this not failure?"

"No, Your Majesty. Not if he does not have *all* of it."

She could not say more because she was sure that none of the women had been told what was really going on. But the Queen understood. She sat down suddenly on the edge of the bed and let her jewelled dagger fall on the embroidered coverlet.

"Are you sure?"

"Yes, Your Majesty. As sure as I can be without seeing it."

The Queen looked away from Thomasina, at the shuttered windows. Her face seemed so naked without makeup, the fine dry wrinkled skin defenceless to hide that there were thoughts beneath it. What those thoughts might be, however, was much harder to say. The room's fire had burned low, and its light distorted rather than revealed.

"Alicia," she said to the pale-blonde girl who was busy quietening the dogs, "go and make up the fire, and then pour wine for myself and Mistress Thomasina. It is well, my lady Bedford. This is good news to us."

The women exchanged glances and relaxed.

"But my brother, ma'am . . ." said Lady Bedford.

"Brother?"

"Robin Carey, Your Majesty," said Thomasina. "He helped me get past Davison's men in the Privy Gallery. He's fighting them now."

"What? And why could you not simply come to me?"

"They are saying I am a traitor, Your Majesty, and have lost your favour, and I heard there was a warrant out for me."

"Good God," said the Queen sharply, then lapsed into silence.

From beyond the door came the sound of falling furniture, a metallic clatter and a dull thud, followed by secondary repeated thuds.

The Queen slipped her narrow shoulders into a fur-lined dressing-gown of pink velvet, wrapped it tight.

"Open the door," she snapped at Lady Bedford, who instantly shot the bolt and opened it.

The Queen marched out into the Privy Gallery, followed self-importantly by her three dogs.

Carey had been overborne by the men-at-arms, helped by one of the gentlemen whom he had not tied up securely enough, and was currently being held by two of them while the other punched him.

"Stop that disgraceful behaviour AT ONCE!" roared the Queen, standing four-square with her hands on her hips, the very ghost of King Harry and also every mother in the world. Selby and Heron stopped their creeping up on them and stood staring at her in horror.

The fighters stopped and turned to her, beginning to look sheepish.

Released from their hold, Carey sank gratefully to his knees, put his hands over his belly and wheezed gently with pain.

At that moment, in a thunder of the Privy Chamber doors slamming open, a herd of men-at-arms and gentlemen came running in various states of undress and waving a wild variety of weapons. At a single look from the Queen they stopped dead where they are, causing the men at the back to bump into each other and some of them to fall over. All of them stared at her, seeing not so much what she was, which was an old woman in her pink velvet dressing-gown unpainted and undefended by clothes, but what they saw in her, which was their most dread and Sovereign Lady.

"As you can see," said the Queen in the voice she used to speak to all of the tilt-yard during a tourney, "we are in excellent health and there is no assassin. We thank you for your valiant loyalty in coming to our aid but you may all now return to your beds."

Some of the men-at-arms muttered and one of the bolder gentlemen stepped forward to ask if the Queen required anything.

The Queen stared at him. "We require nothing of you, my lord of Oxford, and we forgive you your naked blade in the presence of the Sovereign since it was drawn for our defence. Now please leave us."

Muttering and buzzing between themselves, the rescue party dispersed. The Queen turned her attention on the still-frozen tableau farther up the Privy Gallery.

"How dare you presume to beat one of our gentlemen," said the Queen. "If he requires punishment, we shall do it ourself."

Carey lifted his head and managed to combine his expression of slowly ebbing pain with a quizzical look.

The Queen returned it steadily and without the least sympathy.

"Mr Carey," she said.

"Yes, Your Majesty," he croaked, still breathless.

"Are you well?"

"Er . . . yes, Your Majesty." It depended on your definition of the word "well," but he was certainly better than he had any right to expect, seeing that he was neither dead nor bleeding.

"Pick up your sword, come and guard my bedchamber for me," said the Queen.

Carey set one foot on the floor and lifted himself up with great difficulty, slightly bent in the middle. He managed to pick up his sword as well, and the long thin duelling poignard which had cost him twenty pounds, returned it to the sheath at the small of his back and staggered gently to where the Queen was standing, trying to look alert and useful, then went down on one knee to her. Eric put his paws on Carey's leg and wagged delightedly at him and Carey absent-mindedly patted his hairy head.

The two men-at-arms and the gentleman who had escaped Carey's bonds stood and stared at this strangely smaller but unreduced Queen in pink velvet and sable fur.

"You," she said to the men-at-arms. "Go back to your posts and allow no one to pass. You . . ." she said to Selby and Heron. "Who the devil are you?" she demanded when she didn't recognise them immediately.

"Your Majesty," murmered Carey indistinctly, "my father's men, John Selby and Archibald Heron."

"Hmf. Very well. You are both now temporarily appointed to my guard. If *anyone* tries to enter the Privy Gallery from the Privy Chamber, kill them."

Both of them ducked their heads clumsily.

"Ay, ma'am, we'll dae a better job on it than the puir wee mannikins ye had before."

"What?" said the Queen. "What is he saying, Robin?"

Carey translated.

"Ah. Hmm. Yes. Thank you. Do so."

The Queen looked with extreme disfavour on the gentleman who had managed to struggle free of Carey's curtain cords.

"Mr Pearce," she said, "you may fetch me some wine from the Withdrawing Chamber." She glanced at the still more unfortunate courtier whose knots had been better tied, who was still feebly struggling to get free. "As for you, Mr Williams, you may stay as you are to teach you not to drink so much before you go to sleep. What if these had been Spaniards, eh?"

Carey hid a smile. Mr Williams looked as if he wanted to cry.

After Pearce had brought her the flagon of wine from the buffet in the Withdrawing Room and given it to Thomasina from his knees, the Queen swept back into her bedchamber, followed by Thomasina and the dogs. After the bolts had gone home, Carey gently shoved the empty truckle-bed back against her chamber door, and sat on it with his sword across his knees. He hoped very much he would have to do no more than look threatening for the rest of the night.

LXXVIII

A LARGE SATURNINE GENTLEMAN came to the Court laundry that day and spent an hour discussing with Mrs Twiste the cost of having his master's shirts laundered by her, when his noble master came to Court. He went on a tour of inspection with Mrs Twiste through all the washing-rooms and the drying-rooms, being stared at and curtseyed to by the hurrying multiplicity of women and girls in that place, to his considerable enjoyment.

Becket's little reconnaissance took place in the morning, while Mary was on her rounds collecting night-soil. Davison and his men arrived in the afternoon, missing him by only half an hour, and found her bag of money in its barrel, which was not so clever a hiding place as she had thought. That told them they had literally and metaphorically struck gold. Only half of it found its way onto Davison's desk, however, since Munday found it first.

Meanwhile, it was given out that the Queen was sick of a megrim and pains in her stomach and had not gone to Divine Service at all that day. Once more the Court buzzed with rumours about her health and the disturbance in the Privy Gallery the night before. These tales were simply a garnish upon the existing state of confusion and tension at Court, through which Davison passed on occasion, in a hurry to go somewhere else, blandly neither confirming nor denying anything.

Where was Mary? In a boozing ken, naturally, by Charing Cross, celebrating my cleverness and her good fortune that at last she had gotten a dowry to save Pentecost. Each horn-cup she drank was certainly the last, her farewell to dissipation, and each pipe she smoked was the same. God have mercy, how we fool ourselves and lie to ourselves in the dream-world of Time. Without a shred of doubt Mary would have drunk and smoked Pentecost's dowry, just as she had every other penny I earned her.

Where was Simon Ames? Unnecessary to describe it, since we have flown there once before in our sieves, to watch Becket enjoying the hospitality of the Tower. Did you think they would not put him to the question? Lord, what naïvety. But if you thought he would be an easy man to crack, well, there again you display your naïvety, for such little outsiders as he is are often made of tougher and more obdurate wood than big brawlers like Becket. And Simon knows the inquisitor's game better than any other of their victims, for he had played it himself once, from the other side.

However, his knowledge was no good to him, for they had no need to take him into the basement of the White Tower. It was his body betrayed him, not his tongue. He awoke from his faint in the Lanthorn Tower, feeling feverish and his shoulder alight with pain. By mid-morning he was raving, and although much of it was in Portuguese which neither Munday nor Ramme understood, they had already picked out the name of Mistress Thomasina, and Davison had widened his search to include her.

All the time that his family was trying to help him, Simon lay tossing and burning in a small cell of the Tower while Munday sat with him to try and make out what he said. By evening they had become so frightened he might die, they called a surgeon themselves, who reopened the wound, cleaned it, cauterised it and bound it up again. Simon was sick near to death and said no more that night, while Thomasina talked and plotted with the Queen, nor the next day, when his fever began to rise again.

As sunset of that damp day slightly coloured the sky over St James's Park and the Spring Garden and the old lazar-house, Mary heaved herself off the bench in the boozing ken and staggered to the door. From north beyond the old cross of Queen Eleanor, white with pigeon dirt, came the crying of the Court falcons in the Royal Mews, and the neighing and stamping of the horses in the stables there as they waited to be fed.

She belched, waited for the fire to pass, and began ambling down Whitehall, singing as she went. She washed her face in a bucket from the well there, seeing me reflected in it and avoiding my gaze, and made a detour around the stocks where some footpad was having his face turned to pulp by the stones of the London street-children.

Perhaps she threw a couple of stones at the man for fun, but no doubt she missed, since it was hard for her to choose which of two twin sets of stocks to aim at. That could not dent her mood, for she was happy as a lark that evening, sloshing with aqua vitae and the satisfaction of getting Pentecost's dowry.

And so she passed into the queuing area of the Court gate, where the petitioners wait to be searched and show their expensive letters of introduction to Her Majesty's Yeomen Guards, before being allowed to pass through Holbein's Gate or under the Court gate itself. There were only a few people waiting, since the word had gone round that Her Majesty was indisposed and so not to be glimpsed in her Presence Chamber or walking in procession to chapel. No doubt the more desperate of the Court suitors envied Mary as she went boldly to the gate and was nodded through by a yeoman who had absolutely no desire to search her odorous velvets. Perhaps she was singing some hey nonny nonsense while the gate guards looked disgustedly at her, and she passed on, swinging her soiled apron and far worse kirtle, already a living ghost amongst the trim and beautiful courtiers. Yes, the Queen had given her a decent livery of twelve yards of worsted for to make her a better kirtle and she had drunk it as fast as she could.

Mary passed between two buildings to go round the back of the palace kitchens and through the woodyard. Now it happens that for a man to enter the Court of Whitehall is very much harder than for a wagon or a witch. The Queen will not allow Newcastle coal in the Court fireplaces because it is dirty and she does not like the smell. But the cords and cords of wood that the Court burns cannot pass through either the Holbein or the Court gates. Instead they are brought by ox-carts between the buildings of the old St Katherine's Hermitage, past the kilns of Scotland Yard and into the woodyard through a passage way by the river. Occasionally a cart will fall into the river, or be said to in the Board of Green Cloth accounts.

So Mary passed through the woodyard where they were unloading and stacking under canvas yet another load of faggots, not noticing how familiar were the looks of a particular heavy-set black-haired man driving the wagon in his shirtsleeves. She went to the main door of Mrs Twiste's laundry, where Thomasina had seen the courtiers' shirts being sorted and coded so long before.

The place seemed oddly subdued. Mary came in through the door and headed for the lobby where the children and their mothers eat the apples they often roast in the boiling fires at the end of the day. Nobody was there. When she turned at booted feet behind her, there were two gentlemen, one short and plump in grey worsted, one tall and elegant in red velvet.

"Stop!" said the tall one, Mr Ramme, of course.

All he saw was a defenceless, contemptible old witch as she swayed from foot to foot by the mop bucket, and blinked at them.

"Wha'?" drooled her purse-mouth.

"You are arrested in the name of Her Majesty the Queen . . ."

Silly bastards, that they thought so little of her. They had no men to back them yet and had not even bothered to lay hands on their prey before they began their pompous speeches about the Queen's name. Mary picked up the bucket of lye for scrubbing the floor and threw it at both of them, causing one of them to scream when the stuff stung his eyes and the other to wail at the damage done to yet another expensive suit.

Then she clutched up her skirts and ran. As there was no point in going to Mrs Twiste's office, who must have permitted this and would be more than likely to knock her over the head with a candle-stick to prevent trouble, Mary charged straight at them in their disarray and punched one of them shrewdly in the gut as she passed. They fell against each other. As she fled along the passage, she cannoned into the beefy Mr Becket, hurrying from his subterfuge of work in the woodyard to grab her as well. He held her fast.

"Sister Mary," he hissed, "let me help you . . ."

It was a pity, but she had no reason to let him. More reason to fear him since she had coney-catched him and his friend and he had no doubt come for a reckoning. So Mary kneed him in the cods and left him leaning against the wall moaning and shaking his head while she scuttled away.

She went down the narrow stairs skipping like a lamb, fear and triumph and a great deal of booze softening her aches and pains like a drink from the fountain of immortality. She did not feel the burning in her chest which usually came when she ran, indeed she felt strong and fleet.

There in the basement, where the Court slops come, she saw the lids on the barrels had been lifted. They had found Pentecost's dowry, damn their eyes. Anger and the stench of it brought tears to Mary's eyes and made her cough, and she could hear the clatter of hobnails behind her on the stairs.

There is a trap-door, and she went to it. Nothing was wasted of the Court slops and perhaps you may have wondered what happens to the stuff they filter out.

It goes into huge old barrels under the floor where it drains and hardens further. Nowhere else but at the Court of such a pernickety Queen would anyone use valuable barrels for such a thing, even if they are at the end of their lives, black with age and some of them stamped with Henry VIII's monogram. Not only the human waste goes there, but in through a chute from the woodyard go mountains of dung from the horses and oxen serving the Court because the Queen is a delicate lady who has bathed at risk of her health every month since she was a child, and she cannot abide bad smells. No muck-heap may sully any yard she passes through or glances out at. Naughty stenches must be caught and imprisoned before she can smell them.

Therefore, under the floor of the laundry basement lie barrels of shite, human and animal, all commingled. Some clever divine that has addled his brains with reading and righteousness might wish to make a pretty parable of that, but I will not. Generally speaking, they roll the barrels out, nailed shut, at night, when the wind is in the right direction, load them one at a time onto boats, cover them with tarpaulin and bring them downstream to the mouth of the Thames where the gunpowder-makers pile the stuff up, the better to grow saltpetre underneath. Every week, at least while the Court is in residence at Whitehall, a boat goes downstream with the tide carrying ominous barrels, and once one was wrecked going under the bridge and upset the burghers of London Town very much indeed.

But for three months and more the Thames had been frozen and no one had dared to do anything other than store the barrels and pray for the thaw, since no wagon could move fast enough to escape Her Majesty's sharp nose, and then there would be the devil of a row.

Some of the stench could escape from the chute and from little barred windows that gave on the Thames, but not all of it. Above, the little girls whisper of the cellar to each other, and grab each other and squeal in horror at the thought, and they believe that if they make Mrs Twiste very angry, she might force them to go down there. Mrs Twiste would never dream of such a thing, believing firmly that birch twigs answer far better, but so the legend runs and no doubt supports her authority.

Nor had Mary been there, since no person of any sense would wish to try it, and even she pitied the poor men that so needed the money they were paid for conveying the barrels downriver. But she also knew that at the end of the place farthest from the Court was a door to the river, for the barrels to pass through onto the boats.

All this took but the blink of an eye to think of. So Mary went to the trap-door, drew back the bolts and coughed at the smell. She kirtled up her skirts and climbed down gingerly onto the lid of the barrel that was under the chute, into the darkness and stench of hell. There was I also, Empress of Hell. She tried to be silent and drop the trap-door quietly, but she could not help coughing and choking as she climbed down and felt her way between the close-packed barrels. The bad airs were making her head spin, it was already turning like a top from booze, bad airs worse than any diseased breath from a marsh. She had to pause to puke behind a barrel and add to the nameless slime on the floor. When she got to the door that led down a slope to the river, she shot the bolt on this side and found it would still not open. It was bolted on both sides.

Ramme and Munday flung back the trap-door, letting evening light into hell, and there was a moment's silence as their noses told them what was below.

"She wouldn't . . ." said Ramme's voice.

"She has. Look at her boot-prints there."

"Oh, Christ. Why does this always happen when I have new clothes on."

"Yours are wrecked already. You go first."

"After you, Mr Munday."

There was another short pause.

"Get *him* to do it," said Munday and Ramme laughed and called up the stairs.

She heard the stamp of three pairs of feet, and then the soft hiss of slow match on a hand pistol.

"You," said Ramme, with such a load of contempt in his voice that surely any true man would have struck him.

"Yes, sir," came an answering rumble from Becket, and that voice was fairly quivering with fear and submission, Mary had never heard the like. He sounded like a whipped dog.

"Go down there and fetch out the old bitch."

The boots came to the edge of the trap-door and there was a sigh and the sound of swallowing.

"Down there?"

"Get on with it, man; we have other things to do this day. Find her and bring her up."

"Get me a ladder; I'm too heavy for this rope."

Well, that gave Mary a little time. She found one barrel that was free of its fellows and near enough to the wall, leaned her back against the rough wet wall and pushed with her feet. It was immovable. She gasped and sweated, then tried another, and that must have been older and rotted down more, for it at least toppled. The lid came off, letting a genie of rottenness escape and making her puke again.

The ladder poked down to the floor from the trap-door and then creaked with Becket's bulk. He had tied a kerchief round his face to try to protect himself from the plague and jail-fever and all the other diseases that come from bad airs.

Mary took her knife in her hand and ducked behind a barrel. Becket came, swordless, large and ugly as a troll. She scuttled from barrel to barrel where, for all the reduction Ramme had caused in him, Becket was still too wide to pass. He knocked over another one as he tried to catch her, and he too was overcome and had to puke.

Mary crept up behind him, muttering to herself and stabbed at him with her dagger. She did it badly and the knife grated on the bone fencing of his chest. He shouted with anger and surprise, spun and pounced with a lightness she never expected, caught her wrists, hurting them, nearly breaking them, and she screamed.

With an easy twist of one paw he took her knife, but did not cut her throat as she expected, as she would have done; indeed, as she had done once to the upright man who first raped her little girl. He drew her close, so the doglike smell of his breath made a welcome change to the air she was breathing, and growled,

"Where is the door?"

Mary spat and tried to head-butt him and he shook her until her teeth rattled and her eyes blurred.

"The door, you stupid old bitch."

She pointed with her head. "It's bolted outside."

"Fuck," he muttered. Then she saw his teeth and realised he had grinned. "Come on. No doubt I can kick it out."

"What's happening down there?" came Ramme's voice, impatient and rightly suspicious.

"Aaah," said Becket, unconvincingly, "the witch stabbed me. I cannot . . . aarghh."

There was muttering above while Becket half-carried, half-shoved Mary between the barrels, knocking over yet another one that barred his path.

Feet appeared on the ladder. Becket moved faster, still hurting Mary's thin old arm while she beat at him with her fist. His boots skidded on the slope to the opening. The trapdoor boomed as he kicked it. Alas, it held firm.

Ramme was at the foot of the ladder, lit from above by dusk-light and torches, his sword glittering.

"Hand her over, you fat fool," said Ramme in a bored and irritated tone of voice.

Becket made a soft growl in his throat and shoved the witch so she fell into the corner just by the door. Then he turned and moved back towards Ramme.

"When will you learn to obey?" Ramme sneered at him. "You're caught like a sewer rat. Or do you want to spend another day hanging next to your friend, the little Jew?"

Becket roared and charged him, leaping a barrel. How he expected to get anywhere with nothing but a four-inch blade against a man holding a rapier I do not know, but as Mary's little dagger in his great hand lifted and clashed in a shower of sparks with Ramme's long steel, God Almighty Himself leaned down from Heaven.

It was a thunderbolt. You ask, How could there be a thunderbolt in a cellar? Well, is the Lord God who made the stars and sea to be bound by a mere cellar? And there are more ways than one that a flame can be lit—have you never seen marsh-lights dance over a bog? This bolt had the same green colour.

First, in the instant after the sparks, there was a huge flash of light, of searing heavenly fire that began in all places and reached all places, a tiny second of heat which shrivelled eyebrows and set brief light to both men's beards. Then a great *whoomfing* bellow of air, which burst open the bolted door to the river and nearly broke their rib-cages, and then a wild sucking wind which brought the door slamming back against the stones and shattered its sturdy planks to kindling. Daylight shone through, like a beacon. Mary could not get air in her lungs, she had fallen down at God's thunderbolt, more terrified than she had ever been, for surely now she thought Christ Jesus her lost husband would come to her and beat her.

Ramme and Becket gaped and smouldered at each other for a second, rocking where they stood, and Ramme dropped his rapier for sheer fright. Terror was printed all over his face. Then broad shoulders hid him from view as Becket grappled the front of his wrecked red doublet, jerked him close and stabbed him once in the chest under his breastbone, and once, up to the hilt, in the side of his throat so the blood spurted. Ramme staggered and fell in the splattering, his limbs drumming as they learnt last of all that all was lost. Becket bent to him, twitched out the blade.

Mary turned, scrabbled on hands and knees, terror transmuted to animal instinct by the killing. She slithered on her haunches down the cobbled barrel-slope and stepped onto the ice. Becket could follow if he liked, Mary cared nothing for him, only she must escape, she must run from my Son's coming in wrath and vengeance, never mind the pursuivants who had stolen her darling's dowry, never mind Becket himself to whom she had caused trouble by coney-catching him; she thought only of escaping, of running away from her death and the eternity of Hell.

Besides, she thought she saw someone on the ice ahead of her. Her disordered brain made the shape of Our Lady the Queen of Heaven, Star of the Morning, Gate of the Sea, made me out of mists and ice-reflections and wishful thinking, as she always had. It was to her dream of me she ran with arms spread like a child, longing for comfort.

So Mary ran out, heedless, onto the ice of the Thames and behind her she heard Becket shouting that the ice was not safe, that the thaw was come, it was too thin, that she should stop . . . Too thin for you, you fat lummock, she thought triumphantly as she scuttled, and then one of her feet went down through cold shards into colder water, and the other smashed a hole as well and she was running slowly in mingled broken glass and icy water and she screamed and screamed as she toppled and fell and struggled, and even if they had wanted to, no one could have saved her. Nor am I my Son, to walk on water.

Dimly she heard shouting from the bank, and a thin sorrowful cry from a higher window that she knew was Pentecost. Her skirts billowed and supported her for a long agonised second as she gasped icy air into her lungs.

Then the fiery cold of the tide's ebb grabbed hold of Mary in its black arms and sucked her under the breaking ice, turned her over, rolled her down, black cold that paradoxically numbed her heart and eased her pain, bowled her along the riverbed, all spiked with London's waste, faster and faster down a hard rough tunnel. In an eddy her kirtle ripped and broke from her back and another whirl-pool caught her, turned her again. Her petticoats were gone, she was in her stays and smock, and the ancient steel boning protected her chest as she curled around the hard lump of herself and was taken along and along, until her chest was burning and sparkles burnt her eyelids. As she was in Hell, she thought it might be safe to breathe, her mind disordered with ice and whirling, and yet she was too afraid of Judgement unshriven to breathe, still clutched her little life clawlike to her chest.

I came in my guise as the black Madonna, Queen of Hell. I lifted her up on another eddy, her head smashed through ice thin as cast sugar at a banquet, and she gasped and breathed and choked and gasped again.

I took my daughter-in-law once more, bowled her on down through the river, down into the muddy depths, lungs aching, throat full of rocks, up again, beaten and flogged by ice and iron rubbish, her poor head bruised and bleeding from the ice, but given another space to breathe, and then another. At last she heard the roaring of the freed river at the bridge, where the ice queued and ground itself to diamond shards at the constrictions of the piers, where she also would have been ground to a forcemeat stuffing. No, she thought, no, first I must be absolved my sins, oh, Lady, help me. Of course I came, the sweet Drop of the Ocean, even the Empress of Hell had mercy, and a swirling eddy of the tide thrust her through breaking mirrors of ice to the place where three cranes rise above the Vintry steps. The tide washed her up to those steps and left her there to cling and crawl, and even as she lay gasping and shuddering in the light of day, her poor worn heart burst a string and burnt out the inside of her chest, burnt tracks of fire down her left arm and the blue surcease of my mantle came down over her face at last.

LXXIX

POOR PENTECOST, WHO WAS peering out of the window to see the thunderbolt, one of many curious faces making an audience. She screamed and wept to see her grandam fall helplessly through the ice and hid her face in the shoulder of Mrs Twiste's bodice, where Mrs Twiste was keeping her safe in her office. Mrs Twiste was a good woman, although Mary had cursed her often enough for trying to keep her away from booze. She let Pentecost smear snot all over her clean shoulder as the child wept and trembled, and stroked her hair and told her "There, there, sweeting."

Down in the cellar, Becket was well and truly trapped. If the river had been water he would have tried swimming, so afraid was he of the Tower. Had the witch not just proved to him beyond doubt that the ice would not bear him, he might have tried to run for it, even knowing of the thaw. But he was not cowardly enough to seek his death deliberately, for all his boasting to himself that Ramme would never capture him alive. Now all he could do was stare at Ramme's corpse and shake. After a moment to nerve himself, Mr Munday came climbing down the ladder with the pistol, the slow match in its lock hissing and sparking and flaring green and blue from the bad airs.

Becket looked sideways at Munday, who was holding his handkerchief over his face with his free hand.

"Mr Munday," he whispered, "I beg you will shoot me now rather than take me back to the Tower."

"Why should I shoot you, sir?" Munday's voice was flat and muffled.

"To be merciful to me, Mr Munday. Take the pistol in both hands, or your aim might be spoilt, and pull the trigger. I will not move." Becket was panting now, not troubling to try and hide the terror and despair in his voice.

"She had the papers?" said Munday.

Becket nodded.

"What about your friend the Jew?"

Becket sagged slightly. "You do have him?"

"Of course."

"I would have thought he had died."

Munday was silent for a second, not inclined to explain about Ames's fever. "He is stronger than he looks," he said reflectively.

Moving by instinct because he could not see, Becket stuck the little knife in his belt, leaned his broad back against the wall and hid his face in his hands. His shoulders shook as he worked to control himself.

Munday watched him, not unkindly, but without pity. He found it interesting how men behaved in extremity, perhaps one reason why he chose to find his fortune the way he did. To be sure, he had never loved anybody and he found the emotion curious in others. He recognised Becket's concern for his friend, knew it for a weapon in his hand far better than a gun. And he could use words well enough when he tried. He thought and then placed them carefully.

"If I shoot you, sir, or if you try to run over the ice and drown, then on whom do you think Mr Secretary Davison's anger will vent?"

"Oh, Christ," said Becket, almost inaudibly. A moment later he was upright, his own man again. He fumbled the knife from his belt and handed it over to Munday. "Well," he said, bleak as a child in a famine, "let us get on with it then."

He went up the ladder in front of Munday, looking up and blinking as if he very much wished he were climbing a scaffold to be hanged, followed by the impassive pursuivant with his sparkling dag.

LXXX

THEY THOUGHT OF PENTECOST, of course. The great Secretary of the Council, Mr William Davison himself, had her brought to an office at Court. On his orders, Mrs Twiste had taken her little ragged kirtle and smock away and delivered them to his pursuivants, to be carefully searched. They found the ivory figurine of myself as the Queen of Heaven in the pocket of her petticoat, her most valuable possession. The child herself was examined naked by Mr Davison's wife, for any papers or writing she might be concealing, and then, as Davison had given the good woman no further orders about it, my darling Pentecost was washed and given another smock, bodice, petticoat and kirtle and a shawl, all of which were much better and cleaner than her old ones and kept her warm, and furthermore an embroidered biggin from Mrs Davison's own sewing basket. Then Mrs Davison sat her down to the best meal she had ever eaten in her life, of game pasties and manchet bread and chicken breast in a garlic sauce and a pile of honey-cakes, all of which she munched through as steadily as a caterpillar on a leaf. On the whole, though the proceedings were strange beyond her imagination, like all children she was accustomed to the insanity of adults and only opened her mouth to say "Please, ma'am, and "Thank you, ma'am." For her the world had gone alien and far away, an empty place without her grandam in it. God knows, we none of us deserve the love of our children.

So when she trotted in to stand on the other side of Davison's desk, peering over it, she was not as frightened as she might have been, and because she knew only that he was a very important and worshipful gentleman and not the true extent of his power, she curtseyed and waited to see what he wanted without any of the dark imaginings that an adult would have suffered.

Mr Davison attempted to smile at her. It would have looked better if his eyes had partaken of it, but they had long forsworn humour. Pentecost felt sorry for him because she thought he was suffering from wind.

"Ah . . . Pentecost," he said.

She curtseyed again, watching him.

Davison cleared his throat. "Pentecost," he said again, "do you know anything of God?"

She curtseyed to him once more. "Yes, sir," she said. "God the Father made me and all the world."

"Have you learnt your catechism?"

"Yes sir; well, some of it."

"Recite what you know."

"Yes, sir. But you have to do your bit. You have to ask me my name."

Davison smiled thinly. "What is your name?"

"Pentecost, sir."

"Who gave you this name?"

"MygodfathersandgodmothersinmybaptismwhereinIwasmadeamemberofChrist, the child of God and aninheritorofthekingdomofHeaven . . ." chanted Pentecost, delighted to find a use for the nonsense her grandam had insisted she learn.

Davison held up his hand. "I see that you do know it. But do you know what it means?"

"Means, sir?"

He sighed. "Do you go to church?"

She shook her head.

"Why not?"

"Because Mr Christ is there."

Davison coughed. "Oh?"

"Yes. He was my grandam's husband once, you see, but he left her and so she hates him." Pentecost paused and shut her eyes. "Hated him," she corrected herself carefully.

Davison was hard to surprise, but this made him stretch his eyes a little.

"Oh? Er . . . how can that be?"

"My grandam was a nun once," explained Pentecost kindly. "That means she was wed to Mr Christ." Pentecost frowned. "Or is he really a lord?"

"He is, of course, Our Lord."

"Oh. I am sorry. So my grandam must have been a lady when she was wed to him. I believe she was once."

"Ah?"

"So my lord Jesus was her husband, but then instead of keeping her and looking after her like a good man should, and giving her his babies, like Mrs Twiste's husband gave her before he died, my lord Jesus threw my grandam out and abandoned her to starve. Which I think was very bad of him. Do you not think so, Mr Davison?"

If Davison had had the use of his larynx he would have berated Pentecost for blasphemy.

"And so we do not to go to visit my lord Jesus's houses because although he is so rich and has God for his father, he never ever gave my grandam a penny to help her, and so she was on the road all her life and very sad."

"She was a witch," Davison managed to say harshly.

Pentecost nodded. "Yes," she said, "she helps the girls at the bawdy-house, and women in childbed too. She tries . . . she tried very hard to be a good witch."

"Such a thing is impossible," said Davison positively. "Pentecost, your grandam has brought you up in dreadful sin and wickedness, but at least you know that God is Our Father and knows all we do."

Pentecost frowned. "Well, he is my lord Jesus's father, but not mine. I have never met my father, but I am sure he was a rich courtier, a tall fine man with a black beard that had rings on his fingers and a velvet doublet and . . ."

This was a story she had made up for herself, having chosen the man she wanted carefully from visitors to the Falcon. However, Davison was not able to hear it.

"Enough!" he shouted. "Be quiet, you bad child. God is our Father in Heaven, He knows all you do, and if you are wicked and evil like your witch of a grandam, then you will end up in Hell like her!"

Pentecost fell silent. Davison had missed his mark here. I was watching her, making a corner of the room shine with my presence, for those who had eyes to see, which was none of those in the room, and I could see the reassurance in her heart. For had not the worshipful gentlemen just told her a way she could be with her grandam again?

"Now, Pentecost," said Davison, getting a better grip on himself, "I am going to ask you some questions which you must answer very truthfully. God is watching and He knows if you lie. If you lie you will go to Hell."

And be with my grandam, thought Pentecost, greatly pleased.

"Yes, sir," she said humbly aloud.

"Did your grandam give you papers to hide for her?"

"No, sir," she said promptly.

"Did she hide any papers herself?"

"No, sir."

"She certainly had some papers, did she not? Don't lie, for I know she did."

Pentecost nodded cautiously.

"But she said they belonged to the Queen."

Davison sniffed. "I am the Queen's servant," he said, "so I am looking for her papers in her behalf." This black lie might have fooled an adult, but not Pentecost. It reassured her to know that both of them were lying, even though it meant that the frightening Court gentleman might follow her down to Hell.

"Yes, sir," she said uncertainly, wishing someone would tell her what the papers were about. Perhaps they were a map to find treasure.

"Where are the papers?"

Pentecost's brow furrowed. "I do not know, sir. My grandam had them."

"Your grandam had them?"

"Yes, sir," lied Pentecost happily, thinking of the book in the Queen's own Library. I smiled to see her, for no mother would ever have been fooled by her glibness. Mr Davison was, however.

"On her, where? In her petticoat pocket?"

"Yes, sir," said Pentecost with a smile, pleased that she could please the worshipful gentleman and wondering if God would come and take her to Hell to find her grandam soon. "In her pocket."

Davison slapped his hand on the table-top with a sharp sound of finality.

"You are sure of this? That your grandam had her papers with her, in the pocket of her petticoat?"

"Oh yes, sir," said Pentecost cheerfully. "She said they were important, sir."

Davison sighed through his nose. "I see."

"Is God your father, sir?" asked Pentecost, wanting to get everything quite straight.

"Yes," said Davison, no longer paying proper attention to her.

"Then you must be my lord Jesus Christ's brother. Why was he so bad to my grandam?"

Davison gaped at her. "You are a complete little heathen," he said. "We shall find you a place at a charity school to be properly taught the True Religion."

"I know it, sir," said Pentecost with a curtsey, determined to make use of her tedious lessons. "Listen. You say: Whatdidyourgodfathersandgodmothers then for you? Then I say: They did promiseandvow three things inmyname. First that I should renouncetheDevilandall'is works, the pompandvanity of this wicked world and—"

"Then how can you stand there and speak such blasphemous nonsense?" demanded Davison. "I never heard anything so wicked. Mr Christ, indeed. If you were my child I would have you beaten and your mouth washed with soap for speaking so."

Pentecost stared at him in confusion, for she had had no idea that she had annoyed the worshipful gentleman.

He brought out the little carved ivory Madonna she and her grandam had carried so faithfully for so long and tapped it down on the desk in front of him distastefully. "This . . . this thing. This was your idol, was it not?"

Pentecost's mouth fell open because she did not know the word. "It's my BlessedVirginMary," she told him. "She is very beautiful and she has—"

"Silence!" rapped Davison. "You were taught to kneel and bow down in reverence for this graven image?"

"Well, yes, sir," Pentecost said, full of foreboding for her toy. "But you know, she is not really the Blessed Virgin, but only an image of her. My grandam said she is to remind us of the—"

Davison was not interested in this hair-splitting. "It was your heathen idol, your image of perdition, and your grandam taught you to worship it."

Sheer confusion silenced Pentecost. She began to wonder if the gentleman was mad.

"She has the baby Jesus inside," she said timidly. "You can open the door and look."

In case the Queen's papers were hidden in it, Davison opened the little door in my belly and checked. The painting of Christ's passion was there, beautiful in egg tempera, the sky and the mourning Virgin's gown made of crushed lapis lazuli, the blood of Christ and the cloaks of the soldiers made from crimson lake. Only the baby had gone missing, dropped out into Mrs Davison's sewing bag when she searched the image herself.

Davison's face twisted at such an ugly truth as was implied in Pentecost's Madonna: that a mere woman should have carried Christ in her body and therefore also His Passion. It made him ill to think on.

"This heathen image," he said sternly, "can do nothing for you, Pentecost, it is but a mammet, a toy. It is powerless save for evil."

Pentecost knew then that somehow her Madonna was doomed. She put her hands over her mouth to stop herself from crying out.

In a stately manner, Davison took the Madonna, rose from behind his desk and went to the fire burning in the grate.

"Now I will show you that this thing is not to be worshipped and is but a piece of ivory, cunningly carved, nothing more."

He held Pentecost's Madonna near the fire, watching her face. If he had thought of it, he might have bartered the Madonna for the Queen's papers, but he never did think of it, since he had not the wit.

"Please, sir," said Pentecost, with tears running down her face, "oh please, do not burn her, sir, she is so pretty . . ."

Davison tossed the Madonna into the flames and dusted his fingers in satisfaction.

Ivory burns with black smoke and a vile smell. For a moment I shone in the flames almost as brightly as I do in the sky, but then the delicate worn planes of my face and carved folds of my gown and the minute filigree of my crown and collar crumbled to black, the door in my belly warped and cracked and blackened, the painting of Christ-crucified burned and disappeared and all that was left was a glowing cinder.

Pentecost let out her breath which she had held, hoping that the Queen of Heaven would act to save her toy. Then her face puckered and she began to cry helplessly into her hands.

"Only . . . only . . ." snuffled Pentecost, "only I was going to ask if I could . . . if you would . . ."

"What?" he demanded impatiently, wishing she would stop.

". . . t . . . take me to see the Queen of Heaven . . . b . . . because Grandam always said she was the one who . . . was . . . was k . . . kindly . . ."

Davison rolled his eyes.

"If you are referring, as I think you are, to the Virgin Mary, then it seems you have even more to learn to save you from ignorance and heathen superstition. Your idol is burnt but you are a wicked child, Pentecost, and I am sorry for you because your innocence has been so abused."

Most of these words Pentecost did not understand, but misery at the loss of her toy was rising in her, misery in such a tide she did not know what to do with it, only it filled her belly and her chest and her head and lapped out to flood the whole room, misery that sprang more from the loss of her grandam than her plaything.

Davison knew that he was beginning to sweat as she continued to cry with all her strength and a great deal of snot. His own children were too frozen in dread of him to weep so immoderately, he had never heard such a noise even when they had been beaten. True, he had heard grown men howl and weep similarly, but that had always been in the service of True Religion. This ungrateful wailing scoured his nerves and when he stood and ordered her to stop at once and came round the table to try and calm her, she shrieked at his expression, backed into a corner and fell over. She curled up in a ball against the pale oak panels and howled extravagantly, so that he rang for his clerk, and the clerk came in and had no idea what to do either.

At last the man-at-arms standing stolidly at the door could bear the noise no longer. He came in, complete with his halberd, and saw the scene: the Privy Councillor clasping and unclasping his fists, and the clerk flapping his hands from the elbow and shouting, "Hush, hush, or you'll be beaten," while a small creature cowered screaming hysterically in a corner. He was himself a father of six and he lost his temper. He threw aside all hopes of reward and a pension, leaned his halberd against the wall, took off his helmet and put it on the desk. Then he shoved Mr Davison bodily aside with his shoulder, squatted down to Pentecost and gathered her into his large arms, cradled her against his buff-coated shoulder and went to the door.

"I resign from your service, sir," he growled to Mr Davison. "I had never thought to see the like from a God-fearing man. Good day."

With that he stamped off down the passage until he found an antechamber where he could sit and hold Pentecost until she could gulp herself into softer crying, and then held her further until her hiccups had eased and she could blow her nose on the hem of her new white apron.

At last even the hiccups had subsided and Pentecost asked to be taken back to Mrs Twiste. Whereat the man-at-arms carried her to the laundry and handed her directly into Mrs Twiste's own arms.

"I am sorry I have seen the day, mistress, that a councillor of the Queen would lower himself so far as to bully a little maid," he told Mrs Twiste stiffly. "But I think she has not been hurt, only badly upset."

Mrs Twiste nodded and thanked him and sat my sweetheart on her own seat and gave her spiced wine so thick with sugar it was nearer a sweetmeat than a drink, until Pentecost's swollen red eyes drooped and she fell asleep where she was.

LXXXI

DAVISON SENT HIS MEN out, every one of them, to scour the river banks and bridge piers for the corpse of the witch. At last two of them returned with a litter bearing the withered, almost frozen body of an old woman that had been found curled up on the steps at the Vintry. Davison searched her personally: she was in the bloody tatters of her smock and stays, her kirtle and petticoat lost to the river. There were no papers on her at all, nor the shreds of any. Although she was blue and unmoving, a pulse still struggled to beat in her neck and Davison conceived the idea that perhaps he might glean something of use from the Jesuit who still clung to life in a locked room at Walsingham's house in Seething Lane.

By Walsingham's orders a surgeon had been called to take out the halberd blade and sew up the wound. The surgeon himself had protested, saying he had never heard of anyone surviving such a wound and he saw no necessity for causing more pain. In the end, though, he had obeyed, needing the gold and not so very interested in preserving a Papist from pain.

As they brought Mary into the little bedchamber and laid her under blankets on a truckle-bed, Tom Hart lay on his side with his legs drawn up to his swollen belly and his face grown as old and sunken as hers, barely breathing and utterly still. Under half-closed lids he watched them wrap her to warm her and bring in a brazier as well, so that the room grew close and stifling as it heated up.

I had been sitting with him, to keep him company, sometimes visible to him and sometimes not, as his fever waxed and waned. Now I smiled, and in his sight I opened my arms to show him this was by my power. He understood me. In all his doings, Hart was a valiant soldier in my Son's company, and now he spent the last farthing of his courage against the agony and sickness of his belly to say absolution for Mary, to finish what he had left open on the night they met in the mirrored chamber at the Falcon.

He did not know if she heard him or not, but I heard him and said the words of faith first spoken by the centurion to my Son, and perhaps Mary echoed me so softly Hart could not hear her. Perhaps she forgave my Son. Only she knew she had been shriven at last and believed now she would not end in Hell. Purgatory she could face, as being only just.

The servant who brought the brazier had forgotten to open a window to let the fumes escape. With the door shut, there was soon a gentle blue haze in the air, my mantle made manifest. Slowly Tom Hart's eyes shut and his lips relaxed from their rigid line, even his colour seemed to become better as he slept. No one came. They breathed more and more slowly as their lips reddened to a strange semblance of health. At last they were both utterly still.

LXXXII

WE ARE COME TO a caesura in the tale, not the end. For Becket it was a time of great agony, although the pain he suffered was the coward's pain of anticipation and fear, not fact. Anthony Munday had all a courtier's instincts and a great deal of cold common sense. He was quite certain that there had been more going on than his master had told him or indeed knew himself, and without Ramme to talebear he was powerful enough to decide for himself how to treat his prisoners at the Tower. For Simon Ames, he called a doctor and a surgeon again, supplied him with medicines and books to read and saw that his cell was clean, dry and warmed with a fire. After a thorough and humiliating body-search, Becket was as decently treated, although kept in solitude and should have been well-enough had he not been furnished now with too vivid a memory. Ramme's corpse was retrieved with great complaint by an undertaker's servants and taken to the same crypt of St Mary Rounceval whence Bethany's mortal dross had been carried to her grave only the day before.

After Thomasina had told the Queen the truth of what Davison had done, her first reaction was to put him forthwith in the Tower and rescind the warrant of execution. However, on second thoughts, that would have revealed too much of the Queen's mind and she doubted not that her stern councillors who would have arranged the execution would find some way of ignoring her orders. She made it a policy never to give orders that she knew would be disobeyed.

She spent the day after the fight in the Privy Gallery hushing up what had occurred. Carey was sent back to his father's chambers with the assurance of her favour once all had been cleared up, and the two men from Berwick were rewarded. As she said to Thomasina, she could not move against Davison until she knew for certain the whereabouts of her testament and confession, for she was quite sure he would use them against her if he did find them. He might yet do so. Until the papers could be found she must act with as great circumspection as she had when the Lord Admiral Thomas Seymour was arrested and she herself had been interrogated.

She was still desperate to avoid being seen to execute Mary Queen of Scots, and fixed on the idea of making the woman die a few days earlier. Upon the Sunday she even wrote to Mary's gaoler Sir Amyas Paulet, requiring him to do as he had pledged in the Bond of Association, and stifle Mary quietly in the night. Paulet wrote back a letter that was magnificent in its stiff-necked legalistic refusal to do what he conceived as evil, and the Queen raged and swore that the silly man could not see that it mattered not at all *how* the bitch of Scots died, so long as she did so in such a way that her cousin of England did not get the blame. She even let out to Davison that she had dreamt of running him through with a sword, which might have warned him that his hold was not quite secure, if he had paid any attention to the vapourings of women's imagination.

And so, as she had done many times before, the Queen waited, not calmly, not patiently but grimly, until events showed her what God desired her to do.

In the morning of Wednesday the eighth of February, in the year of our Lord 1587, a plump, stooped, middle-aged woman who had once been the tall and willowy Queen of Scotland walked—all in black satin and a veil of white—to the hall of the castle of Fotheringay. There an audience of three hundred of her worst enemies were waiting to see how she died. Her women disrobed her, to show her now all in dark red, the colour of blood, of courage and of martyr-dom—red bodice, red petticoat and red sleeves. Her eyes bound with a white cloth embroidered with gold, she knelt to the block as she prayed in Latin, against the yammering of heretic Divines determined not to leave her soul in peace even at death. Then she stretched out her arms, confided herself to God, and the executioner took off her head with two strokes and a little sawing.

Thus Davison had his great victory.

LXXXIII

IT WAS AS IF the Court were holding its breath. The Queen remained out-wardly impassive, troubled, as she admitted, with her old pains, and she did no business of ruling.

A couple of days after that Wednesday, Thomasina went in some state to the laundry to find out how Pentecost was faring. Mrs Twiste had taken her in for the moment, rather than send her back to her scandalous aunt at the Falcon.

Although she knew nothing of Davison's burning of Pentecost's Madonna, Thomasina brought with her the fashion doll she had often played with in front of the Queen, for Her Majesty seemed not to like that game any more. This she presented to Pentecost and bade her keep it safe in case somebody stole it, and Pentecost squealed and laughed with happiness in the usual faithlessness of the young, clasped it to her breast and declared that never in all the world had there been such a beautiful puppet.

"Keep it away from the fire," Thomasina told her. "See the pretty pink face? It is made of wax and will melt just like a candle if you forget and let it get too warm."

Knowing how it was for a little girl, Thomasina had also brought a box to keep the doll in and this delighted Pentecost almost as much as the doll itself, for it was sturdy solemn box of black oak lined with red satin, and furthermore had a key which could be worn on a ribbon.

"This will be my treasure casket," Pentecost announced as she buried it in the pallet and pile of blankets where she slept.

"You can keep letters from your lovers in there when you are older," said Thomasina with a smile.

"Or the Queen's papers," agreed Pentecost.

Thomasina stopped on the way to the door, came back and sat herself down on the floor in front of Pentecost.

"The Queen's papers?" she whispered, hardly daring to breathe in case she frightened Pentecost with too much interest.

"Yes," said Pentecost. "Can you take the kirtle off? . . . Oh, look, yes, you can, and she has a farthingale and a—"

"That your grandam had?"

"Yes. And her shoes are velvet, and leather soles. Oh, I wish I had a pair of shoes so beautiful, and her petticoat all embroidered, she must be as beautiful as the Queen; look, see the embroidery—"

"Pentecost, my dear. If you have the Queen's papers . . . If you have them and can give them to me, the Queen will give you almost anything you could ask for."

Pentecost stopped fingering the doll's petticoat and looked up. Her mouth dropped open.

"Oh," she said. Then cautiously, "Will she?"

"Yes," said Thomasina.

"Mr Davison said he wanted the papers, but he was horrible and he burnt my Madonna because he thought it was a nidol, which she *wasn't* and he said if I lied I would go to Hell and he said my grandam was a witch and she was in Hell and so I thought I would like to go there, so I lied to him and said my grandam had them when she . . . when she . . . fell in the river . . ."

Tears threatened to flood again.

"Mr Davison is a wicked man himself," Thomasina said at once. "The Queen hates him. If you can find the papers and give them to the Queen, you will make her happy and you will make Davison very sad."

"That was why I lied to him, you see," Pentecost added, pursuing her own thoughts. "So I could go and find my grandam again."

Thomasina put her arm around Pentecost and squeezed.

"My dear," she said, "none of us knows who will go to Heaven and who will go to Hell, but my own opinion is that Mr Davison will infallibly end in Hell and your grandam might well find herself in Heaven. And wherever she goes, when you die, if you want to, I expect you will go there too."

"Will I meet the Queen?" asked Pentecost.

"Yes. If you have the papers to give her, yes, certainly."

"But I will not have to die first?"

"No."

Pentecost laughed. She put the doll in its box, smoothing her down and tucking her up under a scrap of linen, and telling her to lie still and not kick and not snore and be a good girl at such length that Thomasina could have shaken her. Then she shut the lid and locked it and had Thomasina tie the ribbon for the key around her neck. Then at last she stood up and held out her hand to Thomasina and they went down the passageway, to the entrance of the laundry, where Thomasina's two waiting-women were standing and gossiping with the woman behind the desk.

Now a small procession formed and Thomasina and Pentecost walked through the woodyard, round the rearmost kitchens and in at the back of the Kitchens by the Great Hall. Pentecost took the back route of a night-soil woman and followed her grandam's old path exactly so that after a laborious tour about the Court, watched curiously by many men and some women, she came to the Privy Gallery.

Pentecost put her finger on her lips. "This is where the Queen lives," she said. "Be quiet."

Thomasina nodded seriously, and gave the waiting women who sniggered a very black look. "You stay here," she said to them, to their disappointment.

Thomasina and Pentecost walked up the Privy Gallery with its roof that Holbein had painted, Pentecost on tiptoe. Past the Queen's bedchamber, up to the other end where Carey had so narrowly missed dying of a halberd blade, and in at the door of the Library.

Pentecost looked round at all the books.

"My grandam could read," she said in a self-important whisper, "she could even read Latin. She could read any of these books."

Thomasina nodded, hoping Pentecost could not hear the hammering of her heart. The little girl tiptoed round the room, trailing her fingers on the shelf that was just right for her height until she stopped and took a book from the shelf. It was a slim volume, though magnificently bound in red calf and gold leaf. She nearly dropped it as she tried to open it, and Thomasina sprinted over and helped her take out the two stained and folded pieces of paper that had caused the Queen so much grief.

The muliercula was so overwrought, she stood and held them in her hand for several minutes together, shaking with emotion. Shall I look at them? she wondered. Shall I read what the Queen wrote when she was a child of fourteen and thought she was going to die?

No, came the answer. You have no right to go burrowing about in her confession.

Thomasina gave the papers back to Pentecost and told her to hide them in her bodice. Through the closed library door she heard the distant trumpets and the press of feet which announced that the Queen was returning from chapel. She knew that Her Majesty was due to meet with her Privy Council, who would be following behind her in the procession, and receive the confirmation of the Queen of Scots' execution. Brimming with mischief and triumph, Thomasina told Pentecost to wait where she was and do nothing and then slipped out into the Privy Gallery to await the Queen.

The men-at-arms in front of her lined up on either side of the gallery and as the Queen turned to go into the Council Chamber, she caught sight of her muliercula. True to her promise when she asked Thomasina to undertake the quest, she had not blamed her for her partial failure and had received her as gladly as before. Now she stopped and paused.

Thomasina ran forward and sheer lightness of heart made her take a hop and a jump and turn two somersaults in the air as she went, before plumping down breathlessly on her knees in front of the Queen.

"Your Majesty," she said. "Please, may I pray for an urgent private audience?"

"Now, Thomasina?" asked the Queen wearily, who was not looking forward to this Council meeting.

"Oh yes, Your Majesty. Now."

The Queen's eyes narrowed and after only a fragment of hesitation, while the Privy Councillors behind her exchanged irritated glances, she nodded.

"Where?"

"In your bedchamber, Your Majesty. Alone."

The Queen nodded curtly, turned about and went to the door of her bedchamber, causing a flurry amongst her maids, who were not prepared to open the door for her. At last they had sorted themselves out while the Queen waited patiently, with only one growl at the girl who nearly upended herself in her haste to reach the handle. Then the door closed. Thomasina went back to the Library, took Pentecost by the hand, led her to the door, stopped, used spit and the end of her apron to clean a small milk moustache and some crumbs left over from breakfast, and to straighten the now grubby embroidered biggin, and then brought her into the Privy Gallery.

The buzz of gossip and speculation died as Thomasina quietly led Pentecost past all the high gentlemen and ladies to the Queen's door. At the back of the Privy Councillors, Davison saw Pentecost in the midst of his triumph and began to wonder.

Thomasina waited until a maid of honour had opened the door for her and brought Pentecost inside, kicked it shut again herself with her heel.

The Queen was standing by the window, looking out on the Privy Garden, where the fountain lay silent with frost. She was again in black velvet and black satin, wrought with pearls and silver-thread embroidery, with pearls in her ears and a great rope of them round her neck, the false-front of her petticoat a foaming maze of cloth-of-silver brocade, and her ruff and standing cobweb lawn veil as near to a halo as a mortal can come. Watery winter sunlight caught sprinkled rainbows from the diamonds in the small crown she had pinned to her red wig.

Pentecost looked up at her and found everything she had hoped to find when she met the Queen of Heaven. The room smelt sweet, the bed was curtained in solemn tapestry and cloth-of-silver, the floor was covered with white matting and the walls with tapestry and Turkey rugs. It was interesting that the Queen liked animals, since there was a basket full of three snoring hairy lapdogs, but that was only to be expected. And the Queen of Heaven herself, although nearly as old as Pentecost's grandam, was tall and straight and as glorious as a picture in a church.

Pentecost dropped her mouth open and took a long deep breath of awe. "Ohh," she whispered to Thomasina, "she's so beautiful, she's even more beautiful than I thought."

Thomasina smiled and almost laughed. The Queen smiled as well.

"Shh," said Thomasina, "you should kneel to the Queen, you know, and wait for her to speak first."

"Oh yes," gasped Pentecost, dropping to her knees with an ungraceful thud. "I am sorry. Ohhh, look. She has a crown of stars."

The Queen smiled again, more pleased than she would admit by such uncalculated admiration. Thomasina genuflected much more neatly and then helped Pentecost up, who had tangled herself in her new petticoat, and led her forwards.

"Give Her Majesty what you have."

Pentecost fumbled the papers out of her bodice and held them up, smiling shyly.

"Thomasina said if I gave you these you would be happy," she said, forgetting she should wait for the Queen to speak to her first.

The Queen slowly took the papers, opened them, read a few words and then crumpled them against the hard prow of her bodice. Her face was flushed and her eyes suddenly glittered and she paused before she spoke.

"Is that right?" asked Pentecost anxiously. "Are they what you wanted?"

The Queen was folding the papers small, with fingers that shook, and she put them inside her own bodice.

"Yes," she said, smiling and blinking. "They are what I wanted."

Pentecost smiled back. "Thomasina said you would give me whatever I wished, Your . . . Your Majesty."

The Queen looked amused at this. She held out her hand to Pentecost, who took it, although it felt strange, being dry with white powder and heavy with rings. Together they walked to the Queen's carved and brocade-padded chair by the fire, where the Queen sat down carefully and Pentecost stood next to her, twiddling a lock of hair that had escaped from her cap.

"Now, Pentecost, I am not the Queen of Heaven, only the Queen of England," said Elizabeth. "I can give you many things, but not your heart's desire."

"Can I have a dowry?" said Pentecost quickly, not paying any attention to this nonsense. The Queen looked sad and also angry, so she hastened to explain. "Only, my grandam always said I must have a dowry so I could marry an old man with lots of money and then I would not have to be a strumpet like my aunt Julia at the Falcon."

The Queen coughed and said that a dowry could certainly be arranged.

"And could I have a beautiful gown of tawny satin and with pink and purple velvet and embroidery of birds, to look like a sunset in?" said Pentecost, growing in confidence.

"I expect so," said the Queen. "I can have my tailor make you one from the Privy Wardrobe."

"And a Noah's Ark made of sugar-paste with marchpane animals, all two by two and coloured and a house made of marchpane with sweetmeats and a diamond crown like yours and a white pony with a gold bridle and a real bed with curtains and another gown made of white satin and a red velvet bag and a book that has pictures in it and a puppy and a ball and a fur cloak and a palace and a prince and a box of kissing comfits and another box of sugar-plate made like animals and an orangeado and—"

The Queen laughed again and stopped her. "My dear," she said, "if you had such a lot of sweetmeats, would you eat them all at once?"

"As many as I could," said Pentecost, worried now. "But I would keep some for later and eat them tomorrow," she added with unconvincing maturity.

"I would not wish to give you presents that would make you sick or cause you to be too greatly envied. So here is my boon for you, Pentecost. Because of the great service you have done us today, we shall give you your gown and also your dowry, which you have so very wisely requested, and we shall see to it that you are found a good man to marry when the time comes, which it will not for many years. Until then we shall look after you as we do all our faithful servants. And you shall go with Thomasina now and our women shall serve you and bring you food and drink, and you shall make a list of all the things which you desire and which Thomasina considers it is seemly for you to have, and then we shall give you one more from the list. For if you have all your heart's desires, what will you do afterwards?"

"Enjoy them," said Pentecost stoutly, who was not at all philosophical.

"No doubt you shall," said the Queen. "Now you are a good child and have made me more happy than you can understand. Kiss my hand and then go with Thomasina to make your list, whilst I am busy with my councillors." There was a certain grim turn to the last word which Thomasina understood, but which passed by Pentecost, who was annoyed with herself that she had not asked the Queen of Heaven for her grandam to come back from Hell.

Still, she was wise enough and overawed enough to know when she should stop, and so she curtsied, kissed the Queen's elegant hand, and then jumped up and kissed her pink-and-white cheek for good measure. Thomasina took her by the hand and led her out of the room, leaving the Queen still sitting by the fire.

She paused there a moment, and then took the two pieces of folded paper from her bodice, unfolded them and read them carefully through, her lips moving with the words. With slow deliberation she held each one to the flames, watched as the golden fire caught the corner, held up the papers and saw them consumed utterly to crisp black ash which she dropped back in the hearth.

A few minutes later the Queen swept out of her bedchamber like a high black-and-white thunderhead from the wastes of the ocean.

LXXXIV

IF I WERE THE shade of Homer, I might essay to describe the wrath of the Queen when her councillors told her, with great self-satisfaction, that the viper Queen of Scots was dead. She had been bent to it against her will like a damascene steel blade and now, the tension released, she whipped back with devastating effect. She roared, she cursed, she painted bloody and terrifying word pictures, she had Burghley and Davison kneeling and trembling to her, and both of them under arrest by the end of their meeting. Burghley, by reason of his age and long service, she allowed to retire to Theobalds and later received back to Court in March, after a further tongue-lashing.

Davison she shredded publicly and in detail, from the top of his head through his miserable taste in clothes to the soles of his (metaphorically) bloodboltered boots, to his vaunted but shabby learning, his lack of wisdom, his damned overweening self-righteousness and his prideful lack of respect for her sovereignty. In the course of her diatribe she let him know that she had just burnt his weapon against her.

Davison marched from the Council Chamber for the last time, his face stony with shock, surrounded by four men-at-arms. The ice-floes had stopped passing down the Thames, and so Davison went by boat to Traitor's Gate, just as the Queen herself had in her sister's reign. With him went Sir Walter Raleigh, the Captain of her Guard, bearing Her Majesty's personal warrant releasing David Becket and Simon Ames.

At the Tower this new reversal caused a frightened flurry. They needed a litter for Ames, who was no longer delirious, but was still very ill and weak. While they were waiting for it to come, Raleigh questioned Becket in his cell and learnt more from him than Becket thought he did.

Raleigh had a cynical understanding of how to reward a man coupled with the dramatic talents of a Henslowe. He had Davison brought up from the antechamber where he had been sitting in silence. Becket walked out of his prison cell and watched as Davison marched in and sat on the bed. Ceremoniously, Raleigh gave Becket the keys and Becket slammed the door and locked it on the Queen's ex-Privy Councillor.

Becket eventually came to trial for the killing of Mr James Ramme and the jury was told to acquit by the judge after barely half the evidence was heard. By that time Simon Ames, well-wrapped and bandaged, could watch the proceedings and be amused by them. It was rumoured that Walsingham had also lost his Master of Posts, Mr Hunicutt, who had hanged himself in a sudden fit of brain-sickness and no inquest ever found out the truth of that.

Pentecost was made a ward of Thomasina de Paris, to be educated and cared for by her. Robert Carey was released from his father's ward and given a present of gold from the Treasury, with which he kept himself out of the Fleet by paying a few of his more pressing creditors. He had learnt something unknown about himself in his service to Thomasina: that the Court bored him and that his instinct for gambling required stronger satisfaction than playing primero for high stakes.

When it came time for a brave man to carry a message of condolence to the Queen of Scots' undutiful son King James, he volunteered for the task. Unfortunately, he never had the chance to explain the Queen's innocence of her cousin's blood, because King James would not receive him into his realm since the Scottish nobles were planning to ambush and kill him. However, other things came of the couple of months that he spent kicking his heels around the manor of Widdrington near Berwick.

Davison did not hang, despite the Queen's determination that he should, thanks to the lawyerly representations of both Cecils, Sir Francis Walsingham and even Sir Walter Raleigh. Raleigh opined courageously to the Queen that to hang Davison would give him too great an idea of his importance. Raleigh also advised injurious forgiveness and humiliating oblivion. And so Davison eventually stood trial in Star Chamber for his crime of executing the Queen of Scots, was fined ten thousand pounds and lived retired for the rest of his life. Lest he think himself a martyr, the Queen continued to pay his salary until he died.

Prologue

A T THE TIME WHEN the thing happened that eventually brought Mary's
death and that of the Queen of Scots, she had little notion of the day, let
alone the year of Our Lord, her wits already well-fuddled with beer and ale and
aqua vitae. The boy-King had been on his throne for a year, though to be sure
it was a matter of indifference to Mary what he did. They had changed the Mass
again, but she had long since turned her back on her unfaithful Husband. She
gave her reverences instead to me, the Queen of Heaven, since worship was a
habit too deeply ingrained in her by the convent to forgo. Heretically, she prayed
to me for forgiveness and for bread and for comfort, and sometimes Mary could
remember that I had come to her in her dreams and stroked her hair.

It was autumn or early winter, and Mary was cold and already beginning to
be hungry. There is hunger when you have missed a meal and then there is
hunger when every meal you eat is too little, when your stomach knots itself up
and every inch of your body is filled with longing for food, every dream a
thwarted banquet. She had felt that hunger before and knew it would come
again, which made it worse. No matter how you turn it to crumbs and taste
each piece individually and save a little for later, no matter how you spin it out,
a penny loaf is not enough to fill your belly. By that time she had almost forgot
the taste of meat and even white meats were too dear for her, though she gave
some to Magdalen when she cried with the cramps. Mary was too old to whore
for her supper, save with men that were desperate and too poor to pay except
with bread. Little Magdalen was still too young, being only five or six. She could
have whored, of course, but her mother could not bring herself to ruin her so
soon. She still had hopes of finding her a dowry and marrying her off.

But Mary had her Infirmerar's skills and her reputation was beginning to grow, as a midwife and as a witch. Who knows, if she had drunk less of her money, she might have been rich enough.

A woman in a velvet mask came to her one day; there was nothing strange in a fine lady wearing a mask to protect her skin from the ravages of the wind and cold, and to be sure it was only respectable for her to put her hair under a cap. She whispered in a soft West Country lilt and asked if it was true Mary was a midwife and a witch, and Mary told her, defiantly, yes.

She might have need of a witch, she said.

Two days later she was at Mary's door at midnight, hammering and hysterical. The witch must come now, immediately, and would be well-paid for it. She paid half the fee in gold, right there, and Mary put it under Magdalen's stays and bade her hide under the bed if she was frightened of monsters. If her mother came not back, she bade the child bury the gold where she would be sure to find it again and take one piece to a goldsmith and change it to pennies and then buy herself whatever she would. Magdalen nodded, white-faced and tried to smile at her mother, while the velvet-masked lady moaned and wobbled her lantern with fright.

So Mary went with the lady, reeling only slightly with hunger and not at all with drink. They went in a private boat which she rowed herself, badly and very slowly, and Mary let her, finding it funny to watch a lady, as she had been once, sweat to move a boat through water.

In the middle of the river she had Mary put a bag over her head, not a blindfold, which she might have rearranged to peek a little. It was made from black wool, fine cloth that might have been scraps from a fine lady's riding habit, with a draw-string that she tied about the neck. Mary was afraid then, and gripped the sides of the boat, terrified the lady would upset them and she would drown. She has always feared water, and with reason, as it turned out. Only the promise of gold and her empty belly kept her from screaming as the lady caught a crab and the boat spun.

Mary never knew where they came to, never had any notion in the world. It could have been anywhere in London. With her face caught in its bag she could smell only the wool, nothing else that might have given her a clue.

When they scraped against a boat-landing, the lady jumped out, leaving her alone, and tied it up. Mary was reaching out with her hands, afraid of being left, and the lady took her arm and helped her out as the boat gave a splash and a wallow and they both almost fell into the river.

Then she led Mary a long way, up steps, down alley-ways, more steps, a wider street, and another alley-way and in at a back door, and through a flagged room that might have been a kitchen, and up many stairs, until at last they were in a room that stank of blood and where some animal whined and grunted with pain.

Mary was no fool. She knew what she would see when the masked lady took off the hood and she could breathe properly again. She blinked and took her time. The first thing she saw was a table by a bed that had a bowl on it, a silver cup, a candle, pen and ink. The bed was plain, a serving-girl's bed, with a straw mattress and plain rough sheets, but that was no serving maid lying on it.

The girl was about fourteen or fifteen, wearing only a white shift that was fine linen and nicely stitched. Her hair too was crammed tight under a cap and her long slender hands were ringless and smooth, her face also hidden by a velvet mask such as they use for their dances at Court. But her eyebrows were gingery and her lashes too, and her eyes so dark a brown as to be black and her face a pale oval.

Not being gifted with second sight, Mary did not know her then as she would be; she knew only that this was some great noblewoman and that she had brought at least some of her distress on herself, for she was in the ugly throes of labour and blood already soaking the sheets. She squirmed and grunted with it and said nothing. Her waiting-woman moved to pat her neck dry with a linen cloth.

"Well," said Mary coldly, "who did this?"

"It . . . it happened. I was not even sure she was with child and then . . ." The waiting-lady seemed kindly enough but not over-endowed with brains.

"What did you do it with?" Mary demanded of the girl on the bed directly. "This is no ordinary miscarriage."

The girl turned her head arrogantly and would not answer. Mary swept up to the bed, caught her face and slapped it.

"Listen to me, you silly little bitch," she hissed. "I need to know what you did it with and when before I lay a hand on you."

The high-born young lady was tight-lipped and trembling with shock and rage that Mary should dare to strike her. The waiting-woman only stood with her mouth open.

"If you will not tell me the truth, then I am going home," Mary said, and picked up the hood to put it back on again. "Take me back."

"No, no, she needs your help . . ." warbled her woman. Mary shrugged.

"What do I care if some great lord's daughter dies, it is none of my affair," she said. "Great lords have done little enough for me."

"But—"

"I'll help the poor harlots who can do no other if they wish to eat, but I see no reason to help a stupid girl who had all she could have desired and saw fit to throw it away to scratch an itch between her legs."

"No, you do not understand, she is—"

"Shut up!" whispered the girl and the woman gulped and shut her mouth instantly. "You, witch, why do you need to know such things?"

"Do you think all inside you is undifferentiated meat?" Mary demanded. "How much hurt did you do yourself before the pains started?"

The girl was clever enough to keep her voice to a whisper so it would be harder for anyone to know her voice again. "I used a knitting needle and the coal tongs to hold it open. I drove up the needle until blood and water came. And I care not if I die, either, goodwife; it was my woman brought you and not by my orders."

"Oh, my dear," said the woman, crying salt and moved to stroke her damp forehead above the mask.

The girl slapped the woman's hand away. Mary saw then that she had been enraged before Mary struck her. If she had begged then—or told of how some clever unscrupulous man had entrapped her and persuaded her, or taken her by force—Mary would have marched out and left her to die. But instead she said directly, "You have the right of it, I am a fool. You may go now, and my woman will pay you for your trouble."

Then she put her head back on the pillow and said nothing as another pain came and more blood with it. Which softened Mary as no other words could have done; and further she was, I suppose, contrary enough that if the girl had ordered her to stay, she would have gone.

Instead Mary took her kirtle sleeves off and rolled up the sleeves of her smock and told the woman to fetch hot water and towels. Mary had brought some of her own thread made of sinew and gut that she kept in a pouch with her hooks and snips and needles. The physicians in their wisdom tell us that sickness comes into a wound by bad airs and if we burn incense, they will have no power. In monasteries they had a different tradition: they washed their hands like Pontius Pilate before and not after, which the physicians insist only demonstrates their superstition.

Superstitiously then, Mary washed her hands and prayed to me before examining the girl. She had done herself damage, but she had succeeded in what she had set out to do. She was open within, and the babe ready to come.

It came at last, a little thing seven inches long, which squirmed and died. Perhaps Mary baptised it in time and perhaps not. She put it in the basin. Its mother looked at it stonily, and saw it would have been a son. The waiting-woman put it on the fire. Then, grey-faced, she left the room.

Mary did her best to mend the girl where she had torn her insides and she bore it all without a word. At last, when Mary said she had finished, the girl whispered, "Give me back my virginity."

"No one can do that," Mary told her. "You lost it months gone."

"I know that." At the borders of her mask, the girl was white and determined. "Sew me up again. The seeming is all that matters."

"Ah." Mary understood then. For a moment she hesitated. Why should the high-born whore not suffer for her sin as Mary had? But it seemed to Mary that she had suffered already and would suffer more in the future, for there was no knowing what might happen inside her. So Mary nodded and did as she was asked, a careful sempstress as she cut a little to make edges that would heal, and sewed with thread made of gut. Half-way through the girl fainted, which was a mercy for her and also for Mary.

"Will she recover?" asked the waiting-woman when she came back, bringing wine to the girl but not offering a drop to Mary, who was near fainting for lack of it.

She shrugged. "Perhaps," she said. "She is young and strong. She should have a care when she marries, for I have no idea if she can be got with child again and what will happen if she is."

"Why should it matter?" whispered the girl, opening her eyes again.

"To pass a babe through, your cunny should be soft," Mary said, "so it can stretch enough. Now you will have scars there and scars are harder than un-wounded flesh, and less apt to stretch."

She nodded her understanding, her hooded eyes half-closed. Extraordinarily, there was the ghost of a smile round her mouth.

"I will not marry."

"Hah," Mary said, "as if it were up to you. The best you can do is try and have your parents pick a man who loves boys or prefers whores."

She smiled at Mary properly then but was too tired and too cautious to say what was in her mind. She only waved that her waiting-woman should pay the fee and take the witch away, and Mary put the bag on her head again meekly enough and let herself be led by a different route and rowed inefficiently once more by the waiting-woman.

Mary did not care and she was full of glee. So the high-born whore thought she could hide herself behind velvet masks, but Mary would know whom she had attended. Within a few years, no doubt the girl would be married and when she was well-set-up and thought herself safe and her childish stupidity forgotten, then the witch would come back and they would make a bargain that would be Magdalen's dowry.

There had been a book poking from under the pillow. When the girl fainted Mary took it and slipped it into the pocket of her petticoat; all she saw then was that it was small, bound in blue velvet and embroidered with a horse on the front. Mary only thought it would have her name in it, or the name of her noble family, and through it she would get her darling's dowry.

The joke was on Mary, of course. It was that ill-famed book of recommendations to the state of virginity, and on its cover was not a horse but a unicorn, most beautifully and painstakingly enwrought in white silk and silver thread, with a ruby for its eye, and gold couching for its horn. Within the girl had copied quotations from Saint Augustine and Saint Paul, but at the end where a few pages were bare, while she believed herself to be dying, she had written her last will and testament. More than that, in her rage with the man who had ruined her she had told the reason she faced death and named him to ruin him likewise, and she had signed it, flourishing, with her own name—Princess Elizabeth. Mary read it, and gasped. So a witch knew long ago the answer to the riddle by which many Privy Councillors were exasperated, for the Princess settled her claim to the throne (in default of heirs of the body of either her brother or her sister, both then living and looking likely to outlive her) on her cousin Mary of Scots.

Princess Elizabeth must have been in terror when she found the book was gone, but what could she do about it? Mary sewed the book up in the cloth bag that she had worn on her head, and hid it in divers places. Whenever Elizabeth was in procession, whether as a Princess or later as a Queen, Mary took care to come nowhere near the place, but drank herself into oblivion elsewhere.

God knows what it is about Mary, why she was lived so long, in spite of the booze and the hunger and the injunction to all good Christian men that a witch be not suffered to live. To see the girl she sewed back into virtue come to adulthood—that was surprise enough, though Elizabeth was ill for a year or more afterwards, and often subject to pains in the stomach. To see her rule—

well, Mary hardly noticed, being too busy with drinking and living. Whenever there were wagers made on whether the Queen would marry this suitor or that, Mary always bet against and always collected. And always spent what she got. After Magdalen died, aged and raving of the pox in the back room of the Falcon, Mary was drunk for a week, but then bethought herself of her great-granddaughter, only four years old then and not ruined yet. Magdalen never had a chance, for she lived her whole sad life in the shadow of her mother's sin, and died of it. But Pentecost . . . Pentecost was Mary's darling and Pentecost would have a dowry, come what may. And that was why she spoke Latin to the Jesuit Father in the boozing ken and saved him from the Queen's men. All she wanted was a dowry for her darling.

And by my help, by the Mercy of the Queen of Heaven and at the expense of her own life, Mary won.

Now judge if you would have done different?

Historical Note

THIS BOOK IS SET in the period between the death of Sir Philip Sidney in the Netherlands—October 1586—and the execution of Mary Queen of Scots on February 8, 1587 (modern dating), a year before the Spanish Armada of 1588, and four years after the events in *Firedrake's Eye*.

Elizabeth I had reigned since 1558, confounding the confident predictions of most important men of the time that a mere weak and feeble woman could not possibly rule by herself. Her succession had been an accident of genetics and custom. In common with every king of his time, her father Henry VIII had desperately wanted a son to succeed him. His first wife, Catherine of Aragon, had produced one daughter—Mary Tudor—and no sons that lived past babyhood. Henry came to the convenient conclusion that this was because God was angry with him for marrying his dead brother's wife and accordingly sought a divorce. The pope disagreed (because Catherine's nephew, the Emperor Charles V, was controlling Rome at the time) and forbade it. In order to marry his mistress, Anne Boleyn, Henry broke from the Roman Catholic Church, made himself Head of the Church of England and gave himself that much-needed divorce.

Unfortunately, Anne then made the mistake of giving birth to a daughter, Elizabeth, on September 7, 1533. After she miscarried of a boy a little later, Henry had her executed on a trumped-up charge of adultery.

By the time Henry died, his ferocious marrying had given him only one more child, Edward. According to the rules of succession in England, and Henry's will, the Protestant Edward VI became king first, although still a child; after he died, Mary (a Catholic) followed him, and when she too died without issue, Elizabeth became queen.

It was assumed that Elizabeth would marry as soon as she could. She had a wide variety of suitors, whom she seems to have greatly enjoyed teasing, and married none of them—almost certainly because she had no intention of handing any power over to any man. By the middle-eighties, it was clear that she was no longer able to produce an heir of her body and so the choice of her successor became as constant a source of anxiety to her councillors as her potential husband had been earlier.

By right of descent, Mary, Queen of Scots was clearly her successor. Unfortunately, Mary, Queen of Scots was a Catholic, related to the ultra-Catholic Guise family of France, and she had been kicked out of Scotland thanks to a spectacular series of blunders, including being implicated in the murder of her husband Darnley and marrying Bothwell, the nobleman who, she claimed, abducted and raped her and who was also implicated in Darnley's murder. She had been Elizabeth's prisoner since May 1568, a perpetual source of trouble. The ten-month-old son she abandoned when she fled Scotland became James VI of Scotland and was brought up a Protestant. Eventually he would succeed Elizabeth as James I of England and Scotland, but until the very end of her life, Elizabeth saw no reason to be pinned down on the subject.

In the sixteenth century, religion was as rancid a provoker of hatred and killing as politics have been in this century. This is the greatest difference between us and our ancestors. In modern agnostic Western culture, religion has become a matter of private personal choice and faith in God is often regarded as, at best, a quaint form of self-deception. In the sixteenth century, religion mattered enormously. Catholics and Protestants were alike convinced that they knew the only True Road to Salvation and that everyone who disagreed would end in Hell for eternity. Queen Elizabeth herself seems to have been more sane on the matter than many of her subjects, insisting that she would not attempt to make windows into men's souls. However, not even she could avoid the ratchet-effect of contending extremists. The Catholics and Protestants of Elizabeth's reign probably had more in common with modern Islamic zealots than we might like to think.

Elizabeth's head of the secret service (although there was officially no such thing at the time) was Sir Francis Walsingham. An extreme Protestant, he had been quietly stalking the Queen of Scots for years. In the summer of 1586 he had finally managed to get her completely tangled in a thoroughly infiltrated plot against the queen's life, headed by a Catholic gentleman named Sir Anthony Babington, who was executed. After what can only be called a show trial in the autumn of 1586, Mary, Queen of Scots was condemned to death. However,

Elizabeth refused for months to sign the warrant for her execution—for which she has been heavily criticized, both at the time and since by self-righteous and patronizing males. Finally, Walsingham's protégé, William Davison, managed to get her to sign the warrant, and Mary, Queen of Scots had the martyr's death she had probably come to desire by then. Queen Elizabeth has been heavily criticized for this too, often by the same men.

Elizabeth's actions around this time were so extraordinary, even for a highly strung woman under heavy pressure and in genuine fear of her life, that I began to wonder how she might have been maneuvered into executing her cousin-queen. A connection with the vague mutterings of scandal around her liaison with Thomas Seymour, admiral of England in her fifteenth year, became part of the answer—and so the plot of this book was born. I would like to emphasize here that there is *no evidence whatever* that the central thesis of my book is historically true—there are hints and suggestive circumstantial evidence, but nothing stronger.

I DO NOT INTEND even to try and supply a bibliography—I have used so many sources of information, I've forgotten half of them myself, and three house moves in the past four years have buried some of my notes deeper than the lost cities of Troy. Who, for instance, was the author of a wonderful unpublished thesis about the Elizabethan prisons of London, on which I based my picture of the Fleet? Whoever he was, I'd like to thank him for his scholarship and vivid writing. Janet Arnold and Jean Hunnisett's books gave me the fantastic architecture of Elizabeth's clothes; David Starkey, Robert Lacey and Simon Thurley have provided productive quarries of information about court life in their books, and Simon Thurley's restoration of the Tudor parts of Hampton Court Palace should be visited by anyone interested in the nitty-gritty of royal life. Marina Warner's book *Alone of All Her Sex* on the subject of the Virgin Mary gave me my figure of the Madonna.

As before, *Stowe's Survey of London* and the Topographical Society's *A to Z of Elizabeth London,* compiled by Adrian Prockter and Robert Taylor, have guided me and my characters around that strange and familiar city.

Glossary

aqua fortis—nitric acid
aqua vitae—brandy
Ave Maria, gratia plena, Dominus tecum . . . "Hail Mary, full of Grace, the
    Lord is with thee"—beginning of the traditional Catholic prayer to the
    Blessed Virgin Mary

Babington plot—see historical note
bale of dice—thieves' cant for a pair of dice, often false
biggin—close-fitting cap worn by babies and young children
billament—jewelled headdress
Board of Greencloth—department of state dealing with the administration of
    the court, especially practical services such as heating and food
bodkin—small, thin dagger used for opening letters
booze—traditional English slang word meaning *alcoholic drink*
boozing ken—worst kind of pub
Bouge of Court—prestigious state-subsidized board and lodging at court

canions—loose breeches
chamberers—court servants doing the menial work for Elizabeth
cinnabar—red oxide of mercury, highly poisonous, used as blusher
Island of Cipangu—Japan, at this time still in contact with Europe through the
    Portuguese
feast of the Circumcision of Our Lord—January 1
cloth-of-gold—cloth literally woven from very fine wires of gold
cloth-of-silver—the same, only of silver
Cloth of State—a kind of square awning over the queen's seat, wherever it
    happened to be, to show she was the queen
collops—chops of meat

comfit—any kind of nonsticky sweet

complected—the balance of one's humours

coney-catcher—(thieves' cant) Elizabethan con artist

cramp-rings—(thieves' cant) leg irons

cuisse—armour thigh piece

distemper—illness, mysteriously caused—or a hangover

domus providenciae—generic term for all that part of the Court that dealt with practicalities like laundry and food—the service department, under the authority of the clerk of the Board of Green Cloth

ego te absolvo—"I absolve you," beginning of the prayer of absolution said by the priest during the Sacrament of Confession

Egyptians—gypsies

esses—two linked capital-letter *S*'s, Elizabethan symbol of sovereignty

the Falcon—well-known bawdy house on the South Bank of the Thames

false-front—a highly elaborately decorated triangle of cloth attached like an apron to the front of the top petticoat, so it could be revealed by the drawn-back sides of the kirtle

farthingale—hooped petticoat like a crinoline that held the skirts out in a fashionable shape

farthingale-sleeves—very full sleeves held out by hoops in the same way

Fleet prison—a notorious debtors and criminals prison near Fleet bridge in London, known for its riots

footpad—mugger

gard—wide strip of material used to trim the hems of kirtles to protect them from wear and mud

garnish—(prison slang) a bribe

halberd—spearhaft with a blade like a cross between an axe and an old-fashioned tin-opener—still carried by Yeomen of the Guard

hard sauce—like brandy butter, only made with sherry (delicious)

Hermes Trismegistus—neo-Platonic writer much respected as a purveyor of ancient and prophetic wisdom—the Hermetic knowledge—until revealed in the early seventeenth century to be a post-Christian fake

homunculus—(Latin—"little man") the inner self

humour—basic to Elizabethan medicine: four humours combined to make a man: blood (sanguine h.); phelgm (phlegmatic h.); yellow bile (choleric h.) and black bile (melancholic h.)

Infirmerar—nun (or monk) in charge of the sick bay of the convent

jakes—toilet

jointure—income, usually from land, given to a gentlewoman on marriage as part of her dowry but inalienably hers rather than her husband's or her children's, to provide her support in case the husband died

kinchin-mort—(thieves' cant) a girlchild

Knights' Commons—the better class—and more expensive—ward of the Fleet prison

Liberties of Whitefriars—area of London where ecclesiastical rather than common law applied, and so generally a haunt of thieves and debtors

Little Ease—notorious dungeon in the Tower of London, deliberately built too small for a man to stand, sit or lie full length

Marrano—Portuguese Sephardic Jew

morion helmet—curved-brim Spanish-style helmet

muliercula—(Latin—"little woman") a midget or dwarf

orangeado—a Seville orange, partly hollowed and stuffed with sugar

paten—the flat dish used to put the Host on, during Mass

patten—wooden overshoe like a clog to keep expensive leather out of the mud

partlet—elaborately pleated and embroidered linen garment, covering only the shoulders and upper chest and fastening under the arms

peascod-bellied—the lower half of a doublet padded so it stuck out like a paunch—very fashionable

penner—leather pouch worn on the belt and used by clerks to carry pens, penknife and ink

petard—an explosive charge—the traditional ball full of gunpowder with a fuse sticking out of the top

physic—medicine

pike—very long, thick spear used against cavalry by men standing in close ranks

posset—warming or medicinal drink

Presence Chamber—throne room

primero—card game, quite similar to poker

pursuivant—general term for Elizabeth's counterintelligence men

rebato-veil—very fine cobweb linen veil held with wires in a high heart shape around the face and shoulders

recusant—someone who broke the law by refusing to go to church on a
Sunday, usually Catholic

red sanders—Elizabethan food dye

screever—one who reads and writes for the illiterate, later a pavement artist
stays—Elizabethan corset
Saint Stephen's Day—now called Boxing Day
stomacher—boned triangular piece of cloth, often embroidered, pinned to the
front of the bodice
the Stool—close stool—a silver chamberpot in an enclosed velvet-covered seat
sugar-plate—a kind of sugar icing made with gum arabic, which could be
moulded into elaborate shapes, left to harden and then coloured (still
available from sugar-craft shops)

tercio—Spanish brigade of three thousand men
tiring woman—ladies' maid
truckle-bed—small spare bed on wheels kept under a larger bed
Tunnage and Poundage men—Customs and Excise officers
turnshoes—simplest and cheapest kind of slipperlike shoe

veney—sword practice with heavy sticks
Virge of the Court—court precincts where the authority of the lord
chamberlain and the clerk of the Board of Greencloth overruled that of the
common law (virge—from "virgus", rod, i.e. the Lord Chamberlain's staff
of office)

Great Wardrobe—the department of state that dealt with the making and
maintenance of Queen Elizabeth's clothes, based in large buildings near the
Blackfriars
Privy Wardrobe—subdepartment of the Great Wardrobe, wherever the Queen
happened to be, dealing with day-to-day maintenance of her clothes
wet suckets—sticky sweets, usually made of candied fruit
white-lead paint—lead oxide, highly poisonous, used as foundation